Nobodaddy's Children

The Dalkey Archive Edition of
ARNO SCHMIDT
Collected Early Fiction, 1949-1964
Translated by John E. Woods

Volume 1: *Collected Novellas*

Enthymesis (1949) – *Leviathan* (1949) – *Gadir* (1949)
Alexander (1953) – *The Displaced* (1953)
Lake Scenery with Pocahontas (1955) – *Cosmas* (1955) – *Tina* (1956)
Goethe (1957) – *Republica Intelligentsia* (1957)

Volume 2: *Nobodaddy's Children*

Scenes from the Life of a Faun (1953) – *Brand's Heath* (1951)
Dark Mirrors (1951)

Volume 3: *Collected Stories**

Tales from Island Street (16 stories, 1955-1962)
Stürenburg Stories (9 stories, 1955-1959) – *Country Matters* (9 stories
and the novella *Caliban upon Setebos,* 1960-1964) ·

Volume 4: *Two Novels**

The Stony Heart (1956) – *Boondocks/Moondocks* (1960)

_____

*In preparation

Arno Schmidt

Nobodaddy's Children

Translated by John E. Woods

Dalkey Archive Press

First Edition, 1995

An earlier version of John E. Woods's translation of *Scenes from the Life of a Faun* was published by Marion Boyars. © 1983 by Marion Boyars Ltd. Reprinted (with revisions) by permission of the publisher.

Library of Congress Cataloging-in-Publication Data

Schmidt, Arno, 1914-1979
  [Nobodaddy's Kinder. English]
  Nobodaddy's children / Arno Schmidt ; translated by John E. Woods.
        p.   cm. — (Collected early fiction, 1949-1964 / Arno Schmidt ; v. 2)
  Includes bibliographical references.
  Contents: Scenes from the life of a faun — Brand's heath — Dark mirrors.
    I. Woods, John E. (John Edwin) II. Title. III. Series: Schmidt, Arno, 1914-1979.   Selections. English. 1994 ; v. 2.
PT2638.M453A15   1994 vol. 2   833'.914 s—dc20   95-16363
ISBN 1-56478-083-X (cloth)
ISBN 1-56478-090-2 (paper)

Partially funded by grants from The National Endowment for the Arts, The Illinois Arts Council, and the Arno Schmidt Stiftung.

Dalkey Archive Press
Illinois State University
Campus Box 4241
Normal, IL 61790-4241

NATIONAL
ENDOWMENT
FOR ❦ THE
A R T S

Printed on permanent/durable acid-free paper and bound in the United States of America.

CONTENTS

TRANSLATOR'S INTRODUCTION

Nobodaddy's Children may be your first attempt to explore Arno Schmidt's world of literary mind games. Or perhaps you bought volume 1 of the Dalkey Archive edition of his *Collected Early Fiction* and after reading that assortment of novellas find that, maybe against your better judgment, you're intrigued, even hooked on his quirky prose. Either way, with this early trilogy of novels (and my introduction will primarily be devoted to whether they form a trilogy, and if so in what sense), you are about to encounter something very close to the crux of the Schmidtian matter.

It should first be noted that these three novels were—written in an order different from that in which they are presented here—first came *Brand's Heath* (1950), followed by *Dark Mirrors* (1951), and finally *Scenes from the Life of a Faun* (1953). *Brand's Heath,* then, was the proverbial first novel, and Arno Schmidt was hot to leave his mark on German literature. As a first-time novelist, he pushed doggedly ahead with the idiosyncratic experiments of form and language he had begun—to little or no applause— in *Leviathan* (1949), a slim volume of novellas. And at the same time he focused and developed the controlling (and sometimes nearly out-of-control) narrative voice that would serve him, with really only minor variations, for the rest of his literary career. Here we find the ever pondering, sometimes ponderous "I"—a rancorous, whimsical, neo-Romantic, bawdy "I"—that will speak from several thousand pages of fiction. With *Nobodaddy's Children* the "solipsist on the heath" (a title bestowed on Schmidt by the poet Helmut Heissenbüttel) took up for good and all his lifelong conversation with himself.

That conversation is most certainly a unifying thread in these three novels (or better, two novels and a good-sized novella), but, then, in a larger sense that same thread is woven through the entire Schmidt oeuvre. With the completion of *Faun,* after three years of work (December 1949 to January 1953), Schmidt wrote a very cheeky letter to Ledig-Rowohlt, his publisher. Bearing the date of 30 January 1953, it read:

Dear Herr Ledig=Rowohlt !

Previously, for both "Brand's Heath" and "Dark Mirrors," I had to listen to all sorts of astounding statements, evidencing little understanding, from both you (and your editor) concerning form, use of motifs, unsatisfactory ending etc. : do you now see that both were the concluding two parts of a comprehensive and carefully balanced trilogy ? – I beg you: same form // same heath setting // same "loose marriages" // the echoes of the endings always dying in the same vacuum ! And arranged precisely by time : "Faun" 1939/44; "Brand's Heath" 1945/46; "Dark Mirrors" 1960/62. With "Faun", which you now have before you, the composition of the "theme con variazioni" is complete, the keystone fitted in the arch, flap-doodle flapdoodle : do you now see how right I was back then ? –

> With best regards,
>
> Your Arno Schmidt.

Two weeks later, then, he accepted Rowohlt's offer for this third novel, declaring that he had turned down other (nonexistent) offers for the *Faun,* "so that the 3 parts of the grand trilogy may perhaps one day appear to-gether in a *single* volume !"

When it could further his literary cause, Arno Schmidt was a past master of—to put it euphemistically—invention. He most definitely made good use of the art on this occasion. For his "comprehensive and carefully bal-anced trilogy" was in reality little more than an afterthought. This we know because on that same day, 30 January 1953, his wife, Alice Schmidt, re-corded the following in her diary:

A. comes in from outside & says : I've just had an idea. The Faun is the 1st part of Brand's Heath, just think about it. And I instantly catch fire. But of course. What asses we are not to have thought of it right off. Now nobody can have any more objections that you've written another Brand's Heath. And we spurred one another on with the inspiration. Even if it had been intentional, you couldn't have found a better motivation. Suddenly there is a deep meaning to the similarity of compo-nents : the sameness of landscape is now self-evident. . . . No, the rather embarrass-ing similarities now seem to be links in a great chain. Only now is Brand's Heath a trilogy that can strut its stuff. A first-rate portrayal of the times : Hitler years & war; postwar and future.

A patent case, then, of flapdoodle on Schmidt's part. Or was it? Upon first reading—indeed upon tenth—*Nobodaddy's Children* looks, feels, tastes like a trilogy. Is there not some way to rescue the inherent unity of these three tales, despite the author's rather belated discovery of it?

We do know a few isolated facts about the genesis of certain segments in the three novels. Among Schmidt's notes is the statement that he dreamt the dream of Öreland found in *Brand's Heath* on the night of 29 December 1947. In his essay "Calculations II" he states that *Dark Mirrors* "was the Experience Level II of my POW period, in 1945, in that barbwire cage outside Brussels, there was a sound of revelry by night"—and by Experi-ence Level II, he means the mind game he played with himself simply to survive. He goes on to assign this particular sort of extended mind game to the "Captive" category, which he describes as "pessimistic," "black sharp-edged," and "merciless" because the mind-gamer is "tied to the cannon's mouth"; the ending, he notes, "usually depends on the termination of existence" in the real world, whether by "death, Pyrrhic recovery or release." Again from Schmidt's own notes, we know that on 20 December 1952, after three weeks of intense work, he gave up on *Scenes from the Life of a Faun* because it was "too similar to *Brand's Heath* and *Dark Mirrors* !" Alice Schmidt's diaries record his despair, his intention to "dismember" *Faun* and "publish only the linguistic pearls as a volume of poetry." But then, ten days later, she writes: "This evening the idea comes to A. (on the john !!) for the 3rd part of the Faun & all night long he's constantly switching the light off and on & jotting down notes, of which he has a whole packet by morning & carefully copies them out." In a white heat (reinforced by copious use of 100-proof schnapps, Alice tells us), he bombs the novel's world to a fiery hell, finishing shortly before midnight on 9 January 1953. Three weeks later he finds he has a trilogy on his hands.

Like all Schmidt's work, these early novels are mosaics, assembled out of diverse sources: dreams, desperate extended mind games, seizures of inspiration, allusions and quotations from his own vast reading—and perhaps most importantly in this case, out of "unforgettable sequences of images presented to me northwest of Cordingen by patches of woods that warmed and nourished me for four years," as he wrote by way of dedication in his manuscript copy of *Dark Mirrors*. A veritable bombardment of disparate, seemingly random materials—and he picked up the shards and molded three novels from them. The narrative voice in each, although it bears different names (Düring, Schmidt, anonymous), is really a single response of enraged shouts and aggrieved mutterings flung at warmongers, their wars, and the sad rubble that war leaves behind. Why should we, or Schmidt himself for that matter, be surprised to find that such a unified voice tells one story three times over?

The threads that hold these three novels together—themes, objects, moods, images—were woven into the fabric by an author not yet fully aware of the pattern of his finished cloth. What fun for the reader! There are, of course, the more obvious unities of motif and setting, the ones that Schmidt made sure he called to Ledig-Rowohlt's attention. But there are so many others—and all of them very intriguing. Watch out for pilfered paintings, rabbits, operatic tenors, global overpopulation, the kobold antics of gusty wind. Above all, I would suggest you be on the lookout for "elmettals," as the old man calls earth's elemental spirits in the opening scene of *Brand's Heath*. Observe how Düring calls them up for the final grand conflagration in *Faun:* "Come to me from out of air, : / Arise from ocean deep, : / Though fast asleep in darkened lair, : / Or up from fire leap – : Düring is your Lord this night ! / Obey him, every shade and sprite!" (A bit of conjuring, by the way, that Schmidt stole from the fairy tale "The Ghost Ship" by Wilhelm Hauff [1802–1827].) And then search long and hard for elemental spirits in the postnuclear solitude of *Dark Mirrors.*

But what should we make of the curious love affair each hero strikes up with the lady of his heart? In *Brand's Heath* it is Lore (or is she really Undine, who has strayed in from Fouqué's tale?), who deserts her scribbling lover; of course, there's Grete, too, so loyal and so unloved. In *Faun* we find a wife who, we can only assume, goes up in flames without a single tear wept for her and a she-wolf Käthe, whom Düring enjoins to find a man who is "no conceited ass with great expectations." In *Dark Mirrors* the world's last pair of accidental lovers parts because, as Schmidt wrote to Ledig-Rowohlt in defense of the novel's ending, "they have become incapable of living together as a result of previous experiences, decades [sic!] of isolation and absolute independence." (And we ask ourselves, decades? But it has clearly only been five years since nuclear war left these two to fend for themselves. Whose "decades of isolation" are those?) And if love is not, although it is usually touted to be, the solution to humankind's predicament, what then is? Well, at the conclusion of *Scenes from the Life of a Faun,* Schmidt himself suggests: "In the end all that's left are : Works of Art; the Beauty of Nature; Pure Sciences. In that holy trinity." Then by all means, let us keep an eye out for their incarnations on each of these three literary planets.

It was not until 1963 that Schmidt's three novels, rearranged now in the sequence of their historical settings, finally appeared as one, under the title *Nobodaddy's Children.* Responding to Ledig-Rowohlt's idea of initiating a new paperback series with a republication of the three novels as a trilogy, Schmidt suggested the title, pilfering "old Nobodaddy," the anthropomorphic demiurge, from William Blake. ("Then old Nobodaddy aloft / Farted and belch'd & cough'd, / And said, 'I love hanging & drawing & quartering / Every bit as well as war & slaughtering.' ") "You will have to let me know right away," he wrote, "otherwise I'll use the joke elsewhere." He was, in fact, intending to use it as the title for the story that later became "Great Cain" (Dalkey Archive edition, volume 3). And, indeed, the title remains something of a joke, since the reader can look high and low for William Blake here, and never find him. Unless, of course, the English poet is hiding in the name Blakenhof, the cluster of buildings that provides the narrator of *Brand's Heath* with a ramshackle roof over his head—but that would be to fetch even farther than Schmidt would have fetched to further a literary cause. All the more so, since Blakenhof means something like Smolder Farm, a telling name, to be sure, since after all we are on *Brand's* (i.e., Conflagration's) *Heath.* Which brings us back to the final incendiary pages of *Faun,* and to that curious box of matches at the very end of *Dark Mirrors*—and so, once again, to our serendipitous trilogy.

In these early years Arno Schmidt was in many ways the plaything of his own genius—or of the Leviathan, Nobodaddy in person, if you will. So pompously knowing, he was nevertheless often naively unperceptive about the creative process erupting within him—that awareness would come much later. But here at least is a trilogy of raw intellect and raw pain—and pure braggadocio. That should suffice.

A few final comments. Although a translation of *Scenes from the Life of a Faun* I did some dozen years ago is still around, it should be noted that this is a thoroughly reworked translation. It has been retuned to harmonize with the other two novels. And, heaven knows, I have learned a great deal about translating Schmidt in the intervening years. I hope it shows.

A note is also in order about the unusual punctuation of these texts, which is sure to look strange to the American eye. It reproduces that found in the German original (i.e., the "Bargfeld Edition" [Haffmans Verlag], the most accurate to date). But why such slavish faithfulness in a translation? Perhaps Schmidt's own "Calculations III" may help explain:

We are not dealing with a mania for originality or love of the grand gesture, but with . . . the necessary refinement of the writer's tool. I shall begin with punctuation. – It can be used as stenografy ! When I write : ‹She looked around : ?›, the out=come (with an "=", I despise Websterian rules for compound words : it's not an oútcome, but an oút=cóme !) is that the *colon* becomes the inquiring opened face, the *question mark* the torsion of the body turned to ask, and the *whole* of "The Question" retains its validity – no : is far better ! : the reader is intentionally not force-fed a stale salad of words, à la ‹and she asked : "What is it ?"› . . . Let us retain the lovely=essential freedom to reproduce a hesitation precisely : "well – hm – : Idunno – – : can we *do* that . . . ." (Instead of the rigidly prescribed : "Well, I don't know . . ." . . . Perhaps many will wonder why I sometimes place the period *before* the parenthesis; sometimes after; sometimes use none at all : I have my reasons – in almost every case (and with a little thought, anyone could discover them.)

That "almost every" is a hedge—yes, Schmidt usually had his reasons, but sometimes he was careless. Despite his avowals of meticulously orchestrated punctuation, I must admit I often find no real consistency; usage varies from text to text and can even seem out of sync within a given text. But rather than attempt to correct this or that usage or rigorously substitute

American conventions, I thought it best simply to preserve the original visual *text*uality.

With that, my introduction is at an end, but please do not skip these final words of gratitude (the same ones, I admit, that concluded my introduction to volume 1—but then my gratitude is abiding), for any pleasure you may find in reading this English translation of Arno Schmidt is due to the constant support and advice of many people. My thanks, then, to the Arno Schmidt Foundation, to Jan Philipp Reemtsma, Bernd and Petra Rauschenbach, Erika Knop. And especially to Hans Wollschläger, whose spirited, wise, and kindly counsel lives in every word of this translation.

SCENES FROM
THE LIFE OF A FAUN

I
(February 1939)

Thou shalt not point thy finger at the stars; nor write in the snow; but when it thunders touch the earth : so I sent a tapering hand upward, with beknitted finger drew the slivered ‹K› in the silver scurf beside me, (no thunderstorm in progress at the moment, otherwise I'd have come up with something !) (In my briefcase the wax paper rustles).

The moon's bald Mongol skull shoved closer to me. (The sole value of discussions is : that good ideas occur to you afterward).

The main road (to the station) coated with silver strips; shoulders cemented high with coarse snow, diamonddiamond (macadamized; – was Cooper's brother-in-law by the by). The trees stood there, giants at august attention, and my look-alive steps stirred beneath me. (Just ahead the woods will retreat to the left and fields advance). And the moon must have still been bustling at my back, since sometimes sharp rays flitted strangely through the needled blackness. Far ahead a small car bored its bulging eyes into the matutinal night, wiggled them slowly looking about, and then clumsily turned the red glow of its monkey's butt toward me : glad it's driving off !

My life ? ! : is not a continuum ! (not simply fractured into white and black pieces by day and night ! For even by day they are all someone else, the fellow who walks to the train; sits in the office; bookworms; stalks through groves; copulates; small-talks; writes; man of a thousand thoughts; of fragmenting categories; who runs; smokes; defecates; listens to the radio; says "Commissioner, sir" : that's me !) : a tray full of glistening snapshots.

Not a continuum, not a continuum ! : that's how my life runs, how my memories run (like a spasm-shaken man watching a thunderstorm in the night) :

Flash : a naked house in the development bares its teeth amid poison-green shrubbery : night.

Flash : white visages are gaping, tongues tatting, fingers teething : night.

Flash : tree limbs are standing, boys play pubescing; women are stew-
ing; girls are scamping open-bloused : night !

Flame : me : woe : night ! !

But I cannot experience my life as a majestically unrolling ribbon; not I !
(Proof).

Drift ice in the sky : chunks; a floe. Chunks; a floe. Black crevices in which
stars crept (sea stars). A pale white fish belly (moonfish). Then :

Cordingen Station : the snow prickled softly on the walls; a black switch-
wire quivered and husked hawaiian; (at my side the she-wolf appeared,
covered with silver grains. Climb aboard for starters).

The great white she-wolf : growled the greeting, took a savage seat and
tugged out her textbook by one corner; then from her pen she extracted
many jagged inky threads, ducked low, and gazed with her round eyes
into an invisible hole. The red swarm of my thoughts circled a bit about
her, snarling, with round eyes, yellow-rimmed. (But then here came
another, a black one, and I whetted my mouth and stared disapprovingly at the dirty slatted benches : sparkling thickskulled brass screws,
roundheads, beaded through us : how can you escape stuff like that ? !
The she-wolf scratched in the frost on the window, for her girlfriend to
get on : ergo : Walsrode).

"Heil, Herr Düring !" : "Morning, Peters."; and he brought out the joke :
‹Flowers for the gentleman ? ! : – : No thanks. The lady's my wife !›.
Hahaheehee. (Outside a silver claw hacked through the clouds, ripped
open a thin one, pulled back again) : hahaheehee. His glances philan-
dered among the schoolgirls, the curve of blousey silk; the thigh-filled
skirts.

Lovely-browed : schoolgirls with smooth facial secrets, serious immobile
eyes; heads of bobbed sandy hair turned on slender necks, while the
porcelain hand wrote minced English, in the blue notebook. (And add
a little morning sun ! : And there it was now, on time, red between
yellow slits of cloud; hoo-whee-called the train, as if from the
universe's gullet, disinterested and extragalactic).

Stopped in the station : (Somebody close that door !. "Batten the hatch !").

Sunrise : and scarlet lances. (But at the back it was all still stiff and ice-
blue, no matter how high He held up those salmon-red vacant tapestries).

Through the compartment window : the woodlands quite petrified ! (And
beyond, pastel pink and blue); so still that No One could get through
(he would have to balance his way on tiptoe, eyes open wide and arms
at an angle; (and maybe take root like that ! An insane urge seized me,
to be that Some One : to pull the emergency brake, leave my briefcase,

tapered balancing arms, crystal eyes, flint & crown)).

Fallingbostel : "Heil !" : "Good-bye !" : "Good-bye : –" : "Heilittler !"

Commissioner's Office (= Prometheus' rock). Colleagues : Peters; Schönert; (Runge was still on Party detail); Fräulein Krämer, Fräulein Knoop (typists); Otte, male trainee; Grimm, female trainee.

Fräulein Krämer : small and of reptilian grace. She stood at the file cabinet, glanced slyly our way, and then rubbed her pelvis adeptly against the table edge; pulled back her green cardigan into the central-heated air, projecting her subtle apple-sized breasts, and gazed ever so dreamily at her thin smooth finger-sprigs as they snapped among the index cards.

"I'd sure like to get under your skin, Fräulein Krämer !" (Schönert, sighing uneasily. Once again) : "I'd sure like to get under your skin." She stared at him mistrustfully out of the far corners of her eyes (has troubles enough I suppose). – "Yes indeed", he protested piously, "if only this much : –" demonstrated : about 8 inches. – Her mouth, at first pleated nonplussed, relaxed, in eddies and dimples, then she puffed syrupy (even I bestowed an appreciative and managerial smirk : Schönert, the bastard. Sure, he wasn't married !), and went over to her girlfriend, whispered two sentences to her, demonstrated – : (distance of about 12 inches), and she too burst into bright and nervous laughter (but all through the propositioning kept up her businesslike dogearing. Then : her glance slithered cautiously through the furniture over to him, Schönert).

Ora et labora, et labora, et labora : "What a flumper." Peters (the Silesian) grumbled testily over his documents, gnawed at his pencil, thrust his teeth over his lower lip and pondered. (Now that was interesting ! I had often listened in on his primal tones : the unintelligible ones were either botched Slavic or French, from the years of Napoleonic occupation of Silesia, 1808–13. So that on principle he would say : "Agreed, savey" = not "savvy", but "c'est fait"; "Damn 'ansumbul" = not "and some bull", but "ensemble". And now he had just called the so-and-so a "flumper". – Found it later in my Sachs-Villatte : "flambart = lively fellow, jolly chap", so more or less comparable to our "live wire" or "card").

Morning coffee break (immediately after which we are open to the public) : films, soccer, the Führer, jokes, "From the lad who takes himself in hand will grow a man who takes his stand" (Peters), Party Convention, office intrigues, leaf through magazines, chew and rustle : "Well, Schönert ?" –

Most peculiar ! : Schönert, well-steeped in the classics, too, had read the

Odyssey XXIII, 190 ff., and disputed the possibility : it would rot much too quickly ! Why even a pile driven into the ground would last a lot longer (since otherwise the capillaries of the stump would still be intact and go right on osmosing : any farmer knew that). "Not a chance that it could last for 10 or 20 years !" Ergo : Homer the Ignoramus ? ! Right ?.

At the window : white-maned horses stood before long wagons; peeped from stalls; were led at the hands of boys; joggled a hoof against the pavement; greenish figs fell out of them; they pondered and snorted. (Prisoners in leather. And colorful carters appeared and shouted in humanese. All in winter).

And of clients sleek and broad of brow a host (well it only lasts from 10 to 12. And was quiet today). Stamp papers. Two permits. "Yes, and then you've gotta go to – Room 14. One floor up.– Okay ?"

A young girl wanted to get married (red skirt, yellow sweater, broad and happily fecund), and I patiently explained that she was still missing diverse "papers", "required by the latest regulation", birth certificate of the maternal grandfather; a signature was missing here on the wedding license (Oh, she had one child already, which explained the chassis, Grand Canyon : should you tell her : better not to get married ? !)

There is simply no communication between generations ! My children are strangers; just as my parents always were. Which is why in biographies relatives are consistently less important than lovers and friends. We stand around like a group of waiters. (Children only break up a marriage that much faster. In our circles).

Stamp one more : "Go ahead and close up, Fräulein Krämer !"

Lunch break : means munching sandwiches. Then get a bit of exercise.

I don't know (in front of stores); I don't know : for me "department store" is always congruent with "indoor family pool"; erotic fluorescent waves in both, artificial and overexposed.

A bevy of girls invaded with tongues flapping merrily. (Peters also wants to buy a piano in his old age. And learn to play. Ah well).

SA, SS, military, HY andsoforth : humans are never more trying than when playing soldier. (Surfaces periodically among them about every score of years, something like malaria, of late the pace is quicker). In the end it's always the worst ones who end up on top, to wit : bosses, executives, directors, presidents, generals, ministers, chancellors. A decent person is ashamed of being a boss !

The dark red bus purred softly my way from behind, slowly pushed along past me, and for a second I gazed into the faces, some ten of them, bisected by chrome bars thick as your thumb, dully splotched by moistured panes, indifferent and large-eyed. (And then, the mill on the Böhme, and the Quintus Icilius monument).

"Watch out, Dr. D's coming !" Peters hissed as he entered and dug deeper into his passports; Fräulein Krämer's thin lesbian fingertips itched faster at her dark Underwood, and trainee Otte lifted the heavy index box to his chin with a demonstrative gasp, the eye of the Lord maketh cattle to wax fat, behold : he came :

Commissioner Dr. von der Decken : tall, gray and fat; sovereign placidity among the great folds of his foggy face; the eyes swept heavily across the desktops and us other objects. He gazed long at my right hand (constantly twirling its pencil while the mail was rapidly scanned : make you feel pervous, Serenisime ?, next page : turn it over. There he still stood, presidential, monumental, potentatial, iguanodontial, ohgod, how we despised each other, like the Emperor of Aromata, next page : turn). "How late is it, Herr Peters ?" "Uh – 3:30, Commissioner, sir, thirty-four." "Thank you" (grumbled out all deep and Hindenburgish), "Thank you". Then departed. And I read and turned pages; Krämer daintily picked her nose; and trainee Otte removed the box from his sternum. ("Did he ever make a face", Peters eagerly : "like a monkey chewin' putty !"; and we wheezed with laughter at the heroic metaphor : but it's definitely another one of his silesianisms !)

Early dusk today. (Schönert had heard the weather report and prophesied overcast and rainy). The desklamp dyed the green formulas an even deeper Marbusian hue (I seen him serve the Queen / in a suit of rifle-green), and Otte brought me the folder with 500 signatures; yet once more; he had finished stamping them (some ordinance for all localities; for public posting), and he helped me, wordless and already a Stakhanovite. "Düring". "Düring". Five hundred times. (And to think people envy us our retirement benefits ! For cryin' out loud !)

God knows : drizzling already; but the train pulled in through the spritz on time. (Peters wanted to go to the movies).

The haggard newspaper distributor : I had strayed into the car for "Passengers with Extra Baggage", and watched how, as we moved by, he opened the window and shot-putted the packages to the lonely signalmen's huts (so they could then divvy them up in the villages). "Well, Herr Singer, how's the tournament going ?"; and he gave me reticent, Hadleyburgian information. (Was, you see, an impassioned chess player, polygonal and penurious, ‹Walsrode Germania Club›, and so charmingly fanatic that he didn't smoke when "in training"). "Heilittler, Herr Singer".

Stillest moor air : a farmer took shape ten paces ahead; at first just gray, as if puffed from smoke; (then he seemed to wear blue trousers; his stooped back stayed unhued); hands vapored slowly around beneath him; then he pulled himself up to full breadth, cracked his whip making the air moan with pain, hollow : and the shadow-patched horse at his side disappeared, nor did he reappear to me again later. (Had tubered off, I suppose, sown away; somehow).

Lights of the village, and sadness, as the mist resembles the rain.

Late hot lunch : a sailor's fate. Fried potatoes and elastic black-red slicelets of sausage. "Got your Hitler photo yet ?" the Egerland March inquired, only to declare at once : "No, no, don't have it yet / but we'll buy one, you bet !". (Like a photo-flash came Christmas memory : candles shimmered, deft and bemused, little soft faces of molten gold above white slender necks, bowing, dissembling and sanctimonious. Ever so cozy the stench from the mulled wine adulterated with cinnamon and cloves, red in its Sunday glasses; and I too had folded hypocritical hands across my belly, drawing on one of my three fat Brazils. But hadn't been able to endure it after all, and reached for the quaint old 1850 atlas I had picked up for a few pfennigs in Verden. Shutter closed).

(Long ago I kept trying with books. As gifts for wife and children. But for years now it'd been nothing but electric pots, linens and meat grinders; primum vivere roundaboutum. With savage joy my son examined the extralong Hitler Youth dagger, what is headed for a fall should be given a shove; the new dress draped on my daughter at the mirror, candy-sweet face : my daughter. Shutter closed).

Turning the dial (looking for news) : "Kadum Soap beautifies your body. / – Kadum Soap is summa cum laude !". And so sincerely spoken, in a plum-yellow D'youloveme voice; must be Saarbrücken; keep dialing. (They think they're some kind of scenic cultural overview !).

"Pope Pius the Somethingth : gravely ill", and I just raised my eyebrows in disapprobation and kept turning : who still travels by zeppelin these days ? ! (When I consider that of our six great classical authors not a one was Catholic . . . . . When I further consider that half of them – oh, and much the better half : Lessing, Wieland, Goethe (in chronological order !) – were opposed to every revealed religion . . . . : why then, I know what I know !)

"Tired : goodnight". (Have my own room on the ground floor all to myself; with the years and children my wife has forgotten me; permits it only with greatest reluctance). Across the way at Evers's and Hohgrefe's lights still on.

In the john again : black and odorless cold. (I really am tired; well, tomorrow's Saturday). (Ashes drifted over the concrete moon, ceaseless, flushed away by the pallid wind, lured away, carted away, poured away). (Then, hours later, it had edged a bit further along. In my shirt at the window).

4 degrees above freezing, drizzle, windless, for now. (The sheets ice-cold).

I flipped open the pliant, blue Kröner edition, and read the letter that Friedrich Nietzsche sent to Jakob Burckhardt from the Isle of Skye in the Hebrides in 1891 : ". . . . . On the beach among planks and other driftwood warped by storms, while a whole skyful of starfish slowly swarms about me as I write : we are building our ‹dragons› with no roof for the timid; the sail, bordered in red, is already billowing on the foremast. – Two of the boats will set out first, as scouting party, as ravens, as Templar knights. I, leader of the main division, will follow a few days later with the six remaining ships : my next laughing epistle [sic !], will already be sent to you, my friend, from Helluland, just as soon as we have selected the sites for our shanties . . . . ." (but here the text fuddled and I turned the page, and strayed among fragments and glosses until I awoke. – Happens to me often, leafing through books that way. Though it's funny, since I usually can't stomach N !).

Kitchen solitaire : tiled cold and empty. Children asleep; wife asleep; I : awake ! – The silly red thermos bottle with its clayey coffings; two cold-cut sandwiches, two with cheese : lovely gray-golden slabs of "harzer" (not the stinky and runny kind : that I don't like ! Certainly a fine thing for a man to have ‹his ways›. With a sneer).

Wind snapped in the garden and followed up with slurping watery footfalls.

The branches rattled in the night. (My coat billowed now with brief braggadocio). Some rain whispered with the asphalt road. (Like black wet woolen stockings, it meandered a long while down through my thinkways. Or like a hearse, having lost its way in great forests, groans, with black white-edged curtains fluttering behind). Haggard bushes, too, clattered skeletoned sarabands; the pavement glistened up at the lonely streetlamp; stray notions were stirring like lemures up in the attic; my guts twanged out a puff : cozily warm up my back – c'est la guerre !

(I'm no lover of mountain regions : nor of the pasty hash dialect their inhabitants speak, nor of the countless vaultings of earth, tellurian baroque. My landscape must be level, flat, mile-wide, heathered, woods, meadow, fog, taciturn).

(Not just geologically : but intellectually and morally as well, the age is aptly called Alluvial : washed up. Lake-dwellers and cavemen; minds

full of the lumber of pile-work or grottoes; Saxon Switzerland of the intellect. Lovely name : "Bell-Beaker Peoples" ! Neither brachy- nor dolicho- : coeliocephalic ! From forever standing at stiff attention, all things grow prognathous : 'ssir, Herr Neanderthal !)

There will be a delay ! : all trains are late, ETA uncertain (and with brusque, official pride his fiery-red cap deplored this irregularity so fraught with responsibility). So we mutely took the couple of steps and shoved one after the other

into the tiny waiting room : at once dark circles began to take shape around each of us, unthinking, pocket-handed; only after some time had elapsed did murmurs arise (that would last for a good 10 minutes; then they would grow furious, etc. etc., the well-known routine. I took care always to keep my she-wolf in view).

Which she noticed, and pulled snot up her nose, saucy and inviting, above her girlfriends. (The homework seemed still to be much the same : discussions of curves, Galsworthy, Wien's heat law, and "Didja read the fourth act ?". –) The wind grew louder; crouching, it leapt here and there, stretched, breathed cavernously, and rummaged sportively in the slush; then it came to my window, reeled off three sentences in Gaelic, snorted away (for laughter, 'cause o' my mug), and was gone. The dark stains beneath us grew larger; the fellow in red picked up the telephone again; it hummed in his thin cord, and he made cautious and peeved inquiries.

So my thoughts went, and my meanwhile body stood at one corner of the station like an empty bus deserted by its driver.

Finally everything was shivering : from the back of the black iron-serpent it invaded coat collars. Puddles slurped in girls' flats (while the fat dragon sputtered flaccid steam that babbled and wobbled indecisively over the leaden gravel).

Smoking section : they inhaled and dreamed; and pro forma I too extracted a chic Attika.

The she-wolf : she ripped her breakfast sandwich into two handy pieces, slowly and with bemused fingers, so that a thick amber pearldrop of cheese rolled down into the glacial crevices of the wax paper (kindred souls, right ? !). Then an apple. Then Schmeil-Norrenberg ‹Biology›.

"Lord, it's Runge !" (shamming) : "Well ? !" (Peters, Schönert, la Krämer, all of them, surrounding). And he told them, the proud and short of it.

About Bergen-Belsen : (as an SS man he had been assigned to duty on the camp staff, the fat bastard). "Oh, they all work nice and hard there !", with a pinched and lordly smile : "the Jews." Pause. He nudged the index card closer to his big blue eyes; but he just had to let it out :

"And if they refuse – they string 'em up." – ? ! ! ? – : "On a special gallows."

Nothing ! I know nothing. I don't meddle in any of it ! (But this I do know : All politicians, all generals, all those who in any way rule or command are scoundrels ! No exceptions ! All of them ! I still have a very good recollection of the big pogroms; I haven't forgotten how the SA hacked at Dr. Fränkel's typewriter with an ax, how they tipped the screaming piano out the window, till he committed suicide ! : But lo the day shall dawn, you fine sons of bitches. And woe to him who then decides to give you fellows ‹another chance› !)

"Christ ? : castrated himself !"; this was Schönert again, who read Matthew XIX verse 12 aloud with emphasis, the parallel passages, referred to the Skoptsy, and then went on spinning out his mangrove ideas. (But not all that far off the track, is he ? Ventilate the matter a bit more sometime).

A small dark client, i.e. beltenebros, with a quite disproportionately high-set bust, was keeping Peters more than busy, who engaged her in long and excessively official conversation, while performing numerous carnal acts upon her with his fish eyes. (No harm in it : just sad ! "She'd make a helluva triangle on the floor". Luther was the same way : he "could not look at a woman without coveting her" either !).

Then the typists' Saturday plans : "Has the commissioner issued any instructions about this noon ? – Well then : ladies !", and I grumpily reached again for my folders, with a cold textile grip.

An Iron Cross of Motherhood ! : It was old hunchback, drunken Benecke, him with the 14 kids; all of them right out of the funnies, red-haired, cross-eyed, teeth like Mah-Jongg tiles, a set of trolls : paddle his rear !

And so one cross for Mother : and she proudly spread her hands across that fat maternal tummy. (As long as the state goes on paying premiums for tupping, then we needn't wonder when our space keeps getting smaller. – But then : what am I a civil servant for ? !)

When the well-known decree went out from Caesar Augustus, the world's population came to about 50 million. (Schönert confirmed this). Now the productive portion of the earth's surface is pretty much a constant. This agreed to as well. At the moment we have 2.5 billion people, i.e., fifty times as many; and every day they increase by 100,000 : and so ? ! And now the opinions started bouncing off one another. (I'm all for sterilization of men – that's not castration – and for legalized abortion. There simply ought not to be more than 1 billion !)

Argumenum ad hominem : "Okay, then go get yourself sterilized, Herr Düring !" (Challenge and triumph : well ? !) : "Why right away, Herr

Runge ! Sooner today than tomorrow !". And Schönert, too, nodded in voluptuary amazement : "A free ride. And the pleasure's the same !", and bent deeper still over Fräulein Krämer's chair. (Then technical details : how it's done : bayonet in, foot down, and out. Or with a p'tatapeeler.)

"Left ! : – Left ! : – – A song !" (Labor Service), and the uniform marionettes jerked past legs adrumming, obediently laid back those Teutonic heads and burbled enthusiastically : "Oh saycrud land of loyalltee . . ." (and meantime millions were perishing in their concentration camps !) And the dashing gravediggers went on bawling, to be distinguished from a like number of mutton only in rough outline, my face delved deeper wrinkles, I sensed more ruins, more limbed corpses ("And like the eagle's winged flight / our spi-hirits so-hoar on high : fly on !"); No sardonic nod from me; no bitter smile; not me ! Only a damn shame that I, seeing this, will have to play blindman's buff with the rest. (Well, maybe you can just stand off to one side. We'll see). (Elephantiasis of the idea of the state).

Nails chewed at the edges, indifferently dressed, broad face surrounding dull eyes : "A passport, please." (In very subdued clear High German : now that's worth something !). And I questioned a biography out of him myself. (Wanted a visa for England : i.e., to emigrate. Sly devils, these writers. They all had no ‹dependents›, and were freely mobile. While folks like us). "Distinguishing features ?" : "– : Perhaps : wears glasses ? –" he suggested; nods and this and this. (But then it was too much for me after all, and I handed it to Master Otte to fill out in his splendid Sütterlin hand).

‹*Communal Reception, 12 noon*› : and it was another Reichstag session, with Hurrah and Heil and glee club and lusty bellowing; for closers : "passed unanimously". (Plus : "A song !". And were so proud : in England there's always that disgusting pro and con in parliament : but we're united, from top to bottom !). And throughout the populace the serene, happy conviction : the Führer will take care of it ! God, are the Germans stupid ! 95% ! (I.e., the others are no better either : just let the Americans elect themselves a Hindenburg sometime !)

People were carrying on like flags; their lips fluttered, their hands flapped, many of them ran swirling before the others. At the open windows the radios simmered and seethed their snappy music, into which gray wind now blended. Rain-light reappeared between the buildings, and soon thereafter liquid pins were skidding across asphalt seas.

Insensitive to the fate of my countrymen ? : Whatever engages in brown carryings-on, brays marches, and does wild commerce with a groat's

worth of words, is no countryman of mine ! He's Adolf Hitler's countryman ! (A half million perhaps are different, i.e. better; but then we
ought to give ourselves a different name, emigrate, to Saskatchewan, –
oh, it's all a sadness and un, and I stamped my skinny legs farther down
the pavement. Or to the Falklands for all I care).

Rain scratched the panes (of the compartment); it grew dark again in our
iron tube.

Brawl of wind : the hail prattled energetically. (Walsrode).

Woods : the entrance had been hurriedly hung with disorderly fog, whose
lower hems still dragged loosely back and forth over the grass; and so,
one corner raised, and a look inside : – (Dropped it. Damp in there.
Shrubberish. Me).

"Walk on over to Trempenau's. Get some cold-cuts". And I walked along,
stooped beneath the shallow sky hatched with rain, full of domestic
bitterness and resigned.

The great white she-wolf : she laughed through cunning teeth, and bought
rich red meat, and flabby pale sausages. Then she swung long-legged
into the bicycle frame, setting her sucklers aquiver, and slid away, alert
and cloudless. Between rain and sullen trees.

My favorite cat : even with my mere modicum of knowledge of the
universe (tee-hee : what does one star feel when another gets "too
close" ?), I'm sure she'll soon transport her young to the open field, far
off, so that she won't be completely neglected herself. (I've seen her
do it out of jealousy once before !) – Exactly the same with people :
once there are children, the man is neglected. (For years now my wife,
sullen and with sly sincere excuses, has avoided gratifying me ! There
will be consequences !).

"Well, Miss Femininity ?" (my daughter); came up bright-voiced and
wanted a mark for notebooks. "You're sure you're not underage for
this movie ?" I warned reproachfully, and she gave me a ladylike
slap (!) and laughed.

"Water – 's – ready !"; in wooden clogs and bathrobe with bundled towel,
I stalked into the scullery, to the tub of gray.

Naked (and scalded red); but it's almost too cold ! I lathered my chilled
rear and appurtenances; resolutely arose and terry-clothed everything
dry.

Rap at the pane : "Hàlloo !" Käthe Evers (the she-wolf) : she probed with
squint-eyes, recognized me, took a good look at it all, including chest
and legs, and laughed aloud. No doubt of it : her laugh exploded, and
she ran around the corner of the house. M. (Cosmotheoros : doesn't
that mean "peek-at-the-world" ?).

Clean underwear; and then I strode once more among the endless and dreadful, black-red tapestries of life, wailing, menacing, lingering in sleep.

Sitting in the armchair : the clock obediently twitched its little numbers at me. (Sometimes the big one inside would let out a haughty and squeezed laugh : "Ah !"; "Oh !"; then the hum of the courtier chorus returned). The cats pulsed inside their fur; breathing. Pulse means life. Maybe we are born between two breaths of the sun (ice-age; inter-ice-age). Presumably the conception of "time" is also dependent on the size of the living being in question; I have another conception than does a 4000-year-old sequoia, or an infursorium with a second of life, or a δ-cepheid star, or the Leviathan, or the stranger nearest me, or my neighbor . . .

In the shed : the latest thing is for bicycles to get taillights and license numbers : as if they were at fault for the accidents ! I have a better idea : no vehicle would be allowed to have a motor that could propel it faster than 25 mph : that would quiet things down at once. (But more than likely some manufacturer of electric lamps, or the friend of one, was sitting in the Reichstag; probably the simplest explanation).

The sun burned out at the lower edge of the sky (down to cloud cinders); out of the woods a gray moor-ghost arose; grass and withered things dripped much and snored (next to my high shoes, my trousers). I adjusted my head on its leg-stand to horizontal and measured about me : 5 lights, 200 degrees of woods, then marshland and muddled field (and no radio, no newspaper, no Volk, no Führer !). Wind accommodatingly coiffed my hair (which I'm not fond of at all !), and whishpurred washily and figarosy : cut it out !

Across the road, to where the she-wolf was oiling the garden gate. (And I walked in the grayvity of the air, as if through great winter coats, my hands closed tight and ear stilled). Cold. Gray ice-mush lay thin before every step; the woods cast desolate rings around the ashpit world; we gawked into each other's spotted souls (while coagulating gases eddied from our mouths. Hairy meaty troughs, that's us. And locked in the cold carton of slush). A mute return to our respective houses. (Later I saw her again at the window, tugging the curtain to one side. Soon I shall be a white-haired old man, with stump teeth and veined fingertubing, leaky hearted, with tough grisly notions, cluck cluck.)

At the very last : bloody cloud torsos piled in the west, the light's mass grave, drenched in gore, in smokiness. (The woods lay like a blue wreath mourning in silence around my horizon). The lunar wake light burned out quite rapidly too; the squarish houses in the development cast faint furtive glances from yellow nooks, velvet yellow in parlors, very soft images. (While out there clouds were dying !). Wire rattled once along the fence. Sotto voce. All this happening above sheet 3023, ordnance map.

"And spring : comes : tothevalley" : there's just no end to it ! (And wife and kids hummed contentedly along, and even clapped too !). "But in Spain 'tis one thousand and three" : dead, that is, at least; well, the civil war is finally drawing to its close (though with yet another grand tyrant !).

Wind grumbled in the evacuated night; clouds still moved about, whole wagonloads, gray; but it was cold again; the tiny feverish stars were already twitching.

Without sleep and the makis of thought crept quick as cats out of every shrubbery : documents claused with honor; schoolkids collared-sailor; pimply military bullied; punk lecheries stroked almond-milkily about my leg; summer trips of old slunk tigered light closer; in the green willow-basket of woods; the she-wolf sauntered past several times in search of seed; (and therefore not a continuum : a heap of bright illustrated tiles; a museum of flash-shots. I burrowed onto my other side, groaning and) cascades of immature headscarves scrutinized me; numbers painted white obligingly milestoned by (if I stray into algebra, then that's it for the night); and ever more dealings in old curios, neck or naught, until, in fact, I heard the 1-o'clock train whistle to me from Jarlingen.

Cloud isles with melting shorelines, a trim bright red skiff drifted there for a long time. (In the tidelands of my morning thoughts, wheels trundled now and again, a neighbor's lethargic curse. Get up, hop out of my pajamas).

: Me ? : Young ? ! (At the mirror : Ugh !). There is indeed a widespread misconception among the afflicted that they are twice as interesting at age 50 as at 25 : if I tucked in my little round belly, I was tall and slim (sure, and if I had lots of money I'd be a wealthy man). Hair moderately mildewed; behind the glasses goggly eyes : – No sir ! ! I stoutly turned my back on the fixture (then into my trousers and shaving, shaving, o thou delight of swains : that's the most disgusting part !).

A bush, which in lieu of leaves had titmice wearing chic black berets : bent forward with a defiant show of canary-green bosoms, and scolded for food. – " 've we still got a piece of bacon rind, Berta !"; but my wife was apparently still sweeping up, and yelled back in annoyance : "Don't bother me now. – : Later." I closed the door again : bueno;

gave the titmice the word, and read for a few minutes (no "Morning Benediction", not to worry ! Still prefer my "Écumoire").

"Holy Gohod we praihaise thy name :" (from Evers's wide-open radio across the way, while the old lady mugged pork chops and swept out her dress; and then the real gospelization started up). Even on long-wave there was solemn chewing on Cheesus Kraist, organs droning with bovine warmth, and there was no saving oneself from all those dairies of pious kindness. Wait : Radio Moscow, pfweewitt : and some ‹Character Sketch› or other tumbled out of the loudspeaker : I don't understand a thing about music, I admit, but that sure was too crude for me ! Marches, doodle waltzes, oom-pah music : no need for that either !

Rearranging furniture : is my wife's passion; every three months I come home to a strange house. – At first I was upset as usual; then indif-ferent : go ahead and do what you want ! And I helped carry and shove, whistling the while : fine with me ! (Besides which, she was happy that I was so cooperative : voilà, both sides served !)

Cock-a-doodle-doo : cackcackcockle; and they whetted their feet on the ground, plucked, beaked machines, in the bark, (one flapped several feet into the air, gabbling), and were dreadfully stupid. "All leghorns", oldman Weber explained proudly (convinced that came from the Ger-man "legen", much the same as Saanen goats from "Sahne". How awfully ignorant "the people" are and thus so easily deceived ! : when I hear a Führer-speech, I automatically compare it to Agamemnon, Pericles, Alexander, Cicero, Caesar, and on to Cromwell, Napoleon, Wars of Liberation, "Parties no longer exist for me" – and what an ass he was ! – and can only laugh at the resounding charlantanry. While "the people" think there was nothing like it anywhere ever, and don't see the consequences : instead of taking their cue from the dupes of millennia past, and thrashing the rear ends of such mountebanks ! – But ultimately ignorance is its own fault, and no cause for pity, and Weber wouldn't have believed me anyway, because "legen" seems so right, and "horn" sounds so Siegfriedian : therefore I slyly pronounced it just as fecundly as he, and we understood one another, too. And how).

"Foxes snatch chickens. Hawks snatch chickens." (People snatch chick-ens ! – : Wars snatch people; plagues snatch people, death snatches everyone ! – But that's going almost too far; I won't think about that any more !)

And speaking of Weber the cobbler ! : One of those fellows who can go on for hours telling about how they "served under 3 Kaisers," and with pride no less. He had even spoken with one of them : they had been

standing guard in front of the royal palace in Berlin; the coach pulled
up : Present arms ! – ! ! (– At this point he invariably added " 'nd did
we evah !"). "From Pomerania, my lad, right ?" his majesty had remarked affably, and then "Fine, fine" or "Stout fellow" or some other
such unforgettable phrase : what a thrill, right ? ! Weber swung his
spoon-chisel like a misericord and kept stroking away at his (long
since shaved-off) moustache.

Daddy's little girl's pastime : "Just imagine, dad : Käthe Evers from
across the street's a ‹sexion leader› now !" (That was the great she-
wolf, and I lent an ear : "Mm-hm." – Well, in my day, youth movements had flourished too; back then ‹Pluckfiddle Jack› and ‹maidens'
hostels› were all the rage : youth presumably comes only in packs. But
that was respectable at least, compared to this ‹National Youth› !)

Actually I was always a loner – always !

She was singing at the window across the way : a very simple folk song, the
medieval Lochheim school, and with such sweet intensity that I was
immediately suspicious : wasn't it you who almost bored a hole in my
scullery window yesterday ? ! (And right off Gerda sent up a military
salute).

A child wearing gloves, incessantly declaiming the word ‹palikánda›,
recitativo secco, presumably a name it had coined itself to designate
some Spicy Islands or other. (But in time the interminable singsong
proved too much for me, and I made an attempt to silence it by mental
telepathy; in vain again, of course; and so resigned myself to having to
put up with it).

A deer-, a dear-, a wandering deer-vish : at Weber's door, exchanged the
password, and came converting; to the New Apostolic Church, and got
fresh in that pious-familiar way common to all members of his tribe : "I
possess the Book of Books," he insisted with nauseating sanctimony.
"The Encyclopaedia Britannica ? !" I cried with feigned envy : "I'll be
damned !", and we stared in contempt at each other, for a bit, holy
Holbach, is there no end to such idiots ! – "We are here below but a
brief span of time : you must regard all you possess as merely lent to
you : house, money, clothes – –" (his really looked as if they had been).
"Our Lord Jesus : called only the simplest folk to him as apostles to
proclaim his word : who could neither read nor write !" (absurdly triumphant !) "Just keep holding fast to your precepts", I said in disgust,
letting the fellow babble on his way, and Weber met his kismet.

I am a servant of the heath, a worshiper of leaves, a devotee of wind ! (And
I exchanged heated words with myself for having responded to the
monkey in the first place.)

"Field drill ! –" and my wife pointed in distress at Paul Düring, age 16. "Let him do some knee-bends and shake the crap loose"; and my zebraic son, Feirefies, was enthusiastic. ("The expressions you use, Heinrich !"; my wife).

"Let me see your school notebooks"; and he handed them to me haughtily, as if to a lunatic. Leafing through : English satisfactory, French satisfactory, German satisfactory minus. (You have to take a look once in a while. Though my father, in all seriousness, would almost go crazy if I brought home a mere ‹good› instead of a ‹very good›; made dire prophecies, threatened to "yank me out", and played the regular fool). So, I put pedagogical wrinkles on my brow, but said nothing : was satisfactory after all, and that was that. (Above all, avoid lending support to teachers' grandiose fantasies that school is the world's navel or good for life or whatever). Then I weighed the notebooks in my hand, and gave it a try : "Tellmepaul – : you ever studied up on communism ?". He tumbled off his cloud and climbed right back up : "What the –" he began, and shook his head in merry derision; scornful : "Not worth the trouble ! The Third Reich put all that behind it long ago." "Meaning you know nothing about it, and let other people do your thinking for you ?" I challenged him coldly, "Have you compared it to National Socialism ? : You'd probably get quite a surprise.". "No comparison", he said coolly and with infinite superiority : "what we have is a weltanschauung"; and departed, a man once again sure of himself. (No point in saying anything to anyone !)

"What exactly does immunity mean, dad ?" (intended as the hand of reconciliation I suppose), and I explained it to him. "But why Reichstag members exactly ?". "Probably because they'd all be arrested first thing," I said nastily, and we could at least laugh a bit together. (Then I gave them each 2 marks : since human ingenuity has yet to devise a way for us to take our goods with us into the next world, from time to time one must teach children a disdain for money, cautious wastrels : "And spend it : saving is nonsense !" I added. Even if it makes every hair stand on end : I had to endure enough of the damned piggy-bank complex as a child !)

Another hour till mealtime : so some easy-chair reading. – – Hold it.

Ants in the parlor ! : Behind the bookcase, they streamed out from under the baseboard by the hundreds. Gerda swept them up onto the broad gray dustpan, and I sprayed a fine mist of DDT. (What a shame. They're bright fellows. Many murders and catastrophes : how they would rail against the Leviathan – i.e. me !; menacing and desperate, shaking their antennae, stamping defiance and heroic courage with all six feet. And my slit muzzle relentlessly blew poison and death. Hastings and fleeings, innumerably jointed, limberly escapist).

We humans, too, ought to be beheaded : very quickly, before old age and sickliness torment us, quite businesslike, with no transition. In your sleep. Or at woods' edge as you walk to the station, attacked by four hooded figures, dragged beneath the scaffold : plop ! !

At the bookcase : The big Spanish edition of Quixote by Diego Clemencin, 6 volumes quarto, Madrid 1833-39 : like to have that !

Swift, Cooper, Brehm : of the 13 volumes, I've always been most interested in the "Fishes". And then the "Lower Animals". (The most repulsive was always "Insects"). Whoever wants to write a book has to have a lot to say : usually more than he has. – Middle High German perhaps ? : often in castles : Soltane and Canvoleis, Belripar and Montsalvaz, Cardigan and Grahars, and all those other ancient magical names that leave you sitting there moaning at knuckles. Or medieval tales : Herzog Ernst (the journey through the hollow mountain, that especially. And the Agrippinas); Fortunatus and his sons. Great man, Ludwig Tieck (And in contrast how stiff-legged and precocious Goethe's prose seems, so "respectable" and Privy-Councillorish : it never once dawned on him that prose could be an art form; you can only laugh, e.g., at the pompous bungling of his "Novella" !)

Every writer should grab hold of the nettle of reality; and then show us all of it : the black filthy roots; the poison-green viper stalk; the gaudy flower(y pot). And as for the critics, those intellectual street-porters and volunteer firemen, they ought to stop tatting lace nets to snare poets and produce something "refined" themselves for once : that would make the world sit up and take roaring notice ! Of course, as with every other grand and beautiful thing, poetry is hedged in by its complement of geldings; but : the genuine blackamoors are the ones who rejoice in the sun's black spots ! (All of this for the reviewers' albums).

Tierra del Fuego : Young Darwin travels to the Fireland. – Must be lovely : wide dense cold rain forests. Savage light from endless cloudworks. Sea and hard mountain heads. No men and no snakes : lovely ! (I'd loathe tropical jungles. I'm for cold forests, endlessly spare. I'd love to see the ones in northern Canada. And, as noted, those of Fireland. – "Din-ner's-read-dy !")

One still on the loose, a loner, between shelved abysses : give him the shoe ! (That's how I'd like to die too : running darkly among tree torsos, inspecting herbs, puppy-tracking berries : and then hit with a half-ton meteor ! : Jagged flame, compacted head. Sela (probably Hebrew for ‹that's it›)).

Roast with sauerkraut ("Music to Dine By : from German Broadcasting"; and once again the ever-popular favorites, a tilting at melody, opus 0.5). – Cats have a passion for sautéed mushrooms, with onions, pepper, salt, caraway. – "Lie down a bit."

I waited patiently for the dishes to be done.

Last try : I cupped my wife's right breast in my hand, and coaxed : "C'mon". (Swallow). "Let's, what do you say !" – –. "But you've still got such a nasty cold", she sidestepped with hypocritical concern (as if I were a daddy of 70 !), and, when I didn't let go of her mammary flesh at once, added "Ouch.", with martyrific composure. – : Okay, the end. –

Okay, the end ! ! : once-and-for-all the end ! I went to my room, M., and stretched out for a while. (At my age you simply can't think anymore after a good meal. At best maybe a little work. – What I trust most are the beauties of nature. Then books; then roast with sauerkraut. All else changes, legerdemains).

"I'm going for a little walk. – ? – Toward Benefeld.". Shuffling wind waded insolently through the blue and gray puddles, blew rings on them, almost splattering.

‹*Cordingen Lumber*› on the sign above legs discreetly ringed white and blue; (apparently had been yellow and black at one time).

At a village window : the typical knotted curtains of the central Lüneburg Heath, and behind them the vase of asters : cold white, colder wobbling violet. And the wind was running again in great gray groups. The world, a new unplastered construction, drafty, and at best a charcoal stove inside (to dry it out; desolate and echoing, like a deserted ball-room).

"Come : let's play Winter Relief Fund" : She shakes her little box, and He sticks something in; I gave my ten pfennigs and got back a gray fish with button-eye as proof I'd payed my taxes; and they were standing on every corner, collecting, farmers and townsfolk of Brandenburg stock, costumed in brown and belted with shiny leather, caps like French gendarmes, frozen a pretty red, and I smiled, and kept pointing at my fish (my, he's a hard-working fellow : I'll hold on to him, with his blue eye !).

The large munitions factory, ‹Eibia›, with its railroad tracks, streets, giant bunkers (overgrown on top with camouflage forests), and thousands of workers. While down on the Warnau lay the whole little New Town of a hundred bright houses, and very prettily done. – But elderly light gnashed on high and wallowed and weltered, grew gray and severe, the black slowly pushing my way. Bald bushes were already rapping witches' knuckles.

Skat jargon (had had a beer) : have they ever actually been collected, from "pants down" for open nullo, to "the man with the long club" ? Would make a doctoral dissertation for a "folklorist", they shrink from nothing. (But what else should I think about ? ! Death ? God ? : ah, good god ! Even the most beautiful evening sky above the Oster Moor passes away : why should an old stink-sack like me want to be eternal ? ! Swell-headed Christian bunch ! – So head back).

Piece of country road. Moon. Me. : We stared at each other, until old stony-face up there had had enough and with help from the wind sleight-of-handed himself a shade of blue, two against one, smeared the road with pasty white light (and ogled me for a long time from behind gauze, veils, cloths, trays, bales).

The ‹Coaster Express› at the Cordingen station : a lopsided giant carousel with varying circles of light and whetting samba music : ". . . and from the top – : / it's no go ! It's no go !". (Followed at once by "Maria from Bahia", and on the nimbly flowing conveyor belt, the she-wolf with wide calves and cartwheeling coat. And Paul was watching eagerly, too).

Encore une fois : the spongy moon in curdled cloudworks. Left : houses gray and soapy; black ajarred doors leading in; roofs wrinkled clear to the top. On the right : along the sallow rag of meadow, wool and silk, and populated by the shades of enslaved, half-starved trees.

Genealogical research : my son quizzed me greedily (and as usual treated as a sport : who can trace back the furthest). Thankgod it quickly came to an end with my illegitimate father, and disappointed, he jotted it down. Nor in the other lines were there any great men to be hunted down – officers, politicians, artists : had all been very simple honest folks !

"Turn on the news." : weather; results from the latest charity drive; soccer; even now the after-throes of the ‹Day of the Assumption of Power›. Crisis in rump Czechoslovakia (they definitely want to occupy that too : well, I'm curious how long they'll get away with it).

In bed : the days passed, regularly, like tearing pages from a calendar. At once the grave countenance of "my" commissioner appeared to me, and I got the frenzied notion to tattoo something on that broad fore-head of his, with indelible ink : so he'd have to run around forever like that ! I wavered for a long time between "Bon voyage !" and "Vote Communist !" (and his wife gets it big on her belly, just above where the hair starts, – – : "Come in !" ? Nah. – – "Encore" ? Nah. No good. But then it hit me : "Welcome Stranger !", in Bodoni Antiqua, so painstakingly I engraved it; and avenged, giggled off to sleep).

Radium numbers : only 3. To the john, number one; and then to the window : boulders of air with polished edges; across the way, fields and roads done in angular woodcuts by the moonlight, until barely recognizable.

Idea : if we had gospels by women, by Mathilda Margo Lucy and Johanna, you can rest assured that the redeemer would have been of female gender as well. (The death mask of the moon was still hanging in the stonegray sky).

The gaunt silver-mailed face (behind the house) : the Don Quixote of the stars. (And the earth is his fat Sancho Panza with pork-chop heart and big baloney imagination : why just yesterday, didn't "Your Hit Parade" start off with "When Huba plays the tuba down in Cuba" ? ? What kind of insensitive automata could ever

a) lyricize & musicize

b) sing it and cut a public record

c) even buy it

d) broadcast it

e) sit there and peacefully (or excitedly for that matter) listen to it !

(: Who does all that ? ! : your famous ‹Aryan German› ! An employee of Western Christian Civilization, Inc. !)

Achillean fellow, the moon : dragged a stiff cloud corpse behind him around our earthenware Troy (blustery).

Her girlfriend (in the train) : She wore a pair of dark snow-goggles, by the aid of which every modern teen thinks she's donned a spell of wide-eyed mystery (if only they could keep their mouths shut then !). This one had Sarah-Leandering eyes and mutely opened her book, its cover coarse-fleshed, emphatically made for the Volk : – ? – : Hans Friedrich Blunck ! (That too !).

What wretched trash ! (Besides which, she held it so that the gilt edge kept flashing in my eyes ! That too !).

And the poor she-wolf ! : a black fountain pen (with golden belt) rotated in its yellow grove of fingers, slowly and sadly gleaming; josephine baker, cul de Paris; her brow mutinied, her mouth lipped reluctantly on lycéean word-grids; her worn-down shoes stood with toes turned wearily in. (Afterward, came something fervid about "medieval German painting", as she gruffly told her friend, and asked her for a few makeshift syllables. – Pretty sight, the way the young savages brewed away angrily at the spectral stuff : just keep right on rebelling !)

"Sure, Herr Peters !". Outside, white cloud balls rose up from the horizon; the elastic wind bounced by, and then again, like a high-jumper. "Didja hear Goebbels yesterday ?" (And the way he speaks, Quick & Slow,

vaulted words, round as eggs, and all of it crap, invalid and outrageous) : "Sure, I heard him." (Wasn't true at all ! I've got more serious
things to do with my time !). "Now that's a real conviver !" (Peters on
Goebbels. = Shrewd character. From ‹Qui vive› of course).

Take a look around the platform : in the impoverished, red-frozen sky the
solid saucy moon, grin silence. A tractor hammered, jeered stench,
popped impertinent : ‹Pfeiffer Coal Company›.

On past the book store : it still seems remarkable enough : when I was just
a schoolboy, my father gave me an English dictionary one Christmas,
and apparently expected storms of enthusiasm. Today I stand nodding
reverently before the great Grieb-Schröer and would like to have it.

Scandal, scandal : Otte's cousin (the one from Berlin) had used the occasion of his visit to give himself a promotion to squad leader in the SA,
and was now to be excommunicated. : Just like the "Führers" up top,
who are forever thinking up new titles for each other, new ranks and
Arabian-Nights' uniforms. The whole nation is in the grip of a mania
for medals and badges, enthusiastically weaving away on the legend
of its own grandeur ! : The sort of thing that truly fits the Germans to
a T !

In which case, I'd prefer Schönert's snappy smut; "Yes ?", and you really
did have to laugh : he gave me a clandestine peek at Fräulein Knoop's
coat-of-arms – the busy and fat one, pinky-white and frosty – a naked
girl with a candle in her hand, and the motto "nosce te ipso" –. A well-
honed mind, Schönert's (though not a polished one); but he's "against"
them too, as far as it goes, and mutual nausea is enough to create a kind
of working sympathy; and, after all, most people are ignorant to the
same degree they are clever.

That's the musical instrument I hate the most : the people's accordion !
With its bloated, wishy-washy, knobby tones.

HeilittlerSomethingIcandoforyou ?" (and play the citizen, fine, and keep
the nation going; let not thy right hand know. So I raised it lightly in
German greeting, while balling my free left fist : will divide my life
that way : an open half, supportive of the state. And the balled left).

(I reserve for myself any action against the state ! : that's necessary for my
personal security ! For the state can forcibly constrain me to participate
in anything its responsible-irresponsible leaders may feel like thinking
up : whereas in an emergency I do not have the power to force the state
to prudence or justice or fulfillment of its duties. Therefore I must constantly resist the arbitrary power of the state – not forgetting that most
fundamental right : being allowed to leave said state unendangered
and with all my property intact. And don't anyone come along with the

lofty objection : that as a petty civil servant I simply lack a broad overview of things ! ! And may your generals and politicians roar as brazenly as they like about the Golden Age that has just burst upon us : in ten years you'll have totally demolished Germany ! And then we'll see who was right : little Düring, or all the big shots and 95% of the German people ! But I am completely outraged by the notion of joining in the dance, of being forced to join against my better judgment; and I will shape my actions accordingly !)

A telephone call : "Herr Commissioner ? – –. – –." : "11:30, yes sir. – Yes sir." Bang hang up. – "Meeting of all department heads in the boss's office," I explained to Peters, "another major house-cleaning for sure : bewailing of infirmities."

In the Commissioner's office and silence. Naturally he kept us waiting to impress us; eight men and the lady caseworker with the Queen Luise badge on her blue linen Valkyrie breast. All right by me : all gets deducted from our work-time ! (Unfortunately from our life-time as well). Hissing of the radiators.

Above him on the wall : von Seeckt, the "Founder of the New German Army", Heil, with persuasive monocle : a tradition of upper-echelon officers that can be traced to Wodan (cf. Rudolf Herzog's report concerning the Götterdämmerung : ". . . his one lone eye flashed and glinted").

"No, you may go, Frau Woltermann."; leaning back (he looked as if he were thinking very incisively about nothing). "Which of you has – uh –" skillful pause; once more he casually picked up the document (although he knew every detail of the contents; to be followed at once by the customary dressing-down) – "had some higher education ?", he said it with lofty commiseration : "– matriculated perhaps." ("Or whatever" would have been even better. Whereas his diss for his PhD had been on "The economic history of cabinet-making in the principality of Leiningen, its contemporary importance and its prospects for the future" !) "The other gentlemen may return to their work –", like being at the court of Prince Irenäus. And now he looked at us three more closely. "You're only 26, Herr Schönert ? – 27 ? – Hmm. – Yes, well, that won't do, thank you." He looked intensely at the window and gave himself a long pinch under his white chin : God, how difficult it was to make oneself understood with mere-high-school graduates ! "Do you still know any foreign languages ? – Latin or English or French ? –" (Very hesitantly, as if it were hopeless; and avoid the "and" at all cost; and I smiled to myself, arrogant and forbearing, malicious and patronizing : oh god, how we despised one another ! !). "I sure don't 'nymore,

Commissioner, sir," Nevers declined, believably aghast, and so he too left us, alone. "Well then : you do speak English ?" he asked in English, indulgently and with a genial smile; and we exchanged a few ragged idioms, coprolithic phrases, while I labored to imitate his botched pronunciation. Yez. (Yes). "Fine," he said, more soberly and businesslike : "by the way – where did you learn to speak English so – uh – tolerably well ?" "In the first world war, Herr Commissioner. Served in France; and then as an English prisoner-of-war. Was camp interpreter; I still read it fairly often, too." "Ah, you were a soldier !" he feigned surprise : "– uh – your rank ?". "Just an enlisted man, Commissioner, sir", jauntily (i.e. the last three months as a noncom, but I wasn't about to tell him that : with people like him it's best to set boundaries and keep as much distance as possible !)

"Ah yes : And you're already – uh – ?". "51, Herr Commissioner". He nodded, lips pressed tight : "That does nicely !" he said with emphasis; then : "Do you have any particular leanings, active member in a church or that sort of thing ?". "As a civil servant, sir, I know only church-es", I declared as prescribed by regulation : "I do not care if I write ‹catholic› or ‹turk› or ‹agnostic› in someone's passport." He weakly smiled his approval : "Not religious then," he summarized, nodded, came to a decision : "Really is high time such nonsense came to an end." Directed to the clock, more lively now : "Fine, then, Herr Düring ! – What we are concerned with is the following : recently we received orders to set up a kind of archive here in the office, dealing with the history of the district – we'll clear out a room or two in the cellar for it – uh – and we'll have to gather materials, documents and such from the various towns and villages, sift through and file them. Possibly local parish records as well; and – should there be time – perhaps from those of private individuals as well. On the whole a massive task – and of course carries a great deal of responsibility with it" he dutifully interjected, "and then, too, it presupposes – a certain – knowledge of foreign languages. Latin, French, English principally, I'd say – uh – you would have to inspect most items, I presume, out in the field – in" he interrupted himself, and looked over to the large district map on the wall – "– in – uh : Ahlden and Rethem, for instance : mountains of material there I'm sure; Walsrode, too, perhaps; possibly Stellichte, at Herr von Baer's –" he waved this aside testily, as if I had made some irksome request : "– well, I know him personally, so I could – if need be – arrange for your – – being admitted. –" he raised his head in affable candor : "Quite interesting work, wouldn't you say ? ! – You're an intelligent fellow : – ?" (What an impudent

bastard; but I at once gave tit for tat : I smiled such a blissfully stupid smile and gave such a silly obsequious nod that he noticed, and grew deadly serious; he gnawed slowly on his gray sausage lips. Pause). "I should be most hesitant to assign this to one of our high-school teachers," he continued dispassionately, "since those gentlemen make difficulties and demands enough as it is. – Would you want to take it on ?" and with eyes ever so bright and clear, like Nietzsche's mountains in the forenoon. I briefly knit my brow; then (by way of clarification) I inquired as to the duration of the special mission. "Yes, of course," he said with a nod, "I would propose that you devote 3 days a week to it – and I'll add another, older trainee to your department. – Who could stand in for you those 3 days every week ? Whom would you suggest ? Peters, Schönert, : which is the more dependable ?" (Typical rotten trick, passing the question on to me !). "The more dependable is Peters; the more intelligent Schönert –" I said critically, feigning concern. "Which means ?" he demanded (secretly smiling and curious; but I did not betray myself). "If I may make a suggestion," I hesitated manfully, and then ethically : "Herr Peters !". "Fine," he nodded to me with satisfaction, "There are, how-ever, some – further incidental instructions you'll need, and – I also want to satisfy myself fully as to your qualifications – : could you come by my place for an hour or so this evening ?" (‹Place›, how mod-est : it was that 12-room villa on Walsrode Road !) "Shall we say   then – : 6 P.M. – : is that agreeable ? !" (How silly, considering he's the ‹master› and I'm the lackey !); to close the deal, forced a cheese-smile, and nodded into the void with a look of torment and overwork.

"Well ? !" (curious), and I told them in brief. (And Peters was proud to be my stand-in; and Schönert wasn't offended or anything : nooo : relieved ! : Spirit of my spirit ! That's precisely why I did it that way. Would've been a catastrophe the other way around). – Wind springs up outside and clouds.

David Copperfield : Schönert suggested that the name of the supporting hero, Steerforth, be transcribed phonetically into German as ‹Stier-fortz› (= bull fart) (not all that wrongheaded; he's always coming up with something new). Then lunch; sandwiches and a stroll.

Clouderama (like the Judgment of Paris) : a slender nimble one in most clinging white; a proper fatty with baronially rounded butt, and majes-tic bosom of fat, as if built by the Romans. (Later, then, the breezy skinny one with red piratical hair and the narrow bluish back of a busy whore : so She's the winner !)

In front of a movie poster : the she-wolf with schoolbag. She was comparing legs, breasts and blonde giggles with her own (and didn't lose; though her face was blunt and gamy) : "Might I ask a favor of you, Fräulein Evers : –". She merely turned her massive head (was not to be surprised). "Käthe" she said laconically through her teeth, and I laughed awkwardly : "– Okay, fine – : Fräulein Käthe –". "Käthe" she said more menacingly "– what is it ? ! –". Confused and giddy, I swallowed hard : "Please, Käthe", I said (and our eyebrows whipped blissfully : She's the winner !) : "Could you stop on your way home and tell my wife : I'll be taking the late train this evening. And so on." "And so on." she repeated imperturbably, nodded that she was agreeable, and then coolly reimmersed herself in studying the line of the calf : placed her foot forward (and seemed satisfied).

Blue silk sky and embroidered with white (but a pattern, some homey proverb, was not to be made out), and I stalked on through streets frozen dry, and inspected the ancient shop windows : a man really ought to own a Visolett magnifying glass like that. 6 inches in diameter, for maps and such; but they were scandalously expensive too, guaranteed 20 marks, and I then went on to muster the hollow spectacle frames in their perfect rows.

Pooh ! : Bedouin dust pelted an ashen path down the blustery street, cloaks of sand spooked about, setting the wind horses to snorting outright.

A very cool résumé of Hanoverian history : how it all sort of coagulated peu à peu : the principalities of Bremen and Verden; Lüneburg and Celle; the earldoms of Hoya and Diepholz; right in the middle along the Weser, bounded in quince-yellow, the merry little enclave of Thedinghausen. The connections with the Court of St. James; the French and Prussian occupation. (Sure : learned in school).

Memories (school memories) : Max Hannemann and Kurt Braunschweig : those two had great literary talent; essays of humorous social criticism. (All vanished !). – A cloud carefully watered the clearing across the way (but left me in peace), and then drifted off on its mission.

Light in the office : the desk lamps, bent like bobbed-haired women, mutely diligent; the angular printed forms turned an unbearable forest green and gave sweet pain; empty posters of light askew on the walls and overlapping like expressionist paintings. "Not taking the train tonight, Herr Düring ?". "I still have to go see the commissioner. At his place." Lower lips shoved forward in admiration; with Peters it was respectful envy. And rompings of clouds, black and red behind spears of pine.

October pibroch (and here it was February) : and a whole clan of gray
clouds, ladies from hell, marched my way; the fields began to mutiny
hoarsely; skeletal bushes grasped (clutched) one another in despair. At
her shop window, a sporty salesgirl appeared and wrestled down the
iron grating. (Then another girl, superfluous, who helped her : fewer
people !) More fans of bare trees, brown lace fans, giant tracery; more
books and square feet per capita : therefore fewer people !)

The curt moon sat on the rim of the steeple; the one black bell, in the belfry
opening, growled dully to those below.

The lilliputian whinnies of the doorbell : hauntings in the house. First, distant and meaningful slam, then the taking of many more stairs than
could belong to the gloomy flight, a cavernous clang and murmurings,
it dragoned its way to just behind the door and lay there in keyed-up
ambush :

The maid : a wagtail aflutter and proper and affected as a fancy doll ("What
a pair of lung lobes !" Schönert would have marveled). "Yes, the Herr
Commissioner is in". "I know", I said pointedly, "and he knows too.
Please tell him that Düring is here. Dü-rrink." (Well, go on : yellow
stairwell, vaulted; silly pretenses).

From the little mirror in the guest toilet came abrasive shrill light (pictures
of Schandau and Königstein, curlicued soil, as if designed by some
Balthasar Pöppelmann or other : hate thy neighbor as thyself !).

The elegant chairs leaned back with an easy superiority; the table's broad
stump was missing mossy roots (and fungal gelatin of floral yellow on
the side). – I entered, so artfully clumsy that I almost tripped over the
brown tendrils in the carpet : my my, that did please the boss qua boss
(and in general).

Smiling, he approached the round table : he acknowledged me, o joy !
The table lamp (its shade pasted with delicate grasses : looked quite
nice !); first guidelines & recommendations, available resources,
"– my library is, of course, at your disposal –", Dictionary of German
Biography (: know it all better than you ! And we turned our bespectacled faces to one another, benevolently – he – and maliciously – I).

"The records will only date back to the Thirty Years War at best". "In any
case do keep me informed about the more interesting findings." And I
jotted it all down on my pad with zealous nods, thrilled, probably
wrote ‹Mooncalf Moses› between the lines too, smiled submissively,
and dotted the i on ‹compoop›.

"You have a bicycle, don't you ?" : "Yes sir, Commissioner.", and gazed
at him with earnest schoolboy eyes, the beloved instructor of the
Working Classes : which means I'm to pedal all over your district ? !.

"You live in – uh : –", "Colony Hünzingen, Herr Commissioner."
"Ah – I see" : "Yes, sir. Just off the new road Benefeld-Ebbingen –".
"Ah, the one they've improved on account of the powder bakery !" he
nodded, drawing cross brows (was, you see, a big government thing,
top secret, and absolutely not under his jurisdiction, the Eibia !) :
"Well then, obviously you have your monthly rail-pass for Fallingbostel, –" (I tucked a bow like a railroad switch) "and hold other ex-
penses down as much as possible. Of course we'll cover any necessary
items; but : within limits, understood ?" Ductile and tranquil : "But of
course, Herr Commissioner." (but mix in a dollop of petit-bourgeois
pique) : "but of course !" "Good."

He leaned back (therefore, end of the official segment; and now yellow Sir
Lion wants to amuse himself somewhat with the Mouse; and I gazed at
him as intensely as if I were about to paint his portrait – : – ? – ? – :)

She hit the switch with an energetic graceful slap (his daughter) and the
funnel of light took its position in the room around us. I was cut asun-
der between glare and shadow, and I sensed bodily discomfort.

A white face : very pretty, arrogant, barred by two red lip-bolts; eyes cold
and chemical, her young hair made one swift motion (18 years old;
therefore in the girls' high school, therefore in Käthe's class. And it
was too cold upstairs to study).

("Yes, Sir Lion ?") : "Tell me – Düring –" (the pause was wonderful !)
"– hmm; have you ever dabbled with philosophy ? = Kant,
Schopenhauer." (jauntily) : "and so on ?"

(Are you in for a surprise !) : "Yes, in the past, Herr Commissioner; I read
a lot of that sort of thing; as a young man."

He smiled, supercilious and academically blessed; very much amused
with formica sapiens : "Why only in the past, Herr Düring ?" (most
snidely) : "Have you outgrown it ? !". (And his daughter, behind us in
an armchair, her silken legs tucked high, let her book fall very slowly).

I drank down the cognac (unsanctioned; the plebs has no manners); in the
junkyard corner of my brain I searched for something appropriate for
this nandu; and lo, a rusty cerebral spiral lay right at hand :

"At one time I had" (and now the first hammerblow !) : "a wise boss" (and
not a word was true !), "who explained the following to me : let us
presuppose beings with a two-dimensional sense of space – who live
here on a single plane –" (I passed my hand in the air, just above the
table) "– and if I were now to penetrate their living space with the
fingers of my hand –" (I let them dangle like the tentacles of a jellyfish) "– what our two-dimensional beings would perceive now would
be –" : "5 circles", he said, furrowing his brow (so he's been able to

follow thus far). "Yes. 5 separate beings;" I said darkly, "individuals. But without ever guessing or being able to determine that, further up, in three-dimensional space, they are subordinated to another unit – my hand.". "Or : I thrust my thumb down into the plane of their world –" (which I did :) "– and then pull it out again – i.e. it disappears for the guys down-under; and then a little later stick my index finger in at another spot in their world. For them that means : 2 distinct beings, widely separated by time and space; but nevertheless they are bound together in the higher unity of my three-dimensional hand." (He frowned and thought it over; somewhat disconcerted; but I went right ahead, icily : Tu l'as voulu, George Dandin !)

"Then the gentleman," ('twas I myself : the gentleman ! Victory !) "supporting his argument with sufficient proofs, suggested that our three-dimensional world, too, is likewise overshadowed by a four-dimensional one. And that one apparently by a 5-dimensional one; for a description of electron movements, the best choice is a 6-dimensional space, etc. – I suppose I could reconstruct the argument even now" (I threatened obsequiously; and then added casually) : "I then worked my way through Hilbert's ‹Non-Euclidian Geometry›, etc. – : So here we are, equipped with a completely inadequate intellect, (one of the Demiurge's dirty tricks !), splashing about in a sea of imponderables : ever since I've given up the pursuit of metaphysics. Fits of speculation come very seldom. These days I stand here and keep track of what those ridiculous old ladies (the Parcae) may have in store for me and the rest of the world."

He protruded the tip of his tongue (that's not all that ladylike either) and thought for a long long time (surely not an appropriate ‹Weltanschauung› for a Prussian civil servant; but when it came to natural sciences, he seemed to have the usual not-the-vaguest of most ‹academics›, of the ‹classically educated›; easily confused and impressed : so there : I, too, can be antiseptic ! : "Vote Communist", and I gaped all the more 'umbly).

The daughter (very pretty face – but I mentioned that already ? !), with her thighs spread wide and visible a long way up, slowly turned a ring on her little finger, and gazed at me through impenetrable lashes. (Just like in the picture).

Another topic (a Parthian shaft) : "You read a lot, Herr Düring ?" (Just like in the army, when the general sometimes inquires : Children ? Six ? Good man; good man : keep it up ! ! – So then, keep distance !) : "Now and again. Sundays. Herr Commissioner."

"What sort of things do you read ?" (‹sort of stuff› would have been

even better). "Prose mainly, Herr Commissioner". (confidentially) :
"Things like : epics, lyric poetry, ballads : they're not for me". –
"– And what sort of stuff is ?" (finally ‹stuff› ! Now coldly) : "Wieland,
a lot of Wieland, Herr Commissioner; Cooper, Holberg, Moritz,
Schnabel, Tieck, Swift; Scott too." (I didn't mention ‹Expression-
ists› : not to you;) : "and Romantics –" I added, mollifying with sweetness and light (because these fellows don't know the Romantics anyway : not their grand pioneering in artistic form, nor their concerto
grosso of words, don't know Wezel, nor Fouqué, nor Cramer, you
goldbrickers !). He nodded slowly and solemnly at each name (hadn't
the vaguest, and I gave him a farewell jab) :

"*In Germany*, you know, we have a very simple method for recognizing an
intelligent person." – " : ? –". "He loves Wieland." – But he had some
strength after all; he replied with dignity : "I don't know him." "Oh :
but the Commissioner knows so many other things," I said quickly,
making use of the lofty third person, and so insincerely, giving him an
inane and wicked smile and left him to draw his own conclusions
(amusing, how we despised one another; and nevertheless wanted to
impress each other, both of us. Maybe we are two tentacles of the same
four-dimensional jellyfish, slowly swaying, full of bright stinging
vesicles, thalassic; and we can't perceive good and evil either : if I
were to thrust my hand through that two-dimensional world in order
to rescue a kitty meowing down there, a hundred thinking transpar-
ent triangles might very well perish while I'm at it ! One universe is
always emanating out of the other : we emanate the world of techno-
logical forms. Bense). Then a bow to the daughter of the house : long
legs !

The night had a round red taillight of a moon. (Only thing missing was the
license plate; otherwise all according to regulations).

Railroad switches bowed and scraped : respectfully : Düring !; signals
jerked supplicating scrawny arms (with fingerless saucered hands);
squiddy eyes stared red and green out of tin-boxed lids; below, sinewy
iron braced right and left against itself : small station.

Strangely restive in the forest today : ‹The mists lie low. The game it has no
scent, nor clearer view›. Or : ‹Among the branches, rustlings. The
snow it roils and swirls; no breeze, no draught›. Or : ‹Howling in the
woods›. (And so on past, ever deeper. With howling.)

The crow described a grating black line in the echoless air. Moon appeared
and examined me icily from clouded lids of yellow-silver. The emaci-
ated shrubs huddled closer together in the terrible pallor. So I stood for
a long time, imprisoned in the gaunt garment of the garden. The moon

grew sharper, bright, like an orator before a starry mob. Wind honed my face; and after a time solitary flakes shot in from the east (then once again shallow cold). As I entered the house, my steps danced a muffled bumpkin dance around me, the frozen curving path thumping me up to the stiff front door.

"Late aren't you ? Everything's cold." (my wife), and she scolded, the words balling in her mouth, scoffed and ran out of breath (my wife). Eventually I managed to calm her down : the honor : at the commissioner's home !

Beating of war drums along the Memel (10 o'clock news) : how long can they get away with it ?

One thing emanates the others : the n-dimensional emanates the (n-1)-dimensional; and it the (n-2) -dimensional : : but who is N ? ? ! !

1. All that exists refers either to the Invisible or the Divine Pleroma, including what has occurred both within and without the Pleroma, or to those things belonging to the visible world.

2. The Divine Pleroma contains 30 Aeons, of which 15 are male and 15 female.

3. The head, root and source of all these Aeons is the one, invisible, eternal, unbegotten and unknowable God, (N !), who by virtue of these his attributes is called Proarchon, Propater and Bythos, which is to say : the First Principle, the First Father and the Deep Abyss.

4. This God of the inscrutable deep has taken as his spouse a principle which is named Ennoia or Innermost Thought, Sige or Silence, and Charis or Grace.

5. And upon being impregnated by Bythos, this spouse bore to him Nous or Understanding, the Only-Begotten Son, the Father, and the principle or root of all other things.

6. Together with Understanding was also born Aletheia or Truth. And this first Tetrad or foursome is the root and source of all things.

7. Out of this Tetrad arose yet a second Tetrad, consisting of Logos or the Word, Zoë or Life, Anthropos or Man, and Ekklesia or the Church.

8. These two Tetrads form an Ogdoad, that is : an eightfold principle, which is likewise the root and source of all things.

9. Logos moreover has brought forth out of himself a new Dekad, that is a tenfold principle. These ten are named : Bythius or the Deeps, Mixis or Fusion, Ageratos or That-Which-Never-Dies or Never-Ages, Henosis or Union, Autophyes or the Self-Begotten, Hedone or Lust, Akinetus or Immobility, Synkrasis or Moderation, Monogenes or the Only-Begotten-One, and Makaria or the Blessed One.

10. Anthropos sired with Ekklesia a Dodekad or twelvefold number of Aeons; the names of these are : Parakletos or the Comforter, Pistis or Faith, Patrikos or Paternality, Elpis or Hope, Metrikos or Maternality, Agape or Love, Aeonous or Eternal Reason, Synesis or Intelligence, Ekklesiastikos or the Son of the Church, Makariote or Blessedness, Theletos or That-Which-Is-Desired-of-Itself, and Sophia or Wisdom.

11. The whole Host of Aeons consists of this Ogdoad, Dekad and Dodekad, the parents of the first being Bythos and Sige, of the second Logos and Zoë, of the third, however, it is Homo and Ekklesia who are the parents.

12. Not all Aeons are of the selfsame nature, and among them it is Nous alone who exists in perfect and eternal communion with Bythos or the inscrutable God.

13. From this arises a longing of Aeons to find union with Bythos, which longing so heated the last of the Aeons, Sophia, in particular, that in her rutting she would have been virtually swallowed up by the universal omnipleromic creature, had she not been held back by Horos or the Limit, that is, he who is the force which holds all things to their nature, to their bounds and character and which determines and encloses all things that come within his circle and so prevents them from being swallowed up by Infinity; and thus he brought her to herself once again and returned her to her nature, to her circle and limits.

14. Nevertheless Sophia, overheated by her ruttings, conceived, but the very violence of these motions caused her to miscarry, and she brought a deformed child into the world, bringing upon it all manner of fears, distress, terrors and afflictions.

15. It came to pass, however, that Sophia was once again cleansed by Horos and returned to her position among the Aeons within the Pleroma; her bastard child, however, Enthymesis or Desire, and its companion Passio or Passion, were banished from the Pleroma and ejected by force.

16. Enthymesis, who was also called Achamoth because she had been untimely born of Sophia, was from thenceforth in darkness, in the void, having no form, no figure and light; for this reason Christos on high took pity upon her and impressed upon her something of his nature, but then pulled back from her, and left her half perfect and half imperfect.

17. And since through him Achamoth had now received a soul, she had a still greater longing for that light which she lacked; but when she pressed her way toward it, Horos held her back, and she was overcome with grief, fear, care and sadness and tormented by repulsive thoughts. And this is the origin of matter, all liquids come from her tears, all light

things from her laughter, all heavy things or corporeal elements from her sadness and dismay . . . . (and so on, to 40.); gets to be too much).

The black steed of night : with the broad silver blaze, tears, laughter and dismay, kept snorting at my window.

(*All that is incomprehensible* : to resolve it into more comprehensible parts).

II
(May/August '39)

The bright village : awakening it blinked and opened all shiny windows; every house crowed like a cock, and curtains flapped pastel wings to the tune. (One pair had fat red polka dots; pretty, against puffed-up pale yellow).

Bushes in scaly sea-green capes appeared along all paths and waved me, trembling and yearning ever deeper down the road; stood as spectators at meadow's edge; did trim gymnastics; whispered wantonly with chlorophyll tongues, or suddenly whistled loud trills; the bushes.

The maid in her violet smock tipped the bucket and glittering yellow waste water, setting her black flies murmuring below. Blue-scarred cabbage and flabby onion spikes. The nimble door gave another whack : and sealed the silence. Good. (Silence : good !)

Snouts of wind grubbed all through the grass, and snored a bit, blue yearling boars breath by breath. A dog burst on all fours out of his planked gable and bayed back and forth, making his chain rattle-snake and yawping : "Mornin', Herr Vehnke !" (In Rethem).

"I can go right on down now ?" : I can go right on down now.

In the basement archives : whitewashed walls, and mice in all boxes : black mannikins, did inquisitive acrobatics along the walls, leapt arches, dwelt in Rethemic labyrinths, (bring bread crumbs along tomorrow).

With a good cellophane ruler (graduation finely etched along the base) you can actually make reliable estimates to a tenth of a millimeter : wonderful ! And I shoved and aligned the crystal-clear two-dimensional tool back and forth : wonderful !

Plus the magnifying glass : and below it the map, scale 100,000:1 : the thin hill hatchings indicated high points; fire lines scored through forests; every tiny blacktangle was a house, where cows grunted, windowpanes sparkled, around the house the fence had been painted green; and I knotted my fingers for yearning, and pummeled my chin in energetic exasperation : I have to see every one of these houses; every shingle on the roof wants describing; so come on !

And away we went with the year 1760, with "consequential advancements" and "the noble Austrian conquests" : meaning an official report. Meaning keep it – – meaning the ‹Politica› file. (Had folded close to a hundred blue file-covers and divided up all the topics. History on the ‹grand› scale is nothing : cold, impersonal, unconvincing, sketchy (false besides) : I want nothing but ‹Private Antiquities›; there's the life and mystery.

I reconstructed all the old villages for myself with their pastors and bustling administrators : names from parish registers, records, statute-books, newspapers, from gravestones. (This evening still got to make the box for the slips of paper, Din A 8, i.e. about 3 $^1/_8$ x 2 $^1/_{16}$ inches. Bearing names, forenames, birth and death dates if ascertainable; plus a thumbnail sketch of the matter : where found etc.) Read, turn the page; Read, turn the page. Read. – Turn the page –

The carton "French Period", and I hesitated before slitting through the thick dirty twine :

first a quick review of the history of the district of Fallingbostel in those years :

1. From 1796 on, the Army of the Armistice, until the Peace of Lunéville, 9 Feb. 1801.

2. On 4 April 1801, the Prussian General Kleist moves in with 24,000 men; remains until the end of October.

3. Brief interregnum.

4. On 26 May 1803, occupation by the French under Marshal Mortier (after 19 June, however, Bernadotte is in command). – 3 June 1803, the Convention of Suhlingen (down near Hoya), absurd, but probably the only proper thing to do, where the Hanoverian Army surrenders.

5. In September 1805, the French occupation troops (with the exception of the 3000 men left at Fort Hameln – : quite right : where Chamisso was later stationed !) march off to Austria; – meanwhile the area is ‹liberated› by Russians, Swedes, and the German-English Legion.

6. 15 Dec. 1805, Haugwitz's Vienna Tractate, by which Hanover is ceded to Prussia (in exchange for Berg, Ansbach and Neufchâtel). – After 27 Jan. 1806, then, Prussian troops under Graf Schulenburg occupy the territory.

7. Following Jena-Auerstädt (14 Oct. 1806), Hanover is first occupied by the French, "under personal disposition", and heavily taxed.

8. On 14 Jan. 1810, our district is added to the new Kingdom of Westphalia of Everyday's-a-Holiday Jérôme. As part of the Département Aller.

9. On 13 Dec. 1810, it is annexed to the French Empire by virtue of a ‹senatus-consulte organique› (nice term that, isn't it ? !)

10. Then in the fall of 1813, "liberated" yet again, and until its dissolution in 1866 part of the Kingdom of Hanover; since then part of Prussia. Aha . . . . . : –

Ahhhh ! ! ! ! – –

The grand old map ! !

There ran the curly lines of brooks round the black dots of houses; through a charming hill number, the 6 and the 2; melted into tiny millponds; the country roads crossed cleverly over them : many, for my heart too many, brooks (and I followed each breathlessly : to its source on a slope; or to where it cautiously seeped and trickled together out of brackish moor). Angular village markings; circles crossed themselves ecclesiastically; while the post horn proclaimed a relay station. At this spot.

And the forests ! : hardwoods encircled silence; conifer forest spiny and silent. Hunters prowled in fir, pulled red hands out of somber carcasses; deer hurtled (with a ‹t›) in a crouch; cows stood submissive in pastures; wind hummed to itself; grass whisked; the bird of my soul vanished in the undergrowth (of the forest of 1812).

Must one follow through on good intentions, or is it sufficient just to formulate them ? !

I took hold of the map by one corner : the splendid cartouche ‹Le Secrétaire général de la Préfecture de Halem, et le Ingénieur ordinaire des Ponts des Chaussées Lasius›. I folded it at one corner again, with clutching covetous eyes. Then I put it into my blue folder (into mine; the unmarked one).

Fingers drumming : how should that folder be labeled ? – ‹Come with me› ?; or ‹Düring : Private› ? – – Finally I came up with ‹Background Material›, and I squinted an eye and regarded that first-class term : –

That belongs to me ! (Cold as can be !) Me ! : I am the true owner, for whom these things have been lying in wait for a hundred years ! For No One but me do these gentle hues of demarcation gather round and enfold me. No One but me sees here at this house-dot : the two young gooseberry bushes : whispered declarations of love, stretched slender green arms, together, in their hunk of night (beneath star scrapments).

And so : into ‹Background Material› : cold as can be !

The heavy woof of warm air enveloped me at once, and smelled of cabbage and heavy good soups, and tasted salty to smirk of cheeks, and chapped the thigh-sized cudgel arms of the confident farmer's wife. – "Noo, thanks ! Really, I can't eat another bite !"

(A ‹Powder Mill› was in fact already there in 1812, where the Eibia stands now. Before that even, surely).

A.C. Wedekind ? Wedekindwedekind – : ah, he was the editor of the almanac / born 1763, just up the road in Visselhövede (and next to Pape, "the" son of the town). Interesting man all the same : was subprefect of the arrondissement of Lüneburg, where he died in '45; and a historian not to be snorted at either : aha : Wedekind ! –

Lord : Wedekind ! ! : could that possibly have been the famous youthful sweetheart of the poet Pape ? ! Frederike W. was her name, died in November 1794. – And I quickly made a note to myself to check it in Visselhövede. –

What's that supposed to mean, the "merde" written in all the margins ? –, –, –, : oh that. (And continue with precision worthy of a Balthasar Denner.)

Rural outhouse : and the larvae swarmed like rats' tails in the brown papered crap. (Those'll make for some real pied perky flies ! : Only just imagine !)

At any rate the axis of the commissioner's swivel chair is not that of the earth. – – How often my handwriting has changed : from stiff childish gothic, to the roman hand encouraged by foreign languages, then a peculiar blend of the two. With Greek δ for d. These days I'm back to scribbling a messy German hand : and then signing my name roman style !

O my : statute books ! : 35 quartos, the whole series (and for the third time now; first in Schwarmstedt; then in Buchholz; I already had a complete set in the district archives). Well. – Undecided. –

(Then I'll simply take the whole series with me : as background material, before it's destroyed ! If only for the names that keep appearing. Which means making a big parcel; part can go by bike, and the rest by mail : and will I ever lie in wait for them !)

It is certainly only to the good if all these items are available at two different locations : in Fallingbostel; *and* at my place ! Right ? – "Heil, Herr Vehnke !"

On my bike along the Aller (rode by way of Ahlden) : there it was : a blue bright stripe, in which poplars stood; bending closer here to brush and smack with the meadow grasses; on the other side a plowman came to hatch out shallow slanting lines of brown.

Contest question : did Cooper use "Felsenburg Island" in writing "Mark's Reef" or not ? (And/or Öhlenschläger's "Öyene i Sydhavet", which amounts to the same thing). – At first I was sure I knew : yes ! Then again later : No. And I still don't know for certain even now !

Hodenhagen : Düshorn, Walsrode, the turnoff :

Bright blue : the puddles fluttered and pulsed beneath the spring wind; quiver clouds swished about; you walked, pushed the bike, and rode through the green springy cage of twigs. (And farmers rattled past with dung-water. Children spun like tops around houses, hogs gnashed, cars hummed. And the clear cold wind bound us all).

Dark red and wind-flexed : the skirt. Her long legs lifted and lowered the staid pedals; and there ahead of me was my she-wolf, riding no-handed and equable beneath the apple boughs, setting the sky swirling even more than before.

"Vogelsang, Castle of the Order" : my son Paul; yearning fanatic dim-witted : "Better do your homework !"

Reread : Spittler, Havemann, Kobbe, Wiedemann, Pratje, Hüne, Mannecke, Pfannkuche, Reden, Ringklib, Guthe; plus Thimme, of course Thimme above all. And Jansen. (keep calm : in 3000 years it'll read like Homer's catalog of ships !).

And so now for the file box : and I crouched contentedly in the back-yard, and cut the fine boards with jig and panel saws, and rubbed the edges with sandpaper, and glued, and hammered in the fine wire nails : lovely pensive work; in the pale yellow evening ! (Great trade : carpenter !)

Raspberry bushes, red-eyed and silent : in Evers's garden; and out back the she-wolf was binding boughs to blackish lattices. Her plaid skirt knelt at the edge of the bed; the wide yellow calf lurked in the greensward, boa constrictor, shapely (till her father came, and with oldster faces askew we squabbled about something – always think of "pigeons" whenever I say or do that – this time it was postal regulations, parcel sizes and such. Weight limits. Because he, though actually a railroad man, had one of the books).

Wait ! : I might as well nail those two broken laths to the fence while I'm at it ! – (The clouds were still stretching long pointed red reptile tongues toward the sun). – – –

"Morning, Herr Peters." "Heil, Herr Düring ! : You're sure looking good !" (envious; now it was my turn to pretend misery and be care-ful) : "Well, just come on down with me to the cellar and have a look at those stacks of files down there !" (more testily) : "and ‹look-ing good› ? ! : dried up, yes; like parchment : I've lost 17 pounds already !" and : "just you ride a bike 15 miles to Rethem every morn-ing : *and* back again the same evening : that'll soon make an old man of you ! Believe you me !"

"Sure : tanned, sure ! You get a tan whether you want to or not !"

"Seifert was in again.". "Which one ? : Walrus-Seifert or Seyffert-with-a-y ?". The fat old man then; and had managed to produce another illegitimate child, his fifth, with his new milkmaid, and had been proud as a brontosaurus and so drunk that he had even invited Peters to the baptism, and had had to be ejected : "Crazy buzzards !".

Brow furrowings : his thought in fat solemn procession, gave a sly nod, and showed disapproval of the blue-splotched restive morning light : "Yesyes : I've been down to look at your operation," (‹operation› !) : "You've made up a separate file for each locality, and then for events of general interest – –". I coughed, cold and respectful : " 'ssir, Herr Commissioner". "Find anything special ? : –". Concise, but not too prepackaged : "This week – nothing, sir. At the moment most of it's from the days of the Napoleonic occupation, 1810." "aahyess," he said slowly and historico-philosophically, "we did indeed belong to France once – my my –". (Only ‹How time flies› was lacking). "Uhh – not Fallingbostel itself, Herr Commissioner," I reported with fussy delight (just what bosses love, for the lower echelon to be so very typically "lower echelon", body and soul : then they can smile indulgently : so, smile, my Bajazzo ! I'm doing you the favor. And going on simply aburst with zeal, Mr. Dutiful, sharpener of pencils) : "only the north-west half of the district as far as the Böhme : this was ‹Kingdom of Westphalia› : ?" and gazed at him expectantly, blue-eyed, top-studently : are you ever stupid ! (And sure enough : he gave an imperceptibly perceptible shrug, derisively licked his upper lip, his glance wandered off with him : off : to where no one from the lower echelon could ever reach him : "Yes sir, Herr Commissioner !")

"Well then, Heil !" : "Heil 'ittler, Herr Düring !". – "And : Fräulein Krämer : button your blouse a little higher : think of the havoc you wreak among our male trainees !". – "Noo : not outright scandalous; but let Herr Schönert explain the biological effects to you." – And once again : "Until Monday, then. And those lists have to get to the army registration office !". "'ll see to that, Herr Düring."

But outside : sky of porcelain : white bellynesses, blue dust cloth; and here below a draft moved through the spindly bushes as if doors stood open all round (making my shirt flutter at my breast and setting my gray hair enthusiastically on end). Even though this was most decidedly still Land of Bureaucrats : telephone poles escorted all streets, turning stiffly at every curve, each one in its dark brown uniform and straight-edged : they will not rest until every square yard is stretched full of wire overhead and fitted out with pipes below !

The birch antennae brushed against my windjacketed flank; a very yellow leaf arrested me in my tracks; my eyes made sweet haste : mirrors for cobblestones and girls' skirts, houses and trim nylons, nimble cars, deftly dodging, and flickered glances from farmhouse windows. "Hello, Herr Vehnke. – Yes; today is probably the last time. – Yes, I'm on my way down right now", and the stairs ran their striped way before me, a little bit into the center of the earth. (But only a little bit).

The chest let fly with wood rot : boggy, roachy, disgusting –; – and I armed myself with much patience and tweezers (scissors – pencils – pad – magnifying glass – Langenscheidt – avanti !). Insect larvae and cobwebs.

And all higgledy-piggledy : The great cholera epidemic of 1831 (right : Hegel, Gneisenau, etc. died during that one). – For the fun of it, I went over a couple of tax forms from 1824, checking off items : just let Someone rack his brains someday over what the marginal note "Approved : Düring" may mean. (But by such antics I now knew by heart all the species of vanished coins, thalers, guldens, friedrichsdors, etcetera, even Bremen groats !).

Pretty, pretty : a study by the famous architect, Johann Christian Findorf (d. 1792), colonizer of moors and founder of villages . . . : Aha ! : had actually planned the same sort of project for the Ostenholzer Moor; with map-sketch and cost estimate. Interesting item. (‹Background Material› ? ?).

And here : a 16-page register with appraisals "of those effects remaining in Ahlten Castle, having fallen into French hands upon said castle's being taken on 25 July 1803"; and it was superb : they had listed every piece of junk : "1 teapot with a horn handle" along with "cash monies and valuables"; "genuine porcelain"; "kitchen utensils"; "9 pieces of bleumourant livery cloth, together with a remnant of yellow fabric, 2 yards : 162 thalers"; "1 petit point settee"; and believe it or not "6 chamber commodes with divers upholstery : 24 thalers".

Then : muskets, horses, harness, fodder, "firewood" : "One pleasure-garden with more than 200 exemplars of orange, lemon and laurel trees, likewise those of 100 rose and pink stocks"; "1 cabinet of books, historical, amusing and gallant" (Probably, then, erotica, "posizioni" and the like).

And the cellar : "1 aam of Tokay wine from Thomagnini. 2 kegs of Hungarian wine from Rebersdorff. 1 aam of 1704 Rhenish", and on it went. – : "3 hogsheads Pontacq" ? Qu'est ce que c'est que ça ? ! – – : Oh sure : red wine from Pau.

Summa Summarum : 178,278 thalers 18 groschens ! And that was 1803 ! : Leaves your trap gaping ! – I mean, that had been – in today's money –

approximately – in Reichsmarks : well ? – : about two million marks ! : now that's something for the commissioner ! (And naturally I'll make a copy for myself, so I can learn all the old details and particulars !) – And moving on with unflagging diligence, turning page on page; skimming each, reading some : 3 boxes always beside me : "Important", "Dubious", "Trash". The last one is filled and emptied 3 times a day. For pulping).

11 o'clock : means another good hour.

French period again : at that time Hünzingen was administratively (deep in my bones, isn't it ? !) part of – at that time – :

a) the Département of the Mouths of the Weser, "Bouches du Weser", (Prefect, Graf Carl von Arberg; General-secretary, von Halem : ah, the fellow who had helped project that grand map I found recently !);

b) the Arrondissement of Nienburg (Subprefect, Salomon);

c) Canton of Walsrode, and finally

d) Mairie of Walsrode

And had a total of 98 inhabitants. Walsrode 1441. Stellichte 311.

An Appeal to the Populace : to capture runaway French soldiers. Signed : Tourtelot, Lieutenant of the 34th Legion of the Gendarmerie in Nienburg. Reward : 15 thalers a head. Had 25 mounted gendarmes and 5 on foot "under him" ("Nicodemes non triumphat / qui subegit Caesarem"; 5 men always made one ‹brigade›). – About 40 names on the list of deserters; with description of appearance, age, height, unit and full arrest warrant details.

Here again : reports by the village mayors of Bommelsen, Kroge; Forester Ruschenbusch of Stellichte.

Here again : break-ins at isolated farmsteads, thefts of foodstuffs, interrogations and evidence, hams and hard sausage (with signatures ‹Paul Wolters, for me and my brother›). And I looked at the district map : was right in my neighborhood, Ebbingen, Jarlingen, Ahrsen. Apparently always the same fellow, "short and scrawny".

Here again : a farm girl had been approached on the moor one autumn evening by an unknown man and asked in fractured German : if he couldn't. And afterwards he had also relieved her of half a sack of potatoes. (That's really the only reason she'd reported it ! – And once again he had been "short and scrawny"; she hadn't made out his face more precisely in the dusk, "he didn't take off his hat", but an older man : and I pondered lasciviously how she might have determined that. But then I grew serious once more, and took out the list of names again : short and scrawny. Short. And scrawny).

And older : that leaves really only 2 men who could possibly be considered : Thierry, of the 21st Chasseurs à cheval; and Cattere, of the 16th Regulars. Thierry and Cattere.

A werewolf : two farmers had seen its shadow : hanging close behind their wagon. And it had constantly "jangled" : "like with chains" ! So the brothers had laid the whip to their horses, and with quaking voice cried out the appropriate charms, à la "Phol ende Uodan", and just before the farmyard there arose a great and untoward swish in the "upper air"; signed Witte and Lüderitz of Kettenburg, together with that of the village mayor and his clump of red seal.

And so things continued with letters back and forth, for several years. But then I stopped to consider : the lonely fugitive in the moor ! And I puckered my brows and gazed at my windjacket's horsedung-colored sleeve : had simply deserted ! In a single bound left rank and file and leapt onto the open moor (and had apparently lived there in hiding for years on end, ‹and paying thee no notice› : even in the white desolate winter : so you can do that sort of thing !). – For starters then I gathered up all the records (I mean, ‹personnel› is part of my department too, isn't it ? !).

"Eat yondah at Stegmeiah's t'day : he knows 'bout it !"

A distant red tile roof in the flimmering muddled meadows; a moth, dazed by the heat, stumbled after its shadow; wind stretched its hot long limbs, rolled over contentedly once more, and fell asleep.

Still a relatively new house; and the hot glow drew me around the corner, brightly stuccoed, sun-drenched, to the broad servant girl at her whooshing carpet beater : "Yeah : the mastah's home", and the handle flexed again beneath the veined wrestler's arm : the hand that guides the broom on Saturdays – –

An old farmer with toothless stinking voice : "Nope, none a that at ouah place. Nope, don't know nothin' 'bout it. Nevah done nothin' like that."; and he gazed expectantly at me from round puddled eyes. (But soon the son arrived, and grumbled things right.)

The old man was 86, and grew more lively as he ate, and told tales about how the hated Prussians had marched in, 1866 : he was only thirteen, and when he called his sheepdog ‹Bismarck›, they asked him if all the dogs in Hanover were called that; and he had answered : "Nope, jist the sons o' bitches !" And how they had thrashed him there in the field, and then that evening the local boys had surrounded them and given them a terrible beating : broke the rifles over their backs !, warming & growing young in his lies; and we were delighted with him and his tall tales : "Thanks so much ! – Be seeing you." : "Was our pleasuh".

And now for the rest (but then that's it; I'm quitting today at 4; in this heat I'm going swimming).

Baron de la Castine ? : Where have I heard that name before ? Where have I . . . . . (look it up at home). – Two books : Karl Gottlob Cramer "Hasper a Spada" (Lovely items; missing in my own collection, too !).

(Then went ahead and leafed through the deserter story again : curiouser and curiouser !).

The mis'rable bastards ! : were they busy chopping down another whole section of woods again ? The robots ? ! And growling with anger, helpless with rage, I pushed my bike along the soft narrow path, crack, another old trunk came crunching down, causing the terrified bushes to dive to both sides, leaves atremble : these damned farmers !

These farmers ! ! : these bunglers ! ! : Look, here, I'll prove it : in our village there are 25 farmsteads, each with about 120 acres (counting it all, wood, meadow, field) : Each of them has his own threshing machine; every other one his own tractor. That threshing machine is used 10 days a year, no more, then it stands in the shed : so that two of them would suffice for the whole village ! ! And one of the things costs 2000 marks : so 23 times 2000 are spent to no purpose ! What an insane waste of national wealth ! What extravagance at the cost of the consumer ! If all these farms were merged, making giant-sized Canadian farms (or, if you like, Russian kolkhozy !) : and then the farmers were put to work as well-paid 8-hour-a-day workers (they're forever wailing to you about how much they have to drudge, and all for nothing they say : every factory worker lives better : so let's do it !) : a hundredweight of potatoes would sell for one mark ! (And that's just one example; I'd like to meet the fellow who would dare tell me straight to my face that this is "efficient !").

And what unsanitary pigs they are for the most part : nothing but filth and fat ! – The whole thing needs to be rationalized; business on a grand scale. (Or then again : reduce the population. That way the old system might possibly be retained).

It's the same with trades ! : pure antediluvian methods ! How would humanity get along without shoe factories ? : one half would go barefoot, and a pair of shoes would cost 200 marks, and every fifth shop would be a shoemaker's. Trades were the medieval attempt to meet the material needs of a very sparse population, while using what were still childish technologies; only students of German literature and guild masters attribute profound metaphysical value to the system : they live off it ! – But I'm all for Salamander shoes (or Bata; it's all the same !).

And so I rode through the pieces of my life : swaying atop a bicycle. (Haven't the least desire to be a god : much too boring, to begin with. A demigod, now that I'd like !).

A swim, a long one (in Bottomless Lake) : lying on my back, and moving only a little, a kind of coziness about it. Swaying sky with tired white patches (if only that silly paddler weren't here !).

The exotic beach (white narrow sand, with fine black sludge patterns) : girls in green and dark-red swimsuits; brown lads, colorfully bisected by their trunks, with clear melancholy adolescent eyes. And the hard grass, ruffled white-green around the blue-green whorl of pines.

Sunset : the setting sun is itself not beautiful ! : red, fat, repulsive, bloody, blind. – But later then the sky; and the static streaks of the clouds !

In front of the house : the wind gave a Mongol snort from its corner and rolled yellow dust into fibrous rope-ends; sucked the shirt off my chest, and amorously lifted the bell-skirt from the she-wolf (to the waistband, making her toothy face gape with laughter; and she kept her hands on the washline, till it sank back on its own; raspberry lips called motherwards and she made thorny fingers).

Clean and oil the bike (forced to wear an old apron) : "They figure one husband's worth about 3 children, Herr Weber," my wife declared, suggestive and honey-sweet. (And He even laughed ! – take off the rearview mirror and replace the worn-out nut. Remounting the saddle tool-bag is the worst part; they're constructed so that on principle you always have one wrench left over !).

Wind fondled the sable of the night, till they whispered and murmured; an owl screeched at us and laughed lewdly. (Or was it Käthe across the way ?).

Syrupiev Chocolatovich : my son ! : "You're going to turn into pure sugar, Paul !"; for he was shoveling down the pudding literally by the bowl (and I bet him that on Sunday he could eat a basinful : I'll bring the 10 extra packages you'll need from Fallingbostel, ‹Almond›, agreed ? And he say's it's a deal !). Before that, Sunday morning, they have ‹Premilitary Training›, with camping in tents, trooping the colors, and all the apparently inevitable and terribly interesting operatic ceremonial. At 17 he can volunteer for the army : become an officer : "Can I, dad ? ! – Or maybe the gruppenführer can speak to you about it sometime." (An out-and-out cool and deliberate threat, unmistakable); and my wife made honored eyes : "If he becomes an officer ! With his secondary schooling : just think how jealous the Alsfleths would be !". "That settles it of course", I said bitterly, and : "whatever you like !". – "His birthday's coming up in August – : whatever you like ! –" (Rather

than let him set the party hacks on me ! : if a man has such an urge to
stand at attention, then don't get in his way : God, what a different sort
I was at his age ! Had had a solid democratic education ! And whenever
people showed up in troops, always turned my back ! – And is my wife
a fool !)

"What sort of station have you got there ? !" : "Weather prognosis";
"agency dispatches"; "termination of broadcast at 2400 hours" : German, would you please speak German ! – – (Ah, that's it : the Babeling
Swiss, with confederated specialties : "Keep dialing !". But then in fact
a lovely choir : "Vieux Léman / toujours le même"). – And the constant
hassling of Poland ! –

"Heil, Herr Peters !" (that's the only difference : he wears the yoke patiently and even proudly : I pull a face whenever I slip in and out of
it !) : "They have to show those Poles a thing or two !"; and his tongue
deftly whipped up a cock-and-bull story in the dish of his big mouth,
about mutilated German settlers, German loyalty, and lots of raped
women : "No sir ! : they need their toes stepped on !".

The train window rebelled with a clatter in its frame; the sun festered by the
woods; a blue farmhand plowed into the slimy earth; a harrow harped
(acoustical nonsense of course !) : "Do you realize, Herr Peters, that
ultimately that might mean war ?". But he hadn't taken part in the
World War, obstinately scratched the back of his thick head, : "The
Führer doesn't want war !", and sat there silently sulking away. (Just as
if someone would punch me in the face, snatch my money away, and
then scream : "I detest acts of violence !". Charming. And that's what
goes down with the SA !)

"Who's the man-in-green there ? !" (softly to Schönert, and point with my
ear, while he entered a promotion into the fellow's papers : "Gröpel. :
The Forester of Walsrode." "Aha".) And I sociably introduced myself to his red leery-little foxface : they always know the old mile-
stones, hidden paths, and so on : "Good ! I'll drop by sometime, Herr
Gröpel ! – Yes, of course", and a deceptive imitation of a laugh. (Prov-
erbs : "Show me a liar . . ." : that one was made up by a mad civil
servant, personnel department. "Barking dogs . . ." : a forester. "The
public good . . ." : a grand tyrant. – Here are another two nice ones :
"Takes more than a new pair of shoes to dance" : for authors. And "not
everyone with a long knife is a cook" : when iron generals go in for
politics !)

"May I have Saturday for a trip to Hamburg, Herr Commissioner ?" –
" ?" – : "It's for official business – uh : semi-official. – I'd like to find
some reference aids for my project; and look up some things in the

State Archives. – – I have an acquaintance there, a Dr. Teufel !" I lied, impatient and impertinent, and he nodded, convinced and cagey. – : "Reference aids ?" "Yes sir : a few volumes of the Gotha Almanac. And a small technical dictionary. – Naturally at my own expense", ambitious and supportive of the state : "but I am interested in the task assigned me, and I'd like to do it well. Herr Commissioner." (Peters couldn't have said it better : well done !). – "Well, all right. – – Where are you prior to that, on Thursday / Friday ?". "Parsonage at Kirchboitzen, and in the village. Herr Doktor" (a little variety in the title for once; and then came his dry little pestled laugh : "Well all right").

And once again : the morning sun was already melting to gray clouds; heard wind leap, leap and fall asleep, deep. My two feet dolted the bike along for me; so I could watch other things and take note : the field of cabbage, the rows of potatoes, the bands of wheat; barley ponds waved green; the dust rolled solemnly about my front wheel (and the bottle in the baggage gurgled).

Woods are beautiful only when you can leave the path at any time and cut, wade, duck right through them (yet another argument against mountains). I give my vote : flatlands ! (Ah, condemned to be a paperpusher : if only I had a mere 10,000 marks, to knock together a log house, solitary somewhere in the moor and woods ! I turned a piece of fallen brushwood in my fingers, bark, crack, turning, turning, tosshighintheair : another glance across the countryside : far off two farmers were drawing deep lines in their potatoes; then give a lurch : to the parsonage gate. – Was only eight thirty).

Church noises : which means bells, singing, congregational mutterings : I made a wide circle (around the congregation).

With nice puffed-up cheeks and a large, gentle hooknose : the pastor's daughter (and a pretty, dainty garden behind her : the weeping birches lay back in the wind with foliage combed in a sweep, and it shoved them right respectably, hastily blowing their hair from behind up over their heads and sending skirts to the fore, too : just like my big pastor's daughter's here : "Yes. Just a moment please. Herr – –". "Düring. From the District Commissioner's Office." "Ah yes !".

Children (counting out) : Eee – ny – mee – ny – mai – ny – med; : / Fall – inthe – river : – and – you – are – dead ! !"; and with shrill voices, they shoved the lonely dead man, thirsting for revenge, from their midst. (And for me the sun is either two fingers wide, or a belching golem of fire : depending on what use I have for it !).

Green-patterned air, brown soil, gold herringboned. ("In these Christian lands certain small loaves or cakes are displayed, of which the priests say that they are gods; and what is more wonderful still, the bakers themselves swear that these gods created the entire world, though they themselves have prepared them from flour, the remains of which they will show to you").

"Why of course, Herr – uh" : "Düring, Herr Pastor". "Yes, goes without saying !"; but first he let me present all my credentials, proof that I was worthy of processing ecclesiastical files; then, however, he grew quite pliable, brought piles of documents, parish registers, gossiping and cursing in clericalese. I was also permitted to admire his library; praised his Ammianus Marcellinus (who is generally underrated ! Tells many remarkable tales !). And he was pleased; his specialty, moreover, was Alexander : "But Herr Pastor ! All we have there are very late and undependable sources ! And even those based exclusively on the accounts of his followers : a third of the truth ! : but the other side has to be presented as well !". "No, no, Herr Pastor ! : why just imagine if we had a history of our times, the sole basis of which were the diaries of Goebbels and Göring : what then ? !"; and the comparison delighted him no end.

"No, I'll be eating at the inn, Herr Pastor. – Has already been ordered." – "Oh. – : but you will come by later to join us in the garden, won't you ? !". "Would love to, Herr Pastor".

And now at last to business : were a couple of huge piles, and two more ancient mustified crates (ancient : that is, 1800; but gave off an immoderate stench !). First a general survey. And I ill-humoredly bit my lip, not wanting to begin, when what did I pick up first but the papers from the years of occupation : steady. Steady !

Interesting (what a bulwark of a word !) : the famous Continental System : What All was forbidden, a very modern sense of the economics of war in fact :

a) no exports of ores and metals, whether processed or not; weapons and ammunition, as to be expected; leather and textile fibers, wood; foodstuffs of all kinds; even fertilizers.

b) no imports of finished textiles (naturally, all of this directed against England !); but even English buttons, playing cards, horses, tobacco, sugar, soap, rum, etc. etc.

All described in detail; and I decided to take the old public notice back to my commissioner. Amazing : you could go out and paste it up on any street corner ! (And the establishment of these ‹départements hansésatiques› was certainly not attributable to "wicked games the Corsican played with German thrones and dominions", as our frock-coated historian types and teutonizing Shatterhands are fond of expressing it : but quite simply to the bitter necessity of effectively blockading the entire coast against wholesale British smuggling and infiltration by troops of partisans : the Germans were sabotaging Napoleon in any case, wherever they could ! : no sir : was very much the right thing to do !)

"1 stoup of wine" was what he had drunk ? : how much is that ? (Ah yes : does vary a lot, but at least between 3 and $3^1/_2$ quarts : holycow ! And I tucked in the corners of my mouth, respectful and envious : He could polish off that, without singing a duet ? !)

Wait ! ! : waitwaitwait. (Two more reports : that had really been an out-and-out cause célèbre, hadn't it ? !)

Söder ? : that's the large farm directly behind us; the fattener of swine ! And Meyer ? : I leaned back and put my pointed tongue to my lips : Meyer, Meyer : why sure ! : the big-time farmer close by Heins's Inn in Ebbingen ! And Ahrens, the fellow who lives further up the main road, toward Visselhövede.

Had chased him twice : once driving him into Griemer Woods : where he had disappeared in the direction of Söder. The other time from Jahrlinger Road off to the west; short and scrawny. And I took out my map and measured and compared : judging by that, you could locate his lair – only approximately – – and I pursed my brows and rubbed my teeth against my lips – approximately – – –

(To be sure : a cursory glance at the other items too : ordinances signed by Graf Kielmannsegg, Minister; laws about cutting peat; stipulations concerning carriage service, national mourning : but then back to my deserter, Thierry or Cattere.)

Thierry or Cattere : Thierry, born 16 July 1771 in Bressuire, Poitou; single; occupation – yes, how to translate that : well today we would probably say something like ‹skilled mechanic›; 5 ft 6 tall and slender; distinguishing marks : saber scars on forehead and shoulders; speaks broken German (that certainly would have helped him ! Cf. that farm girl recently !). – – And Cattere : born 18 July 1773 in Lisieux – that's in – Normandyaha –; married, 3 children (well, simply one more reason : I thought of my own family and brushed my hand over them); occupation, baker; 5 ft tall and slender; no distinguishing marks, but known to be irascible and headstrong : had stabbed a corporal ! (That would of course provide the basis for constructing a plausible story : argument with superiors. – But that seemed too simple for me : because to desert like that, and above all to remain in a strange country, for years : there's nothing simple about that. That takes a very special mentality !)

And then of course there's another stumbling block ! : We northern Germans are generally right tall and sturdy : would they still call a man only 5 ft tall "short" ? : Nooo : that would be more like a "dwarf". Wouldn't it ? – But then I had my doubts again : and so things stood as they were : Thierry or Cattere. (But an extremely interesting case : the reports were now more than two years apart : he really must have had some sort of permanent base of operations ! And presumably very near to where I live). (And not in the woods : because any forester would have found that at once ! ! – Which leaves, then, nothing but marsh and moor; and I pulled my map over to me again).

In the chaise in the pastor's garden : tanglements of foam, and against blue background (while the lawn and I sailed along below, warm pastoral : old books are valuable not because they tell : of tanglements of blood and mucus, of fingers hooked and teeth straddled ! But because such clouds and cragged lights are captured in them, clever and filthy remarks. – "Why, goes without saying, Herr Pastor : with pleasure !").

A new scale : wind-force 6 : topples chessmen. (Thankgod that's what we had; so a sociable gathering.)

The Herr Pastor had read Vergil's Georgics until he didn't know how to differentiate anymore between oats and rye. But for all that it was a quaint sheltered life (that I must say ! I must !) : he and his daughter had even given names to individual fruit trees : "Our Anselm is bearing well this year !". (but that's perfectly in order, what with their being large individuals; every dog has his : haven't they introduced that among the sequoias in California ? : so there !) – "But just think of the widow of Tekoah, Herr Düring !". (now was the time to make a joke, though I knew my books of Samuel) : "Of Tekoah :" I said tentatively and as if surprised : Is that a noble family by letters-patent ? Or somewhere in the Gotha ?", and he laughed most edifyingly. "You will excuse me for a half hour or so, Herr – uh", he wafted his broad and black way inside to some confirmands or other, and I was left alone with his lovely puffed-up daughter.

A depraved creature by the by !, and we cautiously lechered ourselves awake with all kinds of double entendres; naturally she knew the she-wolf and was even in the same class with her. And the wind haggled lewdly behind our backs, and tosseled with gentle innuendos; screaming, larks snared themselves in the silver loops of the clouds; the plaintive bass of a team of oxen dwindled past the hedge; the red cliffs of evening, almaden alto, towered above the box tree.

Picking plums : I gallantly climbed the ladder, and tossed them into her lovely wide willow basket; bees, bumblebees and wasps hummed about our flushed faces; and I gazed not undeeply

a) into her piebald décolleté

b) into the overfilled sky : with foliage, cloudwork, stripes and colors : it was too much, above and below; and the knife of the moon was already wedged in a branch. (So what : for most of your life you have to park your conscience anyhow !).

Merry ride home (and I thought often of the red and yellow pastor's daughter) : in front of the delicate bracket of the moon was a big fat decimal : all written in silver pen between mellow black clouds and silent tree limbs. (Like some mathematical jargon perhaps : cloud times, bracket, linden ribs).

"Yes, I've got to go to Hamburg in the morning" (professional shrug) : "on office business". (conciliatory) : "You got something special you want me to bring ?" And it was darning yarn of rare hues, that couldn't be had in Walsrode; "Oh, and listen : square mother-of-pearl buttons, too : like these ! I'd best give you a stocking to take along." (And wash the sweaty soles; and between the toes a zooish stench arose : so quick, rub the soap over it !)

Spend the night outdoors sometime, really ought to ! : the brief shower drubbed me daintily. (And across the way, Käthe still had a light on); now and again a leaf ran over; wind snuffled; a hunted star appeared; a branch coughed; now and again. Affirmation of water. Leaves scratched my nape, moist and loden-jacketed, until I laughed and stalked on (still have to see the carpenter : want to have him make a sturdy plywood chest for me, with a lock, compartments and a tray; for the expropriated documents in my collection; stuff of dreams). (The shiny curve of the moon's plowshare dug ever deeper into the sallow dripping lawn of clouds, and I too discovered my invisible path more elegantly into the meadows). –

Window with no curtains (mine !) : I can live only in right-angled brightness (and on my desk a bookcase with firm and fluid contents). Rain smutted lazily and warm down the pane, watery and possibly fecund : and so quickly pack for tomorrow; I can shave early in the morning, and that will surely hold me till I get back. –

And ready, step outside ! : the sky was just turning pale yellow and keen blue, and the gaudy air was like hovering water : good omen for me ! In my tuliped red mouth. On my veined hands.

Good omen for me ! ! : across the way Käthe was washing in catch-as-catch-can style : she balled water in foamy fists and brushed it over her belly skin; jumped wildly about, clapped and crabbed across her back with strong arms; took hold again of her shimmering hips, her great-eyed breasts, and then let herself be wrestled dry by a most enviable terry towel; dressed only in panties, came to the window, tugged the elastic at the front and peeked inside. Then she saw me standing there, and vanished (yet without haste; and started singing grandly : ". . . the clohouds / echo-my-sohong / far over the sea . . .", alto, then whistled another snatch, and flashed and slammed the door : was certainly no more than meet and just I'd say : she had watched me that day in the scullery hadn't she. – And with wistful wide eyes I thought of my prudish wife, who had not let me see her nude fourteen years now : well she can keep her filth to herself !).

It's really cheap ! : 127 miles round-trip (including the Sunday discount for the return) comes to 5 marks 60; I slipped the small official brown cardboard tab into my trouser watchpocket, and picked up Wieland, "Clelia and Sinibald". (: But forever on the move, like a reporter, that wouldn't be for me either : a small wild tract of woods : that's me !).

Change trains in Visselhövede (the first time); and as I walked, I gazed over at the old steeple, where Samuel Christian Pape (1774–1817), the genial poet, had spent his heath(en) youth : another poor devil who fretted too much over the reviews of his poems (instead of telling the caboodle to go to hell, with the sovereign insouciance of Walter Scott or Schmidt; don't read the stuff on principle ! – I had read the lovely little biography Fouqué had written for his 1821 edition of Pape's poems, and had also run across many living relatives in my archive work. Naturally I also know the supplement to them in Gubitz's "Gesellschafter" : if you're gonna do it, do it right !).

Wieland : among us Germans, no one has reflected more profoundly about prose forms, no one has experimented more boldly, no one has supplied such thought-provoking patterns, as Christoph Martin Wieland : but then that was perfectly natural; for only such forms could incorporate both the great store of figures he drew from imagination and life and his extensive knowledge of history, literature, etc. – The stiff-jointed, didactic "Agathon" is still very much of the old school; but almost immediately afterwards, the great adventures in form begin; even "Don Sylvio" and "Danishmend" are chock-full of the most exhilarating artistic devices, from whose charming tempi all moderns could learn. Suddenly everything shatters into anecdotal discourse : the imperishable "Abderites" swirl across the agora, and Sheikh Gebal counters the poetry of the "Golden Mirror" with truth of his own. There is still much undue length and brittleness; he still had not succeeded fully in unleashing his godlike voice; but the very next step brings with it considered, logical, important progress : dialogue. It is after all grammatically self-evident that the living present tense has a much more compelling psychological effect on the reader than the seemingly restrained pluperfect, which is only the twaddling of old maids. (This is likewise the source of the enchantment of lyric poetry, or even optically convincing drama; both, however, commensurate with the lightning-like brevity of their effects, are incapable of absorbing broad-ranging, weighty intellectual matters : only prose can do that !) And so Wieland here tried out the first of the techniques for employing the present tense : Apollonius of Tyana tells his tale in a Cretan grotto; and "Peregrinus Proteus", still far too lightly regarded, sits down with Lucian among Elysian shades. And as an old man he tries yet a second innovation : the epistolary novel. And with all its faults, the inimitable grand mosaic of "Aristippus" is a success (along with the finger exercises "Menander" and "Crates"); for the reader receives each letter in a constantly renewed present; he is addressed from all the cities and provinces of Greater Greece; the most beautiful humane moments appear woven into significant historical events; and the truly invaluable discussion of the "Anabasis" and the "Symposium" are likewise organic parts of the whole – they're boring only to victims of jazz : "Aristippus" still remains the only historical novel we Germans have, i.e., that gives us life and knowledge; aurum potabile. Wieland is my greatest experience of form, apart from August Stramm ! (And what all could be said about his verse narratives, tolle lege; but that would mean intoning a new hymn : take and learn !) – He is the example of how a great writer of prose labored with diligence and profound thought all his life to perfect one of his two modes of expression. – (And by way of contrast : for Goethe, prose is not an art form but a junk bin – aside from "Werther"; and "Truth and Poetry", where, however, there is no problem giving form to the material to begin with – : divergent fragments glued together by force; novellas crudely knotted along the main threads; collections of aphorisms; commonplaces of all sorts – dead sure to be put in the mouth of the least likely person : think of the avuncular, worldly-wise "maxims" he has little Ottilie write in her diary ! – The most flagrant example is "Wilhelm Meister", especially "Meister's Travels" : what he gets away with there, e.g. in chapter transitions, is often so primitive it would shame any well-bred, self-respecting high-school senior. A brazen formal shambles; and I pledge to produce the evidence any time at all (if I didn't have to put my capacities to more serious uses : Goethe, stick to your lyric poetry ! And your plays !). –

In front of the main station (was only 7:52) : a car tallyhonked; in the
distance fire engines tooheetoohawed merrily; the air delicately layered itself from white to blue; and the red-yellow subway stormed
around the curve with lowered head. (The secondhand bookstores are
over on Königstrasse, or on Neuer Wall; Hauswedell is too expensive,
no point in that. Maybe step into Woolworth's first).

Buttons and darning wool : well, let's hope it's right. – Harsh lights
and subdued noisiness. (How did that go ? : ribbons bubble, belts
loop adders, jaws gape barrels, eyeballs rummage – – ? – –. Can't remember !).

Or wait ! That was it : ‹In the Department Store›
: 4th floor : Hands are yapping bright-dyed fabrics jaws gape barrels
eyeballs rummage distance buzzes may-I-help-you's boxes slumber
armchairs settle clothing jungles coated forests ribbons bubble elbows
jostle buttons ogle stockings shelter digits finger D-mark pieces thighs
are reaching down from bottoms.

Instant love is undertaken for a raven Titus head, and while kerchiefs
loiter round other necks, she slyly rends the rustling fabric, so that her
average-sized breasts come bobbing up, the triangle of her face grins
out above the crevice, and while the aged lady floorwalker does her
watching, I wait, among the nylon rushes of massive female legs.

3rd floor. Scanty praises pointing lifting saucers circle vases taper
fatties snarl behind their cheekpads lanterns cable ironing-boardly
mirrors marvel belts loop adders yarn-balls cower motley helots
mouths start stumbling word prostheses calves are reveling hips look
privy cashiers clamor butt-end eyeballs teeth agaping snapping grating
noses farting brain bits out.

Skirt hems slink about girlfriends (high-school seniors); carpet-
stretches, mutely bedded roundabout by housely wives (oilcloth souls,
bodies like shopping bags); records gently playing for us folk wired
for sound, black-smocked girl trainees drag around cardboard boulders, escalator solemnly trimmed with statues, and right next to them
signs blockade atop scratchly cocomats : Only one fifty ! Hey you !
Customer ! And more bovine leather, batteries, smoking gadgettes;
chamoisly the world is off to rack and ruin.

2nd and ground floors : Rifles barrel bamboo vipers glasses twitter
dunes of coffee lips gone crooked buckled clucking words out trotting
rippling toddling hot dogs bronzed with dots of mustard scales with
taloned pointers subtle yellow tiny show-offs thick potboilers brash
trash photos rigid jackets upright stairways ramble rosy gristled ear-
fuls napes of buffet-worthy matriarchs with earnest censure luggage

boxing doorways flailing as you leave. – (It's by Schiller, I think : ". . . Children wailing mothers straying dumb beasts moaning under rubble all are running bolting fleeing . . .").

And hard horse-sausage ! : I can't help myself : I love to eat it ! Near us, in Neuenkirchen, there's another doughty artist in the craft : "Give me a string of 10, please : or better : you can package them and send them to my home, can't you ? – : "Yes ! : add the wrapping and shipping charges to the bill !" (They're easy to keep fresh in summer, too; hang them in a dry, airy place where the flies can't get at them : they just keep getting better and harder !). "And give me another two to take along with me."

At the secondhand bookstore : "Yes please : – this way !", and he led me to the long low row of the Gotha : soft linden green "Letters of Patent"; chalk blue "Ancient Houses"; dark violet "Barons"; dark green "Counts" (I don't need the court annuals). "The price depends primarily on the date : up to 1918, 2 marks 50; after that, 3 marks 50", and discreetly stepped back his vigilant yards : "I'll find what I need, all right ? !".

8 volumes in all (and sorted by the familiar even and odd numbers) : 20 marks. "I can look around some more – ?". "Yes, of course !". And right at home, I strode to the bookcases, leafed through Droysen's historical atlas ("A bargain : only 30 marks !"; nah, too expensive). Read once more page upon page of Galiani's "Dialogues sur le commerce des blés", one of the most brilliant books from that period in France; the "Thessalian Nights" of Madame de Lussan. Then went ahead and bought the complete German edition of Scott, 1852 ff. Stuttgart, with its countless charming brownish foxings (and He even apologized for the fact, the nincompoop !) : 25 volumes for 15 marks : "Pack them with the others", and I gave him my address for the C.O.D. package : "No ! : 64 ! – number 64." (And paid 20 marks of it on account : "And then enter just the 15 marks on the C.O.D. slip !" : because of my wife !).

(Swift : "Gulliver's Travels" : very simple structure :

1st Book : the genius tormented by the termites; and I recalled that unutterable description, oh how often, teeth gnashing, I had wept and laughed over it : the way the wretches swarm on through the triumphal arch of his wide-spread legs, every last bit of Lilliput, generals and politicians at the head : and look up as they pass, grinning at the tattered seat of the giant's pants ! –

2nd Book : the disgust at things organic : where the pores of the skin grow big as the mouths of teacups; he rides astride the oak-barked

nipple of his colossal patroness : the smell almost kills him ! And the
calf-sized hymenoptera rev their motors, circling his life – Gong ! :
3rd Book : against philologists and technocrats, against "pure" and
"applied" sciences : only the magicians know much of anything; but
you're terrified and it would be better otherwise ! The masses ? :
drudge and drivel; and if they don't obey, their sun is taken away (even
though the island of "Laputa" – the ruling "upper class" – can never be
sent crashing down as threatened : they'd end up blowing themselves
kaputa ! The hope is that those down below won't figure that out some
day and emancipate themselves from those "on top" : oh, is it ever
witty !) –
4th Book : the grand final loathing of all Yahoos, not excluding Swift :
and I put down my reichsmark on the Yahoo's counter, and pocketed
the wee thing, for my own travels into several remote nations of the
world.)

Lunch at the fish galley : and I bit into the golden-brown filet, and forked
the cool greenish potato salad, and wolfed down a second helping, and
gulped half an icy liter of beer : lat me heer dwelle al my lyf ! (Like
Herr Walther in Tyskland).

Fine and now ? ! : the train leaves at 2:50, and how should I spend the hour
and a half till then ? – Decided : off to the art museum : nothing
cheaper than that. I checked briefcase and hat down below, and first
climbed to the top, part of my strategy : while I'm still running at full
steam : only need to walk downhill later on !

Homely and slick : the smearings of the Third Reich hanging down every
wall : grainy landscapes with incredibly broad-hipped sheaves offered
palpable support for the suspicion of intellectual crop failure; men of
character sent populist gazes out into an invisible Greater Germany;
maidens stuck in their folk costumes as if in urns : the dauber had
wrapped the squat rustic heads in such anacondas of blond braids that
it made you want to offer the poor things an aspirin. Sculptors had done
stark nakeds, with strict party-line physiques and eternally proud pro-
files, all with a striking family resemblance; nor had they omitted the
irresistibly folksy "Horse Breaker," curbing his stallion single-handed
(but I've served in the horse-drawn artillery and know how it's really
done !) – and it all was so oppressively monotonous, and standardized
expressionless, and forgettable a hundred thousand times over, and
executed with such hopelessly obvious technique; and the contentment
of the master race sprawled like a fat sfinx in every room.

Oh God ! : another "Kneeling Girl" peeking around the corner ! And I
walked wickedly right on in and gaped despairingly at her painfully

to-scale rear cheeks; and the "Meditating Girl" adjacent looked so exactly like her that you could have switched signs and been done with it ! (Me unhappy ? : Me ? ! : I can still think whatever I like ! ! : Have my house, a tolerably stultifying job, and a vocabulary larger than that of all party members put together; moreover, two separate sides to my head, while the brownshirts have only one. Unhappy ? ! : Noo ! !).

But wait : look at that ! (and I had to offer small congrats to the clever management downstairs !) : way at the back and quite casually things grew more angular and less soporifically Aryan, people looked out from under their brutally low brows into uncanny things emanating from them; a hand was once again something white-spidery, and a back courtyard could make you shudder, and Otto Müller set everything to rights again :

"Otto Müller : Girls in the Park" : and the two naked teenagers peered somberly from under their hair at the spectator, stuck out their still skinny legs among grass and wild flat plants, turned aside unvirginally and went on lying in wait for cautious dark-green life : and I smiled wild and triumphant : 'nd they say he's still livin' on Lammer-Lammer Street : 'nd doin' what he pleases : long live our grand and holy Expressionism ! !

Color blindness is rare; art blindness the rule (but should I therefore consider myself perverse or in error ? !). There is even a Sanskrit proverb that says, most people give off sparks only when you land a fist in their eye ! : and so, painter, paint ! poet, write ! with your fist ! (For they have to be awakened somehow, the semi-people behind the boundary line : so simply let yourselves be cursed as "ruffians" by the faint-hearted; as "arsonists" by the firefighters; as "breakers-and-enterers" by the sleepers : they should thank their appropriate gods that somebody has finally awakened them !).

Schnorr von Carolsfeld "Wedding at Cana" : nice colors; but otherwise skim milk.

And I sat and looked and dovetailed my fingers, and missed my train and the next one : Meister Franke "Group of Women from a Crucifixion" (right at the bottom, on the left where you come in, second room).

The Lady in Green : sat there, and glanced over her narrow shoulder only now and then : she had been waiting 500 years for me ! She spread her cloak more cleverly, raised her white powdered nose and laid her intelligent forehead farther back : her slender fingers engaged in a sly and amazed game, branched decamerously (especially the small-stalked ones), and the pointed tongue of grass licked its way lesbically deeper under her robe :

Lord : that hairdo ! ! : the long yellow tresses against the linden-green velvet cloak and the white kerchief : that was no kerchief anymore : that was a cache-nez ! Most decidedly ! (And how chic her halo was perched ! : the others wore theirs in good bourgeois Aryan style, like kerosene lamps. – She could stand up and without further ado walk across Broadway : the guys and dudes would wrench their necks to get a look !)

A reconstruction of this "St. Thomas Altar" on the wall : now wait ! – – Can that be right ! – – :

First : the treatment of the foreground : in his other panels it's only a meandering mud wall; the background a massive ticking-red tapestry of stars. But here : daintiest herbs (as in Leonardo's "Virgin of the Rocks !"), dandelion (ah, when it's painted like that, you simply have to use the magic word ‹Taraxacum› !), and the beaded kidney-shaped leaves of incognita Franckii, leek and buckhorn. (Which then means : immense progress compared to his other – presumably earlier ! – style).

Second (the different format : that too); and the poses of the figures – to be sure, it's a matter of extrapolating from clues; but it can hardly be otherwise ! – : when the official assumption here is that this fragment is from the lower left of a four-paneled square ? Impossible ! ! From both the way the heads are held and the most primitive sense of symmetry, you have to conclude that it's from the lower left of a nine-paneled square ! And doesn't belong in the same series with the others at all : why can't he have painted several crucifixions ? ! (After all, the holy masquerade was the only possibility an artist had back then !)

I appeared at the barred, white-gray window; the guard plodded by glancelessly; my heart flickered and swallowed. Below, an endless red freight train whistled its way out of the station into the dusty summer time : 3:50 (and they close here at 4:00 !). And so I doggedly returned to stand before that overly graceful crouching girl and despoiled her sweetly with my semi-senescing eyes – – no : out of here; very inconspicuously; maybe I can still catch the interurban to Rotenburg. But a photograph of her; and the two girls in the park : 4 marks, there !)

Last rakish strokes of sun along Glockengiesserwall, and the warm air suddenly pivoted, sylph of straw, and laid her soft arm-sheaves about me. Next to the flowing streetcars and trotting workers. Right out on the street.

In the briquette-colored iron of the main station : my furrowed face beside the raging horned locomotive; behind girlish hips on green stilts. And the thundering steam bagged us bumpily, me groper-in-fog, and her plump gold-trimmed suitcase (and beside it, the delicate brown-meshed calf).

"Your attention please ! the interurban for Bremen is now departing from platform 5 : All aboard and please close the doors behind you !"

The pickax of the moon was toiling in the inert cloud gravel : Rotenburg.

I don't want to go home ! : so I stayed the night in Visselhövede : would have been one o'clock anyway before I got home. The giant inn-keeper, erstwhile masseuse : "Wasn't a man who didn't squirm beneath my hand"; fried potatoes and farm sausage (plus the bed, only 2 marks 50 !).

The perennial hotel room : from next door came giggling like traveling salesman and maid; and then the dull rhythmics : you, you, you . . . .

Breaking loose in installments (Piecemeal, breaking loose halfway). (And overhead the indefatigable dance music : I've never danced in my life. And even now I hearkened with no envy to the misshapen tumult : workers in bib and tucker, factory girls and farm wenches, sweated up in dancehall and garden. Then the little music got insistent again; then the tomfools rotated in their well-pressed fabric shucks : yes, if you could run alone with her across a wide meadow, dashing at one another hand in hand, with the she-wolf, howling, and apart-yet-near race back through the bushes : more like that; yes). (Finally something like ersatz sleep).

Outside once : wild cloud waters buzzed like angry insects about my ears, drenched my pajama collar, moist at the elastic banded belly. –

Drink some water : I'm all for water ! At home I drink it by the quart. (And then again some 100-proof; for variety; but seldom. Simply a matter of opposites : civil servant; and – yes, and what ? –. All right, today a little 100-proof !).

Smoky morning, warm; (and the 5 miles are a mere morning constitutional : no : more like sultry ! And smoky as the day when Bedloe strayed into the Ragged Mountains : so most anything may happen to me today !)

The dry heath : I walked across it, a cocksure forester, and my long straight walking stick swung smartly and daringly at my side. The juniper berries were already turning black, though lots of gray-green ones still hung there as well : big handsome fellows, the bushes; 5 feet taller than I – : more than that; so they're at least 400 years old : the days of Luther. (Oh screw Luther !).

Long live whatever struts the earth adorned and clad in green (to wit : the fields and the forests. But I also greeted forester Gröpel : out of respect for the opening of Tieck's ‹Runenberg› : – yes, I greeted the forester,

and his stiff chamois-tuft disappeared, twenty-one twenty-two, into
the new growth alongside his dandy muzzle : gone for good ? – ? – Yes
sir : so let's march on !).

The brown paths with their water welts. Men out in the peat, somber and
slow with shovels, and those big fibrous bricks (bosh : everyone knows
what it looks like !). Distant dots of farmers toiled tending watery potatoes : may they taste bitter in your mouths (do that in any case !). Wind
gave a single crack in the firry frameworks, sailplaning grandly across
the moor, come and gone, come and gone : stopped : very quiet again.
(And smoky; two sheep stand in the background).

Between tracts 123 and -24; then the path down along the edge of the
woods : the wild fern; yellow the old, green the idle young, the strapping lads. Ever more casual and lonesome, my path wound its way,
and probably would finally have come to an end, when I called a halt :
Say ! : this was the area where Thierry and Cattere had kept on disap-
pearing ! (That is to say : Thierry *or* Cattere. – So I slipped my briefcase behind a bush at its stem, and investigated the terrain : –. –. – do a
thing or two, before the jaws of darkness devour me; defy him a little
life : him, Mister Death !).

And they came fuming up ! 10,000 poisonous soft gray beings, with beady
red eyes, and gobbled me up, so I broke into a moaning gallop, and
bellowed like a panicky cow, and slapped my palms, already occupied
by horseflies, against my neck and at my precious face, and still on the
run, scampered round a tree, stormed up its ladder of boughs :

Yow, yow, yow ! – : they were still down there fidgeting above the path and
muttering truculently, and I kept batting at the dot-shaped pain, wherever it appeared, and panted and blinked : horseflies ! – Whoo ! – But
they don't come up this high !

35 feet up (can I ever climb when I have to !) : so then, 35 feet, and heaving
a sigh I looked around :

The reedy surface : really quite large, maybe 400 x 500 yds (and my tall
tree surely equally as old) : the long assegai blades, tempered yellow,
stood motionless and dense, 10 feet high, a botanical army. (Was the
lowest point in the area, trysting place for evening fog and brown
water-slings. – Over on my far right, discernible only by its vaporous
roof : the Söder farm).

And my gaze went stiff and spurred :

Almost directly below me, so that I hadn't even noticed it till now, a gray
steadfast thing : smarter duck of the head, peering deeper still : :

A gray clapboard hut ! – – : I took the daring step, one tree further;
wrapped myself atop the new branch, grabbed wildly at wooden struts,

let myself hang from the brown tree, banged the edges of my shoes to find bark stairs, took a buxom pine lass in my arms (she pricked me, the savage virgin, the second sex, and trembled as I ruthlessly mounted her), fished for bottom and stood.

Right, and where was it now ? ! : looking wildly about me. I picked up the long scrawny bough (wet underneath, ugh !), and I used it, but cautiously, to part the grass sarrisae to my left, Winkelried II : nothing. To my right. A little more : Aha ! I waded a couple steps in that direction (was quite dry, by the way, the ground), nudged sharply with my tool arm : – !

An old thing : small; two yards long, two wide. Or two and a half at most. I lingered long before I uncorked the wooden bar, and the plank door sank, slowly and solemnly, into my arms.

The Haunted Palace : silent ! – –. (A small window, long and wide as your forearm. My head turned above me back and forth).

The thick posts still solid, massive oak, and couldn't get both hands around them; the wooden walls silken gray and lightly warped.

I squinted harder, and balanced over to the corner : a piece of faded uniform on a black rusty nail. A hundred years of dust stirred beneath my finger; rot ripped, weary and relieved; with a very puckered gentle mouth I blew the dust from the shoulders : and into the small hollow of my hand rolled a hard roundness, and I rubbed the button shiny on my sleeve. Gilt brass, beaded rim and of finely grained convexity; I turned the inscription back and forth beneath my bespectacled eyes : 21 (large). And in a circle around it "Chasseurs à Cheval" : Jacques Thierry it was ! ! (And gold-plated for sure; I rubbed it again, silly and eager : my heirloom !).

In the far corner a stubby earthenware bottle, bound with straw : blackish desiccated contents, lemuric and opiate : must have lived like a faun, skittish and all pricked ears. (In a certain sense a precedent for me, is it not ? ! – Value of the historical example : you can do this sort of thing ! – The civil servant always needs his precedent !)

Outside (leaning against the doorpost) : the world invisible; or just the smoky sky. And now and then the slashing cry of a sylvan bird.

Calmly and mechanically I picked up my briefcase (now unchallenged by horseflies) and took the nearest path.

"Well now" (the nodded greeting). "Just now getting home, are you ?". "Yes, that's right," (most peevishly) : "even had to spend the night !" (But the darning yarn covered as alibi).

On the ordnance map 1:25,000 : the hut is not marked ! Judging by that, No One knows about it ! ! (But by way of precaution I'll have a look at one of the 1:5000 plats in the land registrar's office in Fallingbostel. – I was almost tempted to write the flying school in Luthe and have them take an aerial photograph of the area for me; and dragged the wanton notion around with me for several days, imp of the perverse : noo, better not. – But I can write to Bressuire and ask for documents; and I did it at once in my quaint French (high-school and occasional reading); but certainly quite comprehensible ! Oh, so what !).

Hans Fritsche : "They act as if they're sent from heav'n / and coo in English when they lie !"; and then went ahead and applied it to Great Britain : even then, Goethe himself had seen through them ! – : What an ignoramus ! ! And he's Goebbels's right-hand man ! (like master, like . . .). Instead of realizing that at the time, circa 1800, German ‹englisch› was used as the adjective for ‹Engel›, (= ‹angel›); ETA Hoffmann uses "englisches Fräulein" a good ten times, and he's not talking about any old Miss ! But it's typical of these quarter-educated rulers of ours; and "the people", themselves a shade duller still, believe it all of course : no sir ! : out of my sight, you leghorns ! – But seriously : that's no longer a matter of spadework : those are preparations. Against England !

The dahlias swung and swayed in the gray-green Sunday twilight; the pinks indignantly shook their finely fringed heads (probably because my stinky feet in their greasy leather husks were standing beside them !) : "I'm going for a little walk, Berta". "Don't be too long, though; thunderstorm's coming up."

As tall as I (Käthe; within woods' edge; black skirt, white blouse); the moon a flame behind her ear, the single gust of wind as a warm comb for her hair : she bit into her lip and waited for me : "Yes".

The drowsy cloud : once again it opened its reddish slant eyes and purred; warm and still. (Which means "sheet lightning"). The gray dry grass was full of our hands and breathings.

There : she daintily showed one of her little gold-plated claws and purred longer this time (the thunder cat). I quickened my pace, encompassed by white hoops. Once a whole host of air waftlets came through the shrubbery and obligingly fanned and cooled my back. – "You're being careful, right." she murmured past me (and at the proper moment I pushed myself away, as disciplined as a man on his silver anniversary).

Wrinkled brow : "No need for the washboard face" she advised softly, lazily, and observant. (Then one more time).

She combed her hair and scraped the harrow through it so roughly that her face opened up with pain, but in her savagery did not stop for all that : beautiful ! (Spirit of my spirit !).

The black wind leapt up, like the bass giants in the overture to Iphigenia; water appeared all through the air, and within seconds we were pasted in our clothes, from the neck down to our firm thighs.

Parting in front of the house : the she-wolf howled something into the abandoned night, and I, spectacled owl, laughed as if part of the Wild Hunt : tooth of shark and eye of skate, be eternal subjugate !

"My God, look at you !" (accent on "look" : my wife. – And diarrhea later on; had been a little much for me : thrice the she-wolf !).

23 Aug. 1939 : pact with Soviet Russia : ? ! – : it's only a matter of days now ! And I gave it some thought : what had been good as gold during the last war ? : coffee, tea, cocoa; tobacco. And so I brought them with me from Fallingbostel, and the airtight tin of navy-cut. Cigarettes in tropic-proof packages. Rum and hard liquor.

Still 2,400 in the savings account : I withdrew two-thirds of it, and went on buying (a vote of no confidence in the state : Jawohl, mein Führer ! !) : leather for shoe soles and Conti-rubber heels. Hardware items; plus a new axhead and two blades for my bow saw. Shoelaces, matches : "I'm speaking to Herr Pfeiffer himself, am I not ? : Could you still get 4 tons of coal to me today ? And 2 of briquettes ? – That's correct : 4 and 2. – – No, number 64 : I'll drop by during my lunch hour and pay for it.– Fine, fine !"

Oil, sugar; envelopes, paper; laundry soap. – Wait : bicycle tires. Flash-light batteries (but they don't last, damn it all !). Light bulbs : always need to keep the radio in good repair, so a couple of tubes in reserve ! – – Revolver ? : and I wavered for some time; but then it did seem overly romantic, and I stuck with my heavy bowie knife. Then a mas-sive leather belt with brass buckle, nice and wide (good as a corset for the older gentleman, wouldn't you say ? !).

Wait : a pair of rubber boots (the heavy-duty sort !). – : "Was able to buy our winter coal at a bargain price, Berta : special sale : 20 marks a ton", I tossed a lie her way to cover up my purchases; for she was already getting nervous, "and tomorrow there's a case of wine coming, too : it's always better to have something in the house—" (laying it on thick) : "for when your brothers come !" – Then back to the office :

"Well, Peters ? !" : "I mean those Poles are getting awfully big for their britches, Herr Düring !", and Schönert too (well, he was still too young). The most lustfully outraged were the women, Krämer espe-cially. And the August sun burned.

When I was walking down the street (: Hurrah, the cotton down !) / a charming girl I chanced to meet : Hurrah the cotton down ! – : "Käthe ! !". She came up, bumped the wind casually to the side with her hips, and gave her rear a slap with the back of her hand : ?

"Käthe : a tip ! : ", and I hastily explained the whys and wherefores. She wrinkled her face up at once, giving it brief, menacing thought – : "So what ?" she growled; and : "I haven't got any money.". I crumpled a 50-mark bill into her hand, advising : "At least buy yourself some good toilet soap, skin cream, and the item a woman needs most : make it several cartons." "No problem : put it in your briefcase, that way your parents won't notice; and lock it up in your wardrobe at home. – And tell me if it's not enough." She still had the money in her hand and was concentrating with a pout; – "Well, all right," she said hesitantly at last : "Soap, you say ? It'll be scarce ?". "Everything, everything, everything," I shouted nervously : "Shoes, Kotex, toothpaste : depend on it : in 14 days you'll only get it all with ration books !". "Oh, you don't know how it was, Käthe !" (impatient) : "don't be stupid –" (she lifted just one eyebrow, and I apologized at once : all right. It's settled). "Fine," she resolved, nodding thoughtfully : "I'll do it. Write it down for me, everything you think I'll need". "Sure, bon".

And back again : "Try to convince your parents in a roundabout way : that they should buy food and coal; the more the better !". "Mhm.". licking her lips she gave a decisive turn of her head, eyes searching for the nearest shop : "Mhm". Menacingly soft : "But listen, if this turns out to be nonsense . . . . . !"

The Böhme was already moving uneasily in its meadow wash, fields steamed gold, gray soft horseflies bit in notorious fashion; loden coats were still roving about young lads, the sedge had not yet died out. – Wait : back to the hardware store again : "A pair of hinges, please. –. –. No, no : for a very simple door to a shed; but good strong ones." "And the screws to go with them too, please" (two in reserve).

Kites stand atilt above Colony Hünzingen, high up : I gave my wife 200 marks : "Buy new shoes and warm underwear for yourself and the kids in Walsrode. – And when the delivery van comes from Trempenau's, first have him give you the bill and check it !". "Yes, but," she was quite annoyed ! "Don't go spending all our money, you hear !" and her eyes were little nest eggs. "Here, here's the bank book –" I said grandly (she really doesn't need to know a thing about my other money !) : "there's still 800 marks in the account : if you're smart you'll spend it today : all of it !" – "You're really crazy, you and your war," she said calmly and suddenly very resolute (having rescued now this precious member o' the spirit world from evil) : "Only 800 left ! !", and she jumped up and paced back and forth, the wailing wife : "Stop carrying on so wild about it all : Weber's already been asking what's up over here !". And I followed her out into the kitchen : "Berta," I approached her, (dutiful and delighted) : "You know what you have to do !". "Sure, sure", she said over her shoulder, haughty and disdainful. (So there it is : my conscience is clear !)

25 Aug. 1939 : permanent pact of mutual assistance between England and Poland; and the malheur was rolling up into a nice little ball : "Well, Berta ? !". "Oh, you've got a screw loose !", angry and defensive. (Now it's only a matter of hours !).

Actually I ought to go over to Kirchboitzen again today; but I would rather put my museum in order : that's my job, too ! : have an urgent need to augment my knowledge for my tasks ! And whistling, I gazed at the lovely "collected" maps and beyellowed documents, and arranged them in the compartments of my chest, carefully laying the button, wrapped in tissue paper, with the rest. (Then once again with furrowed brow out to the shed : nail the board to the back wall; the readiness is all !).

‹*Wandering Willie's Tale*› from ‹Redgauntlet› : that is a splendid story, and much too good for it not to be commented upon these days; these days, when they're all Kolbenheyering and Thoraxing (or, more precisely : mediocring !).

Inviolable sanctuaries ought to be created ! and while I nailed I composed my letter addressed to the League of Nations :
"Gentlemen :" (or better : Excellencies ! : otherwise they won't lift a finger !).
"Your excellencies :
In light of the tremendous destruction which all wars in all times – and none more than the most recent – have caused to mankind's collections of art and literature; and in light of the far greater dangers to which these will be exposed in the next inevitable armed conflict and in those yet to follow, I – although a German – hereby take the liberty of submitting the following proposal to your worthy assembly.
§1). The erection of inviolable cultural sanctuaries at several sites on the globe – with a minimum of at least 3 –, each to be constructed, maintained and administered cooperatively by all nations. For this purpose, I suggest small and otherwise useless islands located as far as possible from all areas of political and economic conflict – e.g., Tristan da Cunha, South Georgia, St. Helena, Easter Island –, where, upon erection of appropriate facilities, would be collected the largest possible stocks of mankind's books, together with the most valuable of its irreplaceable works of art. – The employment of any weapon whatsoever within a radius of . . . miles would be forbidden.

§2). In order to render impossible any misuse of these sanctuaries and to avoid providing any power with a pretext for intervention, neither the products nor the prototypes of engineering or of any other applied science will be accepted.

§3). One copy of every book published in the future is to be sent by its publisher to each of the "Culture Islands"; likewise the originals of paintings and sculptures or a copy, if possible executed by the artist himself, of equal merit.

§4). Provision is to be made for the greatest living artists and scholars to find security of person and the opportunity for unhampered work at one such site whenever they may wish it (or upon retirement or in case of war). – The decision concerning an individual's worthiness could be left to a League of World Artists, though this too must first be created (but not to the Nobel Committee; one need only think of Rilke, Däubler, or Alfred Döblin – while a turd like Sienkiewicz becomes a prize-winning turd !) – In the future all important men could, moreover, be buried here together, creating world shrines.

§5). Hopeful young talents, who have shown proof of ability, could be encouraged by granting them permission to live worry-free on these islands for a period of time, during which they would at last have the easy access, so necessary for artists and thinkers, to mankind's cultural achievements.

§6). Other intellectuals would also be rewarded with admission for a few days : not, however, physicists, chemists, technicians (for the same reasons already noted); furthermore, entry is forever denied to all politicians, professional military, film stars, boxing champions of all weight classes, publishers, rich gawkers, etc., or to persons merely wishing to find asylum in times of war. – Permission for such special visits is to be extended by each island's administrators. – –

Considering the magnitude of the preparations necessary, (establishment of a commission, selection and purchase of the islands, construction of the physical plants, selection of personnel, transport of items of culture value, provisioning with supplies, etc), all of which, even at a modest estimate, may require years to complete, the project must be begun at once. – I am confident that none of your worthy delegations would wish to veto such an undertaking : mankind will one day tender you its reverent thanks for the preservation of its most sacred possessions ! –

With the deepest respect, I remain your : Heinrich Düring.

P.S. : With reference to §4). I hereby take the liberty of applying at once for a visa granting lifelong asylum : the mere mention of my epoch-making research concerning the district of Fallingbostel should obviate any further substantiation. I am in my early 50s, 6 ft 1 in tall, of no religious persuasion, free of infectious disease, and at no time have I ever been a member of the NSDAP or any of its affiliated organizations."

(Except for the GLF : but everyone had to join the Labor Front. – Well, I'll append it anyway by way of precaution. *"P.S. 2 :* Except for the GLF.". – There. : My conscience is clear ! : yet once more !).

The sun ? ! : a madman careering about up there with his howling molten rivers ! (And we respectable folk still call them "stars" and genteelly celebrate the misty luster of the spawn of hell !). I spat right in the sun's blotched face, trod the earth with hasty, hacking steps, and ripped open the buttonholes at my chest, revealing the sweat and sparse hair below me. I hacked at a fork in a branch with the edge of my hand : that damned duffer up there : Supposed to see everything, hear and smell everything – my heartfelt sympathy by the way ! – and allows a war to break out again ! : ergo he's included it in his ostensible plans for the world ? !)

"Staar-light : Staar-bright ! / First staar we see tonight !" : Children with their brightly flickering paper lanterns, they too want to free themselves of this workaday life : with lights, with words. In the dusk. Not a dumb idea !).

"What's up, Berta ?" : she came hastily toward me : "A call from the Herr Commissioner himself : you're to report to the office tomorrow without fail ! Absolutely no fieldwork". After a pause, from the kitchen : "What's going on ?". "Maybe somebody's sick – ?" (wily, phlegmatic and shrugging). "Oh, that's it" (plausible and relieved : they don't want to know !)

In the night her hand on my shoulder : "What now ?"; for my wife was standing in her nightshirt beside my bed, and a very bitter and crude joke tickled on my tongue. – : "Just listen, Heinrich : motorcycles !"

Indeed ! ! : indeed : there the throbbing machines stood, gaping cyclopsically, over by Hogrefe's fence; then to Alsfleth's. Then – "Go on down there, Heinrich : there're lights on in every house !". – And so slip on a jacket. –

"What's up, Herr Heitmann !" (From the army registration office, in Falling), and at once I recognized the stack of brown cards : "Call-up orders, huh ? ! – On our way; just like '14/'18." And he proudly : "Well, this time it won't last as long as it did in your day, Herr Düring !"; and I raised interested eyebrows : ?. – "I mean, this time we've got the Führer", indulgent and disdainful of my advanced senility.

‹You idiot› I immediately thought, but translated it in citizenese : "Yesyes, of course" (and made to go him one better) : "all be over in 4 weeks !" (don't you notice nothin' ? !). But : "At the out-side !" he confirmed emphatically, and remounted the saddle : "Well then : Heil ! !" (Would I ever love to be that brown !).

Nothing more grisly and pitiful : than two nations going for each other's nation-antheming throats. (Man, the "animal that bawls hurrah"; as a definition).

"What is it, Heinrich ? !" : and with my head I mutely motioned toward the Spreckelsens' next door, where the young wife, tears streaming down, was tying up her pale husband's bundle; at 3 in the morning : she ran into open wardrobes and ripped apart their piles of underwear (and on the occasion of his changing his underpants they did it one more time; without worrying about the open window).

Nessun dorma ! !

III

(August/September 1944)

In a dream : back in Hamburg again, with Käthe (in railroad uniform, with lantern and hoo-whee whistle). And we filed through the window bars, inside we wrapped the paintings in blankets, tilted, whispered, knotted; left behind our briefcase with ID papers (bogus, of course !) as if by accident. "Windowpanes for the boss", we said, as we grumpily showed our passes (from Käthe's father !) at the main station. She had martially draped the conductor's coat over her mighty shoulders, the black bill of a cap set in her hair, her no-small-talk mouth underscored her sturdy mocking eyes. Alone through lamplorn trains, in the rumbling third-class night, travelers with large lightweight burdens, ‹On to victory the wheels must roll›, mostly mute, and my wide condor-lady propped her tubular legs under the seat opposite, oh, timeworn greenish white toothpaste ads around her (and mounted photographs of ‹Wasserburg› and the ‹Hainleite›); the iron rushed round us on its way; we slew straying Polish husbands and wives; towered up out of semidoors; lugged up stairways; crept through chessboard landscapes : black-forest, white-meadow; I bit a red pencil in two, pelted arc lamps, battled in shoes, Käthe encamped in armchairs and me on a breasthunt, in the vertically striped carpet of a blouse, flying houses and migrating birds above Ernst-August-Platz.

(The paintings had to be stashed then behind dressers and bookcases with double backs. I coolly ordered the measured boards from the carpenter. On Sundays we would drag them up out of hiding and silently inspect them; in one newspaper was an article concerning unidentified thieves and coal-filching).

Warm and foggy (at 5:30 in the morning); this evening then : off to Chateau Thierry ! (Quite superfluously – and purely to round off my knowledge –, I'm going to study known cases of lycanthropy : actually, actually you can only giggle over such gloomy goings-on !).

Nowadays all you can do is escape halfway. Given the density of population ! (Or, rather : you must divide yourself; live a double life; but burn out more quickly. Far from any sort of Christian paradise).

Joachim von Wick : had been postmaster in Walsrode; and I affectionately gazed at the letter from my collection (b. 26 Aug. 1756, d. Walsrode 23 May 1827. – I've got into the habit of browsing through my ‹Background Materials› every morning !).

Main road : you walked among these hot days as if among tall columns. (Golden, green-flecked. To the train).

Brief diversion : I imagined that I was a famous corpse and Berta the Widow was guiding people through the ‹Düring Museum› in Fallingbostel : there in the display cases, under glass, lay my manuscripts (e.g., my request of Finteln to finally put his thumbprint on his ID – "his last letter. Yes." – next to it the grand but still unpublished biography of Fouqué). On the wall a portrait of me by Oskar Kokoschka, with only one ear and highly unchristian flesh tones. A re-chording, ‹Celeste Aïda›, warbled by me; : "Here the carpenter's pencil that he always made it a point to sign his name with –" (this was often stolen by admirers, but was always lying there again, one mark thirty a dozen from the Westfalia Tool Company). And out in front of the building with tower (= the church), I stood tall in my metal tux, a hand lifted in polite disgust toward the District Commissioner's Office . . . . "The boots he died in . . .". – "Uhwhat were his last words, ma'am ?" (the ‹Spiegel› reporter with his red morocco writing pad); – : "Uh – ‹Long live art – uh – : Long live the fatherland !›. Uh : Germany, that is". "Ger . . . many . . . : Ah; – : Thank you !". (Whereas I had merely gasped ‹shit› ten times !). The grand finale, the niche illuminated a sulfurous blue where stood the slender urn with my ashes (because I definitely want to be cremated; it's much more hygienic !); the unpretentious marble plaque : – come on, quick ? – ‹Here lies . . . › (aw bull : not lying at all !) – okay ‹'inder me not› ! (without the ‹h›; that makes it especially vulgar). Or better still : ‹Don't get 'indered !›. (Which fitted my case at the moment very nicely, having to catch the train !).

The larks twittered your ear deaf; (and I had to stand again too; since now, during the war, there's one car less : there are too many people ! !).

What would I do with 10,000 marks ? ! : buy 8 acres of wood and moor in the district of Fallingbostel; and a heavy barbwire fence around it, i.e. 7 acres (because fences like that cost money !). which makes about 110 x 185 yds, better than nothing ! – Or finance a new edition of Albert Ehrenstein. – Or a pilgrimage to Cooperstown; and immediately I pictured it to myself : up the Hudson as far as Albany; from there cross-country via Saratoga Springs, then on to Otsego County. And naturally the first thing you have to do is – "Heilittler, Herr Düring" : "Sago-sago, Paleface !" – climb Mount Vision for the classic view of the town. The sun arched through the dirty compartment window, and I was still standing there, hat in hand. (Before his grave).

(If only I could get hold of the ‹Autobiography of a Pocket-Handkerchief›; the travelogues and his historical works on the navy. And the ‹Rural Hours› by his daughter : I still know far too little !).

Schönert was a prisoner in Africa, Peters in Normandy, Runge had been killed in the east in '43 : no great loss there ! (But little Otte, not even 18, now lay by Monte Cassino !).

Wooden buskins with a pair of diagonal straps (there haven't been any leather shoes for ages now !); but they looked chic on long legs, and Krämer had even painted a sepia stripe up her brown calf : and it actually looked like a very elegant seam on a pair of silk stockings ! How grand, Mother Nature, the glory of thy invention ! : "Just how far up does that stripe go, Fräulein Krämer ?". "And who gets to draw it on all the time !" She fixed a dove's pious green eyes on Steinmetz, our part-time drooling dotard : "My little sister does, every evening", she breathed, hushed as a church ("yet He who speaks of ‹evening› speaks of much". This was followed by further remarks about ‹Pandora's Box› and ‹that ball Columbus showed Isabel›; Schönert's spirit was still manifestly among us).

Faithfully following new regulations to use the smallest possible phormat for every letter (looks cute with a "ph", doesn't it ?), I wrote practically nothing but postcards, or used 4 x 6 index cards for frasing in-house memos (the "f" in exchange for the above; for pedants). : All is lost already in the east, and the Germans are retreating through France, and I cheered to myself : a man whose prison is finally bursting open ! ! And even should I have to live for 5 years on water and bread : if these bastards, Nazis and officers, are swept away, then my world is gold-plated ! So I elaborately rubbed my hands, and was so amused that Krämer gave me an astonished smile (any man is a delicacy these days, and in an emergency you'd even settle for me, right ?).

An absurdly fat woman as executive secretary : ‹E pur si muove !› She needs dehydrating too.

Breakfast break (40 minutes today, Saturday. And then it goes straight through till 3 o'clock).

Saccharin tablets in the coffee : and even they had long since grown scarce, only to be had by swapping ‹under the counter›. The cardboard buttons broke when you sewed them onto the shirt; and oldman Steinmetz had actually offered Krämer 4 textile points (= 1 pair of stockings) for a roll in the hay. I had done my shopping well beforehand, and given my modicum of vanity, was completely independent as far as clothing etcetera went; so that I could use my points exclusively for : new lenses in my glasses, soles for my shoes, a handful of nails without an iron ration coupon, and a roll of film once when Käthe was on leave. (Over 16 months ago now; had been in early May. Late ice age).

An outraged Fräulein Knoop : ‹mussel salad› the menu had read, no coupon needed, and they had started to eat it, when Kardel had found the snail feelers : yech ! (Transition to frog's legs, oysters, beche-de-mer, and all other possible exotic abominations, rotten eggs and shark fins). Steinmetz, too, came by, smiling extra elegantly, stroking his imaginary moustache, and told us at length, like the Red Book of Hergest, all about Paris in the old days : "M'syour" they had all sworn : "It tastes like coconut". Spicy, spicy. "Oh," said Knoop, incredulous. "I swear by the pillow of the Seven Sleepers !". (Well, in that case).

"Over by Bergen, they're setting up an officers' training school", Fräulein Krämer informed us; excitedly aware of her serviceability as highclass whore. (If only we could get back to the medieval notion that every soldier is more or less ‹disreputable›, – rightly so : the "foe" never did him any real harm ! – about on a par with the hangman, and to be avoided by every decent citizen !). – Still time for a quick walk.

Summer sun : shadows : Peter Schlemihl ! : Nowadays he'd join a circus and make millions ! If only a ‹man in gray› like that would appear to me, and offer me something for mine, something useful in these times : a tobacco pipe that never burned out; a car that didn't use any gas, a horse-sausage that never got smaller.

Chewing in front of a bookstore : German-silver rhymes scrambled at anchor, bloatings : Blunck, Heribert, Menzel, Kolbenheyer, ‹Choric Verse›, ‹Quex, a Lad for Hitler›, and all the other balladmongers of the Third Reich. A magazine, "German Faith" with an SS-wedding : a squad-leader masquerading as a priest of Odin blessed the couple beside an anvil with a sledgehammer *that* big : magic fertility rites. (Plus "The Blind Goalie"; probably some more of your ballads. Or a soccer novel. Who gives a damn. Nowadays).

Eduard Vehse's 48-volume work, "History of the German Courts, the German Nobility and German Diplomacy since the Reformation" is going to need a supplement that goes on up till 1950 ! : what charming items could be added : the courts of the Wilhelms, of the Eberts, of the Hindenburgs, of the Hitlers, together with their accomplices and successors !

Or : "Correspondence between Two Notorious Personalities : (to wit : God and Satan); and then simply the dates : Hell, April 20th . . . . . ; Heaven, April 22nd . . . . . (And the notation : "The aforesaid individual who goes by the name of Shakespeare has even now arrived . . . .". Etc.).

A *cat approached,* looked at me doubtfully, gave an embarrassed laugh, and I cut one of my three slices of coldcuts into little pieces for her and laid it on a sheet of wax paper : –. – An old woman, perched on a bike, precariousing among schoolchildren.

A *children's choirlet* recited dutifully : "Fold my hands. Bow my head : / The Führer's commands / Give daily bread ! / And free me from all dread !"; and I simply could not help myself, I had to walk over to the hedge and have a look at these five-year-old beings, in bib and tucker, sitting there on the narrow wooden benches. The nurse (who had led them in reciting these vile verses), placed a small piece of glassy candy into the little tin cup each held by its handle, and they all stirred at it with their spoons, ‹cooking› it vigorously : what sort of regime is it that can dream up this sort of thing ? ! (But immediately I recalled that I, too, had learned as my first little song : "The Kaiser is a very nice man (sic !) / : and he lives in Burrlin"; and so it seems to be the universal, inevitable method of providing ‹civics› lessons ! Oh, the bastards, the lot of them ! ! To pump such verbal swill into defenseless, fragile, unknowing beings ! Or the equally senseless harangues about the "Blood of Christ" ! : children ought to grow up in total intellectual neutrality until they're 17/18, and then be put through a couple of rigorous courses ! They could then be presented alternately with the fabulous fibs about the "Holy Trinity" and the Nice Men in Berlin, and, by way of comparison, philosophy and natural sciences : and then you shysters would have to keep a sharp lookout !).

Then the nurse gave a shriek, and a whack to one of the urchins, and I moved behind me. (Still have to get 10.– marks to the parish office; for two schoolkids who copied the death register for me : grinning : money's not worth much anymore !).

"We want to serve you faith-full-lee : / faithful uhunto death. (Yes, death !)" : But why, for heaven's sake ? !

Dust-girded recruits : mindlessly flapping their feet, twitched and tossed their brown-sweated heads, and hurled the heroic words from them : "We want to pledge our lihives to you . . ." : Yes, but why, for heaven's sake ? ! !

With me you're totally wasting your measured syllables ! ! Before you decide you want to die for the fatherland, you'd best take a closer look ! (And "My Life for the Führer" ? ! : for a politician I wouldn't grab hold of my arse ! !). –

A letter from Schönert (just arrived; and la Krämer read it aloud in triumph) : well, this time at least they weren't exposed to the hideous
trench warfare we had in the first World War. (But then aerial warfare
in those days was a silly idyll compared to now ! And outside the next
detachment was already bellowing a song of Lora and Dora, and of
Trudy and Sophy. And I thought of my tall girl, my distant girl. Of
Lena and Irena : of Anne-Marie. – "Hand me those coal ration cards,
Fräulein Krämer, so I can stamp them", and she reluctantly pulled
herself away from the window; her face had pouted itself out of
joint –).

Past noon and still another 3 hours !

Hot in the office, and reverie came to pat our faces with soft, empty hands.
Eyes yawned (it is simply too long without a break !); hands loitered
at official business; under the chairs oblique legs stretched; Krämer
slowly pulled some zipper or other through the silence, and then typed
away at her metronome, distant droplets, on dainty hooves, in a forest
of dust. ("Pan sleeps"; that was coined by some office worker, somewhere around three in the afternoon).

"You're decking yourself out like a bride !"; for she was clandestinely
doing her nails, Fräulein Knoop, and her black mourning (for the 2nd
fiancé already) looked attractive enough set against her white over-
stuffed face; she made heavy chestnut eyes, rolled her anklets down
further, and taking a breath, tugged at her skirt; then dipped and
pumped her fountain pen and counted, listlessly and softly, bookkeep-
ing noses. The new trainee gazed timidly at where the strap of her bra
cut visibly through her fat back; turned his red head away and projected the image onto the far wall. The old man was sleeping now,
quite unabashedly, but behind his green glasses, unconvictable (was
just an old office fox, and still quite useful !)

After half an hour one of them whispered the question : "Do you think
there'll be a thunderstorm today ? – Can we still go swimming later on,
do you suppose ? –" A quarter hour later I answered in an elderly, envious voice : "Both, Fräulein Krämer". A door slammed resolutely; the
old man awoke with self-control, and loftily entered a name in his
book; Robin the Red had moaning visions of Krämer, first with, then
very much without her swimsuit; Fräulein Knoop went to get new ink;
and I rapidly stamped my way through another 80 clothing ration coupons.

"Boss's in a bad mood today !" : and sure enough : he had written numerous nasty remarks on every petition, sort of in the style of Frederick the
(thankgod) One and Only, and then at the bottom a steady stream of

"refused"; "reject"; "no"; "impossible !"; "how dare he ? !". Once he
had even added : "not to be processed in the future" : all the better for
us ! And now for the last folder . . . . . . : "The boss wants to see you
right away, Herr Düring !"

Two or three gusts of wind, and clouds of evil portent. (Through the corridor windows; in passing).

"At one time you told me about that − deserter, the one from 1813 − ?"
(gravelly coughs) : "Just imagine, Düring : they say there's another
one now. In the same area. Been there for years ! I've been following
the matter for some time"; he shoved the forester's report into my
hand, and watched me, with lurking amusement.

Breached bulwark : my face. (No doubt of it : Gröpel, the son of a bitch,
had apparently been spotting me mornings !). And his was an ample
gray rag. (Plus four additional reports by farmers : remember those
names). The rag ripped open in one place; he sneered new words
together, and alertly I countered them : for all I care he can turn my
stomach till the next ice age ! (Has had a more proper education
maybe; but not the man to dare the deed).

"Yes, looks like we'll have to make a raid on our new ‹faun›," he proposed
merrily, daring me. He gazed at me intently : "They say he's about 50/
60 years old. Gray hair; tall and scrawny"; and he brazenly took my
measure; and I stared at him, unshaken and cunning : something different about you today, too ? ! − ? − Ah, well look at that ! ! : all at once
he was no longer wearing his party badge ! (Just like old Häusermann
and the rest of the sewer rats : lookie there !). I ‹took the floor› : I said
coldly : "May I please ask a personal favor − Herr Doktor − ?" (and
he leaned forward more snugly) : "− You are a Party member, are you
not : could you give me the address of the District Party Leader : a
petition on behalf of my daughter : you are a friend of his −" (And
how : for Christmas he had given him a carpet paid for out of our
funds !). − He sat there ever so stiffly; he said politely and flatly :
"Kirchplatz 3". Looked at his calendar : "The raid will be next week
then. September 8th". "Yes sir, Herr Commissioner."

All right, then, that's the end ! ! and I whistled a dry and bitter tune :
over ! : the end ! All right !. (So, clear the place out and set fire to it,
tonight ! − And I'll give the forester a kick in the pants yet. Or two. All
his files and cards and ration books just might get lost sometime : it'd
take him a good six months just to fill out new forms ! − − But it's over,
over, over ! − Oh, Käthe !)

"Well look at that : − it's already started to rain, Fräulein Krämer !". And
"Heil !". "Right. Heil ! : have a good weekend !".

"13 convoy ships sunk !"; the loudspeaker sang and thumped in the human paddock; words met, strict and gray; and the limp watery dead drifted pathetically through our crowd. Rain befingered me. The apparatus bellowed bakelitely and triumphed on : "For we're sail ! ing ! 'gainst Engellannd ! : Engelland !"; Herms Niels and Herm. Löns, the German Hit-Tune Company ! (But the other side's got Vansittart & Wells). I waded mutely through the slush of muttering and teeth; many heads had eyes in trumps; laughter, too, appeared, and two women sizzled "Super !". And still they sailed from every window, spare and manly; No one was sobbing or walking stiffly with cobwebbed eyes; but it was raining harder, silver-gray drops splattered up from the pavement, hand-high, around my walking shoes.

A *dog* leaped, with head turned in the thicket of legs. The dead hovered up ahead with limp bluish arms, hung garlands of eyes about me where I stood, one ate with me, uneasily, from my teaspoon. (And it was lovely out on the main road : you were all alone : no one drives a car anymore ! At most there are the funny wood-gas buggies that Hitler claims will win his war ! – Old grass threw itself excitedly from one side to the other; but now once again, the scudding smoky blue).

The music surged and burst in fragments (here too) : oldman Weber stepped out under his sign : "They'ah keep'n' it up – hah : sunk ump'ty tons ag'in t'day !" And proud. I nodded as piously as I could, and first made to walk by; but then I added : "Shame about all those supplies : why one freighter like that : we wouldn't have to do a stitch of work the rest of our lives !". "Hmmm", and it went on hudibrasing behind me. (Then a shaky bass barreled something about the Rhi-hi-hine : oh happy days were here again, 1944 !).

"Well, Berta !" (still in deepest mourning) : our son had been killed on the Murmansk front 14 months earlier; as an off. cand., doing his required eight-weeks frontline training. First home on proud leave from the school, as admired sergeant and cornet : "Well, dad ?"; as if he had it made now ! When the worst was yet to come ! And I screwed up my face to smile, inspecting the peacock, till he turned away, offended. Explained to him why, too, certainly; but he had heard too much about battle as the ‹tempering of a man›. "When not on duty, I'd rather not mingle with the rank and file !" he had informed me with astonishment when I once suggested that, whenever possible, he go among them from time to time : to hear some good common sense ! Okay, bon ! – Sure, and then when the local Branch Leader showed up, my wife came back hard to earth, threw a bowl of potatoes at the Führer's picture, and went into sobbing spasms. (Me : I felt nothing ! You don't really dare

tell anyone that; but I felt more distant from Paul than from some stranger; for Cooper I can still weep, even now. But I recognized ‹my boy's› shallowness and dreadful mediocrity : his mother's ! : actually I should have said to her : you bear a generous portion of blame in this, you pompous woman ! If only you had helped me preach reason to him, instead of whooping over the silver cord wound about his bird-brain ! !).

(Then the epitaph : "What should we put in the newspaper, Heinrich ? !" implored the Prostrate Lady in Black. "‹Paul fell›" I said sternly, "‹one of many deluded children› !" : I would have done it too ! ! – Oh ! : she didn't want to go that far; particularly since her mite of a conscience did not, perhaps, quite absolve her : for, oh, how disdainfully she had looked down her nose at the poor corporal-drudges from next door. How she had puckered her mouth to a penny, and gone out for a strut on the arm of her son ! How her sassy tongue had let fly when I termed ‹the officer› the most despicable of all beings : "Jealous of your own son, huh ? !"; and had gone off laughing to the pantry, to slip him the last of our supplies ! – Yes, and so she decided in favor of something original, "Fallen for Greater Germany" – well, if that's what you want ? ! – But she didn't let Gerda volunteer for anti-aircraft duty anymore !).

And so : "Well, Berta ?" (as a greeting). Yes, yes. And she had tickets for the 6 o'clock movie, too : "Come along for once !". (And I groaned inwardly : I usually never go; for the same money I can buy an ordnance map ! – Well; once is not a habit; and maybe she would sleep better, and I could disappear more easily tonight). – "Feddersen wants you to stop by, too"; and I furrowed my brow deeper still.

"Heil, Herr Feddersen". " 'fternoon, Herr Düring". And he, craftsman-dictator, rummaged unhurriedly among his fabrics and scissors. (Had ordered myself a canvas coverall, as camouflage in the woods; was quite superfluous now. Or, then again, not : since I would probably always want to walk among trees; so coolly try it on !). And with his heavy gray hands he smoothed the fabric over my limbs. (Did I want stirrups fitted on the trousers ? – Well, I'd think about that); but my heart cursed and flickered within me, and he promised delivery in 4 weeks. "3", he added, after we had complained some about the weather, and I had let him dig deep several times in my large ‹House of Neuerburg› tin. "And don't forget the green peaked cap" (for my prim pate) : "and remember the double seat, too, please, sir ! : the main thing's the durability !". "Sure; the buttons covered with fabric, of course. – Good-bye !".

Facing books (back home again; another hour yet till the movies). Balzac, Balzac : not a poet; no rapport with nature (the most important criterion !). Only every 20 pages is there anything really good, a precise formulation, an allusive image, a sudden spark of imagination. How ridiculous, for example, his deadly descriptions, all of them 2 ungainly printed pages long, of the boudoirs of the haute volée ! : can anyone fit together the fragments of such inane puzzles ? And keeps repeating the same figures, motifs, situations, as only a prolix proser can. He never gets his men right; nothing but incroyables, curmudgeons, journalists, poison-concocting doorkeepers (how soothing, in contrast, even Cooper and Scott). His women : courtesans and wallflowers. Psychology ? ? : o my ! ! : for the one and only ‹Anton Reiser› I wouldn't take all of Balzac and Zola put together !

And then there are the new scribblers in Blood and Soil : compared to them B. is no less than a god ! For example, these panegyrics here on the jacket :
"the captivating charm of unpretentiousness" (when there is no way to hide the total imbecility of it all !),
"a manly and open book" (when the author, with much painstaking embarrassment, manages a weak thrust of his abdomen !),
"that finally fills a gap of long standing" (if by chance the fable doesn't for once date back to Homer, but merely to Hesiod !);
and I lovingly caressed my old Pauly's "Encyclopedia of Classical Antiquities".

As for new poets : it is indeed a great rarity for someone to make the fine distinction between whether that's an office window glimmering there on the horizon or a large heavenly body about to rise. (And when it's finally circling overhead, they lie there in their close-curtained alcoves, breathing raspily, and dreaming of chubby secretarial hocks; or of how they never passed their high-school comps) : for whom do poets write really ? For the one in a hundred thousand just like themselves ? (Because the one in ten thousand who might be a potential reader never discovers the contemporary poet at all; and at best has gotten as far as Stifter). – No sir ! : I would not want to be a writer ! (And ‹nationalist kitsch› is the same thing as moldy mildew : nationalist means kitsch !).

Still need to calculate : when, where, and in what phase the moon will rise tonight. (Yes : it's clear; – for the most part. And blessed be K. Schoch's table of the planets; even the dumbest Düring can manage with it. And it's absolutely precise).

(Long ago, as a boy, I was always drawing stylized maps on large sheets

of graph paper, with right-angled islands and infinitely intricate bays and canals : most probably the ‹labyrinth-complex› of primitives with their edifices, tombs, mines. Now it's in woods; and on a map scaled 25,000:1. Relaxed, so to speak. More natural. More nimble).

And tonight I've got to set fire to my hut ! !

"Hein – rich !". – : "JustimagineHeinrich : Fräulein Evers is home ! On leave ! – Over there !" (No doubt of it ! In the name of him who will one day be my boss ! "Is that so," and show controlled surprise. Words, yes. – Back upstairs : and to the window ! – :).

"Ah – Fräulein Evers !" : innocent, jaunty (and shaking terribly); the hand across the fence said ‹Käthe !›. My breath was violent and mechanical (the way wind mingles with foliage); my eyes whispered (as if vegetal); my heart battered at my jacket (: and tonight I've got to set fire to our hut ! !). "You coming along to the movies ?" choked out hastily (so she'll know where I am). "Oh. Not tonight," and she gave a dry, collusive laugh : "got to clean up first; after the trip. And lie down for a while." (Meaning she might be free to talk later on !) "Goodnight" : "Goodnight, Herr Düring". (And so a good night ! good !).

The movies : first News of the Week : glorious victorious torpedo boats rocking at sea (with the appropriate goading musical accompaniment), and beaming ‹Boys in Blue› : "If only we could die just a little for Greater Germany !". Tank cavalcades and artillery (the French used to be the world's best artillerists ! : they invented it all, hollow charges, trajectory charts; and I thought of the old descriptions of chain-shot and case-shot in the memoirs of General von Brixen, at one time Rüchel's adjutant, an original edition of which adorned my Background Materials. As early as 1795, the French were directing their battles from the air ! For example, at Fleurus !).

Then the ‹Documentary› : the Alps, naturally (also with obligatory heroic instrumentation; the clouds sailed rapturously to a variation of the overture to ‹Der Freischütz›); lakes and ah, such snowy peaks. Patinaed cliffs : stony bijoux 50 feet high, in rusty bushranger outfits, ferny feathers on their hats, sassy tottering bouldered skulls. A milk-white team of oxen forded the river (brass began to swell hymnically, as an accompanying mighty stream). And everywhere in that landscape swept so obligingly clean, were ‹German Men and Women›, patented, heads so full of character and trust in the Final Victory. ("Yes, Berta, it's charming !").

Stupid and saccharine : the feature. Decorative waltzings about ("Aren't the costumes simply dar-ling, Heinrich !"; Willi babbled with Lilian;

and Hans Moser, the sweet little rascal : ah boys and girls, if only there weren't such nasty penalties for 2nd-degree murder !

Inflammatory banquets, with someone blowing smoke right out of the screen, and people drinking beer and smacking their lips (1944 ! – Although I don't doubt that a person with a sufficient dose of punch in his belly can manage just about anything !).

The Kaiser, the Kaiser, His ‹darling Majesty›, actually danced in very person with her : and getting a good grip on her furbelowed skirt, with her curtsying hands, she glided in nearer : giant close-up (Oh Swift in Brobdingnag !), soundlessly unbolted that hangar of a mouth : dental slabs the size of dictionaries occupied her jaw bow, beneath nasal pilasters; her eyelashes bristled like carpenter's nails. From the cavern came an alluring waltz (and the soulless gawkers began to rock imperceptibly to the prescribed tempo, as the Lestrygonian head up there swayed back and forth).

Yes, and so then the Kaiser danced with her, clumsily to an aPaulLinck tune, and it was such a high honor (maybe she'd already done service ‹under› 3 kaisers); but the ‹class difference› proved just a teensy too big after all, and so she accepted the Honved musketeer, dashing and debonair, as erotic surrogate : and it was All so stinking false and absurd, so gushy and German : no sir ! I happily shut my eyes : at least then all I smelled was the sweat around me, and I heard the little thing beside me sob convulsively (probably as the Kaiser strode back to the Hofburg – lonely and tragic as only the Viennese can be). – She deployed herself decoratively on a regal bed, and necked a bit with Morpheus; until her penis in Honved uniform came to rescue her : thankgod ! (And straight for the exit ! – – "Ah, it was all just so lovely, Heinrich !" : my wife. "Wonderful, Berta."; and we middle-classed homewards. 8 o'clock and sunset).

It's the maddest thing in the world, (and you really ought to hear my pencil rustle as I write !), that you can hold 500 years of painting in one hand : Francke's green Magdalene and Mueller's girls in their green park (seems then that ‹green› is the tertium comparationis !). And I went over to the map of the Département of Weser from 1812 : lithographic green was the border around the Arrondissement of Nienburg : where I lived. (Beneath broad leaves; fenced-in by sulky pine needles. Käthe's stockings had been green just now, ah, just a tiny bit of ankle; greenish too the insectile moon in the pink of evening; greenish cow dung and envelopes, pencils and backs of many a book).

Keep your shoes on !

Cloud tongue-lashings above backyard gardeners : we ripped up scrawny pea vines and ravaged ranks of plants (and the globes of our butts, mine behind me included, jutted out foolishly, how disgusting). Beyond, a cutlet of moon was swimming above the night; a breeze came up and called out Ho ! and Evening !; a tardy child leaped and bounced steadily along over the ground, right up to us, beside the black pendulum of its shopping bag. Wind-tears appeared in Weber's eyes (and he let a fat gob slither out of his bearded muzzle, and then carefully rubbed the rest of it around his jaw with the back of his hand : don't waste none of it !).

It is a horror beyond all measure to be me ! !

"Uh – Herr Evers ! ? – would you perhaps still have a piece of fuse left ? – From when you blew up that boulder out at the back of your field recently ? – – Oh; just a short piece : about so – !" and I showed him : 12 inches (I sure would like to get it under the commissioner's skin !). – The yellow chitinous body of the moon crept up black branches. A planet, Venus let us hope, fixed in amber).

Wrestle down the blackout shades (and inconspicuously get ready for the hut : to hell with the rascal with the tattooed brow ! – For the last time !). I gingerly picked up Thierry's button and rubbed it on my sleeve : wicked its sparkle, and fraternal. (And I waxed sullen, stony, like a great thunderstorm : for the last time ? ? ! ! – Rubbing –)

"Come to me from out the air, : / Arise from ocean deep, : / Though fast asleep in darkened lair, : / Or up from fire leap – : Düring is your Lord this night ! / Obey him, every shade and sprite !".

Well ? ! ——— (Listen : ——— ?
——— Nothing : Fff).

I twitched my left, more nervous eyebrow and walked by stiffly. – "Heinrich !". "Don't forget : the current's awfully low again : bring the lamp while you're at it !" And I fetched and bore the good old kerosene glowworm : good thing I bought that reserve canister back then ! (Wise old Düring, right ? !).

The news (but it, too, very murky and low) : all fighters had returned to their air bases; but neither did they forget their customary and timeworn ‹straightening the frontlines› ("Trustworthy as a bulletin from General Headquarters" is how they used to brag !). The Pope was suffering once again from acute apparitions of Mary (cf. Scheffel's ‹Castle Toblino›, p. 398); and enemy bomber formations were approaching as per usual (meaning, presumably, Berlin again).

The hierarchy of the three Christian denominations (and of the countless minor ones as well) goes on feeding obtusely off the same inadequate arguments that were just barely reasonable to intellectual middlebrows of 2000 years ago. Since which time, as understanding has grown with each century and in each individual, there has been increasing exasperation with the disastrous gulf between the generally recognized necessity for charity toward one's fellows and their unswervingly shamanistic arguments for it : a third of the blame for our present desperate intellectual situation can be laid to this contradiction, which still disquiets most people, and has even driven generous men, in the anguish of their rage, to malign love itself. It really is high time to relegate Christian mythology – and all its gods, demigods, seers, heavens and hells (and, of course, all the earthly set decorations, stage equipment and costumed extras as well !) – to where it historically and deservedly belongs, namely, right alongside those of Greece and Rome, etc. : that would settle things down considerably both within and around us. –

The kerosene lamp in my hand took a bound with me, and shook off its frosted bonnet. The cupboard gave me a push, that I parried only with difficulty, and its doors thrashed away at me too. My wife tottered behind the lattice of her apron and held a table in her hands ! The panes snarled clear and savage in their frames; a cup leaped up and landed at my widespread feet; the air jumped (just a good thing that the windows were all standing open for summer !); I lurched through doors with head on the slant, danced about on the staggering staircase, and fell at the front gate into people.

"They're bombing the Eibia plant ! !" oldman Evers clangored and shook like a black coat, I grabbed for something Käthean and we were already galloping, technical emergency corps, behind the wind in the same lurid direction, with pattering soles, vaulting fences; two crows hurtled by; one turned around and screamed at me : cad ! caadd !

Another jerk and throb, and afar the houses laughed, bright and demented, out of windows clinking to shatters. The she-night clapped with thundering paws, Explosia, and countless crashes played tag around the horizon. (Lightning bolts hacked tonight from bottom to top; and each one thundered amply jovian as it vanished into its horrified cloud !).

The long road wrenched. A tree pointed finger masts at us, lurched some more, and closed the branching cage behind us. We scrambled over the red-checked earth, through flame-gorged ruins, our jaws chewed the smoky jellied air, we shoved the brawl of lights aside with the plates of our hands, and our feet doddered along before us, in shoes with crisscross laces, hugging together. The flailing light battered our brows beyond recognition; the thunder crushed pores and glands underfoot,

and filled our open mouths with gagging avalanches : then ponderous
sabers were scarving at us again.

All trees dressed as flames (on Sandy Hill) : a housefront stumbled forward
menacingly, with silky red foam at the corner of its maw and win-
dowed eyes ablaze. House-high boulders of iron rolled tumults about
us, blackish, the very sound of which was lethal ! I threw myself on
Käthe, wrapped her with wiry arms, and tugged at her greatness : one
half of the night was ripped away, and we fell to earth slain by thunder
(but clambered up again, defiant still, and gasped helplessly into all
volcanoes).

Two railroad tracks had torn loose and were angling off like crab claws;
the pincers turned about and in a resounding arc passed lovingly over
us (and we ran and ducked beneath the languid iron lash). From below
came a defiant pounding at our bones; the gaping muzzle of a pipe
appeared and lazily spewed acid.

Every maid wore red stockings; each with cinnabar in her pail : a tall silo
of powder scalped himself, and let his flowery brain truffle over : while
below he performed hara-kiri, and repeatedly rocked his monumental
body above the bleeding gash before discarding his torso. White hands
gesticulated busily in the everywhere; many had ten unjointed fingers
and one that was nothing but red nodes (and beneath us the grand
dance of wooden clogs stomped in rhythm !). Hitler Youth slunk about
werewolfily. Fire brigades wandered lost and nimble. Hundreds of
arms spurted up from the sod and distributed stony handbills, "Death"
inscribed on each, large as a table.

Concrete vultures with glowing iron talons flew by over us screaming
dissonantly, in great flocks (until they spotted a victim over in the development and pounced on him). A yellow-toothed cathedral stood
bellowing in the violet-fringed night : so its fat steeple exploded into
the air ! Clusters of ruttish red flares lilted above Bommelsen, and we
had diachromatic faces : the right side green, the left a cloudy brown;
the ground danced out from under us; we threw our long legs in time to
it; a rope of light looped in berserk curves across the sky : to the right a
bonbon translucence, to the left a deep frenzy of violet.

The sky took on the shape of a saw, the earth a red lively pond.

With black human fish flopping about : a girl, naked from the waist up,
burst toward us barking impudently, and the skin dangled at her shriv-
eled breasts like curly lace; her arms fluttered back from her shoulders
like two white linen ribbons. The red dishcloths in the sky blustered
and scrubbed blood. A long flatbed truck full of baked and boiled
humans glided by soundlessly on rubber tires. Ever and again airy

giant hands grabbed hold of us, lifted us up and tossed us. Invisibilities jostled us against one another, till we were quivering with sweat and exhaustion (my beautiful sweaty stinky girl : let's get out of here !).

A buried tank of alcohol shook itself loose, rolled out like bindweed on a hot hand, and dissolved in a Halemaumau (out of which fiery brooks flowed : a dismayed policeman commanded the one on his right to halt and was vaporized in the line of duty). A fat-lady cloud stood up above the warehouse, puffed out her balled belly and belched a pastry head high, laughed throatily : so what !, and knotted her trundling arms and legs, turned toward us steatopygically, and farted whole sheaves of hot iron tubing, endlessly, the virtuosa, till the shrubs beside us curtsied low and babbled.

An incandescent corpse swooned and fell to its knees before me, offering its smoldering serenade; one arm was still flickering and broiling petulantly : it had come out of thin air, "From heav'n above", the apparition of Mary. (The world was altogether full of them : whenever another roof rolled up, they shot out from the cornices like divers, helmeted or in their naked hair, flew a little distance, and burst like paper bags on the earth below. In God's own scalawag hand !).

The ruby-glass pulsings of a fire anemone in Döblinesque groves; benignly it waved with a hundred hawser arms (on each of them nettledown surged), then cautiously dived deeper into the sea of night, and skirmished on, but furtively. A three-story bunker began to stir : it grumbled drowsily and rippled its shoulder bladings; then it discarded roof and walls with a gurgle and the vertical dawn suddenly made for us gowns of flame-colored taffeta and many faces of fierce roses (until the black thud pulled the earth out from under us like a rescue net : a car with firefighters plummeted whirling from the heavens, buckled a few times, and with a nod perished in the gravel, the corpses propped together in jumbled animation).

(For a while broad silent flakes of fire fell about us, come di neve in Alpe senza vento : with hand and cap I batted them away from Käthe's graven image, interceding all about her : she brushed one from my gray smoldering hair, and went on watching the keelhauling of hissing shadows).

A rigid man appeared in the sky, a blast-furnace in each hand : he prophesied some death and death, so that I pushed against my hand, and saw the bones dark within the fiery flesh. Two long thighs of light tap-danced down those walls there; the road blanched at the sight and melted partly away. Lots of greasy black bags were being carried past us on stretchers : the workers from the third shift, their chief conductor

explained, and with fluttering tongue stepped back into mute van-
guard. Meteors klaxoned through the upper air; farmhouses shook with
laughter, sending their shingles flying down; fire fountains were frol-
icking godforsaken everywhere and sparks geysered in jets.

In the weeping clutch at road's edge, a woman went mad : she tugged her
skirts with fat hands, up to her belly, unjammed her mouth, wooden
wedged, and tumbled down before her coarse yellow hair into the
jiving rubble; all at once the ground before us began to glow : a thick
vein swelled up, forked brighter still, throbbed and blubbed soupily,
and ruptured with a sigh (so that the white air almost throttled us, and
retching we groped into rearward gloom. A pine caught fire and
screamed, skirt and hair and all; but that was nothing compared to the
orders troated in bass from vats of light and to the gnashings of fence-
high flaming teeth).

And now : the fat woman from a while ago rode a hunk of horse through
the air just above us, smoldered and ignited desperate for her mamma !
From behind, a steady wind harried us between the legs, dragging
wheezes and condoling dust with it, and when it took the notion, made
wavering tents of sparks. A penis of light, tall as a chimney, twitched
and thrust into the smutty tangle of night (but then broke off too
soon; but was already replaced on the right by a red-bearded pillar of
flame whooping up a clog dance, till the grit beneath us groused and
burped).

A whistling voice ran toward us, preceding someone who had gone and
caught fire; his forehead got pasted to a tree stump and he wriggled
there for a long time. The jagged boomings flailed at us like morning
stars; the caustic light gnawed the skin around our eyes; beside us
shadows buckled at the knee. Bunker B1107 bellowed like an ox
before tossing its matted concrete skull high : then its gut was torn
open and the red blaze punched the breath out of us. (I pasted more wet
handkerchiefs over Käthe's gaping mouth and big trembling nose).

The black-yellow tatters of night flew ! (Once the harlequin lass wore nothing but red scarves !) : four men ran in pursuit of a giant snake that
leapt over the railroad embankment, up front hissing and slobbering;
they dug their heels in and roared it seemed (but only the faces gaped
wide; and the ridiculous helmets of the brave idiots). Posters of light
sprang up so quickly around us that you couldn't even read all the rum-
blings (eyes were simply pasted shut by the toxic colors, and slit open
again only in pain and reflex : "Come on ! Käthe !". Flaming whores
smacking their lips, all in red, with sharp face and rakish makeup,
made a hot excursion our way, distended their smooth bellies, crackled

laughter, and came closer still into the bawdy strumpet light : "Come
on, Käthe !").

The night licked its chops again with many blank lips and tongues, and
showed us a couple of alluring stripteases, sending bright tassels
drizzling down around us : then endless rattling applause set in (and
foot-stampings to make your head ring). Trucks full of gesticulating
SA drove in a little too close : the lads jumped down, hissing like
lighted matches, and vanished (while their vehicles likewise skipped
and melted away). A whining boy came toward us bearing his arms
askew : like a towel his hide shagged vertically from him; he displayed
coppery teeth, and whimpered in time to the detonations, whenever the
gorilla pounded his chest.

In the earth's interior sound rolled like nonstop subway trains : those were
the grenade cellars ! : Good ! : Better than if they got lobbed at the
innocent-guilty ! All flashing flames slashed at uniformed German
Maidens. And they were still breathing as we carted them off across
lawns by their sturdy legs.

"Käthe ! !"

"Get down ! ! !"

Because right next to us the bunker began to crow, and raised its red comb
so stiff that we did fall a great fall and shared our tremblings, as, with
buffeting of walls, it flew away over us. In its place there first appeared

a morel of fire (and 30 men could not have got their arms around it),

then the Giralda,

then many apocalyptics (and glistening brushwood mountains).

And only then did the sound send us in a seamless tumble onto the grass,
causing houses over in the developments to toss frying-pan caps into
the huzzahing air : "Käthe ! !".

"Kää-tää ! ! !"

I bounded my hand up her legs, scaled her panting belly, enclasped her
shoulders : "Käthe ! !"; her head wailed from stupefaction; horrified, I
ironed away at her face : "Ow !"

A crude block, big as a sideboard, bit the back of my hand : "Käthe ! !". –
She threw her legs up and grappled like an adder. : "Hair !" she roared
with no restraint. And frantic, I felt her all over, her brow, her hollow
ears, the furred back of her head. And tore at her shoulders as she
screamed : "My hair ! ! !"; and still she made no move up !

Her mane : fumed in the hot stony maw ! – I threw myself to one side, and
ripped out my pocketknife, splitting a nail, and turned savage to hack
away at her, till she gave a shriek and pummeled me : "Now ? ! ! !" –
"No : not yet, not yet ! !".

"Now ? ! ?" : – "Ow – I," she tore off the medusan head, scratching me in pain as I lifted. Red brushes sprouted from the earth and stained the screeching clouds somewhat purple; several times the sky collapsed (and the red-black fragments fell below the horizon). Käthe barked and wagged her calves; with a howl we bit at each other's invisible faces, and crept between the heaps of stars around to our left, till we found ourselves once again inside bags of noise, inside the grove of swords, till it grew dark again; till I

"There : that way ! : follow the tracks !"

Along the railroad : we dodged a locomotive hissing down on us, bellied along runners growing ever darker : "Come on, down Rain Strasse", and then the other track, Bomlitz-Cordingen – : now I knew exactly where I was, and led the way swiftly and smoothly : "Can you run, Käthe ? !" "Yes. I'll manage. I seem to be all right otherwise !".

In the Warnau : "Hooooooo –" : "Lovely." "Water !" We wiped ourselves with sand and grass, and helped each other when our arms would stretch and bend back no further. "Damn, I can't get my shoe on !". – – "No, wait. I can just do it." (But she limped away more heavily in my arms).

"Oh ! – : –" : an army of crazies brandished daggers of light above the woods; the blades cracked and yowled (and afterwards, of course, much crimson blood flowed down cloud wadis). The meadows bounced beneath our callous hoofs (cased in leather); blackness prickled round our callous skin; to the world I looked : tame to the touch, middle-class hero, a stiff-nosed office worker : won't you all be surprised !

Little beech brigades, oak athletes, pine archers : they are our bodyguards, as once upon a time in Sherwood Forest : "Such outlaws as he and his Kate"; and with that we pushed deeper into the woods : I knew the disposition of every blade of grass; was that piece of bark lying there like that last time ? : here a fox had scrambled across the ground, there a human, now two humans. Grasped junipers, toed moss and cold mushroom caps, mushroom snacks, the ant making menacing pincers at my Conti-rubbered heel; in my trouser leg the sting of keen foils of grass.

We ran easily and glided in pursuit of our own limbs, across disks of wind-stilled meadow, until I landed in the pliant prickly arms of a broad-hipped young fir (her boughed legs spread wide, lusty pelvic trunk, my hand detected moist mossy wrinkles; and the palpitating breastplate whooped : "Käthe – ?-". "Yes. Right here." (at my sleeve.))

The moon fumbled a few seconds beside us in the brush of the westerwood, distorted, red with rage. Around the corner : there it took its stand, small and ominous, above pine bludgeons, highwayman in rags of cloud, right there in front of us : scram, you !

"Ah, now I know. – But : this foot, damnation !". "Wait. Just a second !". –

Kerosene lamp : the flame was the size of a cedar nut; just above it yellow and blue hair of fire, sulfurously agile. : "C'mon in. Careful with that door !". (Noiseless, the well-oiled hinges. : "Fine !").

"Hm : Fine !" : she stood there looking about her contentedly (the shutters sealed felt-tight), then sat down on the old familiar blanket, and groaned a bit at her foot. "Wait, I'll help you." Unlace it wide; – gently maneuver the heel out : "All right ?"; and she threw back her head against the plank wall and gnashed on a ‹Yes›.

Her big red foot ! : 2 toes were already broken and swollen big as sausages ("Wait, I'll heat some water"); and the tin can, a ferrous brown brimful, crackled atop the folding solid-spirit stove : "Takes 5 minutes, at the most !").

"Ohboyohboyohboyohboy !"; to take her mind off it she looked around : my furnishings : "Just like before." Soap and half a towel; nails in the wall, here and there. Food supplies, 2 blankets, matches, machete and compass. "Have you got adhesive and a bandage ? – Great !". The little telescope, magnification of 15, and very collapsible : "Has come in very handy ? Right ?", and I told her the story of how I had used it to spot the commissioner's car coming down the main road over there; and she examined it, pulled it out full length, turning it over.

Two books : Ludwig Tieck "Journey into the Blue; and Scarecrow". Fouqué "Magic Ring".

Two paintings : Otto Müller : "Hmm –" a repeated show of approval. Franke "Group of Women". "This was the one here, right ?" she asked, and pointed a finger at the Green Courtesan (Heavenly and Earthly Love. No ‹Christus› or bloody whatever !). – (Get the utensils from under the floorboards).

"Come here, I'll wash you. –" : Full bath out of a tin can. (First pedicure; and she delightedly moved her ankle in its secure bandage : "Great !"; praise and confidence). Rub cream on the burns on hips and ribs; and she gleefully braced her downy moist belly against my face. (Then she examined me as well, pricked open three blisters, and checked buttocks and testicles. And we fell ever more deeply into each other).

The cavantinas of the wind.

I found myself everywhere in the lattices of her great fingers, in the yoke of her long arms, the broad sash of her legs. Heavy. (She would say perhaps : I bore him like half a suit of armor; his body hacked at mine; everywhere he found breasts to tweak).

(With these pale yellow bodies of ours, we are badly camouflaged ! Wonder if Indian war paint – apart from the shock effect – might not have had the simultaneous effect of optically resolving man's obtrusive body into more natural images with dark and bright patterns and stripes ? For the prowl through umbrage and underbrush ? Brown from earth ochers; green from plant juices; and fungi yield dyes too; berries. Like our modern tarpaulin : it's exactly the same thing ! – – – : "Yes; I sowed a broader band of reeds around outside : a good 10 yards at least ! And planted 40 pines : almost all of them have taken root ! – – Well, it doesn't matter now : Later." Then RIP-soap, rest in peace, for me : all out of a pea can).

The Ladie's Supper : and she gloried in digging the liverwurst out with my pocketknife : "Manohman !". "I haven't eaten this good in years !"; filled up. (And for tea, a bag hanging daintily from its thread : even Americans use one twice. The English four times. Germans eight. : "Sweetener ?". "Noo ! : Anything but that ! Barbarian !". – – "You really live quite the life here !". "Only for today, Käthe." And she, touched and satisfied : "mmm"). – How late ? ? : well – : past eleven for sure : 11:43 P.M. to be precise. We were, however, a long way from being able to sleep, took the blanket and sat down before the door, half naked as we were : "That'll burn for days yet !" (The Eibia rumpus) : "The fire'll eat its way along the endless conduits – as far as the Lohheide; maybe over to the thieves' den in Munster – just keep moving down all the shafts : ab-so-lute-ly hopeless !"

We watched, with plain eyes and upended faces, reed and wood, as beyond them, distant, constant, the red sea seethed and jostled. I was weary of all words : washed-out words, slurped away by billions of tongues, Dietrich-Ekartish words, worn ragged in billions of baggy mouths, Fritsche-Goebbelsish words, run down at the heel on all airways, broadly bruised by all lips, nasaled, expectorated, stark-baked, shit through brooms : mother tongue ! (Oh, what a charming, ingenious term, is it not ? !).

But when that tongue is burning in your mouth : in Mine ! When thickets are houses to you : to Me ! When the wind whisks your arms and legs : Ours, ours, ours ! (Encompassed by skin, swished by hair, foot tappings, back rustlings : and now they were driving me out of my paradise, by means of commissioners and foresters ? Really ? ! – She rubbed my forearm soothingly : it really is absurd).

"I have one more bottle of beer inside, Käthe." : "Hand it over.". She drank languidly and endlessly; then concentrated her nose, and gave a discreet burp, my charming toad. I quickly kissed her on her cold beer

lips; and eavesdropped for a new grouse in her body – – but this time her chest grew fuller and broader.

"Let's hope all the buildings have been destroyed !". She eyed me critically, and then nodded : compris. Then shook her head : "Doubt it".

"Where do you have to report to next ?". "To Nancy" (lazily). I calculated briefly with brows and lips; shook my singed head : "Noo, Käthe : you won't have to show up there ! – – In – : 2 weeks ! They'll be at the Rhine". Shrugs : "Then I'll just have to report to Karlsruhe". Another shrug. Out of the reeds the most delicate fog flowed toward us : where is its source ? (Lovely image : a mossy foundling, soundless fog bubbling up out of it. Absurd of course. Gone !).

"What sort of stuff do you signal corps girls do ?" "Hffff" (through her nose) : "Telephone operator, lots of that. And office work". And I gave a bitter nod : know already what's coming. (She; icily) : "They won't leave a woman in peace till she's given in. What riffraff officers are. And the creeps at the paymaster's too. But you know the bastards. You were a soldier long enough". "Yes. Unfortunately". – "Enough of this".

The fog licked our toes : now the ground was gone too, then you were just floating off, hands in your pants pockets, an ecstatic head laid back, beside Käthe. (But those were just words again : away with these caprices of infinity ! Better just to sit like this !).

"Another six months. Nine at the outside !" (the war) : "but then hunger will really start stalking ! We'll all trim down ever so nice and slender ! – Have you still got good soap and such, Käthe ?". "Huh-uh" and shook her head; but she gripped my knee a bit more tightly, and I knew that meant ‹Thanks for the tip that day›. "As soon as you're back here, you'll get a couple of boxes." She turned a piece of profile toward me, and asked hardnosed : "Has your wife still got some ? Or Gerda ?". A warm dry current of air had wiped the fog away; our feet were once again propped at an angle to the ground : "No."

"Just don't get married, Käthe ! : No old man, no disabled veteran, no churchgoer, no conceited ass with great expectations. – Someone who's good in bed and who doesn't bore you."

"In the end" – as proof I patted the flat of my hand on me as proof : "all that's left are : Works of Art; the Beauty of Nature; Pure Sciences. In that holy trinity. – And keeping in shape." (Stop that ! Your mouth – my mouth – just trots off, driveling away : Cut it !).

But now I simply had to let loose with savage laughter : "And that is that ! Käthe ! Burn it down ! No other way ! – Tomorrow morning we set fire to the place"; and when she tried to talk me out of it : "They'll come with police dogs, and pick up the scent. And fingerprints : we'd soon be ripe pickings." Shaking my head, in protest : "No sir." (That everyone doesn't do some time in the course of his life is ultimately just dumb luck. Not that you have to be a cutthroat or such !).

"Fine."; and I wrapped her up in the blanket inside : her bright arms knelt beside her sunflower face. "Another log on the fire ?". "Show it to me first"; and she held the humble log in her hand for a long time; simplicity, ephemerality, obscurity, rigidity; and handed it back without a word. (It then cast light onto the flickering ceiling, and muttered to itself. Just as with Thierry. For the last time). (Then profoundest exhaustion).

(Dream fragment : an image ‹Remembrance› : Old man on his park bench. Hedges form individual compartments, and bowers. He sees himself at various stages in life : as a child. Alone in a swimming pool among many halves of girls. Bent over books, walking, in the distance a country home. In the middle of the park a large marble statue of Käthe. No dots).

The night in black tux (with only one button, sewn on slipshod); day, first in a red-yellow dressing gown, then in a sloppy smock of clouds. (Me among reeds : stinking away).

I stuffed the empty bottles, the tin cans, all the non-flammables into the tiny metal stove, pulled out the pipe, thin as my arm, and walked away with it. "?". "Ditching it all in the pond out back" (hard). Whatever'll burn, spread over the floor. (The rest in the rucksack).

We just looked around us, but not at each other.

So then : the match to the fuse ! It was 5 minutes long (and ended in the clump of solid-spirit under the leftover firewood. – Wait : throw the shutters on too; and those loose boards).

I helped Lame Kate up the ladder of branches, down the rungs; the secret path ran noncommitally through fern and dry litter of needles (and we did not look back even when – far behind us now – it started to crackle and pop : most probably ignited by some sparks from last night's fire !).

Hazy and dry now (autumn near) : and view of the woods for a dowry. : In 4 weeks I'll already be walking among black wet tree trunks. On a bloodied parquet. Alone. In my new canvas suit).

In thicket's edge, and we walked more cautiously (hesitantly). The pull of the woods was so strong that our hair pointed to the rear (where now only a thin rope of smoke still dangled from the clouds). A covey of birds eddied slowly across the sky. – "Well, come on".

Something, anything else ! (And the sun rode on high in the dry smoky haze) : Look at : her whittled head : "Käthe : if you were the sun, what would you do ?". She understood; her laugh emerged slowly from beneath stony mourning eyes : "We-l-l-l . . . . :" :

"Sometimes I'd rumble across the sky like a four-engine job". (And disconcerted we raised our faces : ? – : No. Looking. Lips. Smile some more).

"Sometimes I'd come up black. And square. – *And* with a bang."

"For poor people I'd cook soup at no charge. And for artists."

"Sometimes I'd reverse course at noon, my cloud skirts billowing." ("When you had already seen enough."). "Sometimes I'd belt my waist very tight and appear as a Golden Eight."

"The astronomers would constantly have to issue updated reports as to my whereabouts : ‹Reliable witnesses report having seen the sun in Hamburg, lying in a vegetable cart, blinking among the oranges› !" –

"Sometimes I'd throw a veil over me and chase the moon" : a complimentary curtsy ! "Aha !" (resigned). – "Sometimes I'd stop at the window during the day and watch you and that skinny Krämer woman !" (Sfinx eyes).

"Your old gray pants – I'd scorch those ! !" – – "Are they really that abominable ? !" I inquired in surprise and arched my lower lip : in that case, away with them !

A drowsy cow made a childlike bound to the left, and the old farmer gave a loud slap of the reins and cooed the appropriate word of command. To his brindled bass-baritone.

((Käthe sings something like :
"Trees in red and yellow jackets / standing round a farmyard; / and they nudge each other whispering, / once I've walked by.

Along green tracks my heart is shunted / (Leaves are ruffling; let them fall); / eight thousand lads in lincoln green / (Leaves more leaves, let them fall).

The moon's light afloat. Berries berry. / The farmer mumbles curses / ahead of evening's horse with November's face, / enigmatic whimpers the wheel.

Your hand reigns in the flaxen / rigging of my hair; in the / white columned jumble of legs; in the / dusky coilings of my corners.")).

"How long do you have here exactly ?". "Ten days.", and our faces achieved a glorious ease : Nowadays who thinks 10 days ahead ? !

BRAND'S HEATH

BLAKENHOF
OR THE SURVIVORS

21. 3. 1946 : on British toilet paper.

Glassy yellow, the cracked moon lay there, it joggled me, below in the violet haze (and later on as well).

"Rabbits," I said : "plain as day : like rabbits !". And I watched them, a half dozen, swinging schoolbags in the cold air, on shank legs. Three cruder sorts behind them; to wit, sonnies of the local farmers. Parents who continue to bring children into this world should be punished (i.e, fined : made to pay 20 marks a month for the first child, 150 for the second, 800 for the third).

"How do y' figah 800 ?" I looked at him : an old man (more precisely : older). Coarse woolens, boots, a barrow of finest autumn foliage before him, drab, red and reddish. I carefully plucked a leaf (maple) and held its translucence to the light : masterful, masterful. (And what profligacy ! He must be rolling in it !) "Well then," I said affably (I still needed some geographical info !), "all right : 1000. – Don't you think that'd be a good thing ?" "Hmm," he pushed, considering "wouldn't make 'ny difference to me. Theah's all too many in the wuhld : humans." "So there you are," I said summing up (my thesis) : "they won't let us emigrate. All that's left is rigorous birth control; clerical claptrap is quantité négligiable –" (he nodded, profoundly convinced) "– within 100 years, humanity would be down to 10 million, and then life'll be worth living again !" I didn't have much time; and a bitter cold wind was coming down the handsome, overgrown fire lane; I asked the man in fur-lined boots (solid workmanship : for no good reason I was reminded of the word "bearskin" !) : "Still some distance to Blakenhof ?" He pointed with his broad head : "Theah !" he bumped the word curtly : "wide-place-in-the-road" and : "take it you'ah a returnin' POW ? – With Ivan ? ?". "Nope," I said bluffly, trimming disagreeable memories : "Brussels. With the English." "And ? How wuh they ?". I dodged it : "They used one to clobber the other. A little better than the Russians of course." But : "Sometimes we were

constipated for 14 days. In July they made us sing Silent Night, Holy
Night before they'd let us fall out." "What the hell : clean slate's a
clean slate !" (i.e. freedom !) I gathered other questions from his blue
eyes : "District commissioner," I explained with a disgusted frown :
"assigned me to the schoolteacher." "Ah, that's him over theah !" he
pointed with eyes raised : "Up theah, wheah y' see the chuhch. – – To
the schoolteachah ? ? : theah's no lodgin's up theah ! – You a schoolteachah *too* ?" I shook emphatically, made up my mind : "Writer", I
said, "and wouldn't you know right by the church ? Deus afflavit . . ."
(and dismissed it with a yawn). He grinned (don't believe none of it
either : good core here in Lower Saxony !). But he was curious too :
"Writah !" he said jauntily : "for newspapahs and the like, eh ? !".
"Nothing of the sort," I replied indignantly (don't think much of
journalistics) : "short stories; sweet at one time, rabid now. In between,
a Fouqué biography : as a kind of eternal flame." He gave it some
thought and pursed gray lips : "Fouqué –" he said with some meaning :
"a god-feahin' man, – – a baron, 'm I right ?" "And a great poet as
well," I said crustily, "neither of which I am. But nevertheless !" Then
it struck me : "You know about Fouqué ? !" I asked with mild interest
(rough hands, but a helluva nose. And the wind began to whistle again,
as if coming from the Sigyns : the ones with the shaggy dogs). "All us
elmettals round heah know Undine," he retorted with dignity; I hadn't
understood the third word; but didn't want to lose time, and my bones
ached from lugging. I got up from my stool : "So then, that way –" I
said wearily; "Yup; so from heah –" he picked up a stick and scratched
in the sand of the bike path : "Up that rise; the chuhch'll be on youah
right; the super'ntendent lives on the left –" (I passed it off : the only
honorable ones were Palafox and Sarpi; maybe Muscovius too; maybe
some others. Well, makes no difference.) : "– the new one's the school-
house : round theah !" – "Thanks.", picked up my ammo crate (a prize
example : tin lining and rubber gaskets inside, as if made for the trop-
ics) : "Good-bye !". He rubbed a hand across his face and was gone.
(Anybody can vanish these days; I once saw a twenty-eighter land
right beside a fellow !)

The garden hose : at the rectory a man with pudgy hands was stretching it
out : Laocoön or on the limits of painting and poesy. Above devastated
heavens, dreary as an empty potato field, all that was missing were
tractor ruts and hedgehogs, don't ask me why. Imposing figure, by the
way, the fat man, i.e. dead, he'd be worth a good barrow and a half of
manure. And next to the church : I am spared nothing ! – I felt somehow exposed in the open square : what if a shooting star falls on the

back of my head now; and taking offense, I walked around the corner. (A title for a book came to mind : "Listen Here !" = Conversations with God.)

"Oh God !" she said, elderly and lean. I shrugged all my shoulders : "I was assigned here by the commissioner" I said, as if it had been a personal encounter with handshakes all-round, and stared implacably at the stamp and insignia (in hoc signo vinces; let's hope so). "Well alright; come in then, please," she capitulated. I put my stool down in the entryway, heaved the stout crate by its rope handle up onto it, and followed her into a living room : green en suite and gilt-edged. Poker-paintings hung across from me; were once considered elegant and ritzy (by my parents too . . .); a bookcase, which I walked right up to, after having briefly introduced myself; books. Circa 200. "We have a complete Ganghofer," proud; and pointed to the series in hunter's green. "Yes, yes, I see" I answered somberly : so then, pyrography and Ganghofer : it'll feel like mother's. A hoary Brockhaus encyclopedia : I coldly selected the volume F; Fouqué; . . . "after the wars of liberation he lived by turns in Nennhausen *and Paris* (sic !)," I read and smiled icily. Right : and there was the whatnot cabinet, too; with little mirrors, knobs, and pinnacles; a borobudur of mahogany. Genuine. You can make anything out of wood : self-assured and happy, she passed a hand over a buxom curlicued column : the way Tristan must have caressed his Isolde, or Kara ben Nemsi his Rih.

"Shorsh" was her teacher-son's name. Had been an off. cand. And her eyes haughtied as phony as if made in Gablonz. Or Pforzheim. When here all the men were running around in dyed Tommy uniforms; all the ladies wearing trousers. Asinine woman.

"Writer – ?" showing curiosity, and she grew visibly more at ease, assured of her social rank. "Yes, but . . . ."; abruptly : she showed it to me :

The hole : behind, around the corner; on the church square. 8 by 10 feet; but first get rid of the junk; spades, hangers, tools, and I offered to do it myself (I needed hammer and pliers anyway, nails : in fact all cosa rara, right ?)

"Pleased to meet you" he said perfunctorily. Late twenties and already completely bald; along with that offensive behavior characteristic of officers down through the ages. Damn goat. Words, words; stupid, stupid : moreover, one of those who already at age 20 neither smoke nor drink "for reasons of health" (and come Sunday, lots of Them, in bumpkin breeches and open shirts, are out for a hike of no less than 35 miles, and set great store by wooden bowls and peasant flowers in

rustic vases); this one liked to dance; "passionately," as was his wont to phrase it : you've got some notion of passion !

"2 gals put up over there" he pointed with the chin of a jaded man who knows them inside and out : then thankgod class began again and he left; vamoose plenty pronto. Schoolchildren were singing now with sturdy voices; a weakling would have said : with clear; but I was fatally and precisely aware of how those brazen throats could bellow during recess. (Did not know then that Superintendent Schrader had banished their romps from the church square, and that instead they let off frenetic steam on the soccer field). It may be, too, that people thought my fissured garments were an original stroke of genius; out of the blue, I was reminded of Dumont d'Urville and the journeys of the Astrolabe. Marvelous illustrations. But this wasn't the time. I crossed over the tiny whitewashed antechamber : a water tap, dripping to declare itself in working order : that's good ! (i.e., not the dripping; but that there's water close by !)

I knocked : "Excuse me : – could you perhaps lend me a whisk broom and dustpan ? And a mop bucket and rag : for half an hour – ?" – – – A small, quiet girl, about 30, but a plain Jane, or just plain ugly, stood by the table (quite nicely furnished, by the way, even though it was just one room. But a large space; long, at least 25 feet !); she looked at me in quiet embarrassment : "Yes . . . ." she said hesitantly : "– but how come . . . ." and from the back, from where the beds probably stood behind the folding-screen, came a sharp, glossy voice : "Yes : how come ? ! – It's out of the question ! –" She had more to say; but I had already closed the door : "Oh, I'm so sorry –" I added in an excess of courtesy : it was fine to be offended first thing; because afterward they would have certain obligations; which provided a solid basis for hitting them up later on. But for now, here I stood !

What do you call that : a chaise longue with no headrest or springs, and even the upholstery missing ? The teacher-mother sold it to me, and a couple of boards that I sawed to a brusque fit and nailed to the wooden frame (nice and solid by the way). And still had some left over; if I cut up my belt, I can make a pair of wooden clogs out of them; brilliant idea. Bigtime farmers in the village, they say one of them has 28 head of cattle : his name is Apel (we'll just call him the Great Viscownt). Of course woodchips and ancient dirt were everywhere now; walls washed a pretty white; flagstone floor. Can't be locked up either; just an iron bolt and cramp : which means a padlock : okay, then not. Besides which "the gals" appeared to keep the front door locked at all times, the key was always stuck inside. Outside was a

small handwritten sign, although under fancy cellophane (or trans-
parite, so as not to offend Wolff & Co.); praise be the Mil. Gov. : you
always know right off who lives there. Not a woman who can fudge on
her age (like our Albertine Tode : quite an amazing feat, for Fouqué
himself never knew how old his wife was. Absolutely remarkable.).
"Lore Peters, age 32, secretary." "Grete Meyer, 32, factory worker" :
So without question the one with the big mouth was named Peters (or
just the opposite : factory girls are succulently sassy and as worldly as
truckers; no figuring it out now). I took the pencil stub from my pocket
(what a treasure that had been in camp; and paper above all; I had
scribbled on the scarce toilet paper and calculated sigma and tau) and
appended : Name. Likewise 32. Below that, small for lack of room :
professional writer : was as good as an introduction; for even now I
was being discreetly observed through the coquettish casement curtains (windows in fancy aprons). Then I went across the church square
for a whisk broom.

A round pond had lived in the sand-pit for 300 years. But a suspicious Frau
Schrader threw me out as well : love thy neighbor as thyself : quod erat
demonstrandum. I didn't go to Frau Bauer (my God : to the teacher !) :
I already had a reputation to lose. Off by itself stood the outhouse,
proper and three-seated; attractive stone shed, clean quarters; apparently built for the schoolkids; plumbing worked; superb.

"Should I walk all the way to the village just for a whisk broom ? !" (and
not find one there, for sure !) So here I stood on the road again, freezing and spiteful.

Rrrumms and the truck came to a stop; a Tommy jumped down, approached, and asked curtly : "Dees weg to Uelzen ? !" I played stranger
to the language (Dym Sassenach) – nor did I really know if he should
turn right or left –; pondered obediently and obligingly produced my
identity papers, blue, ID No. 498109. Patiently amused, he crimped
his mouth and nodded : that's all right; once again he raised his fingers : "Yult – senn !" he said emphatically : nothing. Nothing whatever. Swung himself back up : wonderful shoes, US-made with thick
rubber soles : Uncle Adolf had never been in the running : bye-bye. If
I'd had my whisk broom, I probably would have dallied, but not as it
was; even as I walked on, I canceled everything I might have said,
shooed off such idle thoughts : man is a funny creature, including
Schmidt. . . . And the girls would already be standing at the door up
there, i.e. one of them keeping lookout; the other, Peters, sure to be in
the Taj Mahal by now; would call Grete in, make fun of my furniture,
plankbedstoolandcrate : sympathy, shame, better intentions : excellent.

Piece of cardboard : will do as a dustpan, and if need be a branch. Twigbroom. I was back at the same clearing as before : the old man had had ditch-digging tools and such for dusting off the forest paths. I hallooed once more; but there was No One to be seen; well he surely wasn't about to spend the evening of his days in that one spot. Irresolute, I walked part way up the fire lane : I'm always bad at cutting off branches and boughs (am an anti-vegetarian in that regard); and never by the roots, and I didn't have a knife; what a mess. Beautiful here. Drizzling too; and I still had to buy bread; in an hour it would be deep-dark : that was the word : deep-dark ! In such a mood, I turned around : there the rascal stood down by the entrance !

I said, breathless : "Sorry I bellowed like that. I only wanted to ask you if you couldn't lend me – your tools – – for 40 minutes. I'll bring them right back." And explained very briefly what was what. "Hmmm – you'ah def'nat'ly not from 'round heah" he laughed contentedly (now, he already knew that from before; what was the point of the remark : because he looked much too shrewd to have made it just as a causeur. He must have meant something by it. – Quien sabe; not I). "Well now," he said indulgently; raised his head, probing : "What wuh y' lookin' for in theah ?" I didn't try to hide it from him; said, however, that I was a friend of plants, a friend of Woods, and what do you know : everything was fine ! He nodded, at first scowling, then in agreement : "Wuhthy sent'ments !" he purred patronizingly : " – wuhthy 'ndeed. – 40 minutes y' said. – –" He scratched his broad, healthy ears : "You'll set the things ovah theah – beside that little jun'pah – when you've done, won't y' ? !" I made a note of the bushlet : "Yes, but," I replied hesitantly : "if you're not here; – and someone down on the road sees the things : comes in here and –". He shook his head, quite sure : "No one comes in heah," he knew that for certain; and : "I'm always somewheah close by . . . .". He handed me the broom, and I thanked him heartily : dandy !

On the right : that's how I carried them : slowly and demonstrably passing the windows of the hardhearted : "Lore and Grete" : oh, ye brothers ! (Actually sisters, I know).

Under the elderberry tree : the song's about the apple tree, but that's no matter. And this time *I* scratched myself behind the cauliflowers; I really didn't feel right simply setting the stuff down in the open hunting lane; maybe he'd come soon (but meanwhile the shops in the village would close, Deuce take it !). I stood there like a painted fiend, nonpartisan and so on. Windy rain bent around the corner and hissed moistly in my ear : can't make it out; I pulled a little brown sheet from my pocket, four by six, struck out two idle formulas (confirmation = Christ & Co.; and "one relieves one's bowels and conscience . . ." : why are you curious.); painted over that in printed letters "THANKS SO MUCH" and crumpled it around the shovel handle; dozed blind to the world : no, no point in this. I walked off, slowly, casting oblique, querulous glances : how embarrassing ! Looked back again : were leaning humbly against the contented bush. Out on the road. Already lights on in the house across the way. Head turned once more : – they were gone ! That can do you in. –

What a wild West store : where you can buy simply everything, a co-op. I waited patiently in the sultry yellow lamplight; signs, ads, Knorrs soup cubes; margarine was weighed out in ounces, to the dram. "A loaf of bread" I said (hard as Germany's youth; ah well; it'll keep longer); "Oleo" : she cut, click, into the crossword-puzzle pattern of the coupons; "Is there any meat on there ?". She made a cursory estimate of the green-tinged pulp paper : "None for normal consumers this month," gruff and hasty, looked at me : "There's still some cheese" she said, all business : that came to two harz clumps a month. "Do you sell knives and forks ?" it occurred to me to ask; the one in the white smock gave me a great big smirk : "Nope ! Ain't nothin' like that to be had yet !" and behind me the hollow laugh of housewives in chorus. Shame overwhelmed me at my own callowness, paid my 1.92 and wandered "home". (You also have to bring your own paper to wrap things in, she had instructed me : the scoundrels are all waiting for currency reform !) A giant pyre stood by the superintendent's fence; at first I thought I wouldn't, but then I pocketed 2 pieces after all : "Let us, then, as knights of the night . . ."

Should I go across and ask for a knife ?" I didn't know. I unpacked my crate : 3 tarps (from Luthe; those buttons'll make for enticing sleep, the princess and the pea, I'll cut them off tomorrow), one whole blanket, one angular reddish remnant. Then I set it up as my pantry : the bread in one corner; pedantically set the cheese beside it, the margarine; on the other side my haversack on a string, add the aluminum spoon : fermez la porte; if I sat on my "bed" and placed it atop my footstool, I had a table. I still owned a towel, a piece of soap (Lux : in that department the English had been quite generous with us; and some wonderful Canadian toothpaste and shaving soap in tubes), toothbrush, razor (with 1 blade : that was something else again !). Tomorrow I'll have to try to build a wall-shelf somehow. And was it ever cold in the stall; but a stove was simply out of the question; I pulled my 2 pieces of wood from my pocket, laid them in one corner of the room, and pensively projected the appropriate stove around them, with glowing maw of fire. Oh my.

Almost dark : poking around outside again; the short one walked past, on her way to throw a tin can on the garbage heap. I overcame my last scruples (ah, is this ghastly !), caught up with her and asked : "Pardon me – are you going to throw that can away – – ?" She stood stock-still; then she asked : "Yes, but do you want –." "Not what's in it," I said genially, "I just need something to drink out of and such." ("And such" was good ! But then why should I in particular always utter words of significance ?). "Oh God," she said; but I didn't give her the time : "may I – !" I asked once again (and had already balled my fist in my pocket : if only I hadn't said anything !), but then at last she held the thing out to me : "There are fishbones in it," she explained timidly : "there was a special ration."; "Thank you !" and I was gone. (Along with the fishbones; I went back out and pitched those. – It's just a little 8 oz can, tall and narrow, I couldn't read the label because it was too dark. Rinse it out a little, and there you are – a cup !)

Light across the way : lovely and bright, has to be a hundred watts (I later learned that everyone up here on the rise, including the church, is on one meter; they keep them burning for all they're worth). Radio sang; a fine, high whistle now and then, as if from the cool, mournful depths of space; they were busy up there among the stars; sorcery. I withstood the temptation to peek inside (they soon turned out the lights anyway); pulled off my combat boots and stretched out : in coat and cap, without remorse; I wasn't to blame for this; so the evening and the morning were the first day. (And those buttons have definitely got to go !)

Öreland : I dreamed all this on 22. 3., toward mor- (bah ! so it gets separated wrong !) ning; not a word has been displaced ! (No more than in the other dreams in my Leviathan ! I'm a veritable bardeur in that regard.) So then :

Öreland : There was once a great city; it was built on piles, massive piles, in the midst of the bleak sea, far out in the North Sea. But the people grew wild and wicked, although storms daily brought sea vapors that hung in the streets; they drank and swaggered, almost all of them; and below them rumbled the gray swells. The sea daemon Öreland, dire and cold, was charged to destroy the city; he laid himself about it as a brown, murky, tumid fog, just above the water. But as he began to lick at the first bulwark with his heavy tongue, there sat a rabbit – where had it come from ? ! – Whereupon Öreland decided that some of them were most likely innocent, and perhaps some of the people as well; he wrapped everything in eddying clouds, in elderly gray clouds; and no man heard again of such a storm.

And when the air grew clear again, the evil city had vanished; only floes of ice and a very few planks drifted about. And from timber to ice, and back again, as it would bear them, a few people leaped about uncertainly, farmers in coarse garb; and of course the rabbits sat there as well and froze.

But a current arose, which swept all away with it, into the howling evening and the long night.

As morning broke, cloudy and wintery gray, they saw, already quite near, a savage land under heavy snow : the tide-stream washed them toward it, into a long and deep bay. They climbed over the tossing debris and onto the shore, and the rabbits dived at once under the roots of the nearest firs. The palisades rimming the fjord were likewise white with snow and full of timbered wastes, and they rose and rose far into an unseen distance.

While they were still looking about them, out from between tree and rock stepped a giant of a fellow, the wind billowing the cape at his shoulders; he was twice as big as a man. He shouted at them, making cliffs and sea and wild timber shudder : "Öreland !", turned abruptly and strode off toward the interior, vanishing at once into the mountain forest.

Among those rescued was a rough young farm lad, who stammered to the others : "Well then – we really ought to – – ask, don't you think ? !", and his legs were already carrying him up the stony shore, on past the brush, here came the first trees, and in steady pursuit of the great tracks; strides so large he could leap twice within them.

The way led straight toward the mountains, without a path between tree trunks, for hours. Finally he stopped and stood looking about; there was deep snow and wasteland, and mountain peaks gazed down from bold heights on all sides. Then he shouted with all his might, what had been called out to him : "Öreland !"; but at once, from the rocks and out of the forest there came back to him only confused echoes, so that he shook his head, and moved on, faster, firmer.

The snow grew ever deeper, and he plodded on silently beneath the heavily laden boughs; he climbed ever higher, and when he stopped to consider, realized that he had long since lost the track. The stillness, the stillness. He stretched himself out in the low fir thicket and shouted again, louder than before : "Öreland !". Waited. Long. Hours later a branch bounced softly; out of the needle-green frozen gorge a sigh returned : "Öreland". From afar the echo came. He turned impatiently

and climbed farther up slopes growing barren now. The sky was whitish and its vault so low that he sometimes doubted he would be able to
move between it and the mountaintops.

But suddenly the high country began to fall away again; again there
were forests and valleys, and as he came around a boulder, directly
before him in a small clearing he saw a rough cabin of dark logs. A
child was running across the yard, and he hastily called out to it :
"What's the name of this place ?". Puzzled, the youngster waited a
moment, then called back in surprise : "Öreland !" and disappeared
into the shed.

He walked on, always following what he assumed to be a path, and
after a long while came upon a second valley : ho, this was almost a
village ! Three, four farmsteads stood there, and a farmhand with a
hale, ruddy face and an ax in his hand was just leaving the first of them.
He walked up to a snow-covered block, shoved aside the pillow of
snow, rolled logs over to it, and began to chop away lustily, sending
the chips flying.

Our wanderer called down from the path : "What's the name of this
village ? !" The other man first looked up in surprise; but his ques-
tioner was no larger than he, and he had the ax. So he laughed, and said
loudly in his dialect : "Öreland." Well well. And on he went.

The forest grew less dense, the land more open, and before he realized
it, he was standing before the first buildings of a great city. Shiny
shops; now and then a wagon rolled past. A young girl in a sleek fur
cap came briskly over the square; at once he approached her and doffed
his own : "Öreland ?" he asked and pointed round him. She gazed at the
strapping lad with quizzical interest : "Hm –" she nodded and walked
slowly on; after a few steps, she looked back invitingly over her narrow, nimble shoulders. He felt the subtle tiny prick in his heart, and
laughed boisterously : no, he had no time for that now !

In his clumping shoes, he bounded briskly across the city, past it; the
boulders began at once, soon grew larger, and soon he was walking in
a deep ravine, whose floor slowly rose : the walls grew ever more somber and steep, until finally they towered to incalculable heights and the
path was as narrow as an alley. "Det er alt så mörke her," he said sullenly to a woman coming toward him : "what is this place anyway – ?"
(in a blue headscarf). "This is the Canyon of Mount Glimma," she
answered readily, and regarded him intently as she walked on. Occasionally on his left, he saw built partially into the rock wall, houses,
before which children played.

After some time the canyon opened again onto a barren plateau; there

stood smooth black crags as if meant to portray stern heathen faces.
They became bigger and bigger, and between them, from a great distance, he perceived a roar that grew steadily louder, and thunder as
from a nearby sea. And then it lay before him; iron-hued and ponder-
ously heaving. He climbed down to the beach, seated himself among
the rocks, and gazed at the water. It roared at the granite, surging hills
forward and breaking them against the boulders. He sat and listened :
nor did it tremble, the shore. This was a good and firm thing, this
Öreland.
Then he stood up; he wanted only to return at once to his people and
to tell them everything. They still had a few axes; they could raise up
a house at once. He would borrow a saw from that first dreary farmstead. Fish schooled richly in the fjord, and surely an occasional bear
would come by. Perhaps they would even give him a few nails. He
could already see himself bounding through the forest with his cardboard box – – (Again : this is a verbatim report of a dream !)

Simply bit into it, is how I ate my bread; water from the can (fetched hot
from Madame Bauer : ostensibly to shave with). As soon as the metal
was warm, the taste of herring came through again (and really will
shave later !). The cheese was wrapped in "Liberation Art," an exhibition in Celle. On the title page an illustration : Barlach : "Intellectual Struggle" : but what drudgery ! (gyrations). Hats off to Rodin's
Thinker ! (Although something's wrong there too : even unclad it's
hard work placing your right elbow on your left thigh like that, *and*
think at the same time !). And Barlach had often carried it off quite
well ! But this was stupid. Was probably the same for us all. – If
only you could stop the damned criticizing ! – For instance, last night,
as the window panels shimmered a yellow-gray, hours on end, light
acreeping up there it seemed, it occurred to me to write a literary
essay : "The First Page"; how they set out to "grab" the reader : has
something like that been done before ?

Kvinnen i mine drömmer : That guy over there threw down the challenge :
"Who wants to be lo-honely in the ni-híght !" (very profound, isn't
it ? !), and I nodded gloomily, thought of the old cobbled-up castle
Akershus by moonlight (with me as a noncom leading the soundless
sentinels, spitzweg-ily); of Herr Ludwig Holberg, bronzed before the
theater : crackerjack fellow, and Nils Klim; along the Karl Johan Gata,
a collage of Överaas, Romsdal, Framhus; better off making a cutting
board.

Did that (there is much gold – as I am told – on the banks of Sacramento;
you've got to tootle something or other. – A schoolboy hurtled past,

hand at his belt : in his image created he him !) Quick and ugly, he ate another piece of bread : a plague o' these pickle herring ! (And o' the cheese.) Like Sir Toby. And gave an encore : "Hear the heavenly music / sing alóng with us . . . (a catch, the neighbors in tent A almost drove us crazy with it, until we sent out our envoys. There are in fact people who consider Treitschke a historian).

Three book ruins, fetched from my coat : Stettinius, Lend-lease; Smith : Topper and The Poor Minstrel (it had been lying out in a tent in Luthe, morning sun all around, I was crammed inside the lining of my uniform and thumbed my eyes : I pocketed it. And would do it again; there you see what Grillparzer could do, demonic ! In any case, more than I; est cui per mediam nolis occurrere noctem. Dostoyevsky's "Idiot" deals with the same theme really, does it not ?)

"Howjacome by that ?" he asked gruffly. (Shorsh : howjacome !) so there. "Aww, it jest bust in two," the lad replied whiningly and held the broken tool up to him. – The way they go into raptures for the Russians in "Lend-lease" : two years and they'll be singing a different song ! (But we're politically immature, right ? ! – Americans don't know anything !)

Lore, Lorelorelore ('ve been over there : was right the first time : her name's Lore ! ! –). Was all business : explained that since they always keep the door locked : – would it be alright if I knocked on the window ? They still had the lights on, and you could see Everything : Me, tall, black and changeable; Grete of yesterday evening small and composed (was just about to leave for Krumau and her part-time factory work). Lore larger, broad-shouldered and lithe; had no need at all for the athlete's patch on her jacket; pale bold mouth, mocking cold eyes : Lore expects every man to do his duty; I looked at her and glinted, so that we both raised our brows. Grete switched off the light, and we said clever and stupid things by the morning dusk. (Am curious if all the postcards have arrived – they surely have –, so I can impress them with work and documents); both high-school graduates, in Görlitz. Know it myself; and we ate ice cream beside the Log Cabin (where you can see the Schneekoppe in the distance), walked through Jakob's Tunnel and stood in the station waiting room. They lent me a knife and a cup; Gretel is nice : she's going to find me a table at her factory. So we know each other's biograms now. Maternal, peremptory, they invited me to spend evenings over there (because I don't have any light !); there's still coffee in the ration books, soap and a little sugar; Lore said she would bring it with her later. And Grete, 100 marks from the Krumau post office (since I've got 1100 marks in my postal savings account).

Woodshed : they showed it to me : behind the house; a space larger than my room; I got one corner. I reached into my coat pocket, pulled out the two pieces of ecclesiastical kindling and placed them decoratively, symbolically. Lore watched me from one side, picked one up and examined its reddish grain : "Wait a minute, that's . . . ," she said suspiciously; hesitated, laughed, flared up proudly, and pointed to a pile in her corner : "I usually take a couple along with me too," she said steely : oh, we minions of Luna among the hordes of the day ! – I could have worshiped her : I am thyne . . . (but art thou myne . . . which I am doubtful of !). I can saw and chop when I get the chance; there's a whole pile of logs to spilt : I can do it : for that I get to sit inside of an evening !

Tieck : is who I'd like to read : Scarecrow, Zerbino, Puss, Eckbert, Runenberg. – Oh : The Old Book or Journey into the Blue Somewhere ! ! (Just thinking of the books I lost makes me want to pull the emergency brake : see "Alexander" : the global-destruction machine !). – Read the misery away.

Evening : Grete's come up with a table, God knows how, for 60 marks; she can bring it back from K. tomorrow on the truck that daily omnibuses the workingwomen around (omnibus, omnibi, omnibo, omnibum etc.). I had new wooden planks on my feet and sat cozily in the warm parlor (if I could have closed my eyes and slept, peace achieved). Grete was darning woolens; and we talked about all sorts of things, about God and the whole of creation, particularly the latter. (When I'm dead, just let somebody come along with resurrection or the like : I'll punch him one !)

They ran me ragged : Grete especially had her bit of erudition touchingly together, and I made the deepest impression (I consider "intellectual" a title of honor : it is after all man's most distinguishing characteristic ! If everybody was one, at least brawls would be fought with pens, or with mouths. Would be a considerable improvement !). From the radio the singing of Rehkämpfer, mozartian and with tintinnabulations (a plague o' this cheese !). Then : "Blind him with your luster now . . . !" (It's already happened !)

Wilhelm Elfers : I told about Wilhelm Elfers and his radio : ho there, it was 1924. We went to his house directly from Hammerweg grammar school, in high spirits, thumbs in our satchel straps, from the suburbs to greater gardenhood : thankgod his mother wasn't there (Marie was her name; widow of a teacher, evenings spent at concertizing with her late husband's colleagues – oh, where are you all : Kurt Lindenberg, Albert Lodz, Tonn our teacher; sometime I'll show them the old photo, where

I'm standing on the steps, in my burgundy and gray jersey). Yes, well, and there on the table he had a little technical tangle : coil of wire, crystal detector, a cooper lead hanging down as an antenna, headphones, my heart ran, here I sit today in Blakenhof : I set the headphones clumsily to my little ears – the crickety whimsies of a violin : I can still see that table and the silly tablecloth. The music spittered softly from Norag (Wilhelm went over to the piano, knew the piece, illustrated with a loud roll of the keys : I reacted with impatient scorn, just listening, a voice spoke obscurities; music withdrew into the distance – –). I took off the earphones then; we-at-home bought a brown box big as your hand for 5 marks 40, strung the wires, hung to that Blaupunkt : where has the time gone; the curse of transience ! (I still have the little box today, as a piggybank, 20 marks in it.)

Why can't you connect other people's brains onto your own, so that they can see the same images, flashes of memory, that you do ? (But then there are the bastards who would)

Coffee : I jiggled my spoon in the lush broth, Odhin's Solace. A mesh of foam lay on top, thickened with stirring, I increased the spin, pulled the spoon out of the funnel's vortex : at first only a tiny rotating disc of foam, white brown and pointless as yet; then the suction pulled in the distant particles : they grouped *in a spiral form*, stood still for a moment, were swallowed up by the ever-growing disc : a spiral nebula ! So spiral nebulae rotate : simply because of their shape ! – I showed my example; demonstrated how it works in the cosmos; proved by analog rotation and contraction : drank it down cold : "Do you know James Fenimore Cooper ?" No one knew the great man; so I went to bed; the alarm clock showed 17 after 10 : the Tommies took away *my* watch in prison, so that I would have the lack of a compass (and you can tell time with it too; one of them had about 200 compasses like that; was 16. 4. 45 near Vechta.)

Sleep : with Lore in the streets of a great city; we walked hand in hand, jostling our way through intricate department stores, light glittering in unending displays; faces weltered; I did not let go of her hand.

Outside briefly : in the spotty night, everything was astir, busy motion, restless treedom, wind in clouds : wind, cold, here below.

Shorsh (I was sitting on my stool in the sunshine of my door). Was reading Fouqué manuscripts, just arrived (that is, working), and he rambled; your cheap small talk, like 222, the red ticket; a creature of clay : spoke of his few houseplants as my "gahrden". And it was as if we were bench-pressing time; we were tough, stuck to it, eiris sazun idisi, like a man on the town council. A farmer marched into the superintendent's, dunking his way along as if shoving an invisible barrow of manure before him : wanted to register a child, Shorsh reported (I mean like rabbits !).

"Hello, Lore !" the swine said ! I would have liked to rend his bodily parts; but held fast to my pencil stub : the dirty dog; grew cold as ice, thought of the most complicated preuves de noblesse : none of it helped.

As bait : I turned the sheet of paper, the letter from King Friedrich Wilhelm IV. (1837, though, so still crown prince), so that the whopper of a seal would be visible, pulled a scratched magnifying glass from my breast pocket and examined it – (: now if that doesn't work ! The package had come today from Baron Fouqué, insured for 10,000 marks : the mailman had never had anything like it, he said. You can't have driven very far. If only I had some schnapps; they say Apel brews some. Apel : the great viscownt).

Resolutely she fetched herself a chair in the glinting light : sat down : beside me ! "Here is where I want to work !" she said (like Undine : beside me ! !)

I quoted : "A gentle breath this life is . . ." "What's that from ?" asked Shorsh after a while, dreamily perplexed. I grimaced casually and shook : "Nothing for you; or just the refrain of a hit tune : it's already somebody's property." But he stared at me, and whispered absent-mindedly as he did : trying it out. (Later I heard him pacing buoyantly about the corridor – preparation for a village promenade – and war-bling : "A gentle breath this life is – da da da dada. Zoom zoom zoom – zoomzoomzoom –," he crouched before the wardrobe, burrowed among footgear, reemerged : "Yes, and it won't last –". "Yes, and it won't last – – !" – : "Yes, and it won't last : lo-o-ong !" – And I nodded, taking note : Ahyes, c'est ca. And poor Fouqué; oh, enough of the monkey. By which I mean Shorsh of course. And's a soccer fan to boot !)

I looked up : sent the flame of my eyes into her face : "French territory since olden days" I replied, and proved to her that this was French Empire, 1810–13; the Böhme was the border : vive l'empereur ! (What all should have happened now; with just one change of underwear, I can't say : I love you !). "I'll let you see my book as soon as it's published;" by way of precaution I showed her the contract; she read attentively : I'm not a misalliance, am I ? !

A divorcée ! I was floored; I swallowed; distraught, I begged : "But may I call you *Miss* Peters ?" She granted me that, after an astonished pause; my table arrived too, thankgod; you could hear the car's shuffling putt-putt out on the road (wood-gas burner : we were going to win the war with those !) and I walked down : why hadn't I got to know her before ! ! (Didn't have a drawer either; but sturdy all the same.)

I came up from behind : and heard them talking : "Why should he insist on calling me *Miss* ?", she asked slyly (when she knew exactly why !). Grete explained dourly : "He's a poet, that's all, and needs the fantasy of his being your first. – You have all the luck."; dispirited (envious), she sighed. Silence. I walked past through the silence.

Coupon L was supposed to be good for 100 grams of prunes per person; Grete got all excited and planned away, and even Lore showed prurient interest. "Give us your book !"; I handed her the raggedy remains; she searched : good ! But we had trouble keeping Grete from taking off on a desperate bike ride : she knew a store in Westensen . . .

At the door again, such a jolly trio : and the weather was just too inviting. Schrader was walking our way, in a dignified dither : sat down : for the first time in the history of the New Covenant, the Mount of Olives was being used as a ski slope ! Only then did he make my acquaintance; awaited our disapprobation, which, however, only a genuinely distressed Grete bestowed. Lore was more curious about what I would say : which I certainly noticed, but went on silently copying the old text (: what a hand Marianne von Hessen-Homburg wrote : it was the height of illegibility; nothing but wavy lines and broad flourishes); what is Schrader to me : de tribus impostoribus; Gautama was the only great man among them, educated. Well now, gradually the Right Raverend's soul lost a few wrinkles; yes : a lovely day; hm (as sure as I live and breathe : and made for better things than ennui, mon vieux ! When would he make to board my ship, do you suppose ?) He obligated his face; inquired with the confidence of a man fully licensed : "Oh ? old autographs !". My nod was mechanical and mute; instinctively my mind's eye saw him in plump geneva bands and jocund gown slaloming down the Mount of Olives : loony world ('nd Holland can't be far behind !); "Fouqué," I said brusquely for the sake of peace (although it was none of his business !). "Ah !" he beamed condescendingly : "Undine : Ozean, Du Ungeheuer . . ." and nodded in relief; I cast him a sidelong glance, but said politely : "Lortzing's text and music have of course no bearing at all on Fouqué personally." "It's been set to music often then ? !" he said in majestic wonder : "I'm not aware of that at all . . . !" Now I had had it; he appeared not just to have believed himself omniscient : no : to still believe it ! "Oh but it has !" I replied charily and went on working, and Lore's skirt was now inching my way in approval, quivering (would I ever like to lay into that teacher-fellow !)

"Research for a definitive edition ?" (Oh, I know what the boys mean
by that : when they serve us up the placenta along with the baby !
The mistress has her stableboy . . .). He started in with "exhaustive
research" and "excerpta" and "palimpsest"; Grete riposted, and so we
all used similar first-class words, for a considerable time. (An erstwhile acquaintance could pronounce "Parerga and Paralipomena" so
that it sounded absolutely filthy; was no dolt, that Amandus !)

Hold it ! It just occurred to me : "Might I check out something in your old
parish records sometime ?" I asked politely : "Fouqué had some connections with this place as well." They all pricked up ears and eyes,
and I gave the brief but precise explanation : by way of Fricke, his first
private tutor (but kept some things to myself). "Why of course" he said
with emphasis; but then : "Assuming your research is not meant to be
prejudicial to the church –". I almost smirked (did he already suspect
me ?); "No, no" I elucidated coolly : "merely some genealogical data,
births and deaths." "Are a great wide sea – !" Grete recited piously, and
the rough allusion gave even Schrader uncommon pleasure : thusly
does one win the hearts of Tyskland's scholars.

Refugees ! : I took a hard look around me, laughed harshly : "I can give you
a splendid case in point, ladies and gents" (Bauer had come creeping
over again as well); I took out the rippling old-yellow sheets, belled my
voice : "1687" I said and raised my upper lip in rage : "The Huguenots
Are Driven Out –" and read :

Brief Accompt of my Flight from France : that I might arrive on these alien
shores to seek Freedom of Conscience and to practice our Holy Religion.

This did occur in Rochelle, capital Town of the Province of Denis,
where lies a harbour to the sea, Anno 1687.

I was of my brothers and sisters the eldest, and in the absence of my
Parents head of our Household, consisting of five still younger members, of whom the eldest was ten and the smallest but two years old. I
had been authorized by my Parents to let no opportunity pass, should
such occur, to flee with our Family – whether in part or in whole – from
the Kingdom.

On the 24th of April of this same year 1687, a good and true Friend,
who begged to remain unnamed for fear of the evil consequence and
hard punishment pertaining upon such cases, arrived and informed me
that a small ship or vessel would be departing for England, and that
upon his intreaty the Captain of said ship had been persuaded to take
with him four or five persons; but that there was room in the ship for no
more than five persons : indeed to that end he would be forced to throw

a butt of wine into the sea and to conceal us among the salt; for he
ran the danger, should he be discovered, of losing Everything, and
demanded therefore a large sum of money to indempnify him. All of
which was no hindrance to my design and our accord. I importuned our
anonymous Friend to bring the ship's Captain to me at the early morning hour of a quarter to four, that no one of our neighbours might sur-
mise anything, with the further intent of employing my Friend both as
interpreter and witness to our Covenant.

The Covenant was made; I pledged to pay the Captain 200 thalers a
head for each of the five persons whom he should convey with him,
being a total sum of 1000 thalers of French coin. The half of which he
was to receive in advance of our departure and the remainder as soon
as he had set us a shore at Chichester in England (a city of that Country), whereto he promised to deliver us.

As our Covenant had been made in the presence of a witness, we
agreed that our embarquement should be at 8 a clock on the evening of
the 27th of April. – On said day, I, two of my brothers and two of my
sisters, dressed ourselves in our best (taking with us whatever we were
able; circumstance not permitting us to dress otherwise); I arranged for
the children's governess to accompany us, for she was party in our
secret.

We made pretense of a promenade in the Castle Square, a place where
of an evening gentle folk gathered. Toward 10 a clock the company
began to disperse themselves; I crept off from my acquaintances, but
rather than return home, we took another way, namely to the place that
had been shown to me, not far from the mole. At the end of which we
found an open door; we entered; we climbed to the top of the stair-case
making neither light nor a single sound; there we remained until 1 hour
beyond midnight, when our Friend appeared with the Captain. I told
the Captain that nothing grieved me more than to leave my smallest
sister behind; that she was my God-Child as well; that she was most
dear to me, and that for these reasons I felt myself more duty-bound to
deliver her from Idolatry than all the others. I was unable to utter this
without great Affliction of heart and streams of tears : I promised the
Captain anything he might have, and many Blessings of Heaven,
should he accomplish this Good Work. My speech and tears so stirred
him that he vouchsafed to take her with us as well, if in return I might
promise him that she would make no cry should agents board to search
the ship, which they would do with dagger-thrusts in two or three
places. I gave my promise in the Hope that God would be my ready
Help and bestow this Grace upon me.

At once my Friend and our governess hastened to fetch her from that other quarter of the city where we dwelt. She took the child from its bed, wrapping it in its clothes and a single blanket, and bore it to us in her apron; it proved God's wish that no one took so much as the least notice. The little child, which was uncommonly fond of me, was most happy to see me again, and likewise promised to be very godly and still, and to behave in no wise other than I told her. I dressed her and wrapped her in what remained.

That very night, at two a clock, four seamen came a shore, bore us all on their shoulders (I had my smallest sister in my arms) onto the ship, and to the place that had been readied for us : the entry was so small, that one man had to stand inside to pull us in after him; where we were so arranged that we sat among salt barrels and could assume no other position; then the opening was closed behind us just as it had been before, so that no one might see the least difference. It was so low within that we struck our heads; ne'ertheless we all took pains to hold our heads directly below the beams, so that should a search be carried out in the customary pretty fashion, the daggers might not strike us.

As soon as we had been brought aboard, the vessel came under sail; the king's agents arrived and conducted their search : we had the Good Fortune not to be found out, either on the 28th or on two following occasions. The wind was favourable, and delivered us at about 11 or 12 a clock from the presence of every Enemy of Truth . . .

"Listening breathlessly" – ? : that only happens in novels; these folks all had robust bronchia; even Grete sneezed in the middle of it. I broke off : it was too much at once; to restore suspense, I said succinctly : "More next round; her story continues : was 17 years old at the time. – She lived quite close by here for years and years; and died here too." And curiosity was aroused : "And she has a connection with Fouqué ?" came the question; "Yes," I replied, still musing on the story : "she was his – great grandmother." Suzanne de Robillard of the house of Champagné. "A brave girl," and Grete valued that (was the same sort). And so each of them culled whatever particularly pleased him; Schrader, her steadfastness of faith (la faridondaine, la faridondon; dondaine dondaine, dondaine, dondon); finally, to silence him, I briefly mentioned the other relative, who in fact converted to Islam : Marquis de Bonneval – my Allah ! You'll find him in any world history text – and his harem avec des belles Grecques : "Now that's interesting ! !" Lore said attentively : "oh : you'll have to tell us all about it . . ." (All : you can depend on it !)

Rest of the afternoon : lazy and malicious. (Like God before creation).

Short story : darkness of night; eclipse of moon. A man crouches by the roadside, hard at work. 2 nearsighted mathematicians stop and stand debating if it's a tree stump, stone, or man. They decide to experiment by striking it with a cane. Sensations of the sitter.

First brush my teeth : so, orts brushed off once more. First back outside, and then to the soiree.

In the jakes : a child's voice came bawling up, in : singing as it did : Sweet Annie from the mi-hill / sat one evening sti-hill / on a big white stone : / on a big white stone. – Water; lingering : . . . in silk and satin gli-hiding . . . : the author sure knew what ropes 'em in !

"Lore's gone dancing !" I sat there mutely copying; 19 letters and letter-tatters from General Fouqué to his brother, à mon très cher frère, Henry Charles Frederic Baron de St. Surin in Celle : was that ever difficult at times, what with the crumbling edges and the old-fashioned French ! Grete helped as best she could; but it wasn't much; she had other work to do in any case (darning and mending).

"I'd really love to be of help in scholarly work myself," she said softly : "but how to go about it. I mean : – you've got no training, and then when you're done it's all stuff and nonsense." She looked at me, and we briefly deliberated this important topic : Just think of it : thousands of manuscripts lying in the great libraries : poets' autographs, documents, what have you : Weightiest Items; and extant only in this one, single, and thus highly imperiled exemplum. Just imagine a bombing raid ! (She nodded enrapt) : How important it would be if there existed at least one copy of each – or better, several copies : done on a typewriter ! – distributed in several places : and anyone can do that. Every high-school student. Every adult; even those with "just" a grammar-school education. (Sure !) Then : collecting materials for biographical studies : retrieving data from old parish registers. Or : if someone would assemble a complete index of names in the 200 volumes of the "Gotha" for us : there's endless work for anyone willing to do it, even for the simplest person; and how grateful scholars would be for the support ! She sat there with watchful eyes : "Yes," she suggested : "but that has to be said and taught everywhere, beginning with the teachers in the schools. – I'd like to do that myself –" and she indicated deferent and shy.

"I can bring you some cellophane," she said all eagerness and sat closer : "we produce the stuff at the plant. And there's an awful lot of waste. – Like this here !" She slipped off to a corner and came back carrying a roll of mirrory mother-of-pearl : "Here : take some," she laid it all

beside me : "and if that's not enough, I'll bring a new roll." She fetched a pair of large scissors, and I showed her how to encase the brittle pages ever so neatly and precisely : now you could handle them again with ease. She drew a deep breath of touching excitement; ". . . We'll wrap them all," she decreed : "then they'll last for another couple of hundred years." I said implacably : "You see : you've already done a good deed; you'd be a colleague. – That's a lot better than producing some miserable froufrou of literature, to which unfortunately I shall be condemned." We cut and folded.

"Beep. – Beep. – Beep : beep : beep :" 10 P.M. : We transmit to you now the Hamburg chronometric signal. "Transmit" and "chronometric"; can't get more bloated than that. We cut and folded.

"Does Miss," I said : "– Peters –; go dancing often in fact ?" Cut and folded. "Yes," she said glumly : "almost every Saturday and Sunday."

(Later, as I was leaving) : "Wait a while yet," she invited : "I'll have to stay up anyway until Lore comes." But I left; she wants some time to herself, too; to wash or whatever.

Is midnight now and gilt moon rides : site solitude with stiffened gentle wind. Jakes darkened. Back in my blue room I drank from the stone-cold, pressured water jet, until I felt my belly taut against my belt. Within I wrote on rough-grained lunar paper :

Poet : should you receive the applause of the people, ask yourself : what have I done wrong ? ! And if your second book is so received as well, then cast away your pen : you can never be great. For the people know art only in combination with -hritis and -illery (no misunderstandings : they may well be doughty fellows, but bad musicians !) – Art for the people ? ! : they yowl with emotion when they hear Czarevitch's Volga song, and turn icy-cold with boredom at the Orpheus of Chevalier Gluck. Art for the people ? ! : leave that slogan to the Nazis and Communists : it's just the opposite : the people (everyman !) are obligated to struggle their way to art ! –

Indiscretions continued to ladder and step-dance gaily in my brain; but I donned my coat, for sleep.

Oho ! : Voices, footfalls, frisky laughter. I stepped up full in the window and watched. The dancers were returning home : 3 gals, 2 guys; cuddling, fooling around, and patting each other good-bye on the shoulders (and Lore right in the middle with stride and lexicon of a fallen angel). Samba, samba : even in the distance one guy was nasaling with sweet hips and in bop time : Ah, methinks / said the sphinx / your sweet winks / come-hither blinks / : mean hijinx / : oh, Germany, my Vaterland !

Came, saw, stood : The moon apparently was not well-disposed toward us, for he shed pure wild light on the dividing wall of glass : we stood opposite one another like two thunderstorms : Lore and I. Mine may have been white; her dark face was diffused into windy, milky hair. There was nothing to say; which was why she gave one short laugh, and then came into the house. Slowly closed the door. Exquisitely slowly. (And now the far door opened; Grete produced light). –

"My teacher and patron, Bishop Theophil Wurm." I was so startled, that he had noticed it and gestured wallwards in explanation, toward the framed photograph : God knows : Theophil, Wurm, *and* bishop; some people have no luck at all ! I was stunned, he took me for moved, and went on bungling about in his memories. (To wit : Schrader; he was free this morning, because the Vicar of Krumau was drilling cathecumens and licentiates, and could not stand him : beatus qui solus. – He had taken the air and seen that we, too, had not gone to church : Grete had work to do, Lore pretended she did, and I let it be known that I was an unbeliever : and somehow we got around to chess.)

So let's play : He was your typical old stalemate fox, and passably versed in theory (I'm no good at it anymore !); we parted $\frac{1}{2}:\frac{1}{2}$. Nevertheless he was surprised and proposed future matches (had probably secretly obtained the primesign allowing him to associate with me. – As to this Wurm : I was reminded of pictures that as a child I had avidly collected from cheap magazines : Johann Jakob Dorner : Upland Waterfall; Joseph Anton Koch : Heroic Landscape; Franz Sedlacek; Dier. But no Wurm.)

Wrenched from Morphy's arms : and now it was the books' turn. Ah well. I remembered that I was at a theologian's and held my peace.

"You should clean this sometime :" an old volume in pale pigskin : Luther (or Madame Guyon, what do I know), but dreadfully greasy; and I explained benevolently to his suppeliant face : "With ammonia. – The binding is still quite solid : it'll look like ivory ! – Try it sometime –", and I handed his tome back to him. He may have thought I was going to borrow it; but my nerves weren't that bad yet; now if it had been Scheible's Cloister. To get rid of him, I gazed straight ahead, blank and long, while he went on leafing through the thing in a pique (pff, nope, I'd rather sleep on a bare cement floor; all the same, he was going to get those parish registers out for me "presently" : I thanked him sincerely and honestly for that, and escaped as soon as I could. In any case, for Them, "presently" means in 4 weeks at the earliest !)

"Stalemate" I declared to Lore : "he's awfully slow poking his men around." "Well, all the same," she nodded in satisfaction : "he's forever bragging about it."

Touched : they even gave me a little bowl of potatoes for lunch, and I had the last half of the harz cheese with them (which was supposed to last the whole month : so there goes supper; après moi . . .)

1714 mercenary trade : Prince Leopold (Old Man Dessauer) concludes a treaty with Whoosis, Landgrave of Hessen-Kassel, whereby in return for every beaver pelt he sends the latter, he receives a tall recruit in return : and hurrah ! for the so-hóldier's life, year in year out ! (Well, they get their due in Massenbach !)

"Ailyen" said Shorsh and drew up elegantly alongside; "Banzai, banzai" I replied in surprise, though recovering quickly : what's the sourpuss want now ?

Politics : we drummed on our chests : ahem, ahem, loosing one ideal after another. "They all swashbuckled with the swastika !" – "Because they had to !" he contended. "Noo, noo" I declared to him contemptuously : "they felt oh-so heroic marching to the Badenweiler or Egerlander : 95 percent of the Germans are – to this day – genuine Nazis !" Closed my eyes; saw – Callot : Les misères et les malheurs de la guerre – the trees full of generals : there they hung along with our political invertebrates, Franz next to Hjalmar; and stridently whistled a mixture of brothers hear the signal-call and allons enfants (but more of allons !)

Then : "The Russians are always carrying on about how their incomparable Red Army won the war; without ever mentioning that Germany was fighting them with just one arm, and that America was supplying." "A one on one : Germany – USSR, would have turned out for them just like for France." Have it your way. "The only winner in the war was America !" Have it your way.

He's right ! Governments are never better and never worse than the people who obey them. – How long will it take before they start looking for millions of hirelings among us; and find them.

Hoffman-Pestman : pleased to meet you : Schmidt. "In the old days (33–45 sic !) everything was better !" "Everything ? !" I asked ironically (thought of concentration camps, deployments, bombed cities, etc., etc.,) "Everything ! !" he answered sharply (under Hitler probably had a fine job in the ammo industry. Ah, forget him; too idiotic for me. – Later I learned that he had indeed whipped up bombs at the Eibia plant, Krumau; I hanged him for it in Callot's trees).

The beasts ! : The specter of freedom rose up before them, and they wrung their baffled hands ! (i.e. I always needed a running start as well; but I could indeed instantly recall my blessed adolescence, when you didn't need to stand at attention for anyone, when there were no "to-gas" : hah ! How I ran down the lambency of night, storming along the Hohwald highway on my bicycle, had hurriedly drunk some strong dark beer, wide-eyed and billow-haired. Those scenes still entered my dreams, that on their restless front bore stars, on mine. Oh, I was ready for rebellion against many a respectability ! Was I ever !)

"Yea : 'm ridin' all this wa – hay 'cause come the break a da-hay I'll see Conchee – ta." he warbled mournfully. – "Polvo di bacco" (Bull durham) he said and laughed roughishly at his own joke (so you can beat him alfresco too, quelqu'un avec quelquechose !)

Excellent (The Loving-cup !) : well, more of that later !

The talk of Blakenhof town : A cyclist had collided on the soccer field with a girl in a warm-up suit . . . "He suffered a severe erection and had to be hospitalized" I mechanically provided the punchline : laughter. – Sports; lots about sports ("Authors to Box Publishers" occurred to me : I took a deep and titillated breath, and imagined it) Shorsh and sports : he was the sort who consider Hans Albers and Max Schmeling Hamburg's greatest sons, and invited me to watch the soccer match. (I have no interest in sports : I can swim fish-fashion; ride a bike; lift a hundredweight in each hand – i.e. not these days : but at one time). Alright, fine : we walked to the soccer field. In his snappy, light-gray suit, he suggested the road through the village; I took the shortcut, down the backway (see map).

Girls; lots of girls : with seducing licenses, classes II–IV. But most of them in such shabby togs, God help 'em; their coats made of Tommy blankets, light gray and stiff, trumpery slipcase. (– Well, nothing for me. – The world as vaudeville, with me in the male lead : I couldn't imagine that even as a boy; more like a gloomy, cupboard-lined corridor that you dash down, head tucked low : nothing for me !)

Blakenhof United – Germania Westensen : they sprang about each other in lethal leaps; the little guy was nimbler : moving like a slinking hyena, he managed to slip past the others, and my companion shouted : "Tulle ! : Tulle ! !" . . . And there was the third guy, slamming his hard, fallow shoe into the little guy's gut, who yelped as his abdomen boomed like a canon shot, and what a disgusting sound against the thin bright whistle of the referee.

"Well ? !" : (God, did he look silly with that bald pate above his off. cand. face !) I cast him an indulgent glance : "Wouldn't it be better" I said cautiously (as if to an invalid) "if these 22 – noo : 23 men *and* the spectators would spend this hour and a half clearing rubble in Hanover

or Hamburg ? Why with those juicy marrowbones, once they set to
work . . ." He caught on slowly, childishly : turned livid : an ideal was
under attack; so much to say at such a moment : he brandished his hat;
with lowered hat he lunged at me – and we were saved by the surging
of the crowd : – :

He pedipulated with such skill, that he seemed literally to hover above the
ball, a hairy, sweating Fortuna, in woolen socks : he fluttered penalty-
areawards, until the sullen hostile defender upended him with a thrust
of his hip : loin du bal. – Amid the general ecstasy, I found this was
taking too long; I left with a contemptuous glance : monkeys all-round.
(As everywhere else.)

Wee stroll in the village : half-timbered houses; crofters, bigtime farmers :
all with horseheads (not wise Houyhnhnms, but up on the gable). But it
was so cold that you froze down to your buttonholes (with Moorose-
clouds now and the wind hooted Brand's Heath at me); simply no mar-
row in the old bones. – Refugees, with their damned little gardens and
sheds and ridiculous crooked fences, make a pigsty of the most attractive landscape ! (I'm one myself, but there's a limit to everything !)

Stood thoughtless for a long time : lots of practice drill in the military : the
girls would be glad to be rid of me for a few hours, too. (Tomorrow
morning I can do some general wood-chopping !). Dusk crept with
heavy baskets over the fields; thrice the gaunt sbirro-faced moon
peered out of cloud alleyways : then I lowered my head (was too lazy
to fall back).

Drunks (so we've got those too now; well, they brew their own); they trod
most heavily. One of them bawdied : "Hey, they ought t' toss one o'
them atom bombs in a vulcaner sometime : would that evah spuhrt 'n
shoot, man !" and they loosed a throaty and genitally vague laugh. Two
men, they stopped in the road ahead of me, studied black me and the
black background. Too long for me. I said politely : "Alau tahalaui
fugau," but not a one moved (so that doesn't help either). They listened
briefly; then the same one said snappily : "Looka him : headin' ouah
way . . ." and they tottered away in greater haste.

"*Oh : It's you –*" said the old man reassured. He had come out of the
woods, tramping over the little ditch, and stood there bulkily beside
me, in his hands a cudgel of splendid proportions. "It's jest not safe
round heah now" he explained agreeably and let me examine and
praise the thing. "Well : how d' youah lodgin's suit y' ? !" I told a spare
tale of my misery; about the supah'ntendent, and that I would soon be
tackling the parish register. "Now what 'd prompt y' to do that ?" he
asked sharply, and I charitably elucidated (in light of his services :

shovel and whiskbroom) : Fouqué – his first tutor, Wilhelm Heinrich Albrecht Fricke – the latter's mother – her father. "Aha !" he said, by thirds grouchy, surprised, and thoughtful : "Well then. –" He rasped the back of his head with his left hand : "Well, then you've got a heap o' suhprises ahead o' y'. – I'll just walk a piece with y'. Fah as the chuhch path." – "Do you actually live in there ?" I asked wearily and woodwards; a growl beside me (was quite dark now) : "O'ah to'ahds Ödern" he approximated, but turned the conversation back to me at once : "And then theah wuh sev'ral o' that bunch in Celle ?" he said with curiosity : "'tain't so fah from heah, is it ? ! I prob'ly have an acquaintance or two theah. – Puhtty town. – Hmm"

Hands in the dark : we shook them as befits strapping fellows. "Well then." "But y' ought to have a club like mine too" he warned : "You'd know how to use it, I'd say." "Sure : but where" I asked indifferently : "Am I supposed to go around filching everything ? ! – 'd be nice, sure." "Well, – 'll see what I can do" he said, apparently a little peeved (but why ?) – and : "Well, then, have a good time with Herr Auen !" "Thanks so much : good night !" – "Good-bye !"

And stood there in amazement : Never would've thought that two defenseless maidens could snore like that. I bent my bollard; – listened; – shook it : I'll be foxed ! !

Or was there some guy in there ? ! – ! – I pulled my fist from my pocket, white and knotty by the chip of a moon : I'll thrash you within an inch ! ! –

No, apparently not. I knocked timidly; Grete was there at once : "Yes ? – Oh, you" slid the bolt on the inside, fled virginally back in : "Lock it behind you, okay ? !" Lore asked sleepily : "What time is it ? – Nine ? : God : what a respectable young man !" (A cheeky creature !)

Slept for breakfast : the topic of sports reminded me of : Byzantium, the Blues and the Greens in the Hippodrome : just like the Avus 500. And though Shanghai may fall and Berlin totter : the most important thing for a New Yorker is that Leo Durocher has been indicted (probably the coach of the "Giants" or whatever) – Living History : I could make my "Cosmas" easy to swallow !

Eastwind : ice-cold but clear. I went over to ask for the key to the shed. – : "Yes, that's a good idea" said Lore : "You see we've got washing to do tomorrow, etc. – laundry use is tightly regulated – and need the wood. – Need some for heat too, anyway." Grete came (from the village, shopping) : "Just imagine, : they say Lebke down below won 537 marks in the soccer pool . ." The new Golconda.

Whispering. Lore called me back; she said sternly : "What do *you* have in the way of laundry ? !". "We can wash it right along with ours !" I lowered my head : I was not a good match after all. "Take that coat off !" she commanded knowingly; reconnaissance; : "We'll put that in last thing." "Give us your shirts and underwear now; stockings and sweaters" (right; she had been married and knew it all down to the last shameless detail). "One of each" I rumbled; they were silent for a moment; then Lore spoke resolutely : "I see : what you have on then. And nothing else . . . ?" Nothing. "Yes, well, what can you wear in the meantime . . ?" Nothing. They had to laugh; but it was rather bizarre. "Well now. Hm" she said clearing her throat : "then it'll just get done all the quicker." – "I'll help of course" I said firmly : "a big part of it is really a man's work : especially the wringing." She gave an appreciative whistle and lifted her clear cold face : "Amazing ! –" she said : "Bon ! We accept. – Hey : we just might get it done in one day for once !" But Grete had her doubts; she whispered anxiously behind the folding-screen, and was checked only by Lore's haughty "pff" : "I'm sure Herr Schmidt has seen worse things in his life than a pair of ladies' panties." You can say that again : noncom with the heavy artillery, mon enfant.

Undressed : I regarded my underclothes with horror and shame : a good thing there were only five pieces. In a flash I slipped into the coarse uniform; it scratched like the devil; and the cheap black dye was sure to run : Little Black Sambo went round the tree. With my eyes closed, I laid the filthy and tattered husks in the entryway and pleaded in disgust : "Best don't even look at them !" "Oh my God" said Grete pitifully : good Grete. But I had to go back again, to show my ration book : "Great : there's still one here for laundry soap" : that was good news. "But none of it's worth anything" said Lore gloomily : "well, I'll go back down this afternoon." – "A saw ?" – "Frau Bauer's got it ! But we don't speak." "I'm on my way."

"Good morning, sir !" she beamed mistrust at me (probably used to being hit up by now); and I was sweepingly obliged (should I unbutton my jacket perhaps ?) : "Herr Schrader there has got the saw." We curtsied and smiled some more : yes, the weather was indeed quite brisk : go to hell.

It was leaning against the woodpile, a bow saw; I just took it with me : nor steed nor yeomanry / guard the tor so high and free / : where princes stand ! (What must Willy have thought about that back then ! How things look inside heads like those, our sort will never comprehend !)

Oh saw, dearest saw : and dull as a hoary village parson (Mr. Lang should
send it off for a good rest-cure). While the ax took two hands just as in
the Song of Roland ("lyest thow an grund of sey" . . I would have pre-
ferred it !)

"Has the mailman been by yet ? !" Lore hadn't seen anyone : "I'll knock
on the wall" – Right; there were only eight inches separating us. Times
in which people lie in wait for the mail cannot be good times ! After
a while she came round back, Control Commission, and was visibly
astounded : a third of the wall was clad in layered firewood : two deep
in fact. Even sitting on the block she looked like my goddess.

"For he's a man without a country now . . ." : Two adenoidal vagabonds
out on the open square (thankgod they didn't see us, nor we them. For
shiftless minstrels one should always have at the ready laurel wreaths,
artificial posies and similar paltry presents; imagine his face if you
tumbled out the door with that sort of applause : for the artist, fit-
ting dandy donation.) "Singing's always easier than working" she
confirmed merrily : was that directed against me as well ? ! "Much
easier !" I said offended. She let the monarchs pass, and then glided
out; the woodpile had grown to a kaaba; well I'll take one more
log. – –

As if to a sleepwalker : she spoke : so cautiously : "You'll have to sign
for it" she said in a monotone : "Come on." I left the saw stuck in the
wood : no, I lustily pulled it out in self-torture, pedantically laid the ax
on a beam, Heautontimoroumenos, reeled to the door, and came.

"Well now" said wee Grete, with candor and soapy hands. And silence. We
stood around the table, and the package lay on it : violet stamps, burgundy : a larger white one : one dollar.

"I've already written my cousin in South America" Lore said with wistful
jealousy. – "Well : let's hope there's something fine in it," and they
were about to duck out; but I grabbed each, one hand each, I did not let
them go. Mute. And they stayed; i.e., Grete fetched tools, in particular a darning needle for picking the knot : "Great string." We had sat
down on my bed and watched idly and busily; Lore shifted her shoulders (was probably sitting on a tarp button); then she actually investigated the components of my bed : boards, two tarps, a gray blanket, a
blanket remnant (reddish : but I've said that already I believe !) Said
nothing. Grete made four rolls of twine and looked at me; I took the
knife from her, cut through the wide band of tape, and we folded the
double layer of stiff brown paper open : every bit of it was priceless.
But the large carton was tied up a second time : alright : Grete. Lore
had already put her nose to the address, and asked from the kaaba : "Is

this your sister ? ! Lucy Kiesler ? !" "'sindeed" I said grandly; "that's her" (and from here on we'll speak only American). Another three rolls. And I took a deep breath, hesitated once more, and began : on top a layer of newspaper : New York Post. "Careful !" Grete shouted : "There's sugar in it !" Right : there was a white crunch : very carefully; (they had already fetched a bowl)

"Ah !" : Bright cans, white metallic tin-heads, mysterious bricks of newspaper : it smelled of – – "real coffee" said Lore in disbelief : 1 pound of real coffee.

2 packs of Camels : "Do you know what that'll mean for you !" "You can buy all sorts of things with those !" – Dexo : "What's that ?" I read on their questioning brows, and skimmed the enamel-smooth text. "Shortening" I said : "but I know nothing else about it." In a sheet of mild silk-paper : blossom yellow and elfin white : 2 pieces of complexion soap : they dolefully lowered their faces and sniffed so charily that it pained my heart; I filled one hand of each (Grete white, Lore yellow; there wasn't a red one, and so I selected the color closest to it) : they promptly laid the bulbs back on the table. I, however, wanted to continue unpacking; I said testily : "Now listen here : I sit over there with you every evening, by light and warmth, and am allowed to bore you for hours on end :" Looked from One to the Other : they held unrepentant silence; I opened my crate and said : "Here : I have one too." Correct, it was my piece of Brussels Lux; they gazed at it dully, but it did have some effect; they breathed and were silent. So then : I laid the pieces in their hands again (She had wonderful hands, and with Grete it took considerably less time). With lightning speed, I led them from object to object : 2 pounds of cane sugar, Jack Frost, granulated. Tea : 16 feathery-light paperbags on a string : "You'll love drinking that" I thought (Thought; had to be careful with these urchins). Mor-Pork : meat. "That's more than a month's ration. Twice as much" said Grete; but held her doughty hand clenched tight.

Shattered : a thin silver bar of chocolate : I tore open the paper so quickly and adroitly that they could not argue; grabbed a few triangles, shoved them past demurring hands and protesting lips. (Mine too !) They puffed air : through the pug nose, through the snazzy nose : and they couldn't talk either, and even I sucked away, using a hand to fend off any further nonsense. (Was Grete opening up her hand once more ? I flashed my eyes around toward her, frightening her into closing it again. The very idea !)

"A spool of thread" : Grete reached for it : "And another" she said devoutly. "But lilac," I objected, staring at the impossible color. She

shook her head vigorously : "Makes no difference !"; tears came to her eyes : "We haven't had any rationed for four months now. And the last was 50 yards of white !" I suggested (while apparently pondering, hand on chin) : "If you would mend my things, you can keep one for yourselves." I got tough : "What do you think I'm going to do, take up weaving ? ! I don't even own a needle !" (True : my sewing kit had likewise caught a Tommy's eye, could probably have also been used for a compass : poor England.) "I'll mend everything for you !" She swallowed softly and swore with a tenfold nod of her head. "And if I happen to be missing a button, can you throw that in as well !" : "Oh sure !"

Then came pepper. Cinnamon. Cocoa. We smelled it and tramped through primal groves. Then –

Yes, I had to sit down : "First take the soap and the thread over to your place, and then come back" I said in a flat voice. 5 seconds; then they were back. "Should you laugh or cry at this ?" I challenged them to decide; Grete reached in and lifted out 2, then Lore and she lifted out the last two : 4 silk neckties (and the image of my little pile of underwear rose before each of us : is this a dagger which I see before me ?)

"Well, over there they can't even begin to imagine what things are like for us here !" I suggested. "Wonderful –" said Lore : "Two of them are lined with silk : look at those colors !" But Grete was instantly resolute : "For bartering" she was calmly calculating (I nodded at once) : "You need, why you need everything."

A diapered baby : I un- un- unrolled the whitish soft material : inside a jelly glass, damson plum. But the material was unusual; the expertesses turned it about, muttering. "Circular knit" (Grete); "It's stockinet" (Grete); two arms stretched taut, measuring : "Almost two yards" (Lore). Embarrassed silence; and then another layer of newspaper. I let out a wild and demented laugh : "Was this really addressed to me ? !"; because there lay a plaid skirt and a quince-yellow blouse. Likewise plaid. Slightly worn. Then more newspaper. The end. pff : pale-violet stripes and some black (in the blouse). – I looked up; they were also mutely examining it : quiet nods : elegant articles.

Review : (we sorted and decided). Coffee, cigarettes, ties, cocoa – : for barter. "This we'll use here !" I said firmly. Newspapers to be studied (a lot of women's fashions : you'll sit a nice long time over those; I know !). Leaving skirt and blouse, and 2 yards of loopy material.

By way of precaution, I placed myself at the door : I raised my hand like the arringatore, furrowed my brow and lectured : "You know all the people in the neighborhood." They couldn't deny it. "Whereas I am a total stranger and regarded with suspicion !" "No ! Not with suspicion !" said Grete stoutly; : "No !"; with another shake; took a breath. "Besides which, I'm *bad* at such things" nervously : "so then : if you two would take over the bartering – you would *really* be doing me a big favor !" I looked about, pleading : "We'll do it all very businesslike : for your work you'll receive this stuff here (i.e. skirt and blouse) : how you settle *that* between you is your affair." I hung them over Lore's forearm; but Grete mutinied : "That's worth more than a couple hundred marks these days – And you can't even get anything that good !" – "Lovely wool" said Lore, her long firm fingers deep in the hem of the skirt : "and it's hemmed so wide . . . ."

But now Grete savagely elbowed her way to the door : for I let the stockinet dangle from my arms, as cunning as an Oriental shawl merchant, gave a voluptuous and many-thousand-nighted smile. – I sang out : "I need – as personal property ! – knife-fork-spoon; cup, saucer, plate; a bowl. Plus the canister that's lying in the shed." (for a wash basin, by the by –). : "Well ? – Is it a deal ? !" – "He's the devil incarnate" Lore muttered respectfully; which I interpreted as acquiescence and laid the fabrics over her shoulder. Then I threw them out.

5 minutes' wait : then I went over with the rest of the stuff. For now the newspapers were all I held back for myself.

"Camisoles !" from the door I heard Lore speaking : "just cut straight across; little hems at the top and bottom : we've still got straps for the shoulders ! – – Lord : we're saved. It'll make 3 of 'em ! With no trouble !" "No; two." Grete said firmly. "Three !" (Lore.) Pause. Pause. "Two." Grete said calmly, but in a tone that caused the tall one to yield. I entered (to divert them).

"Of course !" I could store things in their cupboard.

Very quick conference : "Most of all I need" I counted them off on my fingers : "a wardrobe – a very simple military locker. A chair." – "A shirt, and –" Out of gratitude Grete conquered her shame : "Underpants. – and socks." she said. "A light bulb." Then it occurred to me; I grew guilefully depressed; I began falteringly : "I have one more request ! – : You know of course that I have neither stove, nor wood, nor pot nor pan. – :" Terse : "How many potatoes can you get for a pound of coffee ? ! – But you have to eat them with me : and in exchange you can fix my midday meal every day." I looked at those thin faces imploringly (and it would be really wretched, seeing as how I didn't know how to cook; and definitely had other things to do.) "3 to 4 hundredweights" Lore said pertly. "We're sure to need a hundredweight a

month" I suggested with furrowed brow : "March, April, May, June –
works out just right – doesn't it ? !" And we looked doubtfully to
housemother Grete : she suddenly began to weep, little Dorrit : "What
miserable people we are" she said : "Both of us. And it's your fault,
too, for offering something like that ! –". "But I'll do it," she concluded in a hollow voice, and clenched a somber fist : "We're so
starved ! – – : I'll do it" – Now I played my last trump : "How's the
wash doing ?" I asked as if awakening : they screamed and made a
dash for the soaking tub.

The electric blanket : I kept gazing at the seductive bright picture, where
an American beauty was busy smiling and warming up her midriff.
Shaking of the head. Once again. Automatically I looked at my bunk :
a threefold cheer for Corporal Neumann the medic.

"And I wouldn't even lend him a whiskbroom that day" Lore recalled
ruefully in the laundry. (Excellent : you see ! !)

By 1 Grete had to be in Krumau; she got aboard the old boy's bike and
clattered off. We rapidly put together a plan for our campaign : get
some sleep this afternoon; I'll get up at 11 P.M., Lore too. She'll get
the kettle ready; while I'm heating it, she'll go back and cook for the
three of us (Here I murmured into her ear, and she smiled : mocking
elvish flickers : I'd give the rest of my life for 8 days : but I didn't tell
her that yet !). Eat at 12:30; start washing clothes at one, in the middle
of the night : and it'd all be hanging on the line by – say 8 or 9. (And
Frau Bauer'll be peeved green !) Muy bien.

"Mashed potatoes !" I called after her ! – Cool weather; very cool : but
clear. (Mashed potatoes : good God, for the first time in how many
years ? ! Magnus nascitur ordo.). I've also got to haul wood over to
the laundry; good thing there's paper and cardboard to start the fire.

With pommeling fists the alarm clock raged, insensate, across the Romsdal
fjord, across delphine sea walls; empty-headed, I pulled on my shoes,
shuddering in the scratchy stuff.

Knock, knock ? – "Yes : be right there !" (that was Lore; so she was a light,
nervous sleeper too) : "I'll wait outside !"

Outside : moon hunched silently behind silent yellow cloud facades. Who
knows, whether the gentlefolk in the fourth dimension don't perhaps
take time-lapse pictures of our universe every 10,000 years : and the
earth is just a smudge on the plate !
With a firm step into the square; moving ahead between church and
the Schrader house (Wurm : can you believe it !). Far to the north a
light moved : was it a night freight ? : God, what images press in on
a soldier-man at any words like those ! "Night freights !" : I lowered

my head, cursed, and rattled back : when a bright light came bouncing out of a lady's window.

She came with a light bulb : "Howdy, Mister Interlocutor" she curtsied (wonderful !); the key passed from hand to hand like a steel kiss : "You're tall : you can just reach up to it"; I can, Lore, I can. "If we left it, somebody'd filch it right off." I nodded, profoundly convinced (wouldn't hesitate a moment myself; haven't got one). She had wound a scarf around her head; broad white brow, small sly chin.

I turned about gruffly : I said sharply : "How old is he anyway ? !" – ? – : "The Cousin from Whatsits !" Flattered, she laughed : "Ohh : – rich and single (flirting) – Around : 55 !" Elicited a contented grumble. Went on soaping the wash and then swinging it over into the kettle.

"So !" I had been resolutely working away at the fiery opening for 5 minutes. "You get the fire going now; once it's boiling, knock on the window – oh fiddle : on the door of course. – That'll take an hour and a half maybe. I'll go cook –" We smiled, gourmands, and took deep breaths : blessed be Mrs. Kiesler ! "We'll each finish off with a cup of tea" I said : "with cane sugar !" Les mille et une nuits. (Galland was a great man; not the pilot, but the old man of letters 1646–1715). – Good.

Alone : The stove has a good draft : or burns superbly : is the same thing. Lots of time in between layings on of wood, about 5 minutes, for reveries. (But it's cold without a coat or underwear : brutal !)

Tender starshine trembling in resting clouds : four times the cry circled the house : Wish-ton-wish. Wish-ton-wish : owlet. Great man, Cooper. That's the soldier's curse : never able to be alone; here I was alone : finally ! Cold, true : but alone at last. Except for across the way, the two of them bustling and sleeping; that was tolerable.

With an iron fire-hook : crouching at the stove door : it was all aglow, strange and jewel-like, but so clear that you wanted to climb in. Salamanders are not such a stupid hypothesis. Not so bad, not quite so bad. And naturally I thought of Hoffmann, and Fouqué : my Fouqué : I'd like to meet the man who knows even half as much about him as I ! If the fairy Radiante were to appear to me now, and grant me three wishes . . . I splayed my fingers and pursed my stubbled lips . . . three wishes . . . (well don't hold your breath : because you know a man by his wishes, and I'm not Sir Epicure Mammon !)

Blakenhof : a light. They say young Mrs. Müller is about to have a baby. – "Children bind" (They'd do better to buy a tandem bike : that would make them much more dependent on one another !)

"It's boiling !" She was fresh and properly spruced up now. "Good" she

said : "I'll be back in 15 minutes; dinner's ready too : should I open the can ? . . ."

I cut it into 6 slices : thick ones ! And Grete herself fried them. Gravy from something or other, plus a tablespoon of Dexo : they had yelped in delight at the sight of the snow-white shortening ! – Oh ! (Apel will trade 4 hundredweight for the coffee, Grete said) – Ah, is this wonderful : you can only slowly shake your head. Food, food : Oh : food ! ! –

And the tea-water was boiling now; they hung their bags in the glasses with silver handles (I got my big earthenware cup; isn't this how Muhammad describes the raptures of paradise ?), and there was no sparing of the cane sugar either : "Now that was something" even Grete said.

Wash, wring out; wash, wring out : we worked liked diesels. And were thrilled at how fast it went (Wringing out wash is *not* woman's work, say what you will !). And now onward : 140 pieces in all, I'd say.

Holy Antropov : did my back ever hurt ! It's definitely after 12. ("Midnight has passed : the cross is dipping low." Humboldt's gauchos were always saying : – I was reminded of the Tembladeras, with all the tales and denials, and the whole voyage équinoxiale paraded by, so that in indignation I thought of something else : a cast-iron memory is a curse ! !)

The strong black morning air, in which a tag of moon flickered.

The pewter day drew on from across the soccer field : ductile; and the Bauers were stirring as well. "Shorsh is an ass" said Lore contemptuously. So expressively that it would have convinced one of the Mon Khmer people.

Now it grew pink : and all at once, as vulgarly pink as in a girls' boarding-school around 1900; as if nothing had happened; shameless. And I carried the next tub out to the washyard behind the house, where Grete did frozen battle amid white flutterings. "Not enough clothespins !" she squawked through festoons of discreet items : even my ragtags had come clean.

7:30 A.M. : Done ! "Never managed it this early !" they admitted. And gazed proudly at me. "Now we can sleep again till noon when Grete has to leave." I felt like stone and wood myself; we parted with yawns (but had that ever been a good meal ! : you really didn't feel hungry yet; God bless her.)

I entered : girlish vases stood stiffly atop pedestals, blue glazes and nouveau lines; goblets in vitrines; metallic shrinelets; Peter with the key, Terminus with hoary locks (according to Stägemann). In the next room paintings : drinking women; landscape in the Odenwald; there stood Muscovius, in preaching robes, with a blackbird in his smiling hand : dark brown frame : that was good. An old chest : 1702 . . . Eisleben . . . Henry Cha . . . (hard to read !). I walked slowly through the museum : on glassed-in tables lots of seals from Babylonian cylinders; as a young man I had greedily examined them for hours on end : periwigged griffins stood among people as if among their own, trees with simple stylized foliage draped above unicorns : full beards were the fashion then too. Behind me were two mummy cases leaning against the wall : one still closed; the other's heavy brown face watched me, lofty, Göttingenic, Egyptian. Modern painting : "Red Form," and "The Couple," sculpture, as an old bicycle. Count me out. Suits of armor gaped from empty visors; Fouqué used to gaze with emotion at such things : ". . . wherein once a body bold and stout held sway . . ."; I walked more coolly past the tin cans, and entered the last silent hall : large, large.

From a side door an old man entered, manicured hands, with a tourist guide's big mouth, busy white hair; old, tall and rickety : watch out for flying parts. I took the knife from him with a gesture equal in value to one medium-sized slap, and frowned and cut the paper tape holding shut the side panels of the triptych. They swung out easy and wide. I took my biceps in both hands and stood there. And. Saw. (And behind me, the tinny old man's constant bickering by the corner panel).

Left : Act One : a room. The Lord from Wernigerode at a huge wide desk, ever so haughty and indignantly red : didn't the rascals call themselves highnesses ? The miffed-nosed secretary next to him, old-fashioned frockcoat billowing, a slim cut-rate Jesuit type (as if there were costly ones !). The man in the foreground was silently picking up the books that had been tossed at him; medium-build; the servility of long years in his back; his hands with neglected nails were soundlessly gripping the old formats. "That's Schnabel the librarian" the old man grated at the nape of my neck "and the gentleman is displeased – oh !"; with the back of my head I sent him to his corner and clenched my cheek muscles : then I saw how Schnabel's face emerged from under his arm; I had expected it to be crusty, rusty; but never, not even amid Hogarth's dry genius, have I seen such a wild, wicked smirk, such sublime disdain for oneself and the world (and the prince; and God, of course). There was nothing to do but depart; I bowed as if wearing a gallooned coat (and the doddering mouth babbled on !)

Right : a shabby garret; he lay dying on a kind of chaise longue. A businesslike man in black and white as the doctor; pepper and salt. A mature housekeeper, worried about herself, wrings her hands. But the flabby gray face gazed, in a heart-stopping mixture of deadly fear and laughter, oh the sweat and nausea, out over his feet to the door, where, just for him, in a long row they entered with spectral transparency : Albertus Julius and Cornelia (Bergmann); Litzberg, youths, girls; and Wolfgang the Sea-Captain, who in good cheer and bold reverence approached the disgracefully hard bed, like a tarp laid over planks : he had found the master's hand and pulled him easily up out of earth's stench : for a boat would be waiting outside : then on to the ship : and then away : ah, away ! (And behind me the old fop went on commentating like a Germanist)

There : Get there ! : It shone from the middle panel, enormously large, the island : white walls above the rumbling sea : oh my land of exile ! I could not bear it; I pressed my head to my fists, and sobbed and cursed in random confusion (But cursed more : you may lie to it !) – But then I've already described it all elsewhere.

Half awake : I culled my limbs from my "bed" and bungled my way to the table on sandstone feet. I wrote a supplicant's letter to Johann Gottfried Schnabel, esquire, : that he might once again send out a ship from Felsenburg, manned with messengers : that they should wander the streets by night and by day in wide, rustling cloaks, and stare into every face to see if they were seasoned, tormented ones, mad for peace, for the Isles of the Blessed. They would have to depart at once, for a port city : Captain Wolfgang had always docked in Amsterdam; I knew that well and with savage eyes cursed upon the decision.

Lore looked in : and I bounded over to the wash with her (it was drying very poorly; but there's still another 3 hours of daylight, and the wind is blowing quite jauntily : never say die. – Grete always borrows the iron from Frau Schrader)

Tomorrow we'll have to hang it out again. Half is – well, I'd say still damp – but in momentous tones I was instructed that it was "ready for ironing".

Like Hackelnberg, the wild hunter, Grete arrived on the old Arcona; what a wretched clatter (I'll run through all the bolts and screws tomorrow; the hand brake hasn't worked for years). She approved our handling of the wash : "I'll go right over to Frau Schrader : then I can start ironing early in the morning." I gave a masterful and lordly sign to Lore and she hurried over to the tea : you can make tea with one of those bags 4–5 times : "And then I'll put them together and boil them once more" Grete said happily : "and I've found a locker already !" And she told how at one time – during the war – there had been lots of foreign workers at the factory, lived in barracks, all furnished military fashion. And there were still many things left : old tables, field cots, lockers. And the supply supervisor was a rat and a smoker; the correlation seemed rather dubious to me : offended, I declared that up until two years ago, I too . . . they laughed prettily, and then she went on : he had been bribed for 10 American cigs to sell a one-man locker for 60 marks, official market value : and since cigarettes were going for 6 marks on the black market . . . "For one pack then –" I said in astonishment; and Grete nodded, brave and shrewd : "It's still quite sturdy; pretty crude paint-job though : blue-gray and scratched up. But really quite sturdy !" – : "Well alright then !"

What're you so busy reconnoitering out there ? !" Lore asked irritably, when for a second time she left her tea-glass behind (and elegant glasses they were : looked pretty, Girls with Glasses; but my heart belongs to my earthenware crock), and wandered about in the shallow twilight. "Apel's still due" she explained in surprise : "this evening, with the potatoes : he'll drive up along behind the soccer field, and – ! she looked at me uncertainly, "– then we have to get them into the shed."

Lore had the padlock in her hand and was counting (her too !) the sacks : "Three !". I snorted like a gale; wasn't all that easy climbing a hundred yards up the slope with a hundred pounds on your back ! And the bin filled up : splendid : "Seed 'tatoes" Apel said brusquely : they *were* nice ones; red and yellow. When I came back down with the last empty sack, Grete was still carrying on some small talk, shyly preparing for still further consumption (in case another one came, why we could make a deal for a couple of pounds of bacon ! What an idea ! !) – I took the little broad-shouldered fellow aside for a moment (had already been introduced as the proper owner of the items); he hesitated, grinned, and at last : yes, he made schnapps too. We shook firm, honorable hands : the man knew his man; besides which as a native of Hamburg I could imitate his Platt almost to a T; we parted as partners in crime.

Shining a light on the full bin : Grete, taught by necessity to shade the door with one hand, was a touching sight : what is a madonna and child compared to this vision of a little refugee woman and her potatoes ! (And what a remarkable play of light, as in the "Evening School", or in a Schalcken).

Tomorrow evening I'll be wearing a shirt again.

LORE
OR THE PLAYING LIGHT

26. 7. 1946.

A piano plinkled shyly, and Grete's homely little soprano protested that
slumber ne'er would near her ere she gazed upon "him"; and I devoted
several moments to reprobate reflections (outside everything beamed
and sparkled : so then, a beam- and sparkle-day !).

"I've got a hairy bunch of coconuts" whistled two tramps out on the
road.

And from Brand's Heath : "You numbskull – you, you !" the wild dove
cajoled. ("Lore ! – Are you ready yet ? !")

"5 minutes !" she called : "5 Third Reich Minutes !" And she arrived long
before that : a red head scarf of parachute silk, dangling a sack : thus
we went into the woods for berries and roots; most of all for mushrooms. (Grete would fetch us come evening).

Across the way sat Pastor Schrader in his bower, flushed and elderly
(can happen to Anyone), probably at his sermon; he yawned, in the
manner of the unobserved, beneath a beret of incredible shallowness;
scratched under his arm; again. Finally he broke off a broad sprig of
jasmine and slowly fanned himself (when off-duty, like Epicure's
gods, he took mind of no thing, but sat in his bower, drank fruit juice,
and read from Luther – or Madame Guyon, what do I know : in any
case from the aforesaid greasy volumes, which he had still not
cleaned). "You see ? –" I said with sulky and envious interest : "Lots of
primates do that . . ." and deftly quoted Brehm : Bruce, Hornemann,
Pechuel-Loesche – all to no avail : I had to go along ! (But mine was a
remunerative smile : what more could I ask !)

Some holiness or other : From the side his face had a supracelestial expression; the jakes behind the house, semicircular, like an apse.

Descending : (and the peacock sun swaggered in the sky) the wide hori-
zons, woods-rimmed, miles-distant : people in a telescope : the ideal :
you see them well enough, but don't hear, smell, feel them. (The
soundless, jangless, silent folk.)

Indigent window : the local bartering-place flatirons, old clothes and shoes, automobile for advertising pillar; pass by, pass by.

"You should carry a sickle" I said enthralled; she opened questioning eyes, oh nosemouthandcheeks (Lalla Rukh means tulip-cheek !), and I explained about Pshipolniza, goddess of noon in the Wendish fens. Then : whistling : "The Girl of the Golden West" (Puccini and Abbé Prévost; damn it all, that everything must die; the most melody-gifted mouth, even if it's Richard Tauber's; crystal sweetness and passion).

Asked directions : He answered, but even to me, a possible savant of local speech, it sounded like "bearberryblossomtea"; but I immediately managed a quick-witted : "Oh ! – Thanks ! –" in reply. Lore looked at me expectantly : "No point in it" I said disdainfully : "we can't walk that far – –. – – Best thing'd be : go into the woods right here ! –" And, satisfied, she nodded.

Brimmed mushrooms : there are two sorts : both leather-brown, rolled under at the edge, flat or most often with a decidedly concave cap; one sort with a coffee-dark velvet stem. The somber pine clearing; trunks stared fixedly, brown-black silent columns, fruitful creatures, in frightful order; mute snails silently gruffed into the fungoid flesh, and the plump boletus louted brownish pink amid things coniferous. : "Just imagine if these pillared reptiles could move, if ever so slowly; tormented by 10,000 parasites deep in their wood : if only we could wipe out insects !"

Let's hope there's water this evening ! (The mains are constantly busted by blasts from the dismantlings; howl of sirens before and after.) – Praised : Hans Watzlik "The Coronation Opera" : it's good ! And Jonathan Swift : a great man : he was celebrated, in the middle of 200 red russulas (and our green mosquito nets, which we dandled in our hands in lieu of sacks, filled rapidly !). Soundless burning in the moss.

Watch out for snakes ! I once knew a man who told me : every year, on the same day that he was bitten, a toenail falls off, and a couple of small swellings appear : it's all quite mysterious. So then : precaución !

Green smoldering above the needled earth; the golden heat embraced us as in a dream; it was in fact my first love !

A stranger (although he strode in silence) : what did that gringo want in our delightful duolitude ? ! (Two-toned : oh woods and glass air !)

A tree in the wood : whoever hit it with a scraggly stick from 15 yards away would be happy : Lore hit it; I hit it on the second try : so we'll both be happy ! Bon.

Above Krumau self-important thunder, and then about 5 drops fell (the Gentle Law) : what if I were to make such a racket with every sprinkle ! (And that's quite apart from the His-Master's-voice theory !).

She looked at me crouching there : I said imploringly : "You can recognize elves by the playing light in their eyes !"; I raised my eyebrows, a supplicant in her face : –

Wood's end : an end to the woods. – "Lore ! ! –"

"I think I'm about ready –" she said between her teeth; I answered above the hammering of my heart : "I am too – have been for the past four months !" We didn't laugh (needed our energy just to stand there with our wits about us); I demanded roughly : "Give me the blanket. I've got to hang onto something."

A red swatch of wild thyme.

I couldn't help it : I closed my hand around her sturdy ankle and she smiled a mocking and kindly smile : even in that regard I would be content. – (Has got herself new stockings on the cuff). – I gazed at her, for a long time, had to let my head drop, and joined my left hand around hers. From there I breathed slow and hard, until she laid her head against mine, and our long hair mingled in the wind for a good while, brown and ashen; and was woven anew : ashen and brown.

She sang : soft and scoffing : "A gentle breath this life is . . ." – – "A dying, fading song ! –" And I nodded happily and reverently. Happy. Reverent. For verily there is a difference whether your beloved or schoolmaster Bauer is humming such trash.

"I can't dance." – "You'll learn !" she said menacingly (had apparently read Steppenwolf). "No" I said good-naturedly : "that I won't; – but the most exceptional things await *you* !"

Love oh, I swore it by the nova in Perseus; and I had to tell her about the great meteor of Madrid from 10 February 1896.

Snails' names (to be painted on their shells) : only 4 letters, (because they are such little shells !), and offbeat : "One's named LELA." Pause. She considered, frowned, blazed up at me : "One's named GLOP" she said curtly, and I puckered my lips in appreciation : GLOP was good ! Pause; envious : "GLOP is very good ! !" – "One's named TOSA, MINK, YUTL, XALL, HILM." – "One's simply MAX." – "Then I can go and name one KURT, too" I said insulted : "No, no : offbeat is one of the conditions after all !"; but she proved to me that it was to be spelled MAKS, and added at once : "URR, PHEB, KUPL, ARAO, ZIMA, LAAR" – ah, how happy we were (meanwhile the snail moved on).

"How have you spent your happiest hour ? !" I replied in embarrassment "Reading the poets. Gaining knowledge. –" Said after an unpleasant

pause : "Here, now . . . ." – Nodded : in her eyes; hair to hair. –

There ! : cumuli ! : I looked up : high, furrowed brows of clouds all around : earnest, disapproving, advanced in years, the Gerenian horseman Nestor, all synonyms (thus apparently a mixture of rain & hail !) – "Lore ?" but she, too, knew no charm against it; in the old days women had always known such things ! – "How's that ?" she said sophistically : "Actually all the rainmakers I ever heard of were men ? ! – ?". "Leave off unseemly cogitation" I said sternly : "this is not a matter of making, but rather of dissipating : which is woman's work, quite decidedly. –" and I had to kiss her with my eyes again, of which the felenous wyf immediately took note, of course, and maliciously arched and spread her pale mouth, so that I could no longer look away (Even the hermits of the Thebaic desert conversed for hours on end with the devil. Or even with themselves.)

First the choo-choo train (from Visselhövede, diabolus ex machina); then Grete came clattering up to the trysting place : "Twenty pounds of mushrooms ! !" she marveled. (Resignedly noted that we were using informal pronouns). So we sat on the tiny heathlet at wood's end; the ladies cleaned mushrooms.

"Well ! And what did the movie version do to Storm's IMMENSEE ? !" – "Isn't it a crying shame how enterprising directors can turn a tender legend into a crude technicolor stew ! ?" Disgusted, I rolled over to Lore's side.

Klopstock's Messiah : insania iuvenili, perversitate saeculi, verbositate senili liber laborat. She (Lore) scraped the sense together, "Verbositate means wordy, right ?" she asked; I said it did, and she nodded her disdain : ". . . silly junk . . ." she said. C'est ça. Whom the Lord will chastise, He sends to the . . . (fill in the blank ad-lib)

Grete's eyes were worn brown cloths : from making that damned cellophane ! She gathered up twigs of thyme. Wild thyme. – – "Let's rest a little longer !" – –

Warm and still, the endless evening hid itself in smoke red and field gray; it all drew near from distant hems of pine, smiling and masked; the bull's eye moon glimmered rustically behind the juniper, warm and still.

Indian file over needles and gnarled roots; even Grete whished about, with a smuggler's lust for twilight. A broad meadow appeared on our right; I whispered in puzzlement : "We didn't come by here before – –"; but it looked beautiful : the gray (unmaimed) high grass, even last year's stalks were still moving with the rest; much stillness adrift. But the sharpest eyes were those of my falcon-maid, she hissed : "a lantern – ! – Get out of here !"; and instinctively we turned to the left, running and in honest sotto voce cursing those everlasting guardians of the woods, who ought not begrudge refugees such a little bit of stuff, god knows : "But they'd rather let it rot !" Grete said bitterly : "not until they've pestered 5 marks out of you for a license . . . . ." Another left, a short open stretch : ah, there it is, the highway ! We sprang up onto the asphalt : now just let Somebody come along, and I got a firmer grip on the old man's club : with so many tramps and gangs around it really was invaluable; every night a couple of farms were raided and livestock stolen ! Which was how we got onto Poland in general; then the Oder-Neisse line, and that topic lasted until we got home.

The lamp of evening : I was welcome and entered. "Is that them ? !" Lore asked at once and took one of the little black things in her hand (Schrader had finally forked over the parish registers today; "presently"). "Ah – turn that off !", because "Buli Bulan" or some other fly-by-nighter was singing a saccharin : Little Miss Loni / is my ideal / : 'cause she cooks macaroni / : at every meal . . . . . ergo, commercial broadcast from Bremen, music sweetly suckled and scattered (just remember, in case Someone calls me a misanthrope : I got my wherefores !)

"Well alright" I said all-business (my glance at One of them most unbusinesslike – "it would be a big help of course, because he wants them back tomorrow morning already. You know what to do : Maria Agnese Auen. And possibly her siblings, parents, and so on : just shout out whenever the name Auen appears. We'll then come up with other family names – through marriage –, so that we'll have to go through them a second time, but they're pretty thin books. – We each take one – : –". "I want the marriages" said Lore, emphatic and mischievous : "that's always so interesting – –"; she got it; Grete the births; I, death. "Where do we start ?" Pondering, I shaped my lips : "Weelll – let's be real careful – : 1800 !"

A page. And there another : the alarm clock's metallic shoes pattered in circles. I raised my eyes without moving my head : she had been waiting for that and lowered hers. Here a page. Wind walked about the house, breathing, and nestled against the panes. "Where are you, Grete ?"; mutters : "1780"; – "You ?"; "60." – "Then be careful."

Nonchalant voice from across the way : "Here's something. – Hey !" and we put out heads and hands together : as follows :

1752 on 17. 10. Maria Agnese Auen ! – good, good ! – married Johann Konrad Fricke, a cobbler from Hildesheim : so that's the mother who's mentioned in the letters. Her father : Johann Wilhelm Auen, gardener of the District of Coldingen – "That's right over there, behind Brand's Heath –" Grete shouted excitedly : "I know the place; a girl from there works next to me !", and I listened with the same interest as if this were useful news. "Johann Wilhelm !" I then said, assimilating : "Johann – Wilhelm : that's new : he's the grandfather who was always joking he didn't have a birthday. – A gardener then. – Well, let's keep going !"

1731 : Grete had found her birthday : 4. 3. 1731. Unfortunately there was no mention of Maria's mother. – The things were in good order, by the by; with important remarks now and then : special events, war, natural phenomena, even all sorts of superstitions (would have been good stuff for Bergers !) In mine for instance, and I read it aloud, so that Lore could take it down in shorthand : the report of Pastor Overbeck from 11. 10. 1742 : ". . . . Divers farmers have informed me that this very evening many Lights have been seen on Brand's Heath, and Voices can be heard as well, so that the guileless cattle do grow restless and children and maids fear to leave their homes. Companied by the Adjunctus, Herr von Bock and said farmers following after with lantherns and spontoons in hand, I immediately betook myself to the steeple to investigate the causam. The Night was uncommonly calm, cool, and, specially above Brand's Heath, full of some fog, but such as did not particularly impede the view : thus did we observe in the direction of Krumau many roving lights in the Forest, their numbers perhaps to be estimated at five-hundred; but even the Herr v. Bock, though he had fitted himself with a good Dollond scope, could observe naught besides. These aeiry phenomena continued for an extended time, though concentrating themselves ever more in a vaprous patch of most disquieting diameter. After we had considered said object for a while, we once again left the place of Worship, and in a small oratio I did persuade the Assembly that we were witness of a merely Natural phenomenon, albeit a rare one, to be identified beyond doubt with the ignis fatuus or Will-o'-Wisp; although it can not be denied that the Prince of Darkness likewise holds Power over the armouries of the air, and indeed his participation in matters of Chymistry is so great that he even prepares the aurum fulminans, as one of the most learned scholars of modern times has instructed us, and thus it followed that the most Efficacious Weapon . . .", and then he had "counseled prayer". We read it through again, enjoying the tale. "What are spontoons ?" Lore asked : "a sort of halberd ? ? – Or – ?". "Halfpikes !" I said importantly; she shrugged : "That doesn't make it any clearer : just say it in homespun words !". That turn of phrase was mine too, and I gave a mini-lecture on the ancient art of swashbuckling, or the technique for wielding a cudgel : it's something that must be learned, too; a virtuoso can lay a man low like a fencing master; those then were spontoons. – She made shimmery eyes and licked her lips : God, is scholarship exciting ! –

Here : Grete had found something else : a farmhand, who jokingly sticks out a hand to shake with a branch along the roadside, and though no bigger than his thumb, it holds him fast; and then suddenly more stately branches move in swaying menacingly : and in desperate panic he takes his knife and cuts off his own hand and flees bleeding to the village. – On 29. 10. 1729. – "Downright eerie –" said Lore jauntily and cast wiry eyes about her : I nodded distractedly.

"What's a pochette –" asked Grete in embarrassment, as if it might be something offensive; I looked up, and she read the passage : a count living nearby had had a birthday; big celebration, dance and music : "Oh I see !" I said, and sketched the tiny dancing-master's fiddle for them : "something like this . . . . So –". Once again : "La poche : the pocket; pocket fiddle; thus the smallest version of the viola." And since they were looking at me so disconsolately, we took a quick trip through the whole family : gambas, viola d'amore, their power and quality, but rapidly, for night was on its way, and Schrader was re- morseless; the rock on which you build churches.

I raised my burly hand : they fell silent in the yellow-black light, and I read the breathtaking report :

"To day, the day of Invocavit, the following incidents befell : a band of fifteen lads and lasses in their finest dress, all of a mind to hear the Word of God, on the way thereto did observe by the side of the road a gayly clad Creature, of pale and sweet countenance and slender linea- ments, who, however, did not answer to their salutations, but only stared at the country-folk from out her cold, keen eyes, and, when forced within their closed circle, did execute most strange gesti to fend them off, always taking anxious care to keep within the shade of that wood of evil repute, which is called Brand's Heath. Upon repeated Christian reminders to join them in approaching the Table of the Lord, the aforesaid Creature merely laughed a most ringing laugh, seeking also with all its power to escape the circle, which two sturdier yeomen the while prevented; for by this time it had grown malicious, threaten- ing with diverse gesticulations, and finally from amidst its pleasing features, it stuck out an enormous, redhaired tongue, in such a manner that all those present started, whereat said Creature smiled subtilly once more at those ringed round it, then sprang back into its precincts, crying out several times over the word cannae, and in between, by report of the Steward who was also present, the name of Carolus Magnus (?) was twice heard. Item, a young yeoman, previously known for his precocious and extravagant behaviour, undertook to pursue the Creature into the wood, and of him there has been no trace to the present day . . ." I stared at Lore : the pale wild face : I whispered : "Show me your tongue; – okay ?" and it emerged like a rose petal, pointed and of most disquieting agility.

I looked at them both; I said : "So *that's why* the old man assured me that No One went in there !" And Grete, with a spontaneous yawn, promised to inquire about it among her co-workers. Yawned again : the poor thing had to be up very early for work ! I got up stiffly and collected the books : "I'll handle the rest over at my place : you two sleep ! – And many thanks ! –" Smiled. (For they were waiting for our new evening salutation); I lifted up my soul : "May all creatures be free of pain !"; and they answered with quiet conviction : "May all creatures be free of pain . . ."

Toothpowder : guaranteed harmless : says the label ! (How droll was our world of '46 : not pleasant-tasting, for instance, or a super-cleanser, or with Radium G – no, no : just plain harmless !). And I grinned till my cheeks hurt : y' couldn't find a soup bowl to buy, but if you turned over the death mask of the inconnue de la Seine, 38 marks 50, you could use it for one. "And behold it was all good !" (Ahh, enough of that crap !).

Night (if only you had something to drink). I sat off to myself by the garish light of the hundred-watt bulb, studying the old signs : wonder if my hand will last 200 years ? Lore was with me, though she fell asleep at once : the Nymphe cannae ! Cannae; cannae : Hold it right here : children, maliciously throwing stones and garbage into the woods, are frightened : by sounds, by things in motion (vast forms, that move phantastically; great Brother Poe). Puzzlements come riding the brook out of the woods, like toys; green, wooden, high-pitched wee pipes; little winged horses with embroidered velvet saddlecloths; the baker in Krumau, in town, had got an order to prepare cakes and deliver them at wood's edge come midnight, where an old gentleman in a pointed, fiery-red hat paid him and at once waved for masked servants : beautiful ! I thought of Procopius of Caesarea : Bell. Goth. IV, 20, and Konrad Mannert : I thank you, I thank you for much knowledge : why do asses like Wilhelm get the monuments and not Konrad Mannert ? !

An arrow (have you ever stolen books ?) : I would like to be an arrow, in flight, toward anywhere, Littrow, Wonders of the Heavens. (Outside, that is).

I stood in the darkness like a simple post; from Brand's Heath came wind, casual and vital, blew forever above me, post planted in darkness. From my room monotoned the artificial light : alright : back in !

The blank ones : again little dappled children beside the road, who mischievously asked to be taken along : so the report of farmer Nieber on 24. 6. 1727 : and how they laughed ! Till the clodhopper got the willies, flailed into his defenseless nags, and galloped off to Westensen (see map). – Oh, yet another report from the interior : the solemnity of the columned woods, draped in fog (cursing the local inhabitants, Beck, Felsch, refugees were forced into the trees !).

The paths into it were constantly shifting : I pondered, frowning, geodatic-cool : good, I would step off the distances, and inventory the whole area; make a diopter. – Wind banged on the window and pro tested : okay, no diopter then ! – And read on (Because Schrader wants his books back tomorrow ! Implacable as the Inquisition : just read Maximilian Klinger : The History of Raphael de Aquilla : now that's a book ! Not like Sartre's trash !)

Auen the gardener : I leaped up from my brutally tortured backside, from my footstool : I pulled the scratched lens from my breast pocket : if this be true, then my young life till now makes sense ! – I went out to the entryway and drank two gulps from the dripping tap : sure to be asleep over there : Lore !

Outside : lions and dragons in the sky.

I followed my finger, woodenly lining the lines : In a footman's apron and flowered hat : that was how he had flown from the woods on 24 November 1720, as if driven by the wind. Had fled to the pastor, one eye bloodshot. After numerous appeals and prudent measures, including reports to the consistory, Overbeck had been able to glean little coherent information : but it did not fall short of, much less wide of, his not knowing enough (like all theologians). It was just a good thing that he had taken notes : there was much talk about the nut of the Princess Babiole, which O. particularly supplied with question marks, . . .

But it is this : Around about . . . –teen-hundred, the Princess Babiole, fleeing from King Magot and a marriage very little to her liking, had cracked a hazel nut given her as a present : "Out tumbled a host of little architects, carpenters, masons, joiners, upholsterers, painters, sculptors, *gardeners* (yes indeed : gardeners, Herr Overbeck ! That's the point !) etc., who in moments built for her a magnificent palace with the most beautiful gardens (sic !) in the World. On every side it shimmered with gold and azure. A splendid feast was brought forth; 60 Princesses, more finely arrayed than queens, led by their Cavaliers and with their Squires in train, received the lovely Babiole with grand compliments and led her into the banquet hall. After the feast, her treasurers brought her 15,000 chests full of gold and diamonds, with which she paid the workmen and artisans who had erected for her such a beautiful palace, but upon one condition : that they build a City posthaste and take up residence therein. This then happened directly, and the City was ready within three quarters of an hour, notwithstanding that it was five times larger than Rome . . ." (That of course is an exaggeration !)

I propped my hands against the table (Grete had procured it : goode Grete !) : so old Auen had been expelled from Brand's Heath, a plant-spirit, an elf-child : that was why he had always kept so cleverly silent about his birthday ! (He had come from that nut, too : how long had he been in there : how did he get in it ? ! – For I had no more intention of doubting it than if I had been Don Sylvio ! : I beg you : it was fully documented after all : I had 5 dozen under cellophane myself !)

An elf-child : ah, were I but one, and not born at Rumpffsweg 27, III floor, of concrete parents (are there not two senses of the word ?) –
I kept on leafing for a long time, but less attentively : for what could follow now; and sleep was gliding about the room : "elfin" is actually an ugly word; "fin"; reminds you of something fishy, skeletal, of Cimmerian rattlings, I snapped with my skeletal teeth.

Moorburn : there had been considerable moorburn in those days, I gazed sleepily into the year. That was a word from my childhood; silently the gray Octoberal weft had come over me as a boy, from the north, northwest, northeast; I knew how you can stand and freeze out in empty potato fields, tilled moor : I steadfastly expected such phenomena from life, and only nodded as they came marching out of old books. I strode to my bunk, tossed back the rough blankets, kyss meg i reva. –

She came out of the door and said as if in surprise : "Good morning –"; "And is that all ? !" I replied dolefully, so that she nimbly slipped inside for a minute.

Schrader : like so many people, he had the conceit that his mail was especially urgent (whereas it all came down to mere Enthusiasmus, to use Brucker's clever phrase !); because for every piece of junk he had a poor chump of a catechumen clatter off to Krumau on an ancient girl's bike : – I went over : he wasn't there (Fine, doesn't get his files till tomorrow then !)
"Well now, how are we doing ?" in maternal tones (while listening, as always, with one ear cocked to the simmering java-pot); well, I can be stubborn too : "Fine !" I assured the baggage, and flattered tauntingly :

"Your son's doing well ? !" : and saw him breakfasting in the kitchen with the radio on : happy brute ! With no effort at all, could hold back the tears when it heard the music of Chevalier Gluck : those must be some gods (and I the ass !). She assumed I was sniffing for a cup of her wispy brew, and peevishly offered it : but I made my self very scarce ! ! –

Over there too : Lore watched clouded me, puzzling over my face; finally she asked with solicitous caution : "Does music always do this to you ?" I implored : "LORE : –" broke off; : "yes" I said bitterly : "Art in general ! – You see, for me it's not one of life's ornaments, rococo relaxation to be greeted affably after a day of hard work; I'm inverted on this : for me it's my very breath, the one thing necessary, and all else is excretion and a latrine. As a young man : I was 16 when I resigned from your club. What bores you : Schopenhauer, Wieland, the Campanian Valley, Orpheus : is axiomatic happiness to me; what you find so wildly exciting : swing, films, Hemingway, politics : pisses me off. – You simply can't imagine; but you can see it doesn't make me more "bloodless" or "papery" than your sort : I get just as excited and enthused, and know monsters, and hate." Pause : another topic : ". . . and love . . . !" I concluded gallantly. "You're lying !" she said indignantly : "you love either Wieland or me . . ."; I proved to her manually that one can unite both, until in exhaustion she believed it : ". . . and you think you're an intellectual . . . !" she said maliciously : "besides, you need a shave." – "That's my thanks ! !"

Mail : Lore held it out to me : tolle, lege, and I "unsealed" the brown letter : it's all crap ! – Then Grete arrived and we could eat; she had brought horseburger from Krumau : you got double rations for one coupon. Ingenious preparation; seasoned more highly ("That's our last onion, fella !") : there they sat and tasted leerily; but gradually the suspicious faces brightened, crispies crunched, and I looked about defiantly : " – ? –". "Never would have thought it !" Lore said stoutly, and the little one nodded : "We'll do this more often – ah, if just for once you could – –"; to get her thinking more profitable thoughts I asked (which I should have done long since) about a typewriter. "Have you finished something ? !" and she was curious, but I waved that off : first the typewriter : then you'll be the first to read it ! – Ahyes, the typewriter ! Coldingen, Westensen, Rodegrund. Krumau : "If at all, then at the plant, but they're so . . ." "The only one here is in the village office"; and, theoretically, Apel was in charge there, Apel, the great viscownt : "Well, actually, he ought to . . . !" (I'll give it a try).

Toward evening : "Come dancing with us, Lore !" (Bauer, as if lacquered;

while Grete inconspicuously threaded a needle); her answer from the cheap wood easy-chairlet was clear : "Nah – We're going for a walk later." and gazed at me thoughtfully; he respectfully raised his "finely drawn" brows (which looked odd with his bald head) and bowed many times in confusion : right, beat it !

Soccer : "Old-timers" were playing. A little urchin rode by on his bike and jeered encouragement to the local boys : "Give 'em hell ! The goalie's Old Nick !" And that was aimed at the scrawny 45-year-old veteran from Krumau. – We grinned and walked on beneath the salmon-hued, the silky-yellow, chilly-green, frozen-blue sky, until the smooth roads grew desolate, and echoed. And had much to talk about : how when we were small : a Maecenas would've been good for me (just so long as there was no horacement); how we would like to be sleep virtuosi in winter : when just once every 4 weeks a surly face would appear at the window; sat a spell in Brand's Heath : "You'll have to write a story about it : but a sweet one ! Not one from your rabid box !" (Because she had read my Leviathan). A sweet one then; and I was softhearted and promised.

"If you find the world's sweetest song / : bring it along ! : Bring it along ! : a humming maiden's hand in mine. – –

Sunday morning : "I've got the most dangerous rival there is" she said : "– : an idealized Lore, who's all wild spirit. Flesh too, sure." – "Only the rarest of men do that" Grete muttered in embarrassment : "don't they usually want just the latter . . ?" Sighed. – I lifted her hand from the bowl (of infrequent beans and carrots), and kissed her wrist. – Sky patched gray. – "You still have to see Schrader !"; "Get out of my hearing !" I said, jolted : I had almost forgotten that !

Automatically I stared at Apel's listless bays : *just once* to eat till my tummy's full ! ! : mashed potatoes, Knorrs bouillon cubes, a pickle, and a roast with it : horseburger full (i.e., a pound at least ! – Oh, hell : two !) I swallowed : well, I'll never know the feeling again ! Deep melancholy engulfed me, and I went into

the house : pervaded at once by the odor of Moravian slogans ! A harmonium drawled a chorale (Christian pops : one of their musical hits or other : nasty things were said of a God : that he had in fact created the world. And we must therefore lift up our thanks; – or kneel down to pray, what do I know !) Nope, I made military creases in my face, and assumed an indifferent position along the river of time : you know what you know; I don't care if the last judgment, along with the last night-court judge, does come : they won't find anything at my place !

"Won't you come in ? !" We smiled ever so elaborately, oh so elaborately. Hmm, hmmm. – A chessboard of flint, polished : that at least was lovely ! : "Very lovely, Herr Schrader !" –
And praise of old Kügelgen : his joy was downright touching, that for once we were in harmony.

Le retour of the parish registers : he gave a sour smile : "Yes, yes – : to this day, my dear parishioners believe every jot and tittle of it. – Just recently, one fellow – ah, best church attendance in the parish for that matter ! – watched as his parked bike took off down the fire lane all by itself and then came back . . . ." (I nodded appreciatively : that I would like to have seen !) He nevertheless did not succeed (just as I never do) in convincing me of my immortality.

Valentinians : oh, I could oblige him with unpleasant details : systems of emanation (why else in fact would I have owned the Brucker ? – who was the first to recognize the connections, even the niggardly Schopenhauer called him "doughty" !) – "Wouldn't you care to read from the Word of God ?" – "Do you have that ? !" I asked with such curiosity and ingenious zeal that he settled for a pursed smile : he had my number : "Well then" he said sidetracking : "You're still young : many – and strange – are the ways that lead to God . ." And we made small talk : all we needed were an SS man and a stigmatic; a whore, an adder and a lawyer : and the party would have been complete (9:22 : oh you clock hands, tireless servants : if only I had a watch !) Luther : "the fool desireth the perversion of all sodomiticall kind . ." Even Schrader gave a muffled laugh. – A woman liberated me : she wept with experience, might I say : in streams (if the pleonasm weren't so wild). Well, one certainly has sufficient opportunity in life to learn to sob. – Exit (With Shakespeare it's always : enter three murderers . .) Well then : Exit.

Liberty and impudence : in German there is only one letter difference : Freiheit and Frechheit – Patched gray again : the sky.

"There are hard-rubbery souls, who can refrain from tears when gazing at a hyperbola . . ." Even Grete started : "You could say infinity just as well" I explained sullenly : Oh, Christian von Massenbach ! (Because in point of fact there is no infinity : how much better off we would be when . . .)

Bauer was on vacation : God be gracious unto me a poor sinner ! !

adversus mathematicos : (although I'm one myself !) : I had said : in 900 out of 1000 cases . . . "You mean 9:10" he simplified : I slammed my eyes on the blockhead : "900 out of 1000 is *not* the same thing ! !" I said rough-hewn. "And how's that ?" the nose-it-all asked with a smile. "Well, just stop and think about it –" I replied gruffly : "it's bad enough if you teach that to the kids. – And 9000 out of 10,000 is better still." (And only Somebody who still hasn't realized that the most important factor in life is happiness could look like that !) : "If someone fired a shot at you every day, with the ratio 9:10 you'd be in the happy hunting-grounds by day 10 for sure : but with 1000 chances you might age another 2½ years : because that in fact presupposes that there are 1000 chances !" "Aha" he said amazed : "then reducing fractions is purest fiction . . ." "Well, not exactly fiction –" I said charitably : "you simply have to know . . . ."; he was awaiting revelations and sat there with expectant eyes, but likewise didn't dare press me in my elaborate musings : thus nothing came of his revelations : so there !

This may last long : he had got around to "the meaningful general" (as Goethe would have expressed it : and at his age he should have known that only the meaningful particular has meaning !) – and I unobtrusively began to guilloche the edge of my tome : you could sense time meandering off in spirals (meanwhile spontaneously thinking of stocks and bonds and other pleasant things : an old typewriter asdf jklö; the sky was getting damned musty too, and the horseflies were risking one dive after the other. Thunderstorm coming.).

"So what ? !" I shouted ! "Let me tell you something, Herr Bauer : let's hope the occupation lasts 50 years ! – Don't try to tell me that Hitler rigged those 98% victories at the polls : he didn't have to ! The way they all delighted in epaulettes and cunningly concocted ranks, in the rumble of marching feet and snappy obedience. (Führer command : we obey ! : Is there anything more disgusting than begging for orders ? ! Make me sick, Germans : No sir ! ! –). And every Hitler Youth applicant, every SA jock or off. cand. (he flinched !) had no problem whatever thinking of himself as a potential Führer ! –"

"Had never heard anything different, poor things ?!" : "First of all : they had ! !" – And then : "Try preaching to them the ideal of the tranquil life, of diligent scholarship ! That it would be sufficient for them if they could preserve and pass on the great values of German culture : will they ever give you an earful !" (Nietzsche knew all about it : *and* approved and sympathized ! Which means he's part of the coarsest rabble ! : how does he put it so elegantly : ask some coarse hedgehog on the road, whether he would perhaps like to be a better or wiser hedgehog, and he'll give you an ironic smile; but whisper an auspicious : do you want more power ? ! ! ! : and will those little eyes ever shine ! !)

"Unfortunately, Herr Bauer ! : we're just a pawn for them as well (the Allies); if they need us to fight the Russians in 5 or 10 years, they'll put

us back in uniform, set us down under the nose of the professional man-slaughterers who're on the scrap heap for now, and : away we go ! "Semper fidelis . . . !" –

"Yes : it's true –" I hissed, "great Friedrich did wear his tricorne even at night ! !"; he left at once, for he had asked whether "Lore" was awake yet. –

The day bunched together on high; objects of iron boomed : bright gray rags dangled and flew on ahead; gusts fell emitting howls of foliage-hair (the copper beech in Schrader's yard looked as swarthy as boiled red cabbage – a Homeric image).

The bushes moved in a crouch along the ground, supplely thumping their branches; jumped up and down eagerly; hunching low, I went around the house to the washyard : below they were playing soccer by the naked rosy-blue thrusts of lightning : pretty racy, huh ? ! Then the rain thudded against the black-echoing gravel (and distance vanished) : the bouncing drops sprang as high as my belt !

Washyard (we three, for it had passed) : things up close were cast in clear thunderstorm hues : an oddly skewed and trembling bright green, deftly dripping : and below they were playing soccer again; the colorful jerseys gleamed prettily : pink and white; and cobalt-blue and yellow. (Maybe there is a point to soccer after all : animation of the landscape ? – But the cities lie in ruins ! !) – "And come evening they drink and dance at Willi Kopp's : a gift of the gods, a psyche like that !" – "Are they supposed to do nothing but fret and lament ? !" she asked with mocking obstinance :

"No !" – "But they should be more serious !"

Inside : the weather-maker cleverly pitted Iceland low against Azores high; "shifting westwards"; "winds tending to the east . ." – : "Twaddle on and tell us . . !" Lore said menacingly; finally it was revealed that for the next two days we could reckon with good weather; "occasional thunderstorms" however : "ding . ." sounded the Hamburg chronometric signal.

"I'll set the alarm" she decided : "we'll get up at 2 and be on our way at once, that'll get us back by 5, and not a soul will see a thing." "Have you got the sack – ?" : it was a crazy ragtag patchwork, and with no solid seam : damn it all ! "Use the good thread !" "Okay, and now get out : sleep !"

"The knife –" I heard Grete say nervously from inside the house : "have you got the little knife to cut with . . ?" "Just hope nothing happens to you two ! !"

Sound sleep is difficult, when you've been through so much, have worries, aren't a soccer player : if it hadn't been for my sister . . . . : and then I thought a lot about our common childhood : bless Her : blessed be Mrs. Kiesler : bless Her ! – Good deeds today : set a stranger on the right path – (actually I've never lied much, or broken my word, more than was absolutely necessary; rarely for the joy of deception. : if someone can say that of himself, it's quite sufficient, particularly in light of the normal state of this meilleurs des mondes : haven't another scruple about it, either !) And am supposed to get some sleep ! !

"Damna- . . . . : oh, that's it. – Yes : just a sec, Lore !"

Voilà : an uncombed morning-man yawning : the masterpiece of the demiurge, 'tis said – well, that's not me !

"Have you got everything ? ! –" "Yes" from the kissed whispering mouth : we tiptoed out the tiny entryway.

On the silver kraal of the moon crouched a lion-yellow starriness, bushmanlike, in the yard. Our wretched refugee garb took flight, divinely folded by the wind; down the black church steps, all Christians lay drugged in their curtained chambers : freedom, freedom : hands chained together, we sprang out onto the road to Blakenhof. – "Lore –" : at once she laid her forearms on my shoulders, oh Nymphe Cannae, we stammered and looked deeper still into pure faces, deep in the night. Us – eye-candescences.

"Children –, oh Lore : they live in ³/₄ slavery. Parents have no right : they only wanted intercourse, and we were the most unwelcome of all, to the tune of curses . .''; I was shuddering with rage, and my Lore : my : Lore answered between her teeth : "Hey ! do you think I wasn't an unsuccessful abortion ? ! – My parents would rather have seen a wolf in the parlor than me, Lore ! !" Ah, my she-wolf ! Our teeth bumped, purest tablets of ivory, her hair flowed in my hands, and a noise stepped from the woods on our right : oh my noise ! – We jumped and glided onto the appletree path.

"Psst !" – "Not so loud . . ." – "Isn't it about full ? –" – "I love you : hey !" – "You !" – – "Enough, don't you think : ?" – I reached for a few more red-cheekies, droplings, like Mining and Lining : "My dear friend, that's it : – lord, I can't pick it up ! ! –" I did get it up, my bones would have raised a mountain (or so I imagined) : and the hundredweight soared : ". . . and now home ! . . ." Amid giggles in the stumblewood.

Greasy-livered Galsworthy ! : "The Patrician" : I mean, talk about self-made problems (as if English society itself were one ! – And we stood like junipers on Brand's Heath ! ! – Whew !) – "Typhoid shots next month : series of three !" – "We'll go together, Lore : together" she at once laid her forearms around my poor neck, and our eyes burned into each other's, blue into gray : why was there no wind to mingle our hair ?

Women's frigidity : "Lore : every-man can manage with one woman : but it definitely has to be the right one. – (And she has to know that she's not going to be saddled with a kid every time : Lore, my Lore !)" – The mushrooms gushed fiery red out of the mossy ground : we pruned them with delicate little knives, you could hardly see them in the darkness.

The woods : "Do you know – Lore : where are you ? ! : oh there : – do you know Hiller's "The Hunt" ? – Oh, then you know nothing about Der Freischütz !" Hiller, Johann Adam, † 1804 : – "Lord, I'd love to have a memory like yours !" – "It's nothing, Lore, it's nothing : I've been punished with it : think of the dreams !" (Explained to her that I know every dream of the night, all of it, can multiply two 40-digit numbers in my head : that's a curse; I'm a cursed man : Olé !)

How brightly beams the morning star (Schrader considered it an old German and/or Latin chorale ! – And I still maintain : people know nothing, because they spend 40 years gabbing instead of learning). The trees lent fixed shade; Lore in deep shade : "Are you still there ?" – "Yes : my love !" – Ah, you deep voice : "Ho on, ho en, hos erchetai / Theos hemon eulogetai / nai amen halleluya ! / Theos monos tris hagistos / pater ho epouranios / ho huios kai to pneuma . ." (sounded good, Greek, although the sense of it was probably crap, please turn over !)

Moon (still above our mushroom spot) a delicate sign in the earliest morning sky (like a candle in water : – lovely but meaningless, that image. Nevertheless : like a candle in water !) And the sack was heavy, so that I groaned (but restrainedly) and the sweat ran down my red-spotted face. : "If only we hadn't taken so many !" (concerned). I smiled at her : there walked a nymph wrapped in the wind sounds.

"There are people – moral monstrosities, and their number is larger than one assumes – whom one can only describe, but no longer understand : I once saw a man eat a Wiener schnitzel and mashed potatoes, with bouillon and egg to start and flummery to finish, sat there reading Dostoyevsky's House of the Dead for one whole hour, and concentrated : – to be sure, he was a manager in the textile industry . . ."

From the chorizon, clearest yellow meddled (I wished that I smelled of hay, and not of human, goat. –) She froze stiff in the blueberry shrubs : I in the fir-ness : Someone was coming through the forest – "Psssssst –" (piercing) : Someone was coming – –

Ah : the old man : I threw back my shoulders, expanded my 45-inch chest, brandished my credentials : the oaken club he had given me – : "Oh –

it's you –" he said jovially, and Lore arose seductively out of the blue-
berries; he smiled and nodded : "Well then – – ah : Herr Gaza –" he
introduced the thin gray figure at his side : we shook moist hands and
smiled our confusion and distrust. "Berries and mushrooms – ?" he
asked authoritatively – : "well fine : but always cut 'em off cahrful, and
no tramplin' things down : y' heah ? ? !" A few raindrops fell about us
matutines; with his large rimy eyes he measured me and Lore, my
Lore, me and me; he spoke quite softly : he shook his mighty head as
he did : he was not pleased : "Octobah : Octobah . . ." he raised a
pointed hand; I shook the hand.

I would like to be like the sky : early in the morning (I mean really early;
and not around 5 when farmers get up !) – I wheezed and had to put it
down six times; despite most gritted teeth and Lore's presence : and
icy rosy air : I've had it ! !

Céladon facades, black-eyed (and let him rise up against me who has read
and enjoyed Astrée : and it too was once a best-seller !)

Sang lady-psalms in a nasally voice (that's not malice on my part : it
sounded truly abominable : a refugee in Blakenhof). And since we're
speaking of twice-told tales : the Persian Wars in modern dress,
journalistics :
"We're standing down here at the Hellespont : since early this morning, 4 A.M., the army of the great King has been marching over the
pontoon bridge, whose architect is standing here next to me : "Might I
ask, Mr. Megasthenes, how long the job actually took . . . ?" (And may
God strike these journalists, I insist : whenever we humans cause ourselves grief : with yet another war, more cripples and refugees ! There
they are crowing and making merry : "Exchange of fire on the 38th
parallel !"; for the formulation alone they deserve to be castrated ! –
Turn your stomach !)

In the shed : 1 hundredweight of stolen apples (and my shrouds began to
shudder. But wee Grete laughed : goode Grete –), and shoved us off to
bed.

Hasty sleep : multifissured; at one point I was riding with her in a train
between Görlitz and Dresden; at some deserted station we jumped
down onto the fist-sized gravel of the embankment, and scurried off
into the gleaming long-needled woods; dipped our feet in the firm
grass, set up a tent beneath a fir; between Görlitz and Dresden.

Waters plunging : right side of throat and ear hurt when I swallow; are
thicker too (and turn my head-stocking around and sleep that way).

Country lanes over hills : the sand was dull yellow but firm, and the two
deep ruts were not a bother as yet; and I was soon up top and saw how

the heavy waves of wood fell away on all sides, vaulted gently; was only gloss and green of many hues, snap and mild. The sun, too, was playing a dark game with me; as I was coming up the hill, it stood cold and eventidal almost behind distant blue-cast clouds : now it or another appeared again behind me at high noon, and hot as well; so I walked lightly on (a swollen-fine pain in my ear), into a dell, and up. And the wagon tracks turned off into pure inconsequence : 'tis better always to walk alone than ride with the many; and the clear, sparse-grassed path was much the lovelier; the firs on high flexed their healthy red wrestler arms, hirsute green; I wafted slowly in the gold-streaked silence that for beauty surpasses much understanding. When the path had quite drizzled away, I banished myself to a clearing : above, blue glimmerings with golden unendurable; the air around me waited so hot, that I gently mindlessly hovered off through new brush, around brown-skinned tree beauties : rough and chaste and hot and fine-limbed, they flowed about, behind, and backwards. Long time was I so, shining shade, beforested, when a free spacious hill grew up, whose rim I easily climbed : and stood on the broad terrace of an old castle. Here and there I saw stone figures, little crude cherubim on the massive balustrades; the flagstones of the court were mortised with delicate lines of moss, summer desolation and aging silence; I strode over to the very high arch of the arm-coated portal, looked down the mighty many-windowed facade (and a sharp pain in my throat sundered head and torso); then light of foot I entered . . . .

Naive blue-eyed sky : "Damn, don't come down sick now !" she warned in dismay, and Grete was alarmed as well : "Oh my. – – And you haven't even got insurance !", and in their melancholy clear eyes stood the poor man's constant fear of expense and life-consuming toil. They laid hands on me : fever ! But although I really felt a bit woozy, I wagged my cheeks flippantly : "'d be a miracle if I wasn't –" I said obligingly : "– after all that drudgery; but it's hardly that bad yet." I swallowed painfully, and they noticed, and after some hesitation Grete said : "You still have some cigarettes . . ." "Two packs." Pause; to be sure, we needed them badly. "Maybe if you had something to drink" Grete proposed helplessly : "they say that works for men . . ."; and Lore nodded too, old routinieuse : "Go see Apel in a bit; you can give him a pack for it, and then you go lie down, sweat it out. – That was quite a feat –" she turned to the other : "Just think : lugging over a hundred pounds for almost 4 miles ! On our diet !" I yielded, although it was a mean thing to do, for it would be at the cost of the poor things' diet; you end up a damn ex-human !) "But they're all out in the field now –" Grete sang out eagerly (had ruefully recalled all my good deeds it seemed) : "Take my bike !" Okay. "And go sit in the sun for now !" Okay.

A Bohemian : with a fiddle, a bass drum on his back (that he used an ankle rope to beat), and on his head a little jingling johnny : providing "arty" music and kept coming closer and closer, making my throat ache with every boom. Of course he was from Jablonetz/Nissa (he began at the "b'ginnin'") ate tomatoes, which he called "love apples", and conversed with me a bit : "Street musicians do get around a lot !" I agreed in torment, and told him about Vermann the trumpeter, who indeed lies buried in the Great Pagoda of Lin-Sing. Until it was all too silly for him. (As he had long since been for me); and I went back to writing in the eilikrineia.

Then Bauer arrived : always one damn thing after another; smiled superciliously when he saw the piece of green tricot wrapped at my cheeks (and my throat grew ever sorer; I can hardly gulp or speak !); and he rustled in the wind :

"You, man, not one word against Jean Paul !" I said with an effort; he looked at me nettled : "Why call me ‹human› – ? !" and forced an elegant smile. "Because I want to remind you that we're speaking of spirits : he belongs to a different order of magnitude than – you" (I was being downright crass : I intentionally did not say "we" : why doesn't he just beat it, and leave me alone with my memories of Titan and Palingenesien ! – But nobody home : he was used to it apparently.)

Showed me his new shirt, God knows ! and I examined the ninny's delicately patterned sleeve : "As if manufactured by Aristotle himself," I managed in weary praise; gave him the fright of his life : his eyes queried : Aristotle ? but I passed over it in exhaustion. – "Whoever is no better than his boss, is no subordinate." – "You have to be inferior enough to be a boss, is that it – ?" he suggested ironically; I nodded so indifferently that he got quite angry (whereas I didn't give a hoot about most any topic today !) – Great men : "Only he who takes hold of life vigorously, who constructively changes the world : can be truly great !" he maintained (so he saw violent action as the criterion). "Alexander !" defiant; "Ludwig Tieck" I said swollen; "Bismarck ! !" he shouted bravely; (and my ear tormented me); "Fritz Viereck" I whispered : he listened, his brow barricaded by wrinkles; he soon left, came back.

Pause (lovely !)

"Who was this" (emphatic) : *"Viereck* !". "You look it up in the encyclopedia ?" I asked, curious and frailly envious; he nodded cold and

under control, surly and princely; : "Ahyes – Viereck – –" I mused,
shook my head, distracted, turned up an invisible coat collar (he noticed and left for good) : that had been the most excellent rum I've ever
known; we had revered the fellow virtually as a god : Fritz Viereck,
Stettin . . . . . . :

"Once upon a time at the court of Eisenach –" : Les contes de Hoffmann
(and wasn't it Herbert Ernst Groh ? !). "Well, how you doing ? !" Lore
called to sunshined me : "Better ? ?" I shook my head, so that she
immediately came out to little-old-headscarved-lady me, and crouched
down beside me : and we gazed at each other like that till I asked :
"Don't look at me, Lore : I look so foolish !" "What a grouch !" she
said in exasperation, but turned her head anyway : it was the truth !
I stood up, shook off the scarf, and said loudly, wincing : "I'll give
the viscount a try."; she silently got the bike out for me, and I flew
elegantly down the hill (until I was out of sight : when my ear caught
the draft of the ride, so that tears ran, pox and damnation !)

They brewed and tasted : it was a regular party, all well-heeled, home-
owner types : and Apel received me boisterously : "Hey !" – Could use
"American fags" now and forever ! " 'll get you a beah-bottle full ! – ?
– 'll take fifteen minutes : we'ah jest ventilatin' it !" (and so went in
with him)

V-2 juice : (during the war they'd made that stuff too in Krumau where
Grete worked); you only needed to aerate and carbon-filter it for a
couple of hours to remove the benzene, and voilà, you had the finest
firewater ! (i.e. it would thwack you between the shoulders as you
drank, but they said the effect was : grand !) They sat and glowered.
Was introduced, to lots of gaping yaps, a steaming white-papered peg
sticking out of each : may God rebuke England and you goldbrickers
(because these grangers were once again skimming off the cream :
during the war they spent more time at home than with us out there,
and now they're the only ones eating their fill again, and taking in
trade whatever the rest of the population has left. The other day one
of them said to Grete, when she arrived with a can of coffee : all
he needed now was a carpet for his cow shed ! May they croak, the
swine ! All farmers ! – The middle high Germans called them villân : it
was official knowledge that farmer and villain were synonymous !)

Course : all "old soldiers !" : one of them, already drunk, did the 1914
parade-march for a cigarette : da buffa buffa buffa-buff ! : the faces
rumbled with laughter, spiky hands pointed at the old nitwit, oh you
abdominal rabble : with lies from the depth of crusted souls; manly
smuttings; and went on longer and longer. They all had "tall" tales,

screaming, and step on the gas, till the hell-hole stank : our sort can't even produce contrails like those : what from ! Apel, half stewed, drove out to the field again, and his friend bungled on : "86 proof" he said proudly to me, scholars among themselves right, and the hydrometer bobbed in the vat : "Well : heah 'tis !" : and he even banged me on the shoulder, patronizing and benevolent : may your hand rot off !

On a white stone : on a white stone (with a cheery number on it; and thus a milestone beside Brand's Heath). Another swig : it tasted ghastly; but the spook rose up in my belly hot and obstreperous, and my throat no longer hurt : so much : that is : to hell with it ! In the last light of dusk ! Another ? : Sure : another ! (Because it was only half empty, and would be enough for another time. – But I was already tottering very nicely, swaying : well, who cares !) – The bike was leaning with very round wheels against the tree, I had polished all the spokes to a shine : could I still stand up ? Behind me someone said grumpily : "Well now – !"; I didn't even look around at first; I eagerly explained : "It has to be, dear friends : I am, you see, defective somehow. – I'll move on at once !" and walked over to the circular cycle (no feeling left in my face : so high as a kite !) Looking precociously around, he came over to me and gazed into my face; the swollen cheek, the tongue : nothing pleased him today : "Y' bettah take cahr o' that," he said in rebuke : "shake a leg and get y' home and into bed : not sumpin' to fool round with in times like these !" (Not with my bed : you're right there !) But he meant well; the stars made their rounds : roundabout and inside me the old cognac pump beat me with something like a fist : I gave him a firm handshake : ! : nodded and walked the bike out to the middle of the road : no shallow mind, that Schmidt, is he ? !

Riding on a bike : ssst ! – That was a stone, a stonelet, a pebble; pipelike shoved lightning legs : and stewed to the gills ! Yuckyuckyuckyuck-yuck : I made such a Flemish face at Apel, the Great Viscownt, in his oxcart, that he leaped up churly and snapped at the pausing air : O Calf of Moses ! !

The jagged moon : sawed away in the snoring clouds, till it scattered milky dust : sagflis is the word in Norge : I was there once; my hard mouth puckered out a scornful puff : all so long ago. (To be 17, 18 once again) I swung my body, left leg as the axis (the right wasn't worth much anymore, from the war !) and loaded myself across the square.

And wouldn't you know, there stood Bauer at the window ! : I clattered the kickstand, and walked over to the pair : I finished him off with a daggered glance, and a drunken " 'vnin' ", to which I attempted to give the tone of a grave insult. I turned to her; I said : "I love you !" (As a greeting, straight out !); she didn't answer; so I turned around again : wounded : God knows, you ought to collect Fouqué material and *nothing else* ! Now she called out : "Herr Schmidt . . ."; I whirled around : it had been Grete ! And Shorsh laughed, equivocal and incontinent : we'll settle accounts another time, Messer Agricola ! "Oh, I see" I said ingenuously : "Beg your pard'n . . ."; went inside and leaned against the wall for fifteen minutes, whispering. Then I put all my clothes on (because I had really started to freeze again now) and rolled up (Let's hope the wetting-down helped !)

Didn't get up until noon : to make up for it, I didn't wash either. "Yes, I'm better !" (wasn't at all to speak of !) – In the mail some more lengthy book fliers : all they were printing now were safe old hits from 20–30 years ago. Some of them passable (even though our literature has been dead since Stifter and Storm); most of them, however, just pimps of poesy. Hamsun's "Mysteries" one of the passables; and I remembered : but had what you might call technically "overdeveloped" characters – not because he had managed superhuman, grand personalities, never fear ! – but it's all too long : you know no more about the characters after 300 pages than you already knew after 100; I call that overdeveloped, or more simply stated : too much pointless chatter. Hachoo ! (Give me Gordon Pym : when krakens like that appear, you're in deep seas; not with Hamsun the Nazi. – I can still see him, how with cane swinging and over 80, but still none the wiser, he courted the German guests, visited their U-boat, and enthused over the "blond beast". He isn't much of a poet either : Maybe I'll back it up in detail someday; I'm too sick now : and once again : hachoo !)

At their place : "Well – ?" I drew myself up, hands in my pockets : "Doing alright again"; but was happier sitting on the planks of the window seat; the book on the table : Mathilde Erhard's Cookbook. (Grete had borrowed it from madame Schrader : why in the world !) Read recipes, for a long lecherous while : take a 4-pound saddle of venison; for a tiered cake 70 (sic !) eggs; soap is easily made from the ample fat left over in our kitchens : we would have wolfed it down straight; with illustrations of a good home-cooking kitchen around 1900; care of the wine cellar : and here I had simply stuck my bottle in the crate; so that was how a table set for 32 people looked, and I avidly read the courses, till I felt sick : "Is dinner ready yet ? !" Came promptly : mashed potatoes, and apples roasted without oil : I thought of our supplies, so we'd be having these for the next 4 weeks. (Great taste !)

Outside for a bit : round-shouldered cloud cattle fattening on the horizon, in the north. (nah : actually clear around). "Could we maybe head out this evening – ?" Gretel asked beside me, timid, embarrassed (but we didn't have an ounce of wood left !) : "At twilight, okay ?"

Twilight, okay : making hay on the moors; a buxom rustic moon just above the farmfolk : "They're still at it !" – Picking up cones and wooden debris (my gloomy head swayed among the spidery boughwork, spooky boughwork, hard and coat-gray); long pieces, brought by stooping lasses, I banged against my tensed thigh until something broke. Already at the other end of the wood : sight through the scrub : wind drudged lazily in territory still unmowed; an old flat goldpiece lay, shattered or dustladen, in the haze of heaven, way over there. (Oh, my deathbed it wasn't, but I was freezing and sweating like a beast in panic) plucking; caressing : – "I'm coming."

Each of us has a rucksack, I the big one, with the damned roots. Set it down. Was dark already; and very close to the railroad tracks : "Let's follow the ties, alright ?" – "The last train to Walsrode went by long ago." "Sure !" Tapping, tapping : "Aren't you feeling alright ?" "Nah" I said (being honest is no virtue, but it's usually quicker; you need much too much time and energy for lying) so then : "Nah !" – "We're almost there, – there's the lumber yard just below." "And then we can rest for a couple of days !" Lore decided.

Frau Bauer, the old lady : with ringlets : "Ah, do you think you could finally give me back my bucket ! !" (Here, take your junk !)

With ringlets : it's a painful enough spectacle when individuals can't grow old gracefully : how much worse with nations ! Hitler's Germany already offered one such unseemly show; its Soviet zone now offers it anew, in sufficiently exaggerated and grotesque form : in the last analysis, Europe itself does. Would that it would finally give up its claim to world leadership, dubious now for 100 years and downright ridiculous for 50, and content itself with passing on its languages and old cultural values as intact as still possible to its successors in East and West; and then reduce its industry and its population to 200 million by the most radical birth control. Europe as the Hellas-Switzerland of the earth : it's everything one could reasonably aspire to; I fear we won't even achieve so much as that, or serene extinction : 20 years will tell. – : "I'd go to Trier to worship the Holy Shirt, before I'd go to the Russians !", and they drooped the corners of their mouths in concern : that means one helluva lot with me. (But it's more like vice versa !)

"You're feverish : get some sleep !" my mistress commanded; she's right : "Good night –" I proffered (and she came outside with me : LORE !) – "It was brutal of us" an annoyed Grete said inside : "to make him schlepp like that today. – But he would've gone along in any case ! – –

He is wonderful ! !" (Who isn't happy to hear that ! ? But I've got to go
out and see to myself !)

Outside : lights flowing in the distant woods (or perhaps before my eyes);
I suddenly began a fit of teeth chattering, and it sounded so loud in
the darkness, that I ran back in at once. As an emetic donation, a large
V-2 bumper : I took a slip of paper, I wrote with my best pencil : "To
Lore / (1a) in my heart / : Darling ! /" and signature; and added : A.i.L.
(that's our code for : Assiduous in Love). – I ran to her door, dabbed
softly, and pressed the slip into a maiden's hand, closed the door myself (the light was too dense for me). Stood there : – ? – : a gentle, deep
laugh.

KRUMAU
OR WILL YOU SEE ME ONCE AGAIN

The wind, the wind : plowed on, its weltering buffalo head held low, across
   Brand's Heath, across the busy road, hill-high across leaflessness :
   then it ran out onto the open square, sending gravel flying, at us; but we
   stood firm, our thin arms locked together, Lore, me, Grete.
   (Three houses around us : Schrader, our ramshackle, the God's house :
   but that didn't help at all in such a wind; only our arms).
   For a while the sharp hippocratic face of the moon lay tipped on high,
   in spotty linen cloths, sending us swaying at first, shuddering : strange
   : such pale light and wind : and to be human the while ! But good that
   through the thinnest material we could still feel our limbs, pressed
   tightly to one another (God, what scrawny arms Grete had : women
   should not have to "work" ! But always robota, robota : that's the curse
   of the refrain !)
   It rolled across the black woods, numbed by the moon; : "Here it
   comes," hissed Lore (my Lore !) and pressed me, like a kiss; we lowered our tough brows, and the gust smashed around us and over us :
   whoosh and the macabre-on-high was gone : who can resist Us ? !
   Grete flinched; she thrust her right (free) hand under my collar; she
   said breathlessly : "Hey you !", and Lore purred like a goddess right
   beside : All, Lore ! (We ought to have three bicycles and sweep along
   next to each other, with instinctively insistent legs !) I pulled the flat
   bottle from my coat : Blessed be Mrs. Kiesler ! and they repeated
   slowly and solemnly, echoing : God bless her ! And thus we took the
   last swig.
And wind : it stamped above in the clouds, sending our legs out from
   under us, in all directions. Fencing with the everywhere : that's being
   human !
"Damn : Give me back infinity !" Lore (my Lore) groaned beside me. I
   wheeled (Grete on my arm) to her; I said : "Hey !" Pause. "No !" I
   said : "I can't do that, Lore !" (My Lore ! Grete had simply been
   brought along.) – "Who knows what will become of Us –" (Very true,

Lore : quien sabe ! I don't !) Wind; wind : we bowed low and bounced back up : We bow low ? ! Before Whom ! ? "Cover your heavens, Zeus, with cloudy haze" : 'sindeed !

October rain : but count Us out ! Laughing contempt, we stumbled inside : "Count Us out !"

"And now read us something !" Lore demanded; I looked into her bluster-ing face, over which clouds were moving, shadows moving, and yet clarity of feature : You will go before me to the end of this little life, Lore ! : She came around the shining table, the one with the white cloth, and took me in her arms (so that Grete wept). And the wind rode, a Hun across Brand's Heath, while the heavens shed tears, and our little panes thrummed : steady; steady ! We'll hold the fort ! 6 years a soldier and with the heavy artillery : has to make one helluva racket before it scares us, right ? !

A pencil (: what if we had to produce it on our own ! Just imagine, humanity is gone : and you have to make a pencil ! ! – Sorcery !) and paper matter in hand : I cast my eyes around the circle. Lore; Lore; Grete : I cocked the point of the thing, and read :

"After perhaps several hours he felt himself awakened by a curious noise. It pressed on his ear like some distant thunder from out a deep upland ravine. At first, still half in slumber, he tried to persuade himself that it was the storm in the mountains, yet the sound pressed up ever more audibly from the other side, where by day he had observed the locked door. / Given such surroundings, this awakening by night in a strange place, something always attended by shudders of apprehension, gripped Alethes' mind with doubled force. The insane old man snored, and spoke various mournful words in a dream; restless flutterings, most likely of bats, swept high in the rocky vaults, and blusters and hisses and roars rose menacingly out of the depths. Alethes, overcome by darkness and dread, called out to the old man. With a groan he in-quired what was wrong. "Do you not hear," called Alethes, "yon wrathful turmoil, as if from an immeasurable abyss ? –" "Ho, ho" said the old man, laughing scornfully : "is that all ? I shall let you hear it better still ! –" With that, he was already at the door fitted in the rock, unbolted it, and at once, with a piercing cold draft of wind, the frightful tumult forced its way up with almost deafening force. – "What is that ? What does it seek ? Evil wizard, tell me !" so shouted Alethes, driven to distraction by the uproar. The old man, standing close beside him, for the door was near the couch of his guest, spoke in a voice audible above the din : "This rocky cleft leads deep into the mountain, far down unknown chasms, to a cavern of ice, where lies a bottomless sea.

It is customarily still; but when as today, the storm comes riding wild out of the clouds, it forces its way through passages unknown down to those secret waters, and then it hisses and howls just as you perceive it now. One can glide a short way across the smooth ice into the vaulted chamber, but one must have a care, for three paces too far, and the Abyss will have you in its keeping until Judgement Day. For that reason I have secured the entrance with bar and bolt : one cannot know, for now and again mad things cross men's minds. – I shall describe it somewhat even now –" He said these words with a hoarse laugh, already on the far side of the door, and Alethes could hear him move about, sliding on the ice. But there came over him, lying there on his couch, a fit of giddiness, and it seemed as if an evil spirit were rustling in the moss and whispering to him : lock the old man out, my friend, simply lock him out : and you will have done with his ugly presence ! – However far Alethes was from obeying this evil thought, he was nevertheless anxious that on his own the old man might slip into the icy hall below, and that then the mad notion would become fixed in his own mind that he had sent his mad host plunging downward : he would then never attain certainty about the event, and would perish from tormenting doubt, for there would be no one who afterward could bear comforting witness. The old man returned at last, carefully bolted the door, lay down on his couch and fell asleep. Alethes, however, could find no further rest; whenever he would close his eyelids for a short time, it seemed to him now as if, hurled down by the old man, he lay in the bottomless sea beneath the icy vault, far from all life for all time; now as if the graybeard were howling up from the depths above the wild tumult, accusing him of murder. / Morning at last cast its first light into the cave through the barred vent of the front door. Alethes hurried outside without turning to glance at the sleeping old man; a clear sky, a calm wind, and firm, crackling snow beneath his feet promised a pleasant journey, so that with each stride forward he found himself joyfully shaking off the horrors of the night. Suddenly, however, he was standing before a slope covered with deep snow and offering no possible path for him to continue on his way. One might be just as likely to step into perpendicular deeps beneath the dazzling blanket as to find any sort of supporting stone. It would have been insanity to dare so much as an attempt at descent, for which reason Alethes began a search toward the other side of the mountain. But when confronted with the same barrier in every quarter of the peak, he felt himself in the grip of cold terror and ever growing anxiety, and was forced finally to admit that, perhaps two or three times now, he had walked in vain the circle holding him fast. The sun was already sparkling brightly on the snow when at last, exhausted and forlorn of every hope, he took the path back to the cave. The old man was sunning himself before the door and laughed at his approach : "You intended to run away," he said, "but we are snowed in here for the winter. I noticed it at once last night as the snow was driven with such fury against the mountain. Accustom yourself to it : you'll not have things bad. You are after all my kinsman; you are Organtin, my nephew, though otherwise to be called the devil, for you've a devil in your devices : you see, how well I know everything ? ! You have betrayed yourself with the song that no one except my closest kin can know. Do not fret : with the coming of summer you may move on, or should there be good weather, even at the start of spring. Until such time, you are the guest of Reinald von Montalban ! Make yourself at home, and have no fear of me. Rest assured, I have ever tended my guests well and refrained from vexing them in any way : enter my cave, Organtin !" –

Whom once she's woven mystery / about, cast raiment's somber billow /
o'er youthful locks on youthful pillow : / He'll not escape Eumenide ! :
Most dreadful and oppressive were the first days that Alethes passed with the old man in the cave. The host could not reconcile himself to his guest, nor the guest to his host, and the dismay of the one ever and irresistibly infected the other. Specially hideous, however, did they seem to one another when they awakened from slumber, each staring at the other as a wanderer stares at the savage beast that while he slept has chosen the like resting-place. Alethes, however, was the first to reconcile himself to the constraints of necessity; he even began to answer to Organtin, the knightly appellation with which the old man had dubbed him, as if he were indeed so named, and as his own timidity abated, more and more the old man restrained his brutalized temperament. He rejoiced in human contact, and suffered but seldom outbursts of moods both dangerous and horror-provoking. These would rage most awfully and uncontrollably when in concert the subterranean flood would roar up out of the icy gorge. Then he would dance about the cave in a frenzy, and indeed sometimes, as on that first night, on the slippery, declivitous ground beyond the wide-flung door as well, from where he would wave his guest to join him, and indeed with such peremptory pose that at times the latter could barely withstand the strange behest. It was likewise one of his amusements to fling stones down the smooth abyss, which, now sliding now bouncing and finally falling into the subterranean waters, awakened horrible tones. / One day he had left the cave in search of large rocks for

this game; Alethes then decided to bar the gruesome abyss forever, come what might of such an undertaking. Quickly he snatched the key from the lock, flung it deep into the icy vault, and then with all his strength slammed the door shut, so that it crashed as the lock closed and the brass bolts banged into place. / Hearing the noise, the old man hurried back to the cave; with a glance he surveyed what had happened and let the stones he had gathered fall from out his garments, while raising his other hand in a grave and menacing gesture toward Alethes. The latter kept a watchful eye, but the graybeard, without a word or further display of his indignation, lay down on his couch and completely covered himself with moss, veiling him just as he had been on the evening when Alethes had first entered the cavern. / And so matters remained until the next morning, when the old man sat up and said : "Organtin : dear nephew; it is indeed good that we are kinsmen and dwell together in this fortress. But liberties such as those you presumed yesterday, you must never dare again. I remain master and lord, my dear Organtin, both for now and for all time, here in my cave, just as once upon Montalban. My honored guests from out the icy caverns are mine : indeed so much mine, that may the devil take any man who thinks to snatch them away from me. I would long since have wrung your neck, Organtin; but it is fortunate for us both that your slamming the door shut has done no damage : for spirits, nephew mine, pay no mind to portals of oak and bolts of brass : whither they choose to go, they go, brooking no opposition. Above the deep sea beneath us, their flight rustles, pinions high, pinions low, now brushing the shimmering icy vaults above, now diving into the disk of silent waters. Since long before the days of Carol Magnus they have dwelt there. Ariovistus speaks of his battle with the Romans, and Marbod and Hermann of the German civil wars. Their ancient weapons, strangely shaped, are mirrored in the waters, and bearded lips to bearded cheeks whisper of things ne'er heard. But behold, Organtin, you imagine that you have barred these fearful judges from me : yet as before their journey goes inevitably on, and therefore they have been with me this very night as well : thank God for that, Organtin; for otherwise – –" He screwed up his face to its ugliest, gnashing his teeth, and savagely rolling his eyes . . . ."

She sat shaded and obdurate; she spoke somber and puzzling : "I'm sorry for you. My boy. –" That is : I understood in part at once; I heard a new evil sound and looked eerily into her eyes, listening. Slow. Grete gulped; she said weakly : "Shouldn't we tell him . . .", but Lore flung her strong hand up; I caught it in the air, I begged : "Jamascuna !";

but they kept gentle silence.

"It was very beautiful" (Grete, muffled); she rummaged in stockingdom : "*Too* beautiful –" came the quiet words. I imposed calm and defiance on myself : "So, a surprise –" I observed matter-of-factly, from the one to the other, and only the little one nodded gravely : a surprise ! Then she said to Lore : "Give me that skirt of yours. The one you tore on the bike –" (Lore had been in Krumau again, alone; had made one trip on the train too.) – "Oh, not now –" and sententiously : "Nothing is so urgent that it won't get more urgent if you let it be !"

"Good night." : "May all creatures . . .", and therefore I stretched a hand out to her again : "Lore ! – Jamascuna – ?" (She came outside with me at once; but did not speak the words).

In my dream the harsh gray skies crumbled and crude blue craquelure appeared : badly made ! Much sun (and of course I'm a soldier once again, just out of the infirmary, with a tottery leg and 20 men to the room : damn the military ! The lowings of hebetude !) Like sun-filled smoke, I float down the bright barracks corridors, down the stairs, always "saluting", above the bare gravel of the merciless compound, oh, and ever onward with creased face. On the dike through Ratzeburg Lake, in my long meadow-hued coat : dirty meadow ! From the first door of a middling-sized house on my right, Grete comes : "How are you today, Herr Schmidt . . . ?" : so that all you can do is set a hand to your hard-billed cap, and salute, waving her earnestly inside : she's too good (and at the market another nod : too good !). But there's singing in the willowed lane, stupid and profound thumpings : And so to see me one – last – ti-hime : / come to the station one last time ! : / In the cro-howded waiting-room / you'll see me for the very la-hast time . . . . : Now if that isn't impersonal and abysmal. (And I was still humming it, grumpily, as I got up !)

Freedom : one German writer is free on 31 October 1946 : the Labor Office is happy to be rid of one more; the Tax Office in Solltau is totally impotent, since as a matter of course he earns less than 600 a year : all you really want is to stay healthy, and keep your needs at a minimum : then you're free. (Happy is of course something quite different ! – And you've got a hairy jaw, hideous and beastly.)

Coated sky (like a tongue); then came :

Rain glazing the window; the trees by the church waved perplexed branches, bent around corners, perplexed, beat the few leaves left to them, perplexed : wet, black, and implacably tough, the bark stretched over the intricate creatures : naked oaks are dreadful things, you don't first have to see them painted by Friedrich. The sky wallowed in grayly from the west, always above.

A bush ruffled its whitish-green leaves in terror before me; nothing in the mail either. But Lore got another one of her substantial, yellow registered letters, with lovely stamps : a volcano fumed energetically above the high plain; and some Bolivar or other posed a brazen profile. (British North Borneo used to have beautiful stamps, and Moçambique; they should issue an astronomical series sometime : Mars all clad in his red, with polar caps, etc; Saturn hovering in its ring. Or zinnias like Schrader had in his garden this summer : I've never seen flowers with such curious colors !). And it was a thick one : she went to the window with it, slit it open, and took out a lot of stuff, both written and stamped. Meanwhile the potatoes were cooking, and I was weak enough to check on them myself.

Grete came fluttering in, breathless, trembling in her chair, hands nervous in her lap : the Russians had crossed the border; near Helmstedt; early this morning. (Furrowed brows !) : yes, that's what they said at the plant : near Helmstedt ! "Of course" I said scoffing and morbid : "And Hitler is alive and well : has been spotted working as a tourist guide in the Popocatapetl massif : photo reports in the magazine." She was still flying; because she knew two refugee women down in Blakenhof who had been raped by the Russians, and had given birth to the babies amid curses (That would not be a bad criterion for the various occupation forces : who had behaved most despicably ! Beasts like that should be slaughtered !).

I suaged her with difficulty; talked her out of her late-breaking Tartar news : "In that case the English tanks would already be rolling down on the road, Little One ! Planes in the sky. – Calm down, calm down !", I petted her a bit, and calmer now, she went over to the stove to add wood. Lore came to the table, her jaw jutting and cursed aloud : "Out !" she swore : "Damn it, if you could just get out of this zoo – ! – Well – " and she whispered with the little one crouching there (at which a gentleman leaves for 5 minutes; by way of precaution and spite I stayed away for 20 !)

"Sure ! The whole highway is full of 'em !", Grete protested : "There's tons of 'em ! After yesterday's wind." And we went out into the afternoon, with sacks, to collect acorns. (We had learned how : to peel them, cut them in chips, and roast them without oil in a wide pan : they didn't taste bitter then ! You could munch away contentedly and swallow the mealiness : plugs a hole too !). – The farmers were loitering out in the fields (a harrow harped the earth), digging out sugarbeet pits

(or up; I don't know anything about it); they gawked above spade handles; whistled suspiciously on fat fingers for hypothetical dogs : God knows, the rascals should be eradicated !

Thievish wind blew in the woods, shuffled its feet in the foliage, much smuggler's syllables came Slavic soft : rustled steps through underbrush and cautiously moved the lattice of branches : "It says ‹Ssshhhe t'aime› I asserted, emboldened by twilight, into the shiny eyes of my October maid : how her hair swayed along the curly-mossed bark of an oaken stump.

The old man : he was pushing a barrow of the most exquisite yellow autumn foliage along the fire lane; Lore froze : she whispered : "I must be going crazy . . . Look at that !" And in point of fact : he wasn't raking the stuff up, but was carefully strewing it along little balks, around small trees; he hung a vintage maple leaf in the top of a sturdy fir child and regarded his handiwork with satisfaction. (Apparently didn't see us !)

Evening's early darkitude / and the dairymaid hums her lay. / Thrice the crow barks loud and lewd / while westward move the scraps of day. / Over Apel's clearing much grows bright : / the moon . . . (I was improvising; for Lore had challenged me to see if I could : I'll have you gawking ! If I have to, I'll learn to gush like a buffoon, or a lawyer : what's the difference really ?)

"Look at the acorns ! !" Schrader was at the fence and knocked with delight on the pickets when he spotted the lavish harvest of fruit, bright green and pied brown : "You'ah plannin' to fatten a pig – ? !", and looked about beaming. – "Oh, a piglet –" I grumbled the emotional Hungarian air : "Oh yah : the readin' 'nd the writin' . . ." and nodded to him bitterish : the same diet wouldn't do you any harm either, my good saint ! (And the horizon, beside the church, raised a burn blister on its spongy gray flesh : the sun of evening; and the trees gazed at it perplexed !)

Salvation Army : "Come to Jesus : boom !" – "Step His way : boom !" – "Christianity, in the form that it has existed among us for 2000 years, by which I mean a murky world of hierarchy and obscurantism, is a wretched drag on humanity !" – "Just be glad !" she offered : "you've still got your momentum . . ." (Right there too !)

"The sun's bright hard-edged glances / are slowly drawing back; / the air around advances / and scowls itself to black; / the darkling moon illumines / us with its borrowed lamp; / and piercing earth, the dew sends / its all-embracing damp. – " (They listened critically and with cool interest).

"The beasts in wasteland forests / are stalking, prey-obsessed; / the herd on silent moor is / in search of bowered rest; / and man, beneath the torment / of work weighed down, he stands / desiring ease and dormant, / enfolding sleep's soft hands." – (Grete nodded slowly : she probably would have liked to be sleeping too. "Hmm" Lore sounded, not disapprovingly; I raised my hand and read) :

"The monster wind offended / storms houses in the night, / where fires so closely tended / can barely stay alight. / And when the fogs are lowering, / all trace of life is lost / on fields, where rain is pouring, / where once man's traces crossed." – Grete opened her soft mouth : "Traces twice –" she asked hesitantly, visibly bewildered by high-school scruples; but Lore jumped up in excitement : "That's grand – !" she said, her brow swaying starry white; cursed softly, with a sharp glance my way, and half opened her wild magic mouth; closed it sourly and drummed on the pedantic dresser. Once again she extracted this noon's letter from its locked drawer, and I pulled myself up stiff and straight : "I've got to go back into the village" I said limply.

Outside : what was I doing outside ? ! – I fetched my coat, pulling it on as I walked, and hoofed it.

At the corner : Three roads diverged before me (and every one a wrong one !) : Nope : Brothers, let us then rejoice ... (which means the one on the right : doesn't make a damn bit of difference !) –

Steps : damn, that too ! –

Bauer : (that too !) " 'vnin', Herr Schmidt !" : " 'vnin', Herr Bauer." "Well : out serenadin' – ?" I sniggered dolefully through my nose and pointed skywards : "that's enough of a serenade for one day !" (Right : the wind was fidgeting treetopside, ashen and sober).

"Walk along over to the soccer field ? Round the back way ? ! –" : I nodded obligingly : I'll walk along. Round the back way, too. (Was ripe for bad company Today : baker, baker ! : What is man and what will become of him !)

"Are you not well, Father ? ! : You look so pale !" (The moon that is); and nimble, self-confident cloudfolk were moving about, even in the penalty area. We leaned against the fence and looked out at the playing field where the spectral team was silently training. "The dead soccer players of Blakenhof – huh ?" I murmured at his head, suggestively in the cold gust of wind (the fellows were scurrying about topsier-turvier now); "Shall I –" I hissed wantonly; didn't even wait, and gave a referee's monotone whistle : at once : a wisp of fog rolled up to the penalty zone, lay there bouncing softly : a bright and sassy nub of fog –. Bauer rolled his collar; not canny : "– Well – let's go –" he said,

manly and morose; then later I heard something about "glance through the homework" : fine, fine; glance away, my boy, and thank God : you have an honest, straightforward profession (of course when the Russians come, you'll have to retrain; but we're still young and versatile.) "You want to come in ?" (Briefly !). I jerked my head energetically : "I've still got work to do, Herr Bauer : ora et labora, et labora . . . You know how it is !" "When's your book coming out ?" "Should it please the Lord : beginning of November" I said truthfully. But also : "No need to rejoice too greatly : rabid contents and dismal as well. – I'm just amazed that it's even getting published." Forced a smile. "Well then : –"; and the door went clippety clop, and the cat came hippety hop; and I looked unthinkingly at the black, wet wood rectangle : a door, a door; would that one still had a door; and the image and the word came with me around the house, around the tiny swatch of lawn, through your soles you could feel the sharp gravel, the blackout on the right was good, and again a "door"; I entered my door, unhooked my homemade wire latch, and then put it back, sat down at my table : if I wanted I could carve an "L" in the right hind leg, ni Dieu, ni maître (but it would probably cause it pain; I'd rather carve into my own right hind leg).

The Schrader housemaid : (for he also kept a kind of poor Lowood-orphan of 15) : "A telegram for you : could y' come to the phone please !" Chairs shuffled hastily; boundings occurred; and I sat there stiff and thin at my flat table. –

A long while : she didn't come back for a long while (would chatter on casually over there, stiff and small talk, working it out and gaining time; well, I'll make it all easy for her); finally you heard her steps outside. She spoke sotto voce with Grete (who had gone over with her then), hesitation; then she came in to me, sat down on my lap and laid arms and face on my shoulder.

She said : "You were the last. – : And you've been everything to me : everything !". We held each other and were silent.

She said : "I never thought – never hoped – that there could be a man like you : I've never been so happy : – – –. – You were really the first, too !" We trembled and were silent.

She said : "On Saturday; day after tomorrow; I'm leaving. – I'm leaving for Mexico : I have all my papers. On a plane from Frankfurt; just came through that the tickets are here. –"

She said : "He's 61 and rich; we have each other's pictures." She flinched and held my hands tighter. "I'll be able to live without a care; he had to put up 10,000 dollars. And pay for the flight besides !" We pressed our avernian faces together and bit.

She said : "You ! ! – – First and last !" And her voice shattered behind my neck. – –

Alone : I scuffed across the square, and a dented golden pail hung in the cloud rifts; on the slope a whispered duet : alraunic blackwater and the wind of this night : I shouted : no devil came to fetch me ! (Shouting is hooey, too; especially because of her.) But I wanted to walk off into the light for a few more hours.

Radio and disorder deep in the night : she clutched my jacket in both fists and hurt me up front and said with a wrenched mouth and shimmering eyes : "We've got to pack you know" (and then we also heard that an "Association of Former Minesweepers" had been organized, and had announced its demands !) Grete plucked her back behind the unfolding-screen and whispered : "I'll sleep over at his place later tonight ! – Yes, I will !"; "Oh, no point in it –" said Lore tormented and undone; "I will !" Grete protested fanatically : they whispered briefly; then Grete said fadingly : "Oh I see –". Took a quivering breath : "Yes, then there is no point !". She hastily emerged, curtsied in front of the largest suitcase and said mechanically into the little opening : "You can have my featherbeds when I'm gone. And the bed-frame," and did a reverse knee bend, and set a drawer from the chest on the table. ("In all of Europe – / in all of Europe – / in all of Europe : / there's not another Grampa like him !") Outraged Grete throttled the Representative of our Recovery; I read aloud to them, and they packed, faltered, looked at me lamenting : and I read aloud :

"We were once seated together in the Emperor's great hall; midnight was approaching, but the goblets were not yet empty, and the drinkers grew increasingly gladdened with the noble spirits and the convivial discourse. My cousin Roland spoke of how he had often defeated the heathen, from the Elbe as far as the Ebro (though it was not his custom to speak in this fashion), in the course of which speech, however, there fell from his lips in golden words of Truth, the prophecy of what awaited him at Ronceval : Oh cousin most dear, you have since succumbed to it, as has Olivier your brother-in-law, who then was so hale and happy among us. Archbishop Turpin was disinclined to give credence to these matters at our feast; he suggested that such pronouncements belonged rather to the god Bacchus, and not to sacred revelation genuinely inspired. Ah, and his pious heart has likewise since been pierced by the name of Ronceval : / But at that time we knew little thereof, and sat merrily in company, just as I have described it to you, Organtin. And then it happened that one of the marble plates

of the floor began to move in a most wonderful way. Now it was lifted
up, now it sank again, very like a wave upon the sea by an approaching
storm, and counter to the nature of a well-laid stone. It gave us cause
for mirth, but soon that mirth was changed to lamentation. Though I
grant 'twas not all of a sudden, but rather in the fashion of this world :
long the hauling, but fast the falling. / And now we all saw how a man
in costume of the Orient, bright of colour and shimmering with gold,
climbed out from under that stone and with a wave of his hand bade the
earth close behind him. The stone lay firm once again. He who had
emerged therefrom, however, bowed to all of us in our circle about
him, in a most strange Muhammadan fashion to be sure, yet most cour-
teously. Now he asked our leave that he might amuse us with sundry
exhibitions of his art. Archbishop Turpin cautioned against it. The
hour was, he said, too uncanny, the very entry of the stranger foreshad-
owed his doings, for he had arisen from below; and in short : it was
incumbent upon this noble gathering to guard against menacing evil.
We, however, asserted that such would be a blotch upon our chivalry,
and enjoined the stranger to display whatever pretty and delightful
things he knew to perform. / Ah, and what splendours he now unfolded
to us ! The Hanging Gardens of Semiramis rose up, and then came the
monstrous Colossus of Rhodes, beneath whose straddled legs high-
masted ships sailed on, and then the rest of the Seven Wonders of the
World. And had that but been the end of it ! But the ancient Heroes
strode up, and fought their battles before our eyes : Hector, and Alexander, and Hannibal, and Furius Camillus, each all the while speaking
in his own dialect, which no one of us (with the possible exception of
Archbishop Turpin) had acquired, and yet by this wizardry everyone
understood in manner unaccountable. At last he said : he wished in
conclusion to show the excellent graces of the Gardens of the
Hesperides, but the ladies must also be in attendance, for he would not
open those marvelous gates to men alone, nor had he even the power
to do so. Carolus Magnus, half intoxicated and faltering now, as were
we all, before this wizard's manifold delusions, commanded that the
empress be awakened and that she together with the noble ladies of her
court appear in the hall. They entered, those gracious figures, and the
Muhammadan shot glances searing into their sweet ranks. – "One is
yet missing !" he called out wrathfully of a sudden. – "That would be
my daughter Mathilde," said a venerable knight, "who comes only at
my particular bidding, and I do not desire that she should appear for
these devilish phantasms." – The Muhammadan, however, smiled
mockingly, and spoke into his beard, whereupon the heroic form of

Hector, in whom the venerable knight openly admitted to have taken pleasure, suddenly appeared beside him, and spoke urgently into his ear. – "Fetch my daughter," said the old man after a few moments, sending two maids of honour for her and confirming this wish by giving them his signet-ring. / Mathilde entered the hall, shy, modest, and so beautiful that the eyes and heart of every knight flew to greet her. She, however, the moment she caught sight of the Muhammadan, who was drawing strange signs upon the floor and suddenly seemed quite ugly to the rest of us, had eyes only for him. "Oh, the Gardens of the Hesperides –" she lisped with delicious sweetness "– the trees laden with golden fruit; and Hercules in their shade – ! –" Of these things, we saw naught, but rather how she, most melting with tears, tottered ever further toward the wizard, who suddenly enfolded her in his arms and called out with mocking laughter : "'Twas she I desired ! !" and before our eyes sank with her beneath the very stone from which he had emerged. / Full of rage and dread, we grabbed at the stone, but so firmly and solidly did it lie in place again that we ran from the hall to fetch masons and smiths. On our return we saw the aged father lying on the floor in greatest despair and scraping to reach his only child, and how with superhuman power he had begun to lift the stone. Though truly the blood flowed about his wounded fingers and nails. Yet he succeeded nonetheless, and the stone yielded. But below it one saw naught but firm, damp earth, and a disgusting toad that grimaced at us with fierce eyes and opened its maw to spit; indeed, when the workers who had been called in had ripped open the whole of the marble floor, so many ugly and poisonous worms appeared that we all had to flee the hall. / All Aachen lay in mourning over the beautiful, lost Mathilde, not merely because she was allied to one of its most noble houses, but principally because she outshined all the women of this world for grace, comeliness, and every other virtue, just as I can now assure you, Organtin, that the very thought of her brings true pain to my heart. / The wise Archbishop Turpin consoled us somewhat. He promised : at the very hour upon which Mathilde had vanished, he would the next night force his way into the hall, and, as we should be present, we could watch him call the beauteous maid back from the underworld. / All of which occurred as he had said : the vermin upon the ground yielded to the powerful rites of the exorcist, and when once the ghastly swarm was gone, we heard below us what seemed thuddings of strange dancing music. / "They are celebrating their victory below" Turpin muttered to himself, "but I still have hope I shall disturb them." – Now he began to utter sacred and most prodigious words, which my poor

sinful tongue dare not repeat, and at which the music from the depths
was changed to discordant wailings. Soon thereafter the lament
swelled toward us, ever nearer and louder, the damp dust of earth
turned and swirled upon the spot where Mathilde had vanished, and
suddenly burst open to reveal a yawning cleft. – "Triumph !" cried
Turpin : "Triumph ! The abyss restores her to us !" – But Mathilde
appeared in quite different guise from what we had intended. Half
her body rose up out of the gorge, clad in robes of sulphurous blue
and fiery red, by whose inconstant flickering light her countenance appeared deadly pale at one moment, frightfully aflame at the next. The
while her hair, like snakes, flew about the features of her face, so distracted that she was hardly to be recognized, and with an equally distorted and shrill voice she called out : "Leave me in peace ! In peace I
say, ye pious pack ! I warn ye ! Ahay ! there he stands now, the old man
who did sire me; who believes that I am his own, and he my lord, and
he is full amazed : Father, thou hast kept me like a lackbrained child.
But here below they have indeed diverse and sundry pleasures, and it is
to my liking. I wish to remain here below. Ye will say, thus am I eternally damned : ah, children : there is something passing strange 'bout
saintliness : many a soul achieves it not, though he make most earnest
provision. Therefore I shall hold to certain pleasure. And disturb me
not; I warn ye yet again ! Otherwise I shall come at deepest, blackest
midnight, arise an alraunic dame, and set me on the bed of Carolus
Magnus and frighten him greatly, seize him by the throat, suck out his
blood, plague his ear with tales to muddle brain and senses ! Beware,
Turpin, oh conjurer, thou most of all ! Thou art no innocent lamb, and
hast many a foul blemish wherefore our sort may chastise thee : ye
have made your choice, begrudge me not mine. – Do ye not hear it ? Do
ye not mark it ? Already they are tuning the fiddles below, lighting the
hanging lamps with fire and brimstone : the time has come : down,
down : huzza ! huzzay ! !" . . . . . ."

4 in the morning : We bleated our yellow tired eyes into the light, but had
to work till we dropped. She then laid a sparkly piece of cardboard in
front of me : so that was Him : a scrawny, worn-out face; with no hair
(except in his ears more than likely; you couldn't see for sure); two –
"Corporation lawyer and landowner" she rasped – two dueling scars
clove his left cheek, and my mouth twitched angrily : when the poor
Papuans or the blacks of Australia inflict ornamental scars on themselves, people say : they don't know any better ! But when our students
atavistically hack away at what little resemblance they manage to bear
to human beings : and are proud of it besides : – well, I suppressed such

reflections for her sake and gave her back the scratchated slippage (another inane expression !)

I rumbled up and helped push down at one corner : it closed easily now. I saw the foxy-red, lightly concave surface with its gleaming tin corners; I suddenly began to tremble; I said : "If one had 10 pounds of coffee, one could perhaps – come by some – beams and boards –" I laughed ingenuously and made the silly thievish gesture with a covert right hand : "Build a cottage in the wood . . ." I murmured helplessly and shame-spare (inane !). We stood and stared at each other; then I took a hard and violent swipe at the air with my hand, shook my head, and went out the door (A door, a door.)

Window stays shut : many have indeed frozen, none has ever stunk himself to death. I threw back the tarp and powdered the boards with English DDT insecticide, and with a lavish hand : you never know with those naughty poet types ! Then lie down; positioned for a crouch-grave; and I did not sleep (My brain whirled with mazes of images and words; wildernesses of images and words, too many, too many, until the mills ceased to clatter).

Again almost evening : for the clouds were readying themselves for a long, anonymously wild journey; and the lying moon (like all palefaces !) curved itself into a sneer amid respectable silvered-hairs.

Outside the village I snatched a flint high above my head and drew my arm down with all my might : against this stony star stones I smashed; serves it right.

"Give us everything !" I demanded enterprisingly : "Bread, cheese : whatever's there !" (Was supposed to buy up everything left on Lore's ration book; nothing dare fall into enemy hands, in this case, then, the district office's). – "Couldn't you just give me meat – or cold cuts : makes no difference – or : sugar : for the next decade ? !" – She made sullen thick lips; we were alone in the shop; suddenly she looked at me askance : "You'ah always gettin' packages from America –" she chattered semi-away : "if theah's good coffee in one sometime – –" then with a frown she cut away briskly at the paper patterns, and clip, there a whole corner gone; had a scar on her neck from a glandular operation (that can't be helped : but dueling scars . . . ! !) Well, I crammed it all right into my dapper little shopping bag, which looked as if it were made of raffia (but in fact had been woven from cellophane, by Grete); and into my coat pockets : there was a total of maybe 3 or 4 pounds of groceries; we were getting only 1050 calories a day after all. Pay; we nodded one another down with knavish good cheer, I agonized, until I smiled, and vanished in the duskiness . . .

Apel up top, me with my hand on the rack-wagon : he carefully lifted the straw and showed two giant buzz saws. "You swiped those from the Eibia plant" I said at once, the augur knows his fellows; and : "you going into competition with Westermann ? ! Alright by me ! !" (For he ran the watermill down by the Mühlenhof, charged 5 marks for 10 min-utes, and, when a poor wretch of a refugee came along with some tree roots he'd dug out himself, he snuffled off with : "We don't saw no stumps round heah !" – May Allah do thus and so to him !) The great viscownt giggled agreeably and tickled himself besides. "Suah" he said with dignity and self-satisfaction : "'ll open up one myself : 'lectristy don't cost so much; and I'll take nor moren fifty puhcent : can't y' jest see the ol' man spittin' 'n' fumin' ? !" and like a shot his face unrolled to its edges, he laughed so hard : no shallow mind that ! (And my distraught heart pommeled me as with fists, and my skin moved painfully over me, and my teeth would gladly have chattered : and he gets to build his sawmill, it trotted in my head, as our noises drew apart; and the sky shifted colorless above the earth, restless, sal-low, disagreeable). When I got to the top, rain streamed into my face as well, very cold, and I walked atilt and askew through the windy Hades (Orpheus got her back; but then he, apparently, could sing).

"When are you leaving then. Exactly I mean ?" She swallowed very quickly : "Tomorrow noon, 12:04; the train leaves from Krumau." I laid the items on the table, and Grete marveled with many words at what all I had got : "You take some cold cuts with you, Lore !" she called in delight; a minor battle ensued, but it was just so that the seconds would vanish with each word. And I too, and propped myself flat against the house; wind bickered and I froze as best I could : it made goose bumps and passed the time.

Inside her-my voice was speaking (still : until tomorrow at 12:04 : maybe it would be gracious and late)

She said hurriedly : "– and just imagine what I'll send you ! ! – I mean, I know best what you haven't got : and you just slip it secretly into the food, so that he doesn't notice who it comes from !" Her-my voice banged and swayed, she boasted with a tremble : "You get a sweater right off : first thing ! And skin cream !" She switched off the light; she said, stony and toneless, her last to the sobbing maiden : "Actually, you two could – – move in together; really; into here. – You're just as gone as I am, you know." and quaked and moaned, while the other one screeched in torment : "You are crazy !" And a most strange voice suggested in earthen tones : "He'd only be thinking of you, when-ever he –" and was weeping now at such miserable happiness; then, composed, : "He wouldn't even do it anyway . . ." After a long while Lore murmured : "That way at least I would've been sure of something."

"We're not going to write, you know; no one could handle that."

"Don't be angry, Gretel –" : "Oh no ! !"

Thin maiden fabric rustled and crumpled; buttons tunkled softly against chairs; there were still two warm, solid bodies in there.

"But you'll send me every book, every newspaper clipping; and write."

"I'll send money for a photo and a typewriter." Eagerly : "Hey, keep a diary, Grete ! : And send it on to me !" Then a voice of dark debris fell : "I'll do that too . . ." and then they collapsed into each other. (While I disappeared along the flagellant wall).

Every(wo)man for him(her)self, we very rapidly spooned up yesterday's crusty yellow (re-fried) mashed potatoes. The large suitcase; a medium-sized one, we were ready by ten thirty; Hi-ho safari. (The little one strapped on the back of Grete's bike, which she walked. The big one was just right for me). The wind blew cold, and the sky was gray : I can describe it quite differently too ! !

Schrader appeared in form of a human at the fence; beneath him the trained and extended hands of the orator; but we couldn't take it, and soon moved on. Through Blakenhof (where I shifted the suitcase to my other shoulder) then the lane to Rodegrund, toward Krumau.

A country lane : it passed through Brand's Heath (but there were no more trees on the right; just rusty and greenish flats, with some very rare Grete-sized pines). Two sandy wagon tracks, divided by a grass ribbon; beside us underbrush and timber fidgeted dissonant, indistinct; at one point, as we walked, shoved, stomped past our little heath, she had surly curses; and blew her nose. ("Warm and still the evening hid itself in smoke red and field gray", I remember, I remember : "the bull's-eye moon glimmered rustically in the juniper –"). I jumped up, supplely lifting the fatty on high : it can All happen without comment.

Sweat gnawed into my skull beside my nose, but I was glad that I still felt something else : blessed be our physical side, nothin' but glands and trusty stench, juice and hair, phlegma kai chole.

Creaking skittish clouds just above us on membranous wings, constantly circled, whistled from gray-leather, hollow chests over the treetopped rim, after us, after us. Her hair flew like birch leaves; and a needled blanket, stretched out smooth 10 yards high above us on our left.

The train station : built to the wonderfully mad regulations of 1890, with those officially specified bricks, with inimitable spirelets, and Grete said her anxious farewells; we nestled the baggage below us; they grasped each other by the arms : they had been together in the same class since they were 12, while beside us now freight cars were shunted, with suitable rumpus. Then she escaped on her bike; and we climbed the 5 steps, to buy the ticket.

On the platform the wind blew on the round iron columns; at 11:58 A.M. we held frozen hands (I must look like a seminarian in my tight black coat !) The big hand snapped again, and we trembled as if possessed (You'll soon no longer have to freeze, my darling, let's hope !). It would have been only a poor imitation of a kiss; because 50 other people were now standing on the stony ledge with sacks and crates. We didn't flinch as it roared in.

And how ! They hung in clusters on the running boards; rode the buffers, leaped down from the rounded roofs : and it cracked like bones in hand-to-hand combat. I ran like a swift arrow clear to the back, where 6 freight cars, covered, were hung on and an elderly agent peered out of the sliding door. As I ran I tugged out 3 packs of Camels : "My wife can ride in there, okay ? !" He jerked up indignantly; I tossed the last one, the fourth, into my palm and held them all at his scraped knee : he looked around, and bent down, and : took it. "Get in up front, in the brakeman's cabin –" he hissed : "baggage first –". The page boy ran; while Lore held back ladylike and only slowly moved up along the main line of battle. The bribee scrambled friskily in the iron beams and fitted the luggage in, obliging left the door open and walked coolly around me, one eye closed : and there my wife sprang up in two bounces ! !

12:04 : she stood on the iron steps : in one hand a door, in the other a black rod; her chin flickered; she called : "Give me something. Of yours !" I shrank back : I had nothing; I banged my hand against my left shoulder and discovered cloth; I tore a piece off and tossed it up to her, laughed for a second, and went on adoring her with eyes. A hellish, gurgled rolling began beneath us; the scene above shifted softly to the right : she cast the black square back at my breast and cried out in despair : "You are –" closed her. Wild. Magic mouth. And we looked at each other for yet a little while (iconodules).

I kicked the tatter indifferently aside and walked along rapidly and busi-nesslike, leaped stairs, tested railings with my hand, wooden-coated, put my platform pass into punch-trusty fingers : the empty bright gray square outside was lovely (like my soul : empty and bright gray !) where the high wind danced about me with dusty gestures; we were alone, bright gray and free, ni Dieu, ni Maîtresse. I felt a great urge to imitate the wind's wings with my arms, abstained however, on account

of the schoolkids. Instead, there was a picture hanging in the newspaper box next to the post office : in America's baseball Hall of Fame,
they were showing Babe Ruth's uniform to some kid; should one not
become a Communist after all ? ! (But then they were letting Wieland's
Osmannstadt fall into ruin, too : so better not !)

"Please, could I have a fine-point pen ?" "Sorry, but not in stock." – "Ah,
thanks !"

First fields, then heath, just don't sit down, then the woods swayed ever
closer : you could go in there and despair a few small things; but the
road was more comfortable for trotting, and inside me it was quiet as a
cupboard.

Many white scraps of paper hanging at the village hall, and I had a read.
This coming Friday, Bögelmann, the Adventist preacher, would provide the total remission of sins for all interested parties; on the other
hand the water would be cut off again : so I had to get back up there
right away and draw it, so that Grete would have some for washing this
evening.

Rumbling the water rushed out of the wide rubber hose with which I filled
buckets and basins, deafening and splashing in the narrow stony cell; I
carried them back and forth in both hands; stood outside the door and
dried myself in the wayfaring wind :

So then : Weep not, Liu !

DARK MIRRORS

I

(1. 5. 1960)

Lights ? (I raised myself on the pedals) – : – Nowhere. (So, same as always
   for the past five years).

But : the laconic moon along the crumbled road (grass and quitch have
   crept from the shoulders, breaking up the blacktop and leaving only
   two yards of pavement in the middle : that's enough for me !)

Push on : staring from the juniper, the peaked silver mask – so onward –

Man's life : means two score years of dodging and doubling. And if by
   reason of the toss (I'm tossing often these days !), they be two score
   and five; yet is their strength only fifteen years of war and a mere three
   inflations.

Backpedal : (and it squeaked with the stop; have to oil it all tomorrow). By
   way of precaution, I aimed my carbine's mouth at the greasy wreck :
   the windows thickly dusted; only after I hit it with the butt did the car
   door open a little. Backseat empty; a skeletal lady at the wheel (so,
   same as always for the past five years !); well : enjoy your bliss ! But it
   would be dark soon too, and I still didn't trust creaturiness : whether
   ferny ambush or mocking birds : I was ready with ten rounds in the
   automatic : so pump onward.

Perpendicular to the intersection : once, above the pretty little plain of
   even, rose delicate veils of dust, in which Mr. Gust did pirouettes :
   but which way now ? ! Roadsignings across the way; I shuffled over
   wearily, ‹Cordingen Lumber› stood atop posts ringed in hellish bright
   yellow and black. Beside it, on the raddled balk, a tapered shaft. I
   puzzled a bit at the engraved legend : ah, that's it : a t.p. ! And
   I laughed feebly : a cop once explained to me, and in total naïveté,
   that the police are also in charge of checking all triangulation points
   every six months, to make sure they're still there. And how one of
   them was about a quarter of the way out into a footpath, so he and
   the farmers involved had moved the thing a yard and a half to the right
   into the woods where it wouldn't disturb anyone, and then went on
   year after year quietly reporting that it was ‹in place› ! Since then, I've

mistrusted the secular results of the geodisists concerning the further unfolding of the Alpine massif, or the lifting of northern Germany : cherchez les constables ! – Yes, but to the left or right ?

Alright : capita aut navim. The penny fell, and Edward the Seventh, fidei defensor, and also a great many other things, directed me to the right : Bon ! (And my little two-wheeled trailer rattled and gamboled).

A *railroad crossing* (thangod the gates were up) and a steadily increasing drop. A Tommy bridge (half rotted; left over from the second world war) across the meandering silent watercourse (lovely pond to my right, paneled with the last yellow of evening); then the road bent to the left, and with weary elegance I glided, à la Lord of the World, into the curve : si quis, tota die currens, pervenit ad vesperam : satis est.

I reached back and pulled out my crowbar, and my pistol : ‹SUHM› was written on the door, and next to that a lottery ad. I pried the heavy chisel point into the wood, top; then bottom; the lock sprang open with a bark, flash and report.

As always : the empty husks of houses. Atom bombs and bacteria had done thorough work. Automatically, my fingers kept pressing the dynamo-flashlight. In one room, a corpse : stench intensity of twelve men : so at least in death a Siegfried (rare, by the way, for it still to stink; was all so long ago now). On the second floor lay almost a dozen skeletons, men and women (you can tell by the pelvic bones). So then, six men (and/or boys); five women and girls.

Outside : at one time was probably neat enough; now the yard tottered about the hollow house. Lovely strapping fir trees, though. Gray walls, gray weeds nodding from them, plus lupins and plaintain. Houses were built of gray walls; cities of houses, continents of cities : who could still find a way through that ! Good, really, that it had All come to an end; and I spat it out : The End ! Uncoupled the trailer and dragged it behind me across the threshold (first room on the right; why make a fuss).

It rustled in the next room : a fox ! The red-haired house-warden glided jauntily past all furniture, and out, into the one-eyed night. I unrolled my blankets; fetched water from the brook; the candle smoldered above the kitchen table as I searched the map. (And the stove still had a good draft, and the chair I hacked to pieces seethed the murky water till it moaned; where was that tea now – ah there). Warnau was the brooklet's name, I determined between crackers and corned beef (would I ever love to eat cheese again : green cheese; swiss, edam : oh stinky limburger for that matter !)

In the adjoining fox residence : photos on the walls; family pictures with homemade smiles. (And am I greasy : if I rolled string back and forth over my thigh three times, guaranteed to have a candle in my hand. – So tomorrow a major break and wash-up !)

A piano : I culled together a handful of jarring notes and acherontic thrummings, no use. I was in serious need of Orpheus : he could have luted up a tune for wood and coal. Or a bathtub. I cursed curtly and went back upstairs.

Many in fact still had IDs on their bony breasts : for whom do you suppose ? And issued by vanished authorities, even if they were genuine. I looked long at one girl in her passport photo, beneath wavy hair, at her blouse : and now beside me lay a few bent bones, and some hair as well, yes, dark blond; in the end I'll be alone with the Leviathan (or even be him myself). Soft barking around the house; the little foxes probably wanted to slink about outside, and, yes, I groped for my hatchet (just before Mainz, in Gaubickelheim, I once ran into six wolves !)

Blankets unrolled and into the eternal hunting grounds of fantasy : ought to link the identity of the Flying Dutchman and Odysseus sometime with a story. Wind began and the tall firs spoke deep and bellowy. It still is worth pondering that mankind has in fact used all three geometries for its image of the world : in Homer's day the euclidian (ecumene as plane); then Cosmas, whose terrarium in fact represents a pseudosphere segment, with the ‹Mountain of the North› as its pole, and held good for centuries too; and finally the geoidal surface; interesting. The moon appeared sad and gleaming in the window quad. For five years now I had not seen a human being, and wasn't angry about it; that says something. You couldn't read by the dull yellow light either; I pulled a book out of my suitcase : no, the title alone, ‹Satanstoe›; I shook my hands regretfully (was too lazy to rekindle the light). Best thing was sleep. – The clock ? Ticking on the windowsill. Think no more. And the fox must have wanted to sleep too, for whisperings were behind the walls like beasties and wild straw. Was secured.

Night (and oval stone in ebony frame) : and try as I would, I couldn't get to sleep ! Cursed like a simpleton. At first I didn't want to, but then I took a (little) drink; energy is a matter of luck; and proved myself at once, always a windbag of first rank, indefatigably capable of every absurdity. Calmly I draped myself with two weapons and

blended into the night : bickered with branches, imitated human voices, grew kind to mosses; I must have disturbed the wind from its bush, for it indignantly bubbled leafiness, chased about the periphery a couple of times, and only then disappeared inwoodly with a rustle. Even the littlest firs were stabbing wildcats if you took too clumsy a hold (I've got to shave tomorrow morning too). At one point there was such a stench that I immediately brought my rifle down : no way could that be a respectable plant, only in zoology did it stink like that ! I didn't move in any closer, however, but owled my way into the mountain forest instead; trunks were growing rarer now, shrubs latticing along the edge. I stepped over the ditch in a crouch, and gazed at the empty moor, wild width, sweet and monotone, in the black radiation, till I rubbed my shoulders in my jacket. It's the most beautiful thing in life : depth of night and moon, hems of woods, silent gleaming waters far off in modest meadow solitude – long and lazily, I perched there, head tilted to the right; sometimes a star spark fell, hours beyond Stellichte; at times a slushy windette crept up on me and tousled my hair, like a lackadaisical tomboy lover; and once, even when I had to take to the bushes, she followed after.

The celestial barber's basin was hanging now from the arm of a fir as I sauntered below it. Was high time to shuffle ‹home›, for it was already gassing gray and streaky in the east; and the shrubs, hollow-eyed and bandy-legged, watch-weary, unseemly too, stood around each other (and me). Morning queased toward me; for

a morning sun appeared, so full-bosomed and mother-in-lawly robust in her nice china-doll cloudliness that I angrily hurled a stone at it over the railroad embankment : godknows, the baggage looked ever so freshly starched ! – Then under the blankets (reawakening Fox & Co., who complained about their new, restive renter). – Heracles : ancient carter of dung (and after the feat, I could finally fall asleep).

The sky rustled unrelentingly above me; my hair quaked as I shaved at the window. I had even found clean underwear in a cupboard; the bike had been checked over; and with a few saucy snips of the scissors I had thinned out the hair in back : aren't we lads so pretty and fine ? ! Thus was I ripe for a village stroll, with firearm and ax. (And just to be sure, I took the binoculars along as well).

Housing development, built and arranged quite tastefully; and they had left lots of firs standing, so that I was forced to give an approving pucker of lips (and from down on the left, the riverlet kept on warbling my way, till it wandered off through a little meadowland, under a railroad bridge, very nice !). Up ahead things got bleaker, the walls more naked; a tiny shop window displayed two radios; then the street made yet another turn to the right, and I stopped and stood grouchily on the open square : it's always the same crap !

A little shanty : ‹General Merchandise›. So I entered (maybe there'd be something edible after all); but all there was in the dingy room was dust covering toxic-yellow bonbons, coffee had taken a powder long ago, the tin cans had buckled and burst (I pocketed three with beef; give them a try later). With my foot, I grubbed under the counter : aha : bottles ! vinegar, vinegar, oil (that I can take with me !), vinegar, vinegar (what did they do with the everlasting vinegar ? !); finally a flask of Munster brandy, 64 proof, and I rocked my head disparagingly : well, bag it ! (Flour and bread are the difficulty ! But there's next to nothing to do about it !) So I cast an angry face about me, went down the path a piece and stood once again beside my bike (good thing the tires were solid rubber, otherwise I would have had to hoof it long ago). Well, a little tour will do my legs good.

An athletic field : The grass grew up to my belt, and the 400-meter track around it was almost totally overgrown. Out by the entrance some paper was yellowing in its box, typed notice from Secretary Struve : the team for Benefeld-Cordingen, the roster for next Sunday (which they had not lived to see !) : Rosan, left back, Mletzko and Lehnhardt at outside, Nieber at center half; oh my Leviathan, their merry uniforms might have been white and red, or yellow and black; well just keep crinkling away. Down the far side of the street stood a couple dozen more cottages.

Playing the Gramophone : (‹a singing, swinging swirl of melody› as they would mindlessly have said on Radio Southwest) and it scared me to death : mug to mug with Duke Ellington ! ! (Now that's surely no fault of his; but then to go and produce such acoustical garbage : that makes it a defect).

"Have you met the sheik of Pakistan ?" – ‹Pakistan ?› the toneless, nimble choir asked dubiously,

"Who keeps so many pretty wives – " – ‹Pretty wives› – I played the record, and again, so sweet was the howl from those nihilists' windpipes, and then

"I love you ! !" sware (with an ‹a›) a male chorus with such infernal booming that an icy chill ran up and down my spine; well, another five minutes.

"Afraid in the / daàrk – : walkin' home aloòne . . ." Well, it was time to put an end to this gallant nonsense; would be a pity to do it to Mozart, but Sousa's ‹Washington Post› would serve : "She's got a child – she's got a chíld-ísh-wáy-aboút-her" : "dara-dattá, daradattá : da-dá" : pajamas of the cat, what-all can a man experience in this meilleur des mondes possibles, and/or instigate ! I gave the nameplate of the proprietor,

admittedly a dentist, a complicated kick and left the premises, where tinny brass was still whomping away : "she's got a flea – she's got a fleé-cy-woóly-skirt : daradattá, daradattá . . . ."

The wild May sun was seething so, I sat down on the pavement beneath it, in the middle of the asphalt, and stretched out my feet (bike in the shade, right ? – Why, really ?) But I was just too restless after all and pulled myself up again : operating a bike is wonderful ! And these empty towns lovelier still; I made eight circles at the intersection; when I backpedaled, I stood like a wall.

Magazines : the plague of our times ! Stupid pictures with even more insipid texts : there is nothing more despicable than journalists who love their job (lawyers of course as well !). The ‹Gondola› : as good as naked maids gazing in silent innocence at their thighworks, and I had to swallow hard, and ride back a few houses.

Duliöh ! so I stopped and stood there by the sign and nodded in great delight : damn, 8 miles from here there had been an English supply depot, and I looked for it in my Conti atlas. If there were still some items on hand there, it would mean a longer stay in the area for me, and I looked about me with renewed interest. Best thing would be to grab a bite to eat and then take off, without the trailer. But then I saw the post office and first walked over there for a quick audit.

Smack : the hatchet up in the door crack, pry and bend, and now the bolt sprang apart midship : a small vestibule. The telephone booth opposite; I stepped in coolly, and snatching the receiver, put it to my ear : "Mmyes ? !"; Outis answered; ‹dead› line, so hang up, carefully, hang up.

Interiors : three windows, wooded brown around; three writing desks, a bench for clients, maid in waiting. With a bound I was at and over the pay-out counter, into the holy of holies. Leafing through the books. Registered mail, moneys paid, stamps rose above their desiccated pillows, ink dried red and shimmer-green, the milky-globed lamps hung about, useless, foolish, obsolete as an appendix. Had also been the local telephone exchange; ample maiden hips had ridden over that dust-dulled cushion (but what a ghastly pattern ! ! Blue with broad yellow nonflowers. And the ghostly soprano : Are you still there ? !)

From a multichambered portfolio I solemnly extracted a postcard (to express my abiding disdain for the dead law), the green 10-pfennig stamp was already printed on it : I could go ahead and write one, and I splayed pondering fingers, already seated. (In case some person was truly alive besides me. And happened in here by chance. And saw the card . . .); and I was already writing

To Herr Klopstock (‹Gottlieb› or whatever), Superintendent, Schulpforta bei Naumburg – and I had scruples about the zip code : Naumburg : that was on the other side now, in the erstwhile German Deimocratic Republic; well, we'll just put a question mark in that spot, order is essential.

"Returning enclosed The Messiah" : And signature. (Quite sufficient in this case.)

As I pushed it into the slot, I thought of the mailbox below; I immediately went around and opened the wooden chest with a kick for a key (was just quarter-inch plywood). There lay circa 50 letters and cards : white, ashen, grayblue and green, all with names, numbers, dates, dearest believe me, and lottery notices (I didn't need a letter opener).

"Many thanks for your kind letter. So your husband still has to do guard duty. Well, things have to take a turn for the better again sometime . . ." (the ‹have› underlined; at that I thrust my head back into my neck and grinned from every orifice). . . . ". . . Lux has had seven babies . . ." (‹Lux› : a big sandy-brown German shepherd bitch; I understood intuitively, and nodded in approval; but did not read on, since those pups had just been – – well, well).

"Yesterday I went past your parent's house on Brüderstrasse, and there in the shadow of the church, stood staring at the lamplight, till the windows fogged with envy and humbug, like neighbors' eyes; a sickly pale evening breeze came up, cold and sweet, like a slender grey-haired lover, ‹tender and clumsy› I thought, and ‹fog›, ah, this life of ours." With brows and mouth I formed a stern and bitter frown and studied at the splintered wood, I groaned through my nostrils, nodded, laughed scornfully, read on : ". . . Tomorrow I'm calling it ‹quits› here, and coming to you ! It won't be long now in any case, and we should have at least one hour together . ."

Embarrassed, I refolded the page, and with head and hand greeted my fellow shadow-traveler : go to your Johanna then ! I hope you got there before the H-bomb hovered beside your embraces, once I lived as do the gods and need naught else ('tis indeed cosa rara, and that moreover an opera by Martini).

Another postcard : "Might I be so bold as to request . . . if a meeting could be arranged. . . ." Mumble, mumble . . . . in short : he didn't want to pay for the typewriter. Money. Money. Well, it was too much for me, very soon. So I stood up, and whistling soundlessly, left the situation behind.

Chewing (two of the cans were still good !), and half a canteenful of tea is quite sufficient; will take an hour at the most to get there. – Should I take the trailer ? My rucksack would serve well enough; get there and it's all emptied out, or destroyed, or spoiled, right ? Enraged with indecision, I scratched my head; oh hell, just the rucksack. All the rest will take care of itself once I'm there; it's no real distance anyway.

Autores fideles and autores bravos (as the Spaniards differentiate among Indios) : occurred to me as I pulled the Cooper out of my pack : we're both bravos. (Just as with Schopenhauer and Buddha, where a criminal became a saint with no transition, life has transformed me from pedant to vagrant; not that it still doesn't sometimes make for a strange mix. – And ‹Satanstoe› is good : even witty and with a good plastic sense of cultural history; very fine !)

Following the red-blue signs (and keeping a sharp eye on the landscape) : lovely, the wide disheveled woods, and vacant meadows; a pastel green tunnel of beeches on my right (will have to wait for the return trip : but it is lovely !)

Damn it all ! : there was another telephone pole lying across the road and the wires tangled among the yellow dandelions. (If I'm going to have to travel this stretch often, I'll need to bring a saw and ax with me next time : what a pain ! – Just be thankful it wasn't a metal mast, otherwise I would have had to blast the whole thing away !)

Six : wild horses, weren't they ? Or ! And like a flash I adjusted the center knob : absolutely : horses ! They were moving silently at woods' edge, grazing, helping themselves with broad lips : I was no more than 300 yards away. – That's rare ! Once, near Fulda, I spotted a small herd of cattle, and, after much toil, was able to shoot one. – So there's game here too !

Jerkwater town : Walsrode (Two streets, signs, silly lawyers, sillier judges, thankgod there's an end to everything !)

One civil servant should have survived; one of those who crosses through each form before ripping it up and tossing it away : oh, you bastards ! At which I tossed a withered flowerpot through the windowpane of the district court, and waited, rifle on my ammo pouch, for the first indignant secretarial face – what a shame ! One foot on the hot curb; the other on the left pedal : polythoughts passed through my cloud-laden summer mind, not to sing, nary a lay, not to speak, nary a clause. I bowed my pate, my head, once, before August Stramm : the great poet ! (Albert Ehrenstein, as well, say what you will !)

Shortly thereafter : diarrhea symptoms.

The road was wonderful and I shot ahead as if from a bowstring. A lonely train station without a place : Düshorn, and I nodded appreciatively : no place ! That's always excellent. And right after it *the halls of corrugated iron :* (made a right turn into it; many passages; graveled paths; one shot blasted the padlocks)

The halls of corrugated iron : canisters of crackers : and I cut right into one : all still good; and tasted good too ! – How many were there : five thousand ? Or ten ? ! – My steps pounded in the high metal vaults, muted between racks; can heads twinkled from crates; with my pocket-knife I dug sweet firm marmalade out of gilded cylinders : likewise still impeccable !

Clothing ? Well, that's not so important (but the gentle yellow-green did look nice); at most a blanket.

An office with typewriters : hm.

A small building : schnapps and ammunition ! What was the tertium comparationes ? : fire ? But the bullets were mostly green and damp, though well-oiled. 80 rounds looked O.K.; I took those.

The tap in a barrel : and it even worked ! Mistrustful : should I taste it ? (Better not; the toxins have penetrated everything; actually you can trust only glass bottles and tinfoil lids). And so with a sigh, I poured out the beaker onto the rilled cement. – I no longer smoke (not since '43); so I had no use for the countless packs, Craven A with cork tip : far väl !

Wind ? (I took a cautious peep out) : blue wind rustled endlessly around the building in great banners; even solo clouds moved with pleats and billows and unrest. – But the depot was splendid : you could live off of it for years ! – I buckled a cracker canister onto the rack and rode off bemused, in my rucksack all sorts of hors d'oeuvres.

Under the lyme tree on the heeth (actually in the beech tunnel between Walsrode and Ebbingen) : the spam was good; taste of the spheres; I'll fetch me a whole trailerful of that : well, many damn thanks ! ‹Your dogs : my money›; those are all Silesian turns of phrase)

And the countless granite marbles hummed beneath me, round to the left, round to the right; after seven minutes I was again panting down the asphalt stretch between Ebbingen and Cordingen : signs with lin-seed-oil colors pointed civil-servilely in all directions of the race-track : oh, what reasonable men ! Far and green the late afternoon cradle, tree-tossed, corots everywhere, and the wind was fresh and its pipings sent me homeward via meadows; and I glided, rocking and atop hard-stamping thighs, along the wavy bandage of tar : long live solitude !

Unfinished (halfway, on the right, they had begun to build). I went to the wellshaft and leaned over the damp echoing main (was my bike still there ? – Yes.)

In the modern ruins : this presumably was to be the kitchen. That : a stall maybe ? The living area had a view to the woods around Ostermoor. Evening was coming on, and the sun was at the shore of clouds; but it was still warm-and-bright, and it shone very slowly away; grasses and road banks, decaying light : and far beyond a pair of jays dangling above the forests.

Deep melancholy : I passed my hand over the masonry so laboriously laid; my mouth turned downwards, my feet stuck in floorlessness : this then was the result ! For thousands of years they had labored on : but with no common sense ! If they had at least held the earth's population to a hundred million with legalized abortion and condoms; then there would have been room enough, vespertine room, as now across those charming meadows and twilighted fields, light and plants united in Brook Farming. But all the ‹statesmen›, those washerwomen, had inveighed against it, no matter what letter their names began with – ah, it was indeed good that they were all gone : I spat spamily, as much as I could, setting the sorrel beneath me quivering : no ! ! It was truly meet and right – Then a bike dawdled along the downhill road (on the left the apple lane into a Colony Hünzingen; on the right a branch of Trempenau stores) ‹home›. (Not afraid in the dark, walking home alone). And he who wishes a flying fortress, will get a blockbuster to boot.

Malepartus (but the indignant hosts seem to have cleared out; well : I'll not stay forever !) Is there no paper in this house; I broke into the desk drawers, set them cracking; a stamped leather portfolio, a Parcheesi game (takes two – mocking me), and I grew visibly vexed; finally a book : Rilke, Stories of God, just what I expected; and I ripped the requisite number of pages out of the giltsmithy prose : the very title outraged me; refined bunk; another one of your pneumatomachists : get thee to the guacharos !

This time I gadded around in the opposite direction, toward the factory smokestacks. A walkway led to the left as far as the railroad embankment, right next to the bridge, and now I saw that one of the tracks ran back onto the factory grounds, so followed that, across the peat-brown ties.

Wood, lots of wood ! In massive plank piles under sheds; in plywood sheets, propped together. Beams, too, but fewer of those. In the yard giant logs, elephant gray, mostly beeches, 30 to 40 inches in diameter : what a pity, all those beautiful trees. But the stuff was all superbly dry, would burn like blazes come winter. – Well yes; I stood up with a sigh (picturing the drudgery of sawing and chopping such quantities) and

strolled pensively out beyond the encircling fence, before which there
awaited me the zebraed legs of the well-known sign : this then was
Cordingen Lumber.

Birches out of which sap ran. Somewhere (and at some time) I had read that
you can in fact make wine of it. ‹Birch wine›, a wafting, maiden-
skirted term (getting refined myself, huh ? And shocked, I strolled off
across the ties).

What was that ? : ah, I see. With the binox you could even make out
the primitive ladder to the platform, and I dreamed my way up for
a moment, to where wind brushed skin and hair smooth, far around
nothing but glistening lonely treetops; Natty was right : forests are the
most beautiful ! And I was only in my early forties; if everything went
well (?) I could ramble the earth void of man for a long while yet : I
heeded No One ! –

The train station : wee and proper. Freight-car red : there they stood, alone
and in chains, and I was forced to recall how in the world war before
last (the second one), we POWs were locked up inside, fifty to a car;
the Dutch threw filth and broken bricks at us, setting the walls cracking, dreadful and boring. On a siding, a little handcar, and for fun I
tested my strength on it : relatively easy to set it rolling (but was probably moving a little downhill).

The caravansary opposite : beer signs in lively enameled colors. For
decoration, a teasing, glassed bookcase with the key obligingly left in
it; I opened up one of the volumes : “. . . And thus to slay him / take
thou a bludgeon of doubled mass . . .” and I fled at once. (Still in the
vestibule, and the breath of laughter hissed from my broad lips : apparently back then in the camps of the Hun there were ‹light field-
bludgeons 53›; and then the ‹double FB 17› for heavyweights : to what
ends cannot a rhetorician be corrupted by his word supply !)

Below : a mill between two lovely ponds; the footbridge rotted through,
but I balanced my way on the heads of the beams. Small open spot with
an unusually tall thuja, measured at least 50 feet; a larger farmstead; to
the left the long row of sheds and garages : what was I doing in these
caves of men ? One more look at the everlasting skeletons ? One more
guess : that might have been a fat man contentedly chewing his supper
sausage; this a leptosome with beret and menjou moustache; and that
one there an idiot with bald ovoid head; and here a virgin of Christian
orientation with or without spectacles. A little feisty fellow who walks
like a postman and philosophically smokes a stump of a pipe (but who
secretly plays the soccer pools). – – A brief downpour was in the off-
ing, and I throttled off to the north, to headquarters (pulled the tarps

over the bike and trailer). They also had a buzz saw back there on my
right.

Twilight : I came up with the idea for a fantastical tale : little winged poisonous snakes that, once night falls, whir all about; with dreadful
results (and at once I invented the antiquated title :

A c h a m o t h

or

Discourses of the Damned,

being the

compleat and true Account of the Journey embarqued upon by
Giovanni Battista Piranesi, a Mariner of Naples, in Autumn of the Year
1731

to

Weylaghiri, the City of Hell

containing a Description in all Particulars of that Country and its
People, their Usages (or rather, Vices), strange Infernal Observances,
Institutions, as well as the singular and pitiable Torments visited upon
said G.B.P. on diverse Occasions and to great Danger of both Body
and Soul; the remarkable Colloquies heard also by him; All

according to His Report,

as several times sworn

and as rendered in the Italian Tongue both on the Evening of 11 May
anno domini 1738 and on the following moonlight Night, upon the
Piazza di Pesci of Naples, in the Presence of two Gentlemen long
resident there, doct. utr. jur. Markmann and Volquardt, of Past. emerit.
Stegemann of Dresden then engaged in Travels, and of the Author himself, as well as a large Croud of People from all Stations of Life; which
is intended for the special Instruction

and Spiritual Confirmation

of the participating Publick, carefully and newly translated

into the German.)

Rained a lot.

The wedged moon was driven into a cloud, slowly cleaving it; thin oleo
light fell on the noncom's picture hanging by the door : the Vaterland's
gratitude : which in the good-old-days after the first world war meant :
a barrel organ and a sign around the neck ‹No Pension›. (But twice
more the Germans screamed and begged to sit up on their hind legs,
and "It is so fine to be a soldier" : they asked for it, and they got it !)

I awoke : so hard was the moon staring through the side window into my
mute face. Untiringly they came : day and night. One day I would lie

there somewhere gasping (let's hope it goes quickly; and always keep a bullet in the colt as a free ticket for the trip into the blue somewhere). – I leaned against the wall, my knees in a crouch, and gazed thinking with owlish eyes into the slow shift of light.

Reciprocal radii (and the notion fascinated me for 5 minutes). – Imagine the graphic representation of functions with complex variables, and in particular, the special case just mentioned : a most apt symbol of man in the universe (for he is the unit-scale circle in which All is mirrored and whirls and is reduced ! Infinity becomes the deepest, internal centerpoint, and through it we cross our coordinates, our referential system and measure of things. Only the peripheral skin is equal to itself; the borderline between macro and micro. – In a unit-scale sphere you could indeed render the projection of an infinite three-dimensional space. –)

Pretty and a clever little mind game; for 5 minutes.

The farther, then, that the loved one moves away : the deeper she enters into us. And I pressed my brow to my knees and wove fingers through toes.

(Outside briefly). Moon : as a silent stone hump in the bleak moor of clouds. Dark mirrors lay greatly about; branches antlered my face and dripped hastily. (Which is to say "Rained a lot" in plain English). Hollowsleep.

I tucked the little hatchet in my belt and shoved off, in the last unexplored direction, i.e., northeast. By my field compass the tracks stretch almost due north, and walking the ties is tolerable (except that the distance between them is shorter than a man's step, and, if you skip one, then it's too wide. – Best submit a petition on the matter).

A country lane at right angles (behind, the sun hovered through braided white clouds, burning montgolfier : and I raised a hand in honor of Pilâtre de Rozier, crashed on 16. 6. 1785, the first in that long series, unprejudicial to Icarus); I followed this country lane, which pointed westward in a gentle curve, past a woods on the left; in the middle a 500-yard-wide section that was once fields; and farther on another chain of woods, light and dusky. The wind was cool, swift and kind, and I smiled, a young wayfarer in the green magic circle all round. A blackberry thorn drew a straight red line across the first joint of my right index finger; I gave it a curt and cold glance as I shifted my rifle around, and the tiny pain melted into the woods.

Many mushroom ruins (left over from last year); far within a waterlet dallied through shoots trimmed stern and green, trickled itself together out of a large meadow, lawless and lovely.

I had lost my direction in there, and suddenly found myself again at the woods' edge, in a little clearing, only a hundred yards from the tracks. Junipers built two delicate semicircles : to judge by their size, those must be very old plants (they get to be 800 to 1000 years old; not me). And the ground was so firm and clean that I cosily poured myself out on it with a sigh. Wonderful !

The shrill sun moved behind scudding clouds; the gray greasy fleece distended; twenty minutes later it lay over the whole moor (and for a good hour).

Maying rain : I sat in it placid as a stone : lovely, a soaking rain at woods' edge with the wind perfectly calm (in May-land, not May-ami) and I delightedly shuffled moist shoulders and calves.

My canteen ? : Yes ! – (I've always drunk simply to augment the soul's power of vision; to loosen the flayed spirit from its earthly clogs; to widen the periphery of the unit-scale circle : reciprocal radii; so it does work !). (And from yesterday an image flared like a spark : the lovely lane of birches coming from Borg; a small cemetery with pointed trees of yew; a burly barn of a church – the taste these farmers had had ! Beside a milestone a little elderberry, three feet high)

I took a deep and fiery breath, and stepped confidently into the gray-bright-green postpluvial air : stood : in each hand a rough young fir. Two birds shot up out of a distant jagged cut of trees, curved upwards squawking, flew off, off toward the surf of western clouds, gave yet another Indian whoop, and sank behind the silent wave of earth like castaway stones. (The speed of rotation of a bullet is $N = V_0 \cdot \tan \xi_e / 2 \cdot R \cdot \pi$, with ξ_e as the final rifling twist, and R the half-caliber in meters – because V_0 is given in meters, of course !)

The evening : terrible and lovely ! Fiery red and white fogs emerged from bottoms and groves, like smugglers with silvered and burning tools; came together and conferred in dell and gray grass (and here came the great jays again, making a vigorous foray).

The map : I had the sheet on my knee and estimated : equidistant from Hamburg, Hanover and Bremen. (They seem to have arrived at a decision over there : stooped and gray, the groups dispersed; dwindled soundlessly down the lane of birches, creeping through last year's yellow reeds : one remained, tall and erect at his post).

The English supply depot right at hand : there lay provisions for 10 years ! In the factory below, wood enough for settling in a whole clan. (Now the sentry bent slowly forward and, using to the full every opportunity for camouflage, shuffled off into the forest nursery).

Water : out back was the brook-ditch; and there was more than abundant rain in Northern Germany. And the work of building, sawing and chopping, dragging and transporting, would do me good (to grow fat : the sin against the Holy Body !)

I got up beneath a middling moon; I said : "Herr von Baer (or whatever the owner's name may be) : I thank you for ceding me these woodlands : I will indeed build a house here, and herewith take possession of them" – here I waved my hand impatiently along the horizon – "in their entirety –". (‹Peculiarily and hereditarily› occurred to me as a legal phrase : is there such a thing ?)

I stuck the little hatchet in my belt (aslant !) : the fusspot. And trod firmly down the – my ! – path. The evening still burned silent, its broader glow damped even lower and with silver cloud flames (but was too lazy to read the figures). But I knew well where I was : in the bushbound bottoms to the east ran Wee-Warnau; earth below me; to my back and on my flanks the great heaps of woods – mine ! – woven about with roads; Again the moon appeared at the nape of my neck as a milestone : he ought to have a 17 written on his face (or 18; always generous). Young leaves fell down, obliging and wavy and broad, before my smooth face : trying to flatter your new master already ? (All my companions !)

Before falling asleep : despite weariness, made a sketch for my house. Tomorrow I must return again to the juniper circles and measure the spot exactly, the height, etc. (And for the shed as well. Best thing would be to stake it out with pegs. – Look for some graph paper in town).

Sat there for a long time : (in front of yon supply of planks) : will that be difficult ! – First I'll have to figure out the transport possibilities : up at the train station is the little flatbed trolley from yesterday; I can load it with beams etc., and shove it as far as the crossing (but first I'll have to knock off the rust and oil it); from the station the terrain falls off to north somewhat : that's very good. – What sort of beams can I realistically move ? There were four-inch, six-inch, 8-inch : I decided to use 6 inchers for the house frame and did the arithmetic : specific weight about 0.7; makes a square of 36, gives me the weight, so they weigh almost 30 pounds to the yard, and cursed fervently : thirty pounds ! Stood right up, and tried moving a 10-yard-long monster : and behold ! With lots of force I could perhaps lever it up. – Then I sank back into my study of framing joints, illustrations of which I had found in an old lexicon.

Yes : there she rolled ! (And even the one switch, the one I needed, absolutely needed, creaked and moved : now if that isn't a good sign !). I throttled four of the staked and corded ogres up onto the low platform and began

the trial run : ho-ly-whats-its ! I gawked in a daze at the coarse gravel and my dust-brown hightop shoes, as I braced them from tie to tie : if only I were already up at the crossing ! Sweat dripped, pretty and arhythmic, and I bent low in desperation, put my most noble part into it as well; the trees wandered past me like shades, dear friends, I almost slipped once (‹A slip's not a fall›), and my knees bent stiffer and stiffer with each bend (what if one of them snaps backwards : that can happen, they say !) But now dusty wooden flooring appeared below in my field of vision inching forward : and here came, good God in heaven, the switch. Gasping, I started stamping once again, and got the convoy across the spot : no more rustic outings ! –

Threw the switch : now be careful : a quick push, then jump up on it and move forward to the hand brake : and now it should begin to roll : –

And it rolled gently, the wind wasn't whistling in my beard stubble, but it was steady and deliberate. We rumbled nicely through the woodland walls, more nicely now, the crossing at the lane was already in sight; I throttled back, and gave one last hard pull just before arrival : voilà ! Got it just right. – But the unloading was gruesome, gruesome; because I certainly didn't want to break anything.

Return (pushing slowly) : I can saw all the beams ahead of time; the longest pieces still to come are 15 feet at the most ! (Pushed the dolly back to the lumberyard, enough for today; first I have to settle on an exact design; then come tools, nails, screws).

Three carpenters had lived in town : so I had a choice (and drafting materials en masse from the Walldorf school below); so I sat there a long time, on into the light-twitching night, and pondered : a coal dealer had had his spot right next to the station as well, and a supply of 25 to 30 tons of egg-coals and briquets was stored there; might even have been 50; hard to guess a thing like that; at any rate, carefree heat for many a year. And then you would find quite a lot in the cellars all around. So that's taken care of too.

"Vaubanic front" came to mind as I drew : all the proportions : of face, flank, curtain, cavaliers, tenaille, ravelin. (Interesting; I once read the Bousmard) – But to continue :

Woe to the man who has not rued, at least 10 times in his life, that he did not become a carpenter ! Or who at the sight of a new nail can refrain from imagining tastily prepared wood and a wee chunky hammer !

I tested the brace and bit on the banister : wonder if I'll be able to manage the triple interlock at the bottom ? My plan was to do it this way :

1.) to lay 5 long 33-foot beams parallel to one another, one yard apart;

then

2.) at right angles, the 16¹/₂-foot beams (that part was simple; since I only needed to cut matching notches where they crossed, 3-in deep and 6-in wide, chisel them out; place angled braces at the four corners to create solid triangular joints; then fill the foundation grid with gravel). But now came

3.) the vertical posts : for those I'd have to use the ripping chisel to make square holes, about 2¹/₂ by 2¹/₂, in the joints from step (2), and leave pegs of the same size on the posts. So that they can't just be 7 ft 3 in tall, but need 6 in more at the bottom, makes 7 ft 9 in, and the same at the top – 8 ft 3 in all.

4.) The ceiling : the same 6-inch beams across the top, 16¹/₂ feet long. But for the transverses, the 4-inchers would work this time, and also for the

5.) Roof. The slant : at the base 50, giving me 80 degrees at the top; and an overlapping piece, 2 ft 8 in on each side. So there. – (The frame was the hardest part; boarding it over was easily taken care of; had plenty of tongue-and-groove stuff down below). Good !

So I sat there and calculated. –

(4 weeks later) : and the serrated steel ribbon flowed untiringly within the bright wood; white woody dust inundated the inoperative left foot, good dust, hard as velvet, and every kernel was there : ought to write the biography of each little kernel : every one of them wants to be included ! "Portrait of a Juniper"; "A Fir Grows on My Right"; "Moss like Us"; "My Life as a Hawk"; why shouldn't "a glade" be a being ? The railroad embankment has "its history". A pebble in the gravel : will live longer than you, Mr. Somebody Reader ! "My Footprint". "Pine Cones" (why, they're whole communities). At my window stood 24 flowerpots with tree seeds : and the serrated steel ribbon flowed untiringly within the bright wood; untiringly.

22 July 1960 : Roof-raising ! (Was on a Friday, but what difference does that make ? !). A carpenter would have puckled over with laughter, but the frame stood. And was solid too; I had done more than enough calisthenics in there. (Now came the second, the easier part : nailing on the boards; then fetching the furniture – but first a celebration !). And the bottle never left my mouth (I should run a check on my watch again, too; the next total lunar eclipse would be on 5. 9., then I would also find out whether I was still right about the date. The local approximate time of noon was supplied at the meridian passage : To your health ! And the malaga, Scholtz hermanos, ran like aromatic fire down my carpenter's gorge).

"The stove" I suddenly realized : I hadn't laid bricks for a chimney ! –
　Well; it wouldn't be the first tiled stove whose flue went straight out
　through the wall (but I grew more earnest : I'd have to be very careful
　about forest fires !). – And then, I didn't even have a house number !
　By now I was so chipper that I first gave my achievement another
　cheerful nod, and then, canned and crocked, went off in search of the
　house number.

Across the vaporing meadow : this time I entered the Mühlenhof from the
　rear; the window at the staircase fell out at me at the first rap (right :
　I've still got to pull out whole windows from somewhere and then re-
　install them in my heath-home !), and I swung up inside : wretched
　furnishings : a bed on planks, no pillows or featherbed, just 5 blankets.
　An abraded desk, with twenty stray books in cardboard-box book-
　cases; a tiny cracked stove (well, it hadn't kept this big damp hole
　warm, that's for sure !), in recognition, I gave the cleft iron an appre-
　ciative tap, and looked glumly about. Paper in the drawers; manu-
　scripts; "Massenbach Fights for Europe"; "The House on Holetschka
　Lane"; ergo, a literary starveling, cursed himself as Schmidt. But defi-
　nitely long-boned : must have topped 6 foot at least. This then is life. I
　saluted the bony poet with my bottle (ought to take the skull along and
　set it up someplace); then I swung myself back through the fat window
　socket, and trudged uphill along the little garden run wild.

The athletic field : I leaned against the grizzled goalposts and set all my
　arms akimbo : here, at these simple barriers, hundreds had stood, and
　excitedly issued their caps into the air whenever "Gramps" made a solo
　charge. I ran a ceremonial half-lap to the other goal (and even kept
　right on, scaling the fence; for beyond it was a tiny cement hut that had
　been blown to bits, probably by the Tommies in the world war before
　last, the madmen).

The ruins : table-sized concrete slabs. First the walls had blasted outwards;
　then the roof had fallen in; the hill was teeming with grass and sorrel,
　shepherd's purse and dead nettle : had they had to blow this little thing
　sky high too ! I approached and probed in the debris with my empty
　bottle.

Deep blue and white : and an enameled corner appeared in the depths, and
　I gave an abrupt whistle and did not rest until I had pulled out the
　whole sign : 5 by 8 and B. 1107. And I made wide my eyes and laughed
　with nods and fury : très bien ! So now I have my house number : B
　point (oh : a solid, fat point !) eleven hundred seven. I wiped the dusty
　object clean and blue with my handkerchief : something any prome
　would be houd of (or "home proud of"; same thing). And in triumph

I dragged it back to my old home base, ate, and ate what tasted good (would I have ever loved to eat eggs again !), and killed the rest of the (hot as blazes) day : tomorrow I'll put the flooring in, with two-inch planks ! (– Crap : of course the roof comes first. There was tar-board up at Hogrefe's; so much that I could use it two-ply.)

Three rooms. I marked off three rooms, each extending the whole width of the house (except for the first); I used double planking on the exterior walls; then on the dividing walls too : I had time and materials.

Back to the lunar eclipse (that was the pedant again, worried about the date !) – By my calculations, total occultation should begin on 5. 9. at 5:23 A.M. CET; the sun would then rise at my spot here shortly before 6; so that an hour before, the moon would be just above the woods in the west; alpha was only 0.5 degrees : so that there was almost a maximum angle of immersion : so the spectacle would begin around 3 o'clock. – Well that was still a month away.

Windows : I set two large three-paned ones in the living room; in the kitchen, a small one to the east; a very small one (from a toilet in the development) in the north wall of the entryway (and very high up). Before I learned to use the plane correctly, the house was finished : it's always that way (but it worked to the shed's advantage !).

At the shed complex (but I was still living on Shore Street) : the projecting roof was no small matter (and I ended up making it an extra six feet wider; I'd have to store a lot of things in there. Including my bicycle and all sorts of tools !).

I painted a sign ‹Private Road› and fixed it at the start of the footpath that led to the left, down through the woods (the way you ought to go ! sic !), and to the center of Colony Hünzingen. I left open the old forest lane along the tracks that wound to my place : psychology, mon vieux ! – All supplies went up in the attic of course, beneath the roomy gable.

With a birch-broom in hand (like Puck) : I had swept it all out, and the stoves (one with brown tiles in the living room; the one in the kitchen; a kettle with a flue in the laundry) were already in place. And otherwise : spidery clearing of firs; and I drank till the gray-haired fellows reeled about me.

Totally uncalled for : a fiery brunette of a moon with cloud ruching. – I'll take two days to gather furniture; or better, three. Then it will be 2. 9. Until the eclipse, I'll take care of details (search for books; spades, hoes, rakes; the saw-horse was still good). On the 6th I wanted to take off for Hamburg, to procure the ‹showpieces› of my decor; cash in on some rare musty volumes, too, etc. Get back on about the 10th. Then I would be faced with the issue of heating; so then, 4 weeks for hauling

coal; sawing and chopping wood; food supplies from the Düshorn
depot (and don't forget the water-detox tablets !) That would definitely
take care of October/November; and then came the splendid lonely
days, for many years : tomorrow I'll fetch the gutters and three more
vats for catching the gray rain. Pots, basins, pans : will I ever fry your
Mor-Pork ! Maybe I can even lay out a kind of potato field for the
coming spring (although for me, farming is about the most repulsive
work of all; except for the military of course; the military and textile
manufacturing).

The splotchy, thumbed-over besant d'or (I had set the alarm for 1 o'clock
and stared into its yellowed disk); how nice, sitting square in the light
armchair, out on the road, and the sky was pale and clear above the
great forests on both sides. In Hamburg I would find myself a good
astronomical telescope; for now the big binox and my pocketwatch
were sufficient. All was still and coolish; dampish too; not a strident
cricket left; only now and then breath flowed through the plants to the
right to the left. In the past, ‹a train› probably came through here at this
hour : far away to the north a soft trundling, came closer, emitted organ
tones, deep, far and near, swelled, lumbering on in jagged thrusts,
lights flowed by on pearly strand, disappeared in the south : soft trundling. Now all was still : and lovelier ! In the past, car lights glided
soundlessly along the ribbons of asphalt : now only the moon still
reigned :

The copper gong ! Hangs pale, a copper gong, still high in the ether.
(So I've got the date exactly right !). Those curious swollen lights
on the disk. Mädler had done a lot of research on them; those were the
real moon authorities : Lohrmann, Mädler, J. Schmidt, and maybe
Fauth. An owl began to moan deep in the forest : did the phantom disk
look different to it as well ? (Let's hope the bridges over the Elbe
haven't been destroyed; otherwise I'll have to get across by boat).
Down in the village I had found the almanac, ‹Handbook of Hanseatic
Departements 1812›; this was old French empire here : so I too was a
citoyen. Whether there was anyone left besides me ? Hardly probable;
maybe somewhere on the southern tips of continents, that presumably got the least of it; ought to be able to get a radio working. Wind
brushed in from the west like a great careless bird; the grasses swayed
with slim green hips, softly grumbled the firs, swearing from the
juniper, brownish broad the moon. And so I passed that night. (And :
dic mihi . . !)

At the intersection beyond Schneverdingen, imperial highway 3 : well
that won't work ! I can't come back this way with an overloaded

· trailer. (As far as Visselhövede the road was still good; but then all the
way here completely grown over, sometimes up to my axles; beyond
Neuenkirchen the only way I could recognize where the highway had
been was that the young pines were still so small : that's what cobblestones get you, this soon ! In 20 years No One will be able to find roads
in this world; maybe you'll still recognize the autobahns, but they'll
be gone too in 30). Here the broad imperial highway was still quite
acceptable in the middle; although a lot of sand had drifted in : I'll have
to take the detour via Soltau on the way back : Soltau, Fallingbostel.
Right : then to Walsrode and come around from behind ! – I stood up,
stiff-limbed (had been taking too few long-distance rides of late), and
took another look at the omnibus whose running board I'd been sitting
on : looks charming : a vehicle with lush grass on the radiator ! And
here I didn't even have a third of the trip behind me; so then : ‹to your
steeds !›

Right after Sprötze (where the main Bremen highway merges) : and the trip
through heath and meadowlands had been magnificent; only you
needed to be very careful on the long bridge – what's this ‹you› ? : I ! I
can in fact strike the word ‹you› from the language ! – first, the planking rattled dangerously, and then every fourth board was missing. But
all of that was not "the problem", rather it was this : outside of and
around (and in) Hamburg, a major battle had ‹been engaged› (with
countless air strikes by both sides) at the very start ("Everyone is cor-
dially invited"); it seemed puerile to assume that even a single one of
the bridges over the Elbe could still be intact ! So it would be safest to
try a small town somewhere on the lower Elbe; that's where I'd have
my best chance of finding a usable rowboat as well. – Still 15 mi to
Neuenfelde; and 3 in the afternoon already : well, it'll stay light till
7:30, including twilight; and the sun singed ‹your› thin linen shorts (I
never used to be able to wear shorts : the insects had eaten me alive;
while other people strolled about unmolested, they hung around me in
clouds ! But now that the multipurpose bombs had exterminated or
decimated most species, and the birds easily kept the rest in check, it
was a pleasure to walk around with bare skin). And there weren't any
observers left either : so I just slipped off the shorts too, and roasted
myself for an hour : in the middle of the intersection.

Damn it anyway ! (It had turned into two hours !). I grumpily rehung the
trailer on my rear axle and raised myself on the pedals to ride away
(with a sunburn in all the ticklish places !)

Wulmstorf : good thing the signs were still correct; otherwise I would
painstakingly have had to identify every town (by breaking into a

mailbox and reading return addresses; or trying out the stamp at the post office or the mayor's : whichever was closer !) And now, sitting on the steps of the barbershop, I took that nip of whisky I'd promised myself : cold and very strong ! – Another little one : the idea was to dose it out precisely, so that it would last till Blankenese. Only fools or etiolated aesthetes are teetotalers : they can never have known what wonders schnapps works on total physical exhaustion. Besides, I can't stand people who have no lusts. – None at all !

And with whisky verve along the dikes : the water stood high at the little landing, and on the left were 5 small boats. (A gust of wind invitingly opened the doors of the little deserted inn, and a club of gulls was just leaving).

Where was the wind exactly ? More or less in the west and with a force of 2-3. Which meant I could take even the smallest sailboat (in which lay a pair of oars; how well-behaved of it).

Mainsheet in the right hand, rudder in the left, and it was time that I got across, since I intended to take that familiar big sleep. How did the rule go : the sail should bisect the angle formed by the direction of the wind and your course : so I glided over the blue long current, tomfooleried with the graceful wavelets, for fun held my course for Flottbek a while, glancing back often to get an exact fix on the Neuenfelde buoy as my target for the return trip.

Carefully moored the boat (and gave the rope a little slack, for when the water would fall later on). Then I climbed into the nearest classy villa : nah : was too musty in there; so I unrolled my blankets on the veranda.

Jungfernstieg : I sat down in the streetcar standing there in front of a department store, and intended to gaze out with melancholy; but I was no good at it, and I climbed out again : left hand on left handle; and on a nasty whim, jumped off in the opposite direction, then walked around behind the yellow tin arch to the balustrade. –

Scratched things off my list, muttering : luckily I had already found flashlight bulbs 2.5/0.1 for my Dynamo (it's not all that easy : you can find plenty of 0.2 etc. everywhere !); four lovely gilt wall brackets, each for 2 candles (still need the brass screws); scratch out nos. 6, 7, 8 as well; that leaves, above all else, the books and one or two paintings.

Maybe a portfolio with graphics, hmm ?

An Alster steamer came out from under the Lombard Bridge, ship ahoy, swung around, started rocking dangerously (for a fresh wind was running through the rubbled streets with a shout), and bobbed up and down indecisively for a while (appeared to be the last one still afloat; the mooring lines of the others had rotted through long ago, their sides battered in, sunk : over on the left you could still see one with three feet of roof tilting up out of the water). This one here had some awful dents in its whitish gray bow, too, and I found it too painful to watch it give another bang and rumble against the stone wall.

In front of shops : did I need another pointy hat ? Or patent leather shoes (likewise pointy) ? My hair flew in the wind (which I don't appreciate at all !), and I stepped for a moment beneath the portal of St. Peter's Church, to set myself aright (a brief glance inside : no, noble Nazarene : Thou art no problem ! God bless you; since, after all, in your opinion that's God's job).

And again I broke down doors, busted basement windows, forced my way through walls, my ax ripped open cupboards, dust-besparkled displays (piles of bones, rib cages don't bother me nowadays : may not heaven be nothing but an invention of the devil to torment us, the damned, all the more ?)

Checkered paper, the kind used in children's sum books, has charmed me since I was a little boy; and so I took along one crude booklet (although it was nonsense : I'd find that in Soltau too !)

New Metamorphoses (in the style of Ovid, came to me in a field of rubble) : Fleeing the Russians, a woman from Berlin is changed by the wind god, Flöse, into a moaning chimney. Or a weapons smuggler, pursued by the cops, into a tramp steamer of the Rickmer Line. In the underground passages of the Dammtor Station, they were still sitting erect, grim or praying, on suitcases and hatboxes, in muted and plaid clothes; a mummy child pressed its face into the scrawny lap of its gray-silked mother : and with my carbine on my ammo pouch, my finger on the trigger, I sauntered resounding down the rows of leather-shod skulls : and behold, he had said (stroking his hairy belly), behold : it was all very good ! At the barrier, where a hill of corpses was piled, I turned around, and walked back down the promenade : for this, then, man had been given reason.

I was so hate-full, that I raised my rifle, aimed it toward heaven : and through his Leviathan's maw gaped ten thousand nebulae : I'd like to pounce on the dog !

A lawyer's office next door ? That too ! – The venal pack : paid to be theatrically verbose on demand; full of the gestures of justice for money; for professional reasons instigators and agitators of all commerce : even murderers, Ilse Koch, generals, thieves, greedy old ladies, can always find their attorneys at ‹law› ! You need only bear that in mind to realize what a dispensable lot they are : in antiquity, the sycophant was the most despicable of beings : just being rid of that pack reconciles me again to the great catastrophe. They ranked below the prize fighters, who clubbed each other in the face while people gaped and paid : good thing it's all been swept away ! (And when I'm gone someday, the last blot will have disappeared : the experiment, man the stench, will have come to an end !) Such contemplations put me in a cheerful mood again. To that same end, I found myself reconciled to the entire missing front wall of a theater that allowed me to walk directly from the street into the orchestra.

Before the gold curtain : with tenor eyes rolling now, I spread supple (or so I imagined !) arms : "There you stood before my ey-hys / : I gazed at you – : and I was shaken / thou, my bliss, my delight . . ." (enunciated and very soft) : "Thine is my heart !" "And I am eternally thiiiiiiiinnnnnnnne ! ! !" (and nodded contentedly : but where was the applause ? ?) Wounded, I stopped and walked off with nettled steps (If I had just sniveled something about my cute-cute-cute canoe; or "singin' in the rain" – and there I was whistling the latter).

In the university library (Admission to students only : please : stud. scr. et cun. !). So here I was in the reading room and began with possessive gestures to handle the reference works : I would have needed a truck ! (Thankgod the most important lexica were on hand in Celle as well).

In the catalog. Very businesslike, I checked through my list of desiderata : baroque novels; a major work on costumes; Ellinger's ETA Hoffmann (there were 300 volumes at home already; I needed about 200 more).

Look at that : our old Franz Horn, Shakespeare's baladin : had he ever written trash ! And I gave him a bittersweet nod. – Ranke; Ranke the ‹historian› ! (Just how careful he was about the truth is easily seen in what he said in 1850 about old Marwitzen's memoirs of Friedrich Wilhelm the Third : it was too soon : too soon ! sic ! to rob the people of their belief in their ‹departed› king / Therefore, too soon for truth ! – And he dabbled in seances, too !) So I schlepped armload after armload down to my black tin-box. But they didn't have good maps; it was all cut and dried : if only a publisher had had the courage to bring out a major atlas of just topographical maps ! Political borders changed every 10 years anyway ! That would have been a meritorious deed; now I simply had to look for what individual items I could find. At least there was enough Cooper for me to complete my selected edition at home; but, of course, no biography here either. –

At the hardware store : a small whetstone, please, one you can bolt to the tabletop; if possible with interchangeable stones : since no one came to wait on me, I chose for myself and added a couple of steel blades (my plan is to make myself 2 spears, and a bow and arrow; shots make too much noise sometimes). I boastfully pressed a hundred-mark bill on the counter : always noble, Robert ! ("Blind him with your luster now" !).

The naked bronze rider (in the art museum) with his silly little hat (if he didn't have anything else on, he would still don just such an arty crash helmet !); shaking my head, I walked by the aforesaid fellow, and stopped again in the lobby. Glassed cases : here you could buy photographed copies for 20 pfennigs (but I already had three originals, and in their frames; although the gold-scrolled ones would definitely not fit my log cabin). – I took another undecided look at the poster : Exhibition of the Society of Graphic Artists; and another; ogodogodogod; but then I walked down the stairs, sighing and mistrustful.

Tables with pamphlets : (floor green-linoleum covered); frugally laden with pamphlets. Behind one of them, I projected a short, buxom, earnest girl; clerical worker, with stubby, upright breasts and a blue cheviot skirt; she countered my lascivious smile with secretarial detachment, the sun splotched rhombs about us, and when I took another swig of my 100 proof (cold and disparaging, her eyes wrote me off), I heard as well the hum and juggling feet of the afternoon's visiting public. I pulled my beret more on a slant and went for the frames on the wall.

"The Rumor". A. Paul Weber. I was stewed, but at once I muttered : "the best allegory since Leonardo." (Likewise "The Great Paralysis" : the only thing the kraken was lacking was Hitler's cap !) So then, A. Paul Weber. And I winked at the imaginary employee, but with no hope by now : if only she were here; je pouvais prendre un chien, Tucholsky had said. The tubular chairs were of less interest to me, and I simply kicked the cheekiest one out of the way.

"Cow by the Sea" : Nah ! I pursed my face, and stared into the unspeakably disgusting green : nah ! – Frames hung down over the walls, proper and pretty : I tipped one up, to see how they were fastened : aha ! : buckles on the back; so you could easily remove any etching. But pooh to you, dear friend : not your bull.

Magnus Zeller : pleas t' meetcha : hic ! But he was good too : lunar landscapes; and the "Italian City"; that one especially. I rocked on my ankles and fumbled a long while before I had the sheet and put it with the other two (and then both those full moons as well). Have to make a note of that "Magnus" (though I found "Zeller" thoroughly odious; was the name of a bastard of a first lieutenant back in the second world war : would I love to have him here now ! The leptosome bastard ! I'd shoot him in the belly, "till his guts spewed out as big as your feet" – it's by Schiller, in case you don't recognize the style !)

"The Leap", *"The End"*, *"Bon Voyage"* : A. Paul Weber again and I banged my fist against the wall : voilà un homme ! (And into the rucksack !) Way at the back Marc's "Band of Monkeys" with beautiful colors; likewise an original staircase painting : not bad at all. Then, however, on a pedestal something made of sanded yellow wood looking sort of like a female thigh (. . Bemberg silk). "ZEN (veiled)" writ below, and I stood before it, left hand on left cheek : "veiled" : so for those two swellings you had to imagine the essentials on your own. (Appeared not just to be in a family way, but absolutely "tribal"; and there were cracks in it too !) : Head shaking. Head shaking. – Then I took the staircase lads and walked slowly onward.

The sun broke through middling clouds, blue gray, like a shot from a bow, and I froze in the midst of the picture-laden chamber :

At first I saw nothing : d'abord je ne vis rien; mes yeux déshabitués de la lumière se fermèrent brusquement : I had expected nothing like this in our day ! ! I knelt down, Magnus Zeller at my back (to hell with the son-of-a-bitch : the officer, that is !)

"Children with Paper Kites" : one of them raised his hand. The other, ah wee-limbed, ran barefoot along beside, the roll of string under his green arm, and the blue wall of sky, frayed with white, rose above the grass ! I banged my head in the silent golden air; I puffed through my nose; I raised my numb hands : there ! : He was flying !

The demon : benevolent and golden-arched; divinity and wily attendants, created and set free, behind a blissful reveler. A blissful reveler, to be such is all my desire. – I walked up to it, and brushed my finger along the yellow frame; and laughed as the twine burst beneath my knife : ah, must take it along !

And praise be the Society of Graphic Artists, Hamburg-Langenhorn 2, Timmerloh 25 : for of our graphic artists I have seen the greatest : A. Paul Weber ! (In the etching gallery still more of them were hung; I selected "The Swing" and "The News" : especially that one).

Piranesi's "Caceri" and Callot, "Balli di Sfessania". Then upstairs again : nah. Portrait of a girl : soft-boiled blue eyes, myopic, like beer, stupid, thin and pale yellow. Nevertheless : the domed sweater, and I looked at it for a long time : more like strong stout. – A monk in watch-out position before God. – (Then I found myself in a helmet collection ! ! Out of here and off to Flottbek !). (That evening, a thunderstorm).

The village of Welle was burning : (The heat was so great that I hesitated to use the broad imperial highway, above which the immense vaults of flame hissed). Lightning must have struck yesterday; first it smoldered for a couple of hours, then the fiery geyser began. (And I labored on faster : I still need to set up a hand pump and water barrels !)

2 full days it took to get home, and walked ever so pooped from the drudgery; once inside, I slid the (unnecessarily wide) bolt shut, and contrived all manner of sleeping and eating feats. – Two days later collected 20 large baskets, for hauling coal, from the farmsteads in the area : 15 of them, in 5 rows, 3 to a row, fit in the trolley.

In 4 days, transported 4 tons of coal and 2 tons of briquets. Swore a lot.

In the lumberyard below : my muscles were stiff and swollen : but they chopped; broad chips, buxom logs, I slammed through knots like a hooligan. Every evening I swam in prisms of wood (tomorrow I would haul and stack them, beneath the overhanging roof). I licked upper lip, corner of mouth, lower lip, corner of mouth, corner of mouth.

Silent killing (because those 300 rounds wouldn't last forever). First came the cudgel; lovingly fashioned of oak, and fitted precisely to my arm (not "of doubled mass"). A six-foot-long cane of bamboo became a whopper of a spear, light and firm. (I gave up on the bow and arrows; my eyesight's probably too poor for that). So in the end I made another shillelagh, one that would have made Mike O'Hearn jealous. – Practiced with my spear for a long while : it's difficult (and even at 50 feet I didn't always hit my plywood target. Hmm). Rained a lot.

Boletus subtomentosus Linné : it occurred to me that the caps grew darker and darker as the year progressed and got more reddish flounder dots; plus the celadon hymenium : it looked glorious. (Once, I studied fungi, du fond and know Latin names long as the arm of a nine-year-old boy). And the wood mushrooms tasted like tenderest chicken. Long evenings reading Dickens's "Master Humphrey's Clock" : that and Bleak House are his masterpieces.

A cat – ought to be possible to tame one (so it could warn you the way a dog does, right ?) I suspected some dogs and cats, gone wild now, were occasionally getting into my garbage pit, behind the railroad embankment (that is to say, this was probably already the fifth or sixth wild generation; nevertheless, it ought to be easy enough to redomesticate them).

Irresolutely holding a spade : sure : I still had six canisters of potato flakes. But I really should lay out a little garden before the stuff in the old fields went hopelessly wild. I swore softly, and decided to dig on the far side of the path. A sullen half hour later, I had had it up to here with the proceedings ! I thrust the spade into the ground beside me (so that I could find the spot again), and went for a read. (Later, however, did clear around 600 square yards, my manure, scattered with a shudder, added the personal touch, and fetched potatolike stuff from the fields. – Won't amount to anything, I'm sure !)

A crystal detector (I know : it was crazy !) but I tried it anyway. Near Appenrodt's I pulled up a copper strand for an antenna; good ground. – Nothing. Sat there in front of it for three hours one night, with headphones; after that I was ready to believe I heard a whistle at 42.5, way in the background, "in remotest land of Turks"; but it was probably only self-deception; for, later, I picked up nothing. Could you run a vacuum-tube set with a bicycle dynamo ? And I cursed my semi-education (rather : my teachers !), who told me nothing about that. Maybe a simple voltaic pile. Maybe there were a couple groups of humans sitting out there in South Australia, Perth, and I would have liked to listen to them chewing the rag. I would like to know why I am still diarying away; I've lost all interest in poking around at inanities : what a tidy and solid life I, working man, could lead ("Oh, could I but be a carpenter"). My hands smell of cheddar cheese; my butt itches : hate to think what it smells like ! (That's no joke, but disgust at things organic).

Wild boars; and I shifted my rifle gears : should I ? ! (Because of my potato patch !). But the last sunshine faded; a cloud Mau-Mau crept across it, the whole body haired with flax and gray white. So I got up off my knee, and stalked home through bush and wild growth, home, to Juniperville. – Last lovely days; Indian summer (Evening and still 65 degrees).

Totally vacant : the sky. The dashing third-moon left only 20 big stars, huzzah, the mighty. And in the clarity, the wind raged, till my hair did eddy and bob. Shiny and bright gray was the side of the house with its shadowed waiting-door; above the roof ran black sheen and heavenly silver blue, black and blue, till my soul did eddy and bob. So I stood there in the dark wooded farmstead, setting my shoulder skin freezing beneath my shirt, and the only choice left me was to imbibe or nap my way between feathered covers :

I walked into the moon, my rifle riding shotgun, in my armpit, trouser-pocket cloth taut across the pistols. I turned supplely to the right and glided into phalanxes of pine, he glided along up top : ever faster. Rollings in the tree corona and whorlings in the blackly carved underwood, the babbling of leaves sped and coiled me forwards. I bounded myself behind the thickest fir trunk and roughed into the radiant clearing : swishing branches, waving herbage, wary hunters, stroke of moon. Reached for my rounded hip and turned the top of my canteen; the chainlet clinked and shied. I closed lip rim around the aluminum threads; my larynx pumped; and the brightness grew ever steelier. Wind assaulted, straight across the clearing, first alone : You're attacking me ? ! I bounded over old stumps, danced along beneath the branches, the wood unfolded : just ahead the road flows.

Road still with hard wagon tracks from human days. I drove along it before the wind as far as my homestead; on past; the apple trees grumbled in disrhythm. Speedier was I, the skin of my lips was already numb, and my thighs rode beneath me along the level bike path, one, two, should I rest, then I rust.

Colony Hünzingen : once there had been lights here for the nightly wanderer : a man read from his calendar, a girl played with her panties, money was counted, the powerful bulbs beamed, announcements radioed "from the world of sport". Plows slept in shedded darkness, dogs stood roaring at chain's end, the poplars at the watering hole watched ducks by day. Was. Watched.

In the second house on the right (and in my indefatigable hand the lamp burred). Four thrusts of the ax and the door staggered open : a kitchen. The dull aluminum was still screaming, cups and plates had blue flowers too. My fingers went rigid and at first total darkness arrived; then all at once the moon through the window square. I tapped upon gloomy stairs, banged fists at doors, a chamber opened full of much promise : a maiden's room ! At the broken window the frigid mongrel wind yelped; I thrust my head between the privy pillows and heard the nettle scratching at my beard. Princely weariness overcame me, dangerous, and I gulped down the small dregs, tottering afoot and gasping.

And down ! across the street moon's light spurted. I returned, legs hotly asprawl; this one time only, and more slowly, down the paths. The fields, though bright with moon, left me cold : I put them down with a gesture of the hand : what did that wild enameled white grain want : I would have loved a mouse (that is, to have seen one !). Or a dentist. – I hastened back deliberately on yielding legs and sat down before my house : enough ! –

Who created cultural values ? ! Only Greeks, Romans, Teutons; Indians in philosophy. – The Slavs are a typically cultureless sort : my God : chess and a bit of music !

Rain days on end. The hoary wind stood about the house like a billygoat, fret wind, fret wind (and the vats filled themselves with lovely dull water !). I went to the other window and gazed to the east.

Outside (had pulled on my shoes after all and swept my cape of tarp about me; comfier walk down the path, and in my camouflage cloak No One saw me before the fir backdrop). The rain tap-danced at the brim of my cap, fingered at my shoulders and Morse-coded nimbly; as I leaned around the corner, the gusts held back as well.

The railroad embankment : the flat artificial wall pointed grainily into distance and rainy haze. There they had drudged with their edge-runners, measured and cut; laid iron shoddy down, and were driven upon it for filthy lucre : now it was all overgrown. Drippings in the underwood, and from the puddles came seethings, cold and silken gray, bubbles leapt and floated : if only they had listened to Malthus and Annie Besant; but by 1950 things had gone so far that the earth grew by 100,000 every day : one hundred thousand ! ! I looked contentedly through the black pine stalks : good that it had turned out this way !

November second broke off the leaves, sheets of copper lay all about, one fiery week long; then I vanished into the early and hard winter (another match with the eleven-year sunspot cycle, wasn't it ? !) In January the brook froze and I had to melt a lot of ice; the stove thundered and gave a broad-hipped glow by white-blue day and by zebraed night.

The moon flashed sharp shadows about me and appeared ever and again in its velvet abysses. Once a stormwind blew from the east for 50 hours straight, and the reading was twenty-eight below. (That same morning an occultation of Jupiter occurred.)

The black dome of night : from the orbicular upper light at the zenith it came, toxic clear and so jeering bright that the snow burnt eyes and soles. I sat down on my two top wooden steps, and wrote on a large sheet :

Fermat's theorem : If $A^N + B^N = C^N$, given whole natural numbers, N can never be larger than 2. I quickly proved this for myself as follows :

(1) $A^N = C^N - B^N$ or $A^{2 \cdot N/2} = (C^{N/2} - B^{N/2}) \cdot (C^{N/2} + B^{N/2})$, therefore

(2) $A^{N/2}$ = the root of the right side; let $C^{N/2} - B^{N/2} = x^2$ and $C^{N/2} + B^{N/2} = y^2$, that automatically gives (3) $A^N = (x \cdot y)^2 = a^2$ and further it is demonstrated that :

(4) $C^N = [(x^2 + y^2)/2]^2 = c^2$ just as (5) $B^N = [(y^2 - x^2)/2]^2 = b^2$

The equation $A^N + B^N = C^N$ can therefore always be reduced to the quadratic equation $a^2 + b^2 = c^2$, wherein x and y are fundamental integers. For a, b and c to be whole numbers, x and y must likewise be whole numbers, besides which $y - x = 2$ m. etc. etc. (And immediately several possibilities : for $y = 4$; $x = 2$ the result is $8^2 + 6^2 = 10^2$. For $y = 5$; $x = 3$, the result is $15^2 + 8^2 = 17^2$; so that an 8 can appear twice, depending on whether it is a or b.)

And now for the Meaningful General : in the case of whole numbers, every expression of $A^N + B^N + C^N + D^N + \ldots\ldots = Z$ may in its simplest form have N elements on the left side, no less ! And – as above with the example of 8 – the same number value may occur at most N times, depending on whether it is A^N, B^N, etc. E.g., for $N = 3$ the result is : $3^3 + 4^3 + 5^3 = 6^3$; $18^3 + 3^3 + 24^3 = 27^3$; $36^3 + 37^3 + 3^3 = 46^3$. The symbols drew themselves out nimbly from my pencil, and I bungled merrily along : just imagine that : I'm solving the problem of Fermat's theorem ! (But time flew in exemplary fashion all the while).

With all its numberless goings on of life / inaudible as dreams : read a lot of ST Coleridge. And the lays of Marie de France as well (Here, then, is the model for Fouqué's "Elidouc the Knight". I.e., it could presumably also be Gottfried von Monmouth).

Concerning the Universe as an Extension of the Sensory System.

II

(20. 5. 1962)

USA-Culture : No One is so small that he doesn't like to be called grande at home ! I flung the Reader's Digest against the wall, heaved a sheet of paper into my typer and rattled off (oh, was I fuming !) :

Professor George R. Stewart, University of California, U.S.A.

Dear Professor :

I read, with great interest, the instructive excerpts from your new book, "Man, an Autobiography," which appeared in the Reader's Digest of July, 1947, on pages 141–176, and relived, with profound amazement, this history of humankind.

The anonymous author of the brief foreword quite justly praises the "originality of your writings" and your having made a "rattling good story" of an old theme without getting buried under a mass of confusing names and dates. In these parts, to be sure, many folks are still somewhat taken aback when matters of cultural history start to rattle; all the more reason, then, that they should value further assurances of "the care with which you gather your facts."

First, a word hereto. Years ago I made an extensive study of the geography of the ancients, and for that reason always take notice of the subject even nowadays. Therefore your statement (p. 170a) touched me sorely and did not contribute to an especially favorable opinion of your knowledge or your accuracy : "In spite of Phoenicians and Greeks, the peoples of the ancient world were essentially landlubbers, keeping along shore. But with people who faced the Atlantic, it was navigate the Atlantic or stay at home. They navigated, and built better ships, and sailed farther – the Northmen, the Flemings and English, the Hanse merchants, the Bretons and Portuguese . . ." (I will disregard the ingenious "either – or" : the lion roars if he is not silent). – When you (and others) engage in constant praise of the Vikings, you are apparently thinking of the first discovery of America; you forget, however, that not one of these pirates ever reached Vinland by sailing directly from Norway or England, but always with stops in Iceland and

Greenland (which, by the way, lie within sight of one another !) : none
of these stages demanded more than 600 miles on open seas at the
most; and the last one was often made unwillingly.

I will not apologize for the ancients by pleading that on those seas
by which they lived – the Mediterranean, the Black and Red Seas –
there was simply no room for such long distances. As soon as they
had sufficiently investigated these waters, they of course left the shore
and regularly sailed across the flood in all directions; and from Byzantium to Phanagoreia was a journey of over 450 miles ! (Nor will I
unfairly pass over navigators' reports that there was one point along
the route where a knowledgeable sailor could simultaneously discern
in a haze both Cape Criumetopum in the north and Cape Carambis in
the South).

But there is yet another major example, namely, the trade with India !
After Eudoxus, as the first Greek, had officially opened the sea route
to India in the days of Ptolemy Euergetes, commercial enterprises
assumed truly gigantic dimensions. I recommend you include the
really interesting "facts" in your repertoire : how they sailed up the
Nile from Alexandria to Coptus; and from there traveled by caravan
to Berenica on the Red Sea, where the India fleet was waiting with up
to 120 (!) large freighters. They necessarily remained close to land as
far as Oecilis at the exit of the Red Sea, of course; but from there
the convoy traversed with the July/August monsoon, *sailing 40 un-
interrupted days on the open sea*, my dear Professor, the 1800 miles
to Barygaza, etc., on the Malabar coast; and returned in December.
And from the time of Hippalus the Sailor on, this voyage was undertaken with massive escort for centuries, year after year, causing Pliny
to declare the value of exports at 50 million sesterces, the imports at 5
billion.

The Chryse voyages across the Bay of Bengal (800 miles on the
high seas) belong in the same context; for such journeys were made
regularly, and Ptolemy speaks of them as common knowledge. – Nothing like them was undertaken before Columbus, not by any of those
nations whose superiority you praise with your either-or; and even
Columbus, in fact, set sail with information about Vinland.

: You, however, contrast them with the ancient "landlubbers," do you
not ? ! I charge you with ignorance !

Not that I would reject all of your views; for as you quite correctly
remark (p. 165a) : "Continual talking is likely to be associated with
some thought here and there"; by that dictum, however, one ought not
compose books, at least not works of cultural history.

But for your "man" the overriding issue is "civilization," i.e., to use your definition from p. 175b : "the mass of such things as agriculture, metalworking and social tradition" (not art or science, of course, none of that ! The word culture does not even occur in your work – except on p. 169a where in an ironic line you speak of those who are more enthusiastic about poetry than about plows); but civilization : that gives "control over the outside world" and for you that is the essential "rough and easy way," the decisive criterion by which to compare epochs, or, as you state it more clearly and precisely, to "test" them.

And as if hastening to make us palpably aware of the full weight of your test of civilization, you also apply it with remarkable impartiality to the Greeks.

First you make the rise of Hellenic culture so easy to comprehend : "Not having much regular work to do, they had to pass the time in various ways. *Thus the Greek citizens were able to develop art, athletics, and philosophy*". Sounds quite plausible, doesn't it ? And so simple ! – How true : for thousands of years before and after them, rulers and priests had no such idle time available to them ? ! And the equally work-shy South Sea Islanders, or Teutons, or the denizens of cloisters, etc., had none either ! And nevertheless, not only did they not develop any of the arts and sciences (not to mention philosophy), not only did they not understand them when they met up with them, but in fact did their best to suppress them ! For certain people – around 99 percent – culture is, after all, boring : do you know that ? ! – True, the artist and thinker requires his leisure; but that sentence, like the one about pigs and sausage, does not work in reverse.

"A great deal of nonsense has been written about the Greeks in general and about the Persian Wars in particular . . ." : granted : I have your book here in my hand !

"The supreme misfortune of the Persians was not to lose the war but to let the Greeks write the history of it and pass it on down to later nations . . ." Sir : someone can babble away that Herodotus' report – for he is the source, after all, not "the Greeks" – was a misfortune for the Persians, only if that someone has never read it ! For : "What Herodotus of Halicarnassus has researched, he here describes, so that what occurred among men may not in time be lost, nor the great and wondrous deeds accomplished, *by Hellenes no less than barbarians,* fade without echo !", and in fact the Persians certainly do not come off any the worse.

Which was indeed something that your beloved "intelligent Egyptians or Babylonians" or those "in many ways more admirable" Persians could have learned from the Greeks : how one writes universal history, with objectivity and apt comprehensiveness, instead of with the narrow-minded, overweening, false, and wooden tone of the chronicles of the Egyptians or the local gossip-columns of the Old Testament. Following these introductory remarks, you then mercilessly apply your "test" (and here I will pass over your cheap though hardly original comments about the relationship between language and thought; a certain James Burckhardt left us – before the University of California was ever founded – a discussion of the agorazein that yields the reader decidedly greater rewards). You summarize : "Throughout the breadth of the world, there is in use no important invention which can certainly be credited to the Greeks." On the basis of which I (even I, Professor George R. Stewart !) conclude, "that the Greeks neither made civilization nor saved it, nor even re-made it very notably." : Thank you ! Now at last, we occidental neurotics, so long hindered by our *praejudicium antiquitatis,* can see things clearly !

Granted, some decades ago now our "Fliegende Blätter" instructed us about cave paintings in Arkansas; Mark Twain about the press in Tennessee; and a few months ago I was profoundly moved to read in the "New York Post" of how for five million dollars the Football Hall of Fame, of which we have been so long deprived, is to be erected in Cazenovia (a borrowing from the Greeks by the way : they were forever building their brawlers and gambolers monuments to Olympia); but we had to wait for your book, this bonanza of nonsense, to inform us about how the history of humankind is taught in the US !

We have been accustomed till now to ascribe in brief the following to the Greeks :

that they were the first to develop and employ the spirit and method of Western research. We owe them such important independent findings as the exact measurement of the earth's sphere, and, as a result, maps with objects fixed by longitude and latitude. In astronomy, star catalogues, geo- and heliocentric world views etc., are likewise Greek discoveries; biological systems are based on their work; : could you solve diophantine equations ?

Compare Greek cultural achievements – statues, temples, epics, dramas, etc. – with any and all previous and contemporaneous achievements : greater men than either of us have been enraptured by them !

Philosophy – – well, you folks over there have not got that far yet. –

We are and shall remain of the opinion that, in spite of the Stewart test, the totality of our intellectual existence, emerging out of the last two crests of culture, the renaissance and the classic-romantic age, is

based, as were those crests themselves, on the Greek way. You observe
that there has never been a "fall of civilization," and given your definition, I can only agree with you :

but you had announced your theme to be "man," sir. "Man" – not your
comical civilization ! The equation of the two is original, I grant, and
your intellectual property; but I doubt that you will find many who
therefore envy you. It may be humiliating that your nation has as yet
made no contribution to great culture – with the exception of Edgar
Poe; but even that day too will come !

(Though not through your efforts !)

> May your toilets always flush;
>
> with sincerest contempt :

Fold, envelop; the traditional 30 pfennigs pasted on it and borne by bike to
the mailbox down in the village : what a flunky ! (And on the way back
kept losing my temper every hundred yards : godknows, what with the
production of atom bombs and corned beef, they ought to have had
more than enough to attend to : you can't do everything after all !)

The bachelor moon (still almost full) I had not yet regained my composure,
and decided, thirsting for vengeance, to set up a test myself (felibre
can't leave writing alone) so then : here goes :

1.) Do you know and value Meyern's "Dya-Na-Sore," Moritz's
"Anton Reiser," Schnabel's "Felsenburg Island" ?

2.) Are you of the opinion that an artist should thumb his nose at the
taste and niveau of the public ?

3.) "Man has no free will." – Do you believe that ?

4.) Do you prefer Wieland's "Aristippus" to the "Forsyte Saga" ?

5.) Did you at times despise your parents ?

6.) Are you superstitious ?

7.) Do you have a friend who in all seriousness recommended that
you read Klinger's "Raphael de Aquilla" ?

8.) Do you hate all things soldierly and uniformed ?

9.) Can you give a brief summary of the contents of Jean Paul's
"Campanian Valley" ?

10.) Do you consider Nietzsche a mediocre intellect (but a great orator) ?

11.) Do you find boxing, films, fashion, etiquette quite ridiculous ?
Then the devil gave me a jab and I wrote (I can write and shout
Everything : I'm alone, you know ! !) :

12.) At any point in your life, have you entertained the least suspicion : some holy book or other, if used as toilet paper, might singe
your butt ? –

Give yourself a +1 for every yes; a –1 for every no and total your score :

You had best hang yourself. (And with that I put the matter behind me).

Give photography a try (am curious if the film is still good; and I've never done any developing either; but it's good for the mood and passes time). So I began to take snapshots : sunspots; a parlor-sized clearing; rusted barbwire (at the train station, where the old iron lay about); larva-corroded fungal ruins; a branch in the woods, oh form forever fleeting; once into the middle of a German cloudwork through a straddly little fir. Naturally myself as well (with delayed action) : on the steps to the house, sunk heavy-witted in a folio (but – as always – I made such a stupid face that the negative already set my stomach turning).

Heinrich Heine : very nice reading (very nice forgetting). Had he written only one volume – using my four-volume edition as the measure – he would have been a great man : but financial misery doesn't permit that to any writer : necessity makes everyone the muse's pimp, her sweet Mack (i.e., in plain German : brewing droll stories for the newspapers; arranging this and that for RIAS; diligently translating the work of foreigners etc. – a fine thing, too, that such magic was over forever !)

Stretch of good weather, and added many things to the large map 1 : 10,000. (Had selected as my starting point a line from the aforementioned hunting lookout to the erstwhile flak-tower, across from farmer Lüdecke's, and fixed an ample number of points; for the small areas in between, compass, optical square, and pacing-off distances sufficed). I want to have my region under constant control. –

Set up emergency quarters in the Düshorn supply depot just in case : all quite crude : tidied up the room, laid out blankets, some clothes and tools; you never know.

24.6. : with mad hands leafing in the shrubbery (and the kettle's steaming and will boil soon; can only report when I rest in between).

While walking blithely the edge of the wood : literally : quite without purpose. Like Robinson with 2 guns, and, because of the noonday sun, beneath my white visored cap (let that be a lesson to me : never run around with such a goddam target on my head !). I saw something glisten over in the shrubbery, and propped my binox against a scrawny branch for more comfortable focusing : that it put me behind a pine tree probably saved my life; because by then bark was flying round my nose, and the angled shot bumblebeed into the underbrush behind me. With presence of mind, I immediately fell into the ditch (and half stabbed myself from behind on the lumpy bolt of my gun).

Assembling my thoughts : well this was something new ! (Calm down;
ever so cool : I knew the terrain, that guy over there didn't !) So first I
carefully raised my reserve rifle and blasted a low shot in the general
direction : left it lying on the level woodland floor beside the ditch and
shoved my cap over the round bulbous rock beside it : then crept very
cautiously 10 yards to the right (toward home as it were). There were
still 20 yards left until the ditch would be almost too shallow.

Sighting 500 (telescopic sight was set for 300 and 500 yards) : and there
came another flash from across the way, and the mud simply flew
around the hypothetical ears of my magic cap, so that it slipped an inch
lower : superb ! Means he'll try again for sure. – After brief reflection,
I wriggled another 30 yards farther through needle sweepings and
ground litter. Climbed up in the fir thicket, and ran into two junipers at
woods' edge : –

Now I could see the guy quite clearly in my binox : he was lying behind a
heap of stones, and was fidgeting, trying to determine the effect of his
shots; but he wasn't about to trust the iron repose of my dummy and
laid his (apparently capped) head back deeper into his duds.

Behind the railroad embankment, gasping : fast as lightning, past the
house, across the tracks, crouching along the righthand side, I ran,
and was now on the same level with him – approximately –, right :
there he still was ! The insatiable fellow was just raising his gun to his
shoulder (and I leapt up again, knowing that he was busy, and trotted
into the woods' edge : crack ! !; yessir, my boy ! Keep yourself nicely
distracted !)

But now things got difficult : I was standing 20 yards behind him and I
considered –

One possibility : cut him down before he could say Jack Robinson. (There
was his girl's bike leaning against a crooked fir. With straight lower
frame tubes : a minority of German brands had had those; contrasting
reddish brown and bright yellow; dirty; cardboard box on the luggage
rack. A flabby rucksack in the grass : canteen dangle, cookware, map-
case). (Maybe he had thought – as I stepped behind the tree, and
pricked up my binox – that I was aiming at him, and that he just had
time to get the jump on me ? –)

Take him prisoner and ‹neutralize› him : most of all I would have liked to
scratch my head : what does neutralize mean in this case ? ! What if the
jerry torches my cabin two days later, or butchers me in my sleep ? ! –
He clawed an itching thigh and jiggled with such fury that I had to grin,
but immediately I got serious again : he might very well stand up now
and make for the other side !

Another 8 yards (gray hair already, huh ? !) I took one more deep and unhappy breath, then gave myself a push, rushed him, and struck – well :
a light blow for starters – with my rifle butt !

In overalls and cap : there she lay ! ! With white ragged hands.

Immoderate glances : hands, shoulder, a face. Hands shoulder a face. Eyes
lip a mouth : hey ! – Gasping, I stood up and emptied her pistols into
the ground; I automatically pulled the ammo clip from her rifle.

Her small very soft breasts : her small very firm hand.

With staggering fingers I groped for the rum flask at my hip, and held it
fearfully to her limp bowed mouth of pallor (there : beneath the short
gray hair you could feel the thick lump now : oh, what an idiot I am !
But clean-shaven thankgod).

Swallowing : finally ! I'll write a hymn to it ! Swallowing. – Then I laid her
head back onto the folded blanket, and my hands like clasps across her
thin shoulders.

Gray eyes (still unconscious : gray and frosty : lovely !)

Like a bullwhip (and with astounding strength) : was how her body
thrashed ! But I got a firmer grip : "Lie peaceful !" I said very still :
"And in 8 days you'll be rid of the bump," Smiled. And she breathed;
irregular and irresolute. Pause. I took my hands away as a test and
squatted down close to her right flank (but kept on looking at her).
"What's your name ?" it occurred to me to ask. "Lisa" (nor did I fail to
notice how amused she was that the last two human beings used formal
pronouns with one another; but nevertheless) then I explained; slowly.

She marveled wearily : "And you haven't raped me." I laid a hand to her
temple, sympathetic; gave one shake of my head : "Poor thing; the
men you must have had to deal with !" (As I took my hand away, the
fingertips glided down down along the cheek.) Above the dust-gray
path, sky solitude burned blue; I slowly turned my lieless face inward
and admitted : "– I couldn't help but think of it of course. For a moment –". Now the exhausted ailing mouth laughed a little, wise, mocking, and kind too : "You're lucky you admitted it !" Sly : "Cause I
would have thought less of myself if you hadn't." Rest a little longer ?
(I've got aspirin over at my place, really).

The wildcat : I had barely got to my feet and was about to gather up her
stuff, there she stood in front of me : in each hand a mauser, her mouth
half open in wrath, her eyes cold and wicked : la donna è mobile (Or la
belle Dame sans merci, that's it !)

"So, my boy" she said stonily and low : "now first raise both hands !"
(Well, why not ? : I can bring them down on you all the easier that
way !) I did it good-humoredly; but when I realized that she was about

to go for my rifle, I leapt to block her path : and felt both barrels deep between my ribs. We stood breast to breast and looked into each other's faces.

She took my measure : height, shoulders. – I suggested (why should I shame her and let her pull the trigger to no avail ? That way, later on, she would always have a feeling of equality, of having acted on her own); I suggested : "Let's conclude an armistice. – Till tomorrow noon, for starters. –" Then I found it in my heart and added : "Please." She wrinkled her brow and harkened to the clash of her motives. Finally I raised (very slowly) my right hand and laid it around her left; let it lie around it in earthly lust for one minute, and then gently pulled the weapon to the side (while we gazed into each other's eyes as earnestly as two screech owls). She resolutely pulled her right hand away on her own; with feigned coolness she decided : "All right ! : Till tomorrow noon !" – I loaded the bike, and we walked off, relaxed and with a little amble, to my place. (Now she has to wash; the water's boiling). And I lugged the bucket and filled the large tub in the laundry, while she sat inside eating a bite, crackers and spam, and drank sweet tea (with rare cane sugar; that really is something different from our beet stuff !); then she had to stretch out on the couch.

Quite softly crouching beside her (a long time).

"Lisa –" (touching with my voice; very lightly; dabbing). And now I realized at once that she hadn't been sleeping at all, but had been savoring the adoration, and iris and teeth shimmered like scamps, entrancing. : "The water's about ready" I announced, thus wounded, and there I was gazing again into that dawning face.

Hands at the wood (of the door frame : my God, I haven't seen a woman for 8 years now ! And across the way, splashings accompanied by wild whistled potpourris, Marion Kerby couldn't have done it better. Ten times I was just short of : ‹Come into my bower of love› : well you can just go to hell !)

"Lisa" : I tasted ‹Lisa›; spoke into the whispering grass ‹Lisa›; breathed wide-nostriled (all down by the brook), and was in mentionable bliss : Lisa !

Potatoes : she was beyond bliss and peeled them very fine (sitting on my steps, between two shiny little basins), and I nodded in deep contentment : good for squaw to do that. (All the while she looked out of her eyes with such apparent kindness, her gaze running over me, that I almost fell for it : had she not had to pucker her mouth in amusement just once : because there I was rapt to my elbows, as if before a picture in a gallery).

Added sugar to her potato cakes : made her home, therefore, east of the Elbe (Right : let's get down to business !)

And she reported : deep in the armchair, very still, with no riffraff of eyes nor conjure of hands (only once did I give a shout : Lisa was about to water down her rum !)

She had come from the east (so we complemented one another to a T; I had had to tramp the west and southwest) : from the Ukraine, where she had been dragged off to; up the Dniester, Lemberg, Krakow, Warsaw (spent two winters there). Posen, Stettin (had wanted to try to make her way by water, but couldn't handle a sailboat : she almost starved trying to get off Usedom against a strong, contrary wind). Berlin (another winter; exactly as I had done in my wandering days : holed up in an apartment; chopped up furniture and heated with that; plundered stores – and I nodded gravely : who should know but I !), then on to Dresden, Prague : but heading south from there she came across one of the radiation belts, where even now, for hundreds of miles, not a plant grew, not a bird flew : so she had turned back around to the north, via Carlsbad to Leipzig. But had left there – for some reason or other – just last November, and come straight through the Harz Mountains to Quedlinburg, where the early and cold winter had caught her by surprise; only with difficulty had she still been able to stock up on provisions. She had started out again in May : Brunswick, Hanover, Celle; for 10 days she had lain in bed in Fallingbostel with a wretched cold, until three days ago. Then Walsrode (spent the night); she had just started out the next morning, when her bike broke down in Borg, and she spent the whole day patching it up. Had grabbed some sleep at a farmstead; then by mistake she had ended up on the road to Ahrsen, and cursing had taken out her little map, and was intending to head west to the highway, ‹straight through Kansas›, when she had seen ‹some guy› at the edge of the woods, who had immediately taken aim at her : so I had guessed right ! (And she consistently avoided the subjunctive, apparently for fear of wearing it out). But she wasn't tired yet, and, although the wind raged, intrigued to learn my trick; so we walked the 400 yards by the last light of evening.

The wind blew in the sails of her locks, white shoulders sauntered ahead beneath her dress; her eyes emerged on the right, on the left, now compact and scornfull, now widened and horizoned, and all the while my huntress whistled, that it would have done your heart good to behold.

She was stunned (and I ditto : even from a distance of 20 yards it looked sensational !) "Well if that doesn't beat everything" she said enraged, pointed at it with both her attendant hands : most optical illusion,

ahyes. Had been a splendidum mendacium (although that actually
‹means› something else; I know, I know). – But now she fetched the
cap, challenging : "Well, noble grouch ? !" : gave me a few willies
indeed, when I saw the two holes above the brim : and she vanished
triumphing in the niagara of wind, maid of the mist. (That's really
quite a feat : at a distance of at least 400 yards, and without a telescopic
sight ! Although you see white against black resplendently. But nevertheless ! – That's something !)

Her slender celadon face floated by, triangular in the thorn-dusk, her
body's supple stem shifting it mercilessly back and forth; slow somber
goddess with weapons of iron.

Again in armchairs : the petroleum lamp glimmers peacefully. (And very
much like a dream for us both – a sentence in which ‹very much
like› carries both meanings). But the most important question still
remained :

"Didn't you, in all those years – in all your travels – find any other
people ?" – At first she didn't want to deal with it; but then she saw
the importance of combining our experiences, and began :

"Oh yes – twice." – "Once, still in Russia, four women : three young ones,
one old. A man with them." – "The old woman poisoned the young
ones first. Then just to be on the safe side I gunned her down." – I
choked it out : "And the – man ? !" She shook her head in the negative : "Blood poisoning. 6 weeks later." Silence. I stood up to no
purpose and found myself at the bookcase; then I turned, and leaned
shoulders, hair, knee-hollows, palmed hands against it, everything; I
asked with hoarse good cheer : "And ? Affair number two ?" – She
crumpled her yellow-shone face : "Lay dying : an 80-year-old Polish
woman." Pushed air through her wrinkly nose : "Wasn't pretty !" Another shake of the head; looked my way with an embarrassed smile :
"And you ? Whom have you met ?" I shoved out my lower lip, musing,
taking what I'd heard to complement the general picture : "No one." I
could report. – "So that south of Prague is one of the atomic waste-
lands.". "Apparently that's the corridor" she interrupted eagerly "from
Danzig to Trieste that they tried to use to separate east and west at the
start of the war – and I found a way across near Lemberg quite by
accident – ?" "Very likely", I admitted, and got out a map of Europe :
"I've seen the second dividing line, Genoa–Antwerp. – Passed over
Switzerland" I explained to her inquiring eyes.

In summary : "From our autopsy, then, we know that all of Central Europe
is void of humans –" She nodded. "And in the adjoining regions there
can't be any groups of people worth the mention, otherwise over the

intervening years they would have seeped through long ago." That too seemed logical." Have you ever seen an airplane all this time ?" Personne. "Russia and the USA have completely finished each other off : so not much is going to be happening there either." (By now we had opened up the map of the world in my Andree).

"So what's left really" she said pensively, and I nodded in approval : straight to the point ! "In my opinion," I declared icily, "the situation is as follows : Asia, Europe (or better, Asiopa) –; likewise North America –" I brushed my hand across the blue and yellow northern hemisphere, and she pinched her lips together in agreement. "South Africa got it too; likewise the industrial centers of Australia and South America.". "My theory is : that, separated by very large spaces, here and there a few isolated individuals are still nomadizing about. Perhaps at the southernmost points of the continents there are –" (automatically I resorted to catchwords I'd thought out) – "still small communities left. – The individuals, unaccustomed to the harsh life and raw disease, will quickly die out." She took melancholy and cozy breaths : by lamplight it sounded like a book. "Eventually those aforesaid tiny groups may pave the way for a repopulated earth; but that will take – well – let's hope a thousand years." "And that's all to the good !" I concluded defiantly.

Reasons ? : "Lisa ! !" : "Just recall to mind what humanity looked like ! Culture ! ? : one in a thousand passed culture on; one in a hundred thousand created culture ! : Morality ? : Hahaha ! : Let every man prove his conscience and say he wasn't ripe for hanging long ago !" She nodded, convinced at once. "Boxing, soccer, the lottery : how those legs did run ! – Very big when it came to weapons !" – "What were a boy's ideals : auto-racer, general, world-champion sprinter. A girl's : film star, ‹creator› of fashion. The men's : harem owner and manager. The woman's : car, electric kitchen, to be addressed as ‹milady›. The old codgers' : statesman –" I ran out of air.

"Let us posit the case" I began again in the words of the old novel, "that there exits – on whatever planet you prefer – a species of creatures who come into their world with such poor ability that barely one in a thousand can be brought to a level of merit worth mentioning – and that indeed only as a result of the most painstaking and diligent culture, together with a convergence of the most favorable circumstance, not one of which dare be missing : what would be your opinion of the species as a whole ? ! !"

"The human race is equipped by Nature with all necessaries for perceiving, observing, comparing, and differentiating objects. For such

purposes it not only has all such objects immediately present and lying before it and can grow wise not only by using its own experience : but it also has lying open for its use the experiences of all preceding ages and the observations of a number of perceptive persons, who, quite often at least, have seen things correctly. As a result of such experience and observation, it has long since been determined by what Laws of Nature mankind – in whatever sort of society and condition it find itself – must live and act in order to be happy after its fashion. Pursuant to them, it has been incontrovertibly proved what all is useful or harmful to the species as a whole, in all times and under all circumstance; the rules, the application of which can preclude all error and false conclusion, have been found; we can know with satisfying certainty what is beautiful or ugly, right or wrong, good or evil, why it is so, and to what extent it is so; no form of stupidity, vice, or wickedness can be invented, whose illogicality or perniciousness has not long ago been proved just as rigorously as any theorem of Euclid : and nevertheless ! Notwithstanding, human beings have kept on spinning about in the very same circle of stupidity, error, and abuse for several thousand years, growing no wiser either through their own experience or that of others, in short, becoming, in certain individuals at best, wittier, more perceptive, more learned, but never wiser."

"*Human beings, namely,* usually do not reason by the Laws of Reason. On the contrary : their inborn and common mode of conceiving is as follows : to deduce the generality from isolated events, to draw false conclusions on the basis of fleeting occurrences or those viewed from only one perspective, and at every moment to confuse word with idea and idea with object. The majority of them – which means by fairest calculations 999 of 1000 – base most judgments about the most important events in their lives on first sensate impression, prejudice, passion, whim, fantasy, mood, coincidental connection of word and notion in their brains, apparent similarity and covert prompting in behalf of their own interests, as a result of which at any moment they will take their own ass for a horse, and another man's horse for an ass. Among that said 999 are at least 900, who in addition do not employ their own organs of perception, but out of incomprehensible laziness would prefer to see things falsely through strangers' eyes, hear badly through strangers' ears, be made fools of through the unreason of strangers, instead of at least making fools of themselves on their own. Not to speak of a considerable portion of that 900 who have become accustomed to speak of a thousand important matters in important tones, without ever knowing what they are saying and without worrying for a moment whether what they speak be sense or nonsense."

"A *machine,* a mere tool, that must allow itself to be used and misused by strange hands; a bundle of straw that at any moment may burst into flames from a single spark; a down feather that allows itself to be driven in a different direction by every breeze – those have not, since the world began, been regarded as images by which the activity of a reasonable being might be described : and yet they have indeed been employed since time immemorial to express the manner in which human beings, especially when pressed together in great masses, are wont to move and act. It is not merely that desire and loathing, fear and hope – set in motion by sensuality and delusion – are customarily the driving force behind all such daily actions, which are not merely the work of instinctual habit : but rather in those most essential instances – precisely where it is a matter of the happiness or despair of a whole life, the prosperity or misery of a whole nation : and most of all, when it is a matter of what is best for the whole of the human race – it is the passions or prejudices of strangers, it is the pressure or shove of a few individual hands, the glib tongue of a single chatterbox, the wildfire of a single fanatic, the hypocritical zeal of a single false prophet, the shout of a single man of rash action who places himself at their head – setting thousands and hundreds of thousands in motion, though they see neither the validity nor result of their action : by what right can such an irrational species of creatures . . ." (first catch my breath).

And so : "The mummers, quacks, jugglers, prestidigitators, bawds, cut-purses, and swashbucklers divided the world among them; – the sheep stretched out their muttonheads and let themselves be shorn; – while the fools gamboled and somersaulted. And the clever ones, if they could, went forth and became hermits : the history of the world in nuce, in usum Delphini."

"And who's at fault ?" – "Why, the primo motore of it all, of course, the creator, whom I have named the Leviathan, and have tediously proved." During my fine speech, she had – apparently in an excess of concentration – closed her eyes, and only opened them again now as the millwheel ceased to rumble. "Well yes," she said slowly : "And I've got a bit of a toothache too." "Then you must invoke St. Apollonia at once," I was quick to advise, but received only a nasty glance : "Thanks to your rifle butt !" she muttered (with a stylishly elliptic twist).

Make up the beds : She slept on the giant couch (four feet three inches wide !), and : "I'll lie down in the kitchen," I stated depressed. "Uh-

Huh." she said, not without goodwill : this held promise of becoming a
novel, with all avec. "Good night" she said sweet and forestalling (and
fumbled pensively in her décolletage); – "Good night. – – Lisa !" I
appended with lightning speed, heard her acknowledging purrs and the
clack of the bolt, and hearkened absentmindedly to the soft, in-
souciant noises adjacent : sorcery ! This morning – : oh hell : this very
afternoon – ! Suddenly a great wave of tenderness and bliss came on :
I lifted my head and laughed aloud in the beblustered chamber; I leapt
to the door, propped my palms against it, and called – oh, some inanity
or other : "Does it still hurt ? !". "No : not at all now !" it came so swift
and beaming, and a splendid little laugh followed, that all was good.
– "Good night : Lisa !" "Good-ní-hight." came a song so merry and
weary from the bed, that the springs rang fine and aeolian harpish,
magic fluty, paganinian, music at night, till I finally took my hands
away and tenderly regarded the wood.

Once again outside (checking the kettle; whether the embers might not still
do some damage).

Then to the window shutter (with my free right hand parry the wind : so that
it's quiet for a moment –) : Breathes within, and regularly.

Sixty-three degrees already ! (And it's only 5:30 !) Outside the pied silk
cloth was stretched high and taut above the pine tops, blue and pale
yellow and pink. In the kettle the water was still a bit tepid from yesterday; I shaved à la maître, and for my naked brown torso I donned just
my long gray seducing pants, 12 inch cuffs, and the wide black belt
with pirate-sized brass buckle (underneath, a pair of sea-green athletic
shorts : for it's definitely going to be hot today).

With little fists it hammered at the door panel :
"Can I wash ?
How late is it ?
Have you been awake long ?"
I conscientiously provided all desired information, also placed the
filled aluminum basinette on the stool in the kitchen, and then fled up
and down the path a bit : cibiat ischtinem : there were really no larger
surfaces to wash (but more complicated ones, I realized, I realized; and
best of all : tea, crackers with marmalade, and peanut butter : we shall
orientally pamper, enervate her !)

Rough-pelted wind gnawed back in the bushes, while here the green moss
swelled through her pale yellow toes and fingers, they hovered within
it and suppled.

"We'll need double of everything now," I said beaming, and rubbed the
basin hollow dry, kneeling before her, in my arm the gleaming round,

like the shield of Hephaestus. "Why is that –" she asked frostily : "How do you know I'll be staying ? !" And my heart congealed, freezing my fingers on the tin rim; I lowered my large head and breathed silently : right ! : Who had told me that Diana would stay. (One to nothing for Lisa).

"What shall we eat today ?" She dreamily stretched one leg out into the fresh blue air; snapped her toes (sic !); musing : "Yes, if I could have my wish – –". Sighing silence, maiden-dreaming : "Macaroni" the amiable enthusiette murmured : "Macaroni and cheese; with green peas. One helluva roast; tomato gravy. – And on top two eggs sunny-side up !" she concluded awaking savagely, and her gaze clasped me broadly and full of transcendent bitterness : "WELL," I said cheerfully : "Macaroni, cheese, . . mm, . . . m : well except for the eggs it's all here : so come on." "Is this true ?" she asked mistrustfully, already swinging to her feet (and I had to get the fire going at once, and open the appropriate cans as vouchers).

12 noon ! There we stood with the steaming bowls in hand, and she hissed like an adder : "The armistice has run out ! My rifle ! – And ammo !" I hastily set the tasty circle down on the table, ran and gave it to her : "Where's the bolt ? !" she baited, vicious. "Yes well – there's an armistice," I said cheekily : "I still have that from yesterday !" She breathed uneasily : the aroma of roast ! "Let's extend it !" I suggested; walked up to her, very close : so much virility and aroma of roast ! I turned serious; I said : "Lisa –" (hoarse) : "for a hundred years, alright ?" She nodded with her head to one side : "Good –" she rasped with a strange smile : "for a hundred years to start with." And then in triumph we marched out with the tray, hunkered in the grass, and puttered with pointy and round instruments, invented by missing persons. (Subsequently she wished to lie down a bit : "Just an hour," she begged and mollified and laid her hand across my shoulders. "Fine" I said recalcitrantly : "I'll count to 3600" and in reward the hand stayed three seconds longer, and fingertips probed my skin. Hey you).

The thunderstorm stood above Stellichte with ponderous forged clouds (air like hot gray glass). All birds in hiding; except for the distant pair of jays squawking mechanically.

She came out of the house, just in briefs and the narrowest halter and mutely crouched down on the gray blanket, right at the edge, by the needled floor; her skinny back to me, knees to her chin, arms like narrow thongs wound about her shins. Behind the green carved trim of pine, the iron drum rumbled like a trooper; dust wind drew a quivering breath; then the black heat sank down again, setting our hides

shuddering and shrinking. At first it still glowed greenly at the woods'
flank, and the muddled field before us was dusty and toxic yellow; then
the whole dome closed over, and the clumsy janissary reeled and
thumped nearer. My white savage; the wind ruffled her hair and I
muttered jealously : he can cut that out ! The pink-striped ball did
not answer; but her rib clamps buckled more clearly as she took and
released one deep breath.

(Deepest dusk) : the pale slim-trained body almost throttled me. Rain
rushed howling high and by. Hands knew no rest; limbs crooked pup-
pety in the savaged night; sometimes I looked listlessly into bustling
touring cloudwork, touring winds, touring wild :

Graybrite Station : We helped us into the open house, bore us in wooden
hands across the hall. We. Us. Hall.

Still night still : "Get into your coat !" I commanded implacably; her coat
draped about her, resting strangely awry and coffee-brown in the air.
"I'm really taken with you . . ." she said, still with artful menace (but
was deeply touched by my solicitude); her face opened stormily beneath my own; we kissed fire from our limbs; she took my ear in her
mouth and whispered lawless things, until we did them. Then into the
warmish night; but :

"Hey listen : that scarf !" I said energetically : "that's close to piracy –"
(and she giggled snugly) – "all that's missing's a breadknife between
your teeth" (with gracious disapproval), "a bottle o' rum in your hand,
and bare chest." She nodded with emphasis and total conviction :
"Now wouldn't you like that," she murmured behind sharp double
teeth : "well we'll see : later maybe –" (And sauntered into my left
arm). "I'm a real gypsy type." and I nodded concerned, anxious :
truetrue.

So I'm for drinking honestly and dying in my boots. Like an old bold mate
of Lisa Weber. So then : Bibe Gallas ! (‹Bibe Piccolomini› she replied
imperturbable; once learned always learned).

"An Oetker Cookbook is what I want" (Varium et mutabile semper femina)
"Just imagine what I could cook for us then !". "Well alright" I agreed,
resigned and stodgy, and she laughed aloud and moved close at once :
"We'll have to eat sometime, you know," she said cosily, and : "but
you won't have to sleep in the kitchen today – I was so pooped yesterday –" she now confided remorsefully. (Dahlias : they're proper and
without fraud; also logarithms. So I'll initiate her in all of it over the
next few days).

"Wouldn't you think that'd give people a weird feeling ? . . ." (camped in
the vault of spreading firs) she reflected and explained : "– to have

invented those novels set in the future ?" (She was reading one from her rucksack : Jens, Accused; our daily work was done : fetched two more loads of provisions; I had methodically sawed and chopped for another hour : we'd not be spared winter). "Not so much because of the majestic flow of thought" she said, anticipating my requests for more precision, "but rather : when, for instance, someone creates a beautiful evening at the end of June, 2070 . . ." and she shook her head, falling profoundly silent. "Well" I said circumspectly : "it's already as good as settled what the weather will be like . . ." but now, a supple ermine, Lisa from the wood, she was making her two bounds, and knelt above my chest : "What do you mean by that. You Philistine ? !" (So quickly did she instinctively draw all and sundry conclusions; including those touching her admirer). She had one hand at my gullet, while the other one searched : "You take that back. What nonsense !" she fumed, free outraged thinker, but I set my brows askew and shook my head in regret.

She stabbed me in the chest dramatically with the broad green blade of grass, and did it so free-swinging and natural that I grew thoughtful deep within, though the surfaces were curling for laughter : the old wildcat ! And I grasped into the gray fur, while she hissed and spat ingeniously, so that her neck bent far back and her mouth gaped.

In the light wooden armchairs on the lawn. The bottles stood between us and sparkled deftly in the last red-golden lights. Her feet on a stylish little footstool, she was smoking slowly from a pack of Camels (but was required religiously to place every single butt in a tin can – no flicking !)

"Yes : now that's a man." she gave a lazy sigh, heavy with significance. Quiet and coolness. The fresh blue evening, set off with yellow, would last for a long time yet. I turned my face to her : "Enough prolegomena" I said sternly "now let's have the apropos : who's this that's so especially virile ?" And added, to rouse her to readier reply, a ‹huh ?›. She waved the dust-jacket posters, and I recognized the cruder image : "Oh I see," I said weakly, and came to demi-consciousness of my task, ‹Hemingway, both farewell to arms and to have and have not.› "Nope," I declined, "I'm more for the pinnacles of US development, your Poe and Cooper : what do I need that missing link for – ?". "And Wolfe and Faulkner ?". "And Wolfe and Faulkner." She pouted a few seconds and stroked the dust-jacket : "But there's such vitality and gusto for life" she proposed huffily. "An even bigger shoot-'em-up in this one ?" I asked out of curiosity. "Or boxing match : whiz-bam-slam ? The world consists of nothing but bartenders, kidnappers, veterans; not a maid

sans nymphomania; driving cars : God, America must be beautiful !"
But now she was flourishing menacing legs in the air : thinking takes a
lot out of you, and you need peace and quiet for it too. Sighing. Then
she threw her largest pine-cone at me; said weakly : "Give it back to
me; I want to play with it –" and reimmersed herself in the enticements
of the new world. (‹What strength he must have›; just like Frau
Salabanda among the Abderites !)

Suggestion : "Lisa : do you want to find a sailboat in Hamburg ? Fit it out
and travel the world o'er ?" (For she definitely was the gypsy type).
But when I looked around me, the idea didn't have a lot of appeal
(besides which, I knew the sea, from 3 years on the coast of Norway,
and didn't much trust those rotting cutters anymore : but I still would
have done it). She shook her head soberly (perceptive : knows me). A
triangular bright yellow sail bobbed up on the horizon, latin sail above
invisible boat; and she too was furtively watching it rush on, master-
fully wistful : isn't Stellichte forest still left to us ? Hazel bushes : are
they no longer filled with little shadings ? (The Camel : doesn't it taste
good ? and the latter rhymed with copulatings). The heavenly pilot
landed afar on dusky shoals; my restless passenger had her hands at
the back of her head and whistled, delicate, vespertine, and broken "I
kiss your hand madam –" (as in 1930 : where have the years gone ? ! !).
"And dream that it's your mouth" : well now, it's yours for the taking.
And I laboriously pulled myself up. (Cold night then; subsequent
stretch of rain).

Lisa had her dignified period today : already at breakfast she shoved two
cups about fatidically and wanted to set the table, all gracious matron,
as if any moment now she would ask for knitting needles. I swigged
tea in gloomy silence, and when she slid a chair upside down onto my
desk, I discerned my kismet : housecleaning ! Windows open, sweeping, dusting, fetching water, scrubbing floors, fetching water, no mention whatever of love, but go shake out that cloth, and as I passed,
merely gazed at the couch with a sigh : whereupon she suggested sanc-
timoniously, that it be beaten too : "Did I guess right, darling ?" And so
we artfully thrashed the poor fixture, in gratitude for happy hours, per
ben fare (And did it ever dustify, and at the least we'll have to bathe
this evening, worthy dictatrix !)

"Soap my back –" she muttered bathing in languor; and I let my hands
carefully travel across the curved foamy surface, felt the shoulder
blades, the thin ribs, and more. – – "Mmm" she went, lazy and savoring : and so once more, da capo al fine; – "but the front's already –" the
devil declared slowly (and only after it was several times too late).

While cleaning mushrooms : "Tomorrow's my birthday" she confessed nervously (i.e. 22nd Aug.; as a gentleman, I did not inquire about the year, because 50 sounds too cast-iron, so she would admit to 35); "mine's not till next year, 18th Jan." I reciprocated the confidence : "Hey : let's throw a grand orgy tomorrow." The knives snippered nimbly, then she raised her broad brow : "I have a special wish . . ." she remarked, skulking, cool and collected; "Well : Lisa" I countered, benevolent and royal : "Whatever I can do : go ahead and wish – : – ?". "Word of honor ? !" she asked mistrustfully, and I wrinkled the corners of my mouth in surprise : what could she want now ? ? "Don't be silly ! –" I said vexed : "Say what it is you want, and I'll do it : all right ? !"

She pulled the preputium back from a wood mushroom, circumcised the rim and slipped me the maimed vegebody ("These pollywogs !" she grumbled petulantly and blew through the lamellae of the next one) : "I want you to tell me about your childhood : where and how you grew up – parents and so on." and gazed over at me coldly : now *that* I had not expected ! I was completely perplexed; I scratched my head; I begged : "Lisa ! – Dearest Lisa : can't I write a garland of sonnets in your honor instead : just think : 14 poems, and the 15th, the master sonnet, composed solely of lines from the others ? Imagine that ! !" Now it was her turn to fill up with doubts : "A garland of sonnets ?" she asked with interest, and confessed in the same breath : "No one has ever done that for me. – Hm. –" And the irresolution was great and vain. "Damn it !" she shuffled back and forth and cast me a most indignant glance.

20 minutes later she stood up resolutely, fetched the two dice (I had taught her to use this informational tool when the arguments stand 50 : 50), and obtained an 8 for the sonnet garland, alas; then for the recollections of youth an 11 (although it was a ‹liner›; since one of them lay directly on a paring !). So then : –

22. 8. : rat-tatta-taaaaaa ! ! ! – I approached the modestly adorned lady, held a small oratio, and led her to her presents : a genuine Feuerbach was among them ‹Girl Playing a Lute› (from the Hamburg trip still); new binoculars 12 by 60 Leitz (because hers had been only a very ordinary 6 by 40); a large colt (you really do need a dependable barrel revolver; pistols are too complicated); a few books : 2 Coopers (in German, to be sure), Victoria Regina (women are always interested in that sort of thing), and Wieland "Don Sylvio of Rosalva". Touched and delighted, she thanked me (at the official kiss, however, skillfully letting me feel her tongue, quite unladylike) and pointed with her thin

naked finger to the 10 handwritten pages : "Are those the memoirs ?"
likewise augustly remarking in reply to my mute nod : "Damned
scanty, my dear." Then we created our symposium : Twenty bellows
blowing those ovens ablaze at once now / multitudinous breath out-
sending of wind enkindling (and the thundering meter pleased her
exceedingly well : and then on the fire she set unruly oil in the sauce-
pans; nodded her approval : kai tote de chryseia pater etitaine talanta :
for now she measured flour and sparkling jam in two bowls).

Golden and hot-headed the afternoon flowed : "Next week we'll dig up
potatoes" I warned nagging; but she wrinkled an indignant birthday
nose and shiftlessly put her hands to her tympanum. A tag of wind (and
tiny white lamb-locks at the foot of the Ahrsen woodlets : only visible
through the big new Leitz 12 by 60 : the instrument pleased her !)

Lamplighted window wafts wide : I groaned a little more, but then un-
hesitatingly handed the pages over to her, a man of my word, and she
read (comfortable in her armchair, totally bekissed, beneath the floor
lamp : my memories. I could watch mutely).

. . . *the parlor* was not locked; for you could, though that happened rarely
enough, walk straight on through it, in the coarse twilight of the ugly
flesh-toned curtains, to the hard granular balcony, which jutted like a
naked stone box out of the tenement's third story. So heavy and
gloomy was the balcony, its side walls handspans-wide and unriddled,
that you felt you could walk onto it only on tiptoe, always struggling
with your quickly doubting heart, which quailed and suggested you
leap voluntarily into the rockbound street ravine below rather than
tumble down along with the rough massive load.

True, the long green flowerbox at the front was sufficiently inviting;
but it stood at the edge; with the scanty wilderness of its tiny weeds,
which the mindless adults carefully pulled up, with numb and unpun-
ished hands; crude befisted folk.

Thus the ‹balcony› served as the start for strange dreams of flight, in
which you left the muffled shouts and scoldings of parents behind,
and slanting downwards, arms wafting wide around the corners of
houses, you glided just above the night-gray streets forlorn of people –
not all that far; mostly you set your foot down between Kentzlersweg
and Louisenweg – and strode ahead then, floating along beneath the
round gray-locked treetops of the predawn avenue (in the direction of
Hammerweg school) . . .

. . . *so bright and empty* was the world with its immense spaces and pure
cold play of color. From broad wooden bridges you looked down onto
the railroad tracks that ran with thrilling inexorability straight ahead

into a sky turning pale; clodded fields moved into the farthest blue; haw hung like clustered blaze in rigid wire of thorn bushes; solitary sheaves as if of nodding golden wire bundled on the fields; flying everywhere magic colored leaves and tolling wind among red branches. Along bare suburban streets, white peaceful mansions lay behind gardens defensive and railed all round; rustling you wandered in the cool evening gold. And when you lifted one of the large yellow leaves on its soft cold stem, a red glowing chestnut lay beneath : the slender sprite in his red silk coat had a noble home. Then came a short cold gust of wind that turned the shuffling leaves, and you knew that it was a being in itself, of whom many must dwell in these great soughing suburbs. In long rows the children moved, usually kept in order by the taller girls, along the quiet smooth streets, past the green and yellow sky, with the bright spheres of their ribbed paper lanterns, in which little clumps of wax glimmered.

Once the evening grew so alien and icy-sharp and so high, that the sky, the guardian beautiful vault vanished. More indifferent than stones were the countless glittering stars swapping nimble, mocking needle rays : why did they exchange dainty and iron glances when you stood by the lamppost with frozen little hands ? All grew alien.

Upstairs the kitchen was warm and bright yellow and there was hot tea, which the boy drank beside the flat iron stove, while the others – the adults – exchanged quiet speech and dull wit. It was always quite curious how they overlooked it – with basalt souls and warm hands – how, in order to bear life, they detached little pieces – parlors – from the world. What was it that gave them this horrifying certainty, this ghostly forgetting, so that they did not hear the holy and singing calls from the stove (unfamiliar high and deep voices, serene and sorrowful, that exchanged incomprehensible signs from the depths of the night; polite and inexplicable calls, disparaging); how outside the noble trees threw themselves back, anxious and sinewy, in the vagrant ice-wind; how metallic star-arrows shot in glorious and deadly arcs out of Nothing into Nothing, from the Alone to the Alone ? They had drawn borders within and about themselves; they measured and weighed : but things immeasurable ? things that could not be weighed ?

(Since he found no borders within himself, he hated everything that was border and boundary post, and whoever had erected them).

. . . *After he* had carefully drunk the thin tea, which had a tiny sharp sugar taste at the last swallow, he placed the cup on his child's table and looked into the sparse fire, where a longish briquet was silently changing from a dull-black imprinted brick into the Other. Fine red cracks pressed in on it from all sides, and along the outer edge, there already lay a leafy white layer of ash, from which now and again soundlessly puffed tiny blue flames with bright yellow points whenever streams of gas bellied out of the dark unknown bowels of the mountain. For a moment you could stand at the foot of the cliff-high wall and gaze deep into the wild mutely blazing crevices; and wander too into red rocky highlands and glimmering deserts of sand; or cautiously set little paper ships onto a still black piece of coal and wait with fading heart until the red sea soundlessly struck at the charring planks, woe to the spellbound crew.

The gray-brown upholstery on the sofa, and he gazed up and down along the old-fashioned high back : by gaslight, when the short-piled wall of plush, worn bare in many spots, stood there wild with shadows, he sometimes took two, three pins and a piece of thread long as his finger, and began from below, where the seat and arm thrust together, to let the needles wander upward : soon you were alone in the midst of an ineffable mountain world, among thundering rubble, beneath overhanging walls, from which the flapping heavy rope swayed.

. . . *the large sun* had risen pure yellow and red and shone through the frozen panes, upon which, since the kitchen had not yet been properly warmed, the spectacle unfolded.

Once he turned his head and called to his mother, who was busy cooking and kneading sweet yellow dough in a bowl : "Hey look !"; then he pointed to the window, on which the ice plants stood, slender and bent in the silver shadows. She came over hastily – as far as the boundary post – gazed into his small, bright face for a moment, said quickly : "Hm – Jack Frost." and then looked again expectantly, one finger on the gas tap, at the churning water. The little boy watched too, how the delicate hot bubbles rose up from the unfathomable dim depths of the great pot, how contorted waves streamed from the edges to the middle and blustering softly sank again.

Then he walked back into the frosted garden, down among the fanning leaves, bent like thin hoops and mighty with feathers, along a narrow white path, which – you could see it quite clearly – led to the level shore of a wide frozen sea with the pink sun rolling at its edge.

He would have loved to know the names of the proud, strange plants – not what they were called – that was something quite different; for he had noticed that of the world's things some were called rightly and some wrongly. Jack Frost's "ice flowers" was wrong; surely each of them had its own name : but that notion did not make him feel all that easy; for he remembered with dismay how the flowers, grasses, even

the tall trees of summer, ostensibly had no names of their own. In
the stairwell, he had often encountered a big, slightly warty man, with
a loud red face, who was called Pfeiffer : why was he called Herr
Pfeiffer, and why did the six slender poplars that he loved so and that
grew on the Bauerberg, with their cheerful leaves and long beautiful
branches, have no names ? He did not want to ‹give› them names; he
only wanted to hear their right ones !
He looked again at the window and noticed with astonishment that he
no longer was running about in the garden but was sitting again on his
two-seated chair; stiff and dull silver, the magic park stood in the distance and waited . . .

The cup appeared in the air (at first I had not seen it at all) and it was
moved impatiently back and forth, without eyes being lifted from the
page : that meant, then, ‹pour me some tea›, well all right; I arrested
the tottering object along with the pale fingers and refilled. "Pre . . ." I
began; but then she was holding it straight again, and only for the sake
of completion did I whisper the ". . . caución". (She looked good in
the squared reading glasses and the long, narrow dress; but after 8
years a man would see a Helen in every female figure, came the critic's
reminder). Presumably her interest was meant as a compliment to me.

She nodded slowly and without looking at me, reached for the next sheet :
(Wouldn't interest anybody anyway).

Midnight long since past : she folded the pages carefully together and held
them firmly in her hand. I stood at the window and watched the quarter
moon (crescit : he lies) creep slowly and slouched across the meadows;
meadow moon through autumnal silence; all clocks are dying down;
one ought to be a spirit : hovering above autumn meadows, that's how
my dewed paradise would look. She stood behind me in the curtain;
she laid her hand on my sleeve : "Was that very hard for you ?" she
asked, bemused-rueful; naturally I did not answer, and we listened as it
pined and husked about the house.

Walking up and down the path : "I can't stay forever" she said aloud to
herself : "I have to find more people." Night cold. I spoke in slow
time : "And if you meet No One else ?" (U-turn on the tracks; standing
still; the moon sank slowly into needle branchings and haze ribbon :
the silver being had turned reddish, the lower points gone now, below).
"Then I'll come back again" she whispered consolingly, breathing
high and deep. Sad and beautiful. –

Silent fog grounds in the Ostermoor : soundlessly digging up potatoes. The
earth was glowing black and red; we burrowed slowly in the cold
clods, with splotched burgundy hands; pressure beneath our black-

rimmed nails. The cloud fire soon turned to ash; the pasturelands below remained cold and dusky green, while I knotted at the lumpy sack.
The air took on an edge, and the bushes eddied a little with the black
foliage. The silence lay autumn-hale over the ‹whole› country.

She asked : "Why do you still keep on writing really ? – Why did you ever
write books ?" (Answer : to earn money. Words my sole knowledge.
"That's not true !" she said outraged. Tried other things. Then too : I
enjoy fixing images of nature, situations, in words, and kneading away
at short stories).

She whistled the March of the Finnish Cavalry : püpüpi : püpüpi :
püpüpüperüpüpü (og frihet gar ut fra den ljugande pol); she said
pursedly : "So never for your readers then ? Never for some kind of
propagandistic or ‹ethical› purpose ?"

"For readers ?" I asked in profound astonishment; and ‹ethical purpose›
was new to me too. "I simply meant –" she mollified, but gently bored
further : "but tell me : – ?". "I've always been an enthusiastic reader
of Wieland : Poe, Hoffmann, Cervantes, Lessing, Tieck, Cooper, Jean
Paul – I have imagined that sometimes : whether they'd be satisfied
with my work, or Alfred Döblin and Johannes Schmidt. But ‹readers›
in general ? ? – Nah ! !" (Know nothing about it).

"Hero worship ?" I snorted contemptuously : "Dear girl !" Whoever has
lived as long as I have with me, no longer believes in heroes (a few
perhaps, but they are definitely long since dead). Nevertheless I
begged : "Lisa : stay !" but she was already too far away, at least ten
furrows, and was refilling her wire basket with soft pale-stony tubers.

Frost at midnight : the wooden parlor was white and black with lunar fib-
bing; a thick red dot slept in the stove. We awakened frostily, and she
bored her beloved shoulders sharply into me. I caressed my way over
everything with hands, said : "I'll build a fire," kissed into sleeping
hair, and hobbled, nocturnally clad : streaked as in the bagno to the
splendid stove. Now I blessed our saws, and all the woodchip after-
noons; I reached into the shadowed kindling and quickly built an ingenious lattice around the red dot, blew dolphin-lipped sleep-drunk, and
at once the flame pullulated in the iron vault, stretched out eager and
spare through the drafts, my head tottered onto my cold breast, and I
stumbled back to Lisa.

After 15 minutes the wave of warmth flowed over us. She groaned contented, vegetal lack-willed (and I scurried off again and shoved more
beech logs in). We shunted hands around us and braided legs together,
peaceful and secure. When it was nice and warm, she said debauch-
fully :

"C'mon : let's go juniper !" I arose, agreeing without contradiction, for the moon had made me mad as well; we disguised ourselves, with taut brows and nimble, and walked one behind the other through the plank walls.

Juniper moon : he twinkled and white-blued amply. The plants were standing sylky-black with anomlous gesturings (have to drop the ‹a› for the sake of sentence rhythm). Once again : Lisa glided into the house for the bottles. – We drank, hunkered in the firm needle parquet, still and restrained.

She stretched her neck, her voice said : "I'm leaving." I saw the junipers scurrying about me, sitting; I grabbed my neighbor branch : "Why ?" I asked dryly and un. Across from me the bottle glass blinked in the open light : "Life's too good here with you" it came in a breath over three moss smudges. In one thundering bound I was beside the white one and took hold of her flesh : "Lisa ! !"

I said : "Lisa ! : –"

"My skin quivers when I see but a piece of your clothing. And my heart is like a foundling chick if I but think of your name : shall we not live as princes. My champignonne ?"

She answered shrilling : "I'm not wearing shoes." (Right : her feet were naked !) I ripped open my jacket and propped her soles against my breast, her knees lay in my hands. The innkeeper moon poured his white over us; to her right lay a yellow hand, to her left a striped hand : and they approached my body. I rubbed her knees and pressed closer to her; but she tensed her legs and drove me back.

"Tomorrow I'm leaving : just in time, before I get too fat and sassy. You're too strong for me." She pushed herself up; she said calmly : "You can help me get ready : check over my bike and trailer; I'll get dressed."

Inflated the bike; hung the trailer on. I went into the house; she was standing in the kitchen and packing a rucksack with tin cans and bottles. I called : "Stay !" (Glass and tin resounded no less muffled).

"Lisa !" but a cord made knots and rustled. So I went outside and gaped at how the frost was forming on the earth.

In overalls and cap : and so she grabbed hold of the handlebars. She took another addict's drink; held the glassy container out to me, and I kissed the cold moist bottle mouth, the cold brandy-moist woman mouth, trembling with cold and misery.

"I have to" ! she declared with determination, "here with you – I don't know – I'm getting heavier and more classical. – I'm sure it's just my gypsy blood and that I'll be sorry before 8 days have passed. – You're staying here, and I'll always know where I can find my final

refuge : – ? !" She held onto my hand across the frame, and I grabbed her by the flesh of her neck and kissed what I found till we almost toppled.

"I'm crazy !" she asserted with a moan : "But nobody can change her nature. Uprooted by 3 wars, ah –" She broke off and commanded : "Step back. Into the shrub circle." I did so. She calmly took her seat and looked around her once more :

The meadows glistened silent and airy in the swill black frame of firs. The moon as keystone in the sharply tapered vault of sky. I said pointlessly : "Do you have matches too – huh ?". She awoke and replied with interest : "No ! – Get me some : okay ? !"

In the house : now where are they ? ! I ripped drawers and packing paper : now where ! ! –

Gone : She was gone ! Of course ! And I stood with bowed head as in a blue stone. Stupid face. Midst plants. In my right hand a box of matches.

Toward morning cloudworks arose (and rain showers). Fresh yellow smoke wafted toward me : my stove ! So I left the wood and pushed onto the house : the last human being.

Once more head high : there he stood green in the bright red morning clouds. Frost in meadowscapes. And wind came up. Wind.

A NOTE ON THE TEXTS

Scenes from the Life of a Faun (*Aus dem Leben eines Fauns*): written December 1952-January 1953, published Hamburg: Rowohlt Verlag, 1953.

Brand's Heath (*Brand's Haide*): written January-September 1950, published (with *Schwarze Spiegel*) Hamburg: Rowohlt, 1951.

Dark Mirrors (*Schwarze Spiegel*): written May 1951, published (with *Brand's Haide*) Hamburg: Rowohlt, 1951.

The trilogy *Nobodaddy's Kinder* published Reinbek: Rowohlt, 1963.

The present translations were made from volume 1 of the *Bargfelder Ausgabe, Werkgruppe I*. Eine Edition der Arno Schmidt Stiftung im Haffmans Verlag, 1987.